A LITTLE
OUT-OF-PRECINCT DETECTION . . .

Burton's torch beam sliced through the darkness and picked out a light switch. Frost tried it. It worked, the dim bulb revealing a plastic-topped table that could be folded back and two bunk beds stripped of clothing. There was a lamp and a small radio on the table, both connected to an electronic control programmed to come on at different times of the night. Frost pressed the manual button. The lamp lit up and the radio came on. A burglar deterrent.

The bottom bunk was over a storage area. They opened the door to reveal bedding and table linen jam-packed. A partitioned section was the kitchen, its oven powered by propane gas. Opposite the cooker was the sink.

"It doesn't look as if anyone's here," observed Detective Sergeant Maud, rather redundantly.

Frost switched off the light and closed the door behind them as they descended the wooden steps. Then he stopped dead, a finger to his lips. "I heard something," he whispered.

A rustling in the grass. Someone moving about. A dark shape loomed, then another. A white, blinding glare as torches were shone straight into their eyes.

"Hold it! None of you move. Police!"

"Oh, shit," groaned Frost.

Also by R. D. Wingfield

A TOUCH OF FROST
FROST AT CHRISTMAS
NIGHT FROST

HARD FROST

R. D. Wingfield

BANTAM BOOKS
New York · Toronto · London · Sydney · Auckland

HARD FROST

A Bantam Crime Line Book / October 1995

CRIME LINE and the portrayal of a boxed "cl" are trademarks
of Bantam Books, a division of Bantam Doubleday Dell Publishing Group, Inc.

ISBN 0-553-57170-2

Bantam Books are published by Bantam Books, a division of Bantam Doubleday
Dell Publishing Group, Inc. Its trademark, consisting of the words "Bantam Books"
and the portrayal of a rooster, is Registered in U.S. Patent and Trademark Office and
in other countries. Marca Registrada. Bantam Books, 1540 Broadway, New York,
New York 10036.

PRINTED IN THE UNITED STATES OF AMERICA

OPM   0 9 8 7 6 5 4 3 2 1

HARD FROST

The man crouching by the window at the back of the house gritted his teeth as he forced the blade of the screwdriver between the wooden frames. Through the glass he could just make out the cot on the far side of the darkened bedroom. He couldn't see the little boy, but knew he was in there. He had watched in the dark from the end of the garden, hands sweating with excitement, as the mother put the boy to bed.

The blade was in far enough. He took a deep breath and levered. Wood splintered and he felt the screws tear free. A sudden swish of noise from behind him almost made him drop the screwdriver. He turned in fright, ready to duck low and run zigzagging across the garden. But it was a firework, a rocket soaring up to the night sky, where it burst in a cluster of bright green puffballs.

His heart hammered and cold sweat trickled. A long, deep breath to calm himself, and then, very carefully and very quietly, he eased open the window, heaved himself up on the sill and swung inside. Three careful steps across the room and he was able to reach the chair next to the cot and wedge it under the door handle to stop anyone from coming in. At the door he listened. Voices. The late-night film on television. Just the woman on her own—he'd checked.

The cot creaked as the child snuffled and wriggled. He froze and held his breath. A tiny yawn, then shallow breathing. He relaxed. The child had settled into a deep sleep.

He took the knife from his pocket. Quietly he tiptoed over to the cot.

Chapter One

Halloween. October 31—Night

A lone sky rocket clawed its way up to the night sky, scrabbled feebly as it started to lose height, then burst into a cluster of green puffballs.

PC Mike Packer, twenty years old, barely gave it a glance as he turned the corner into Markham Street. This was his first night out on the beat on his own and he had other things on his mind. He patted the radio in his top pocket, reassured he could call for help if he needed it.

A clatter of footsteps behind him. Two teenage girls, heavily made up and dressed as witches, tottered past on high heels, trailing a cloud of musky perfume. They whistled and called to him, blowing wet-lipped kisses. On their way to some Halloween party and already drunk. Someone was going to be lucky tonight and, grinning ruefully, Parker wished it was him! But no such luck. He was on duty on this cold and windy night, pounding his lousy beat until six in the morning. He drew his head tighter into the snug warmth of his greatcoat and watched until the girls turned the corner. The wind snatched away the last whisper of their perfume and he was on his own again.

He cut through the narrow alley which brought him into Patriot Street, a backwater of small lock-up shops and an empty space that was once a secondhand-car site.

The street was dark, its single streetlamp vandalized long ago.

The hollow echo of his footstep pattered behind him, giving him the uneasy feeling he was being followed. Once he even stopped suddenly and swung round, but there was no one there. Outside the shops, piled up on the pavement, the shopkeepers had dumped plastic bags of rubbish, ready for collection the following morning. Packer weaved his way around them and flashed the rock-hard beam of his brand-new torch into shop doorways, rattling the odd handle to make sure all was secure.

The end shop, long empty and boarded up, was once a butcher's. A sign swaying gently in the wind said This Valuable Property to Let. The sign had been up a very long time. The shop's doorway was piled high with rubbish sacks which had obviously been dragged there from adjacent shops. Why, Packer wondered, had someone taken the trouble to do that? Again he clicked on his torch, watching the beam crawl slowly over the pile. He half-expected to disturb a dosser or perhaps even the boy they had been told to look out for, the seven-year-old who had gone out with his guy and still wasn't home at eleven o'clock at night.

Packer stiffened. There was someone there. Someone crouching behind the bags in the corner. Someone keeping very still. "All right—I can see you! Come on out!" No movement. Keeping the torch handy for use as a weapon if necessary, he started pulling bags out of the way. Then suddenly the figure lunged at him and the face . . . God . . . it wasn't human . . . it was green and malevolent. Dropping the torch, he fumbled for his radio. The radio . . . he couldn't find the bloody radio. . . .

·   ·   ·

"Denton Police." Police Sergeant Bill Wells stifled a yawn as he lifted the phone to his ear and muttered into the mouthpiece. He wasn't really concentrating on what the caller was saying. He was still simmering with rage. He had been going through the new duty rosters to the end of the year and was livid to see that Mullett had yet again put him down for Christmas day duty. Well, Superintendent flaming Mullett had another think coming. Let some of Mullett's blue-eyed boys do their share of holiday nights for a change, because the worm was about to turn. Wells frowned at the agitated voice. "Try and take it easy, madam . . . just tell me what happened. . . . What? . . . Where? How bad is she?" His pen scribbled furiously. "Don't worry. I'll get someone over there right away."

He snatched up the internal phone and jabbed the button for Wonder Woman's office. Detective Sergeant Liz Maud. Let that flaming tart do some work for a change instead of painting her lousy fingernails. He'd noticed from the roster that she had all of the Christmas period off and she'd only been here two bloody weeks.

"Yes?"

The impatient edge to her voice always put his back up, so his tone was curt. "Seventeen Crown Street . . . break-in and stabbing—little boy, one year old."

"On my way," she said. "I'll need backup."

"We haven't got any," said Wells, happy at last.

Packer was sweating with relief. Thank goodness he wasn't able to get to his radio. They would never have let him live it down. It was a guy—a child's guy—and the green face was Guy Fawkes. He pulled some of the sacks away to get a better look. He froze. Behind the guy, a rubbish sack, propped up against the shop door, looked wrong. He touched it and his hand jerked back as if he had received an electric shock. Packer had never seen a dead body. Part of his training would involve a visit to the mortuary to view a postmortem, but this had not happened yet. Burton had said that the pathologist always cut a long slit under the corpse's chin so he could peel the face from the skull like a rubber mask. Packer had hoped he would be able to see it through without fainting when the time came. But now, before he was ready, he knew he had a dead body. Too small for an adult. A child.

As he reached out, it toppled over and he thought he heard a grunt. Still alive? Was it still alive?

He tore off his gloves with his teeth and fumbled at the cord tying the neck of the sack. Then he was staring at a face. A young boy. Brown masking tape bound round the eyes as a blindfold. More masking tape, pulled tightly into the mouth, forcing the lips back into a mockery of a grin. Vomit dribbled from the mouth and nose. Packer dropped to his knees and gingerly touched the flesh. Ice-cold and no sign of a pulse. The brown dribble of vomit had a naggingly familiar hospital smell. He opened the plastic sack wider, holding it by its extreme edge, and shone his torch inside. The dead boy, knees bent, was naked.

He straightened up and pulled his radio from his pocket, then took a few deep breaths and called the station. To his surprise he managed to keep his voice steady. He sounded as if he met Death in the street every day. "Packer here, Patriot Street. I think I've found the missing kid . . . and he's dead. Looks like murder."

"*Stay there,*" ordered Wells. "*Whatever happens—stay there!*"

Packer moved out to the street and waited. An eerie silence seemed to hang over the area; the tiniest sounds were magnified. The rustling of the wind on the exposed plastic sacks. The creaking of the For Sale sign over the butcher's. The hammering of his heart.

Then just audible, but getting louder, the wailing siren of an area car. Wells wasn't going to send out the Murder team until he had checked. Not on Packer's first night out on his own.

At the station it was chaos and Bill Wells was in near-despair. Everything was going wrong. A murder investigation and no senior CID officers available. Detective Inspector Allen, who should have been on call at home, had left a contact number which rang and rang but no one answered. Jack Frost was on holiday and that stupid cow Liz Maud must have switched her radio off, as he had gone near-hoarse calling for her. He was now ringing the divisional commander's home number, but knew he would get short shrift there. He could hear Mullett's sarcasm now. *"Surely you are competent enough to sort this out for yourself, Sergeant?"* The phone was hot against his ear and the ringing tone went on and on. Then he was aware of a tapping on the desk in front of him. A tubby little man in a camel-haired coat was trying to attract his attention. "Be with you in a minute, sir," Wells said.

"You'll deal with me now, Sergeant. I'm in a hurry."

Wells groaned. One of those pompous little bastards. Just what he needed tonight. . . .

His attention was snatched back to the phone. Someone had answered. Not Mullett, but his half-asleep, disgruntled, toffee-nosed wife peevishly demanding to know who it was. "Sorry to disturb you at this time of night, Mrs. Mullett, but is the superintendent there? . . . No? Do you have a number where I could contact him? Yes, it is urgent." Of course it is urgent, you stupid cow, would I be phoning if it wasn't? "Thank you." He scribbled on his pad and hung up the phone.

The man was glaring at him. "I am still waiting, Sergeant."

"Please take a seat, sir. I'll deal with you as quickly as I can." He looked up hopefully as PC Lambert came in from Control.

"Still no answer from that Inspector Allen number, Sarge."

"Keep trying. If the damn pathologist arrives to find there's only a detective constable in charge, he'll do his nut. Any luck with Wonder Woman?"

"Not a dicky bird!"

"Bloody cow's useless." Wells ripped the sheet from his pad. "Someone else who's useless . . . see if you can get Mr. Mullett on this number."

Lambert glanced at it and frowned. "This is the same number I'm trying for Mr. Allen, Sarge."

Wells looked at it again. Lambert was right. "Mullett and Allen, both out together at eleven o'clock at night. I wonder where?"

"A cut-price knocking shop?" suggested a familiar voice, helpfully.

Frost! Jack Frost in his crumpled mac and maroon scarf, beaming at them.

"Jack!" cried a delighted Wells. "I thought you were on holiday."

"I am. I've just nipped in for some fags. Did you get my comic postcard?" He struck a pose and declaimed:

> "I cannot get my winkle out
>   Now there's a funny thing.
>   The more I try to pull it out
>   The more I push it in!"

Wells grinned. "I stuck it on the notice board, but Mullett made me take it down. He said it was pornographic."

"What's pornographic about a man eating winkles?" asked Frost. "So what's all the panic?"

"Patriot Street. Body in a dustbin sack."

Frost grimaced. "Where did people hide bodies before

dustbin sacks were invented? We find more bloody bodies than rubbish in them these days."

"This one's a kid," said Wells, "and someone killed him. We've got a murder investigation with no one higher than a detective constable in charge, the pathologist on his way, and Mullett and Allen conveniently unobtainable. A proper sod-up!"

"Not as good as some of my sod-ups," said Frost, "but I'm glad I'm on holiday. I'll just nick some of Mullett's fags and go." He disappeared up the corridor.

Seeing Wells with nothing to do, the man in the camel-hair coat sprang across to the desk.

"Perhaps you can now spare me some time. I've lost my car—a metallic grey Rover, registration number—"

"Stolen car, right," said Wells, pulling the forms toward him. The quickest way to get rid of him was to take the details.

"I didn't say it was stolen. I just don't know where it is. I drove down from Bristol for the firm's function. I parked it down a side street somewhere. I must have got confused—I can't find it. My wallet, credit cards, everything, are inside it."

"It's probably been pinched by now," said Wells cheerfully.

"I'm sure it hasn't, Sergeant. It's fitted with antithief devices."

"And you've no idea where you left it?"

"If I did, I wouldn't be here, would I?"

Wells put his pen down. "So what do you want us to do about it?"

The man sighed as if explaining to an idiot. "I would have thought that was obvious, Sergeant. If one of your men could drive me around the side streets, we could look for it."

"I've got a better idea." Frost had returned with one of Mullett's best cigarettes dangling from his lips. "Why don't you piss off and go and look for it yourself? We've got more important things to do."

The little man spun round angrily, jabbing a finger at Frost. "I'll have you," he spluttered. "You don't realize who you are talking to. I've got friends in high places. I want your name."

"Mullett," said Frost. "Superintendent Mullett."

"Right," said the man, scribbling this down. "You haven't heard the last of this." He stamped out of the station.

"You bloody fool, Jack," said Wells.

"He won't take it any further," said Frost, but now beginning to have doubts himself. "Anyway," he said, brightening up, "I'm on holiday so Mullett won't suspect me."

"If you were dead he'd still suspect you," said Wells grimly.

Lambert slid up the dividing hatch to the Control Room. "Still nothing from that number, Sarge. I got the exchange to trace it for us. It's the Clarenden Arms, a big pub and restaurant over at Felstead."

Wells's eyes narrowed. "What the hell are they doing there? Those two are up to something, you mark my words. Why isn't anyone answering the phone?"

Lambert shrugged. "They say there could be a fault on the line. We'll have to send someone over there to pick Allen up."

"We can't spare a bleeding car," said Wells. He groaned. Lambert was right—there was no other option. "All right— send Charlie Baker. We want Allen back here. Tell him it's a murder inquiry."

The hatch slammed shut. Wells spun round quickly, just in time to catch Frost before he sidled out. "Hold it, Jack."

"I'm on holiday until the end of the week," said Frost.

"We've got to have a senior officer over there. . . . Please, Jack. I only need you to hold the fort until Allen arrives—fifteen minutes, half an hour at the most. . . ."

"All right." Frost nodded reluctantly. "But you owe me one."

The door was closing behind him when Lambert slid up the hatch. "I've got hold of Liz Maud, Sarge."

Detective Sergeant Maud was late arriving at the house. She still didn't know her way around Denton and the ancient, well-thumbed street map Sergeant Wells had given her was falling to pieces. Lots of the street names were unreadable. After twice retracing her route she pulled outside the front door just as the doctor was leaving. "Kiddy's not too badly hurt," he told her. "Couple of superficial wounds to the upper arm, which only required bandaging." He glanced back and winced at the hysterical shrieking and sobbing from inside. "That's the mother. She's in a worse state than the kid. I offered her a sedative, but she chucked it at me." He edged past her. "I wish I could stay, but I've got other calls. . . ." He plunged out into the street, relieved to get away from the noise.

Liz switched off her radio. She didn't want her interview with an overwrought mother interrupted by trivial messages. She homed in on the crying, which was now accompanied by a banging noise. It led her to the child's bedroom, a tiny room with a single cot, its walls decorated with nursery wallpaper.

The banging was caused by a middle-aged man who was hammering nails into the window frame, which had been forced open by the intruder. A young woman, probably the mother, jet-black hair, pale olive skin, was sitting in a blue painted chair, rocking from side to side, moaning and sobbing continuously. Liz sighed. She obviously wouldn't be much help.

A plumpish woman in her fifties was standing next to the mother, holding the child, who was wrapped in a blanket.

The child, an infant, his face flushed and tear-stained, had cried himself to an exhausted sleep.

The mother, wild-eyed, seemed unaware of Liz's entrance, but the older woman looked up inquiringly.

"Detective Sergeant Maud," announced Liz, holding out her warrant card.

"Took your time getting here," said the man, knocking in one last nail and putting down the hammer. He gave the window frame a testing shake. "That should keep the bugger out."

"If you could try to avoid touching things," said Liz. "There could be fingerprints."

"You wouldn't need fingerprints if you got here earlier and caught him," said the man.

Liz ignored this. "Are you the husband?"

"I'm her next-door neighbor—George Armitage." Armitage nodded at the woman with the baby. "And that's my wife."

Liz addressed the mother. "What's your name, love?"

But it was Mrs. Armitage who answered her. "Lily—Lily Turner. She's in a bit of a state, I'm afraid."

"Is there a husband?"

"Well—there's a father—not sure if he's actually her husband, if you follow my meaning." Mrs. Armitage lowered her voice. "He's inside . . . doing eighteen months—stealing radios from cars."

Liz gently touched the mother's arm. "Lily, I'm from the police. Can you tell me what happened?"

The mother's only response was to moan louder.

"She's upset," said Mrs. Armitage. "Doctor offered her a tablet but she threw it at him . . . not that they would have done much good—he's not much of a doctor. He gave me water tablets once and I was never off that damned toilet—"

Liz cut her short. "Perhaps you can tell me what happened, Mrs. Armitage?"

"Half a mo!" She put the baby down in the cot and pulled the bedclothes over him. There were little flecks of blood on the sheets. "The baby was in here asleep and Lily was in the other room watching telly. She heard little Tommy crying. She tried to get in here but couldn't get the door open."

"The bastard had jammed that chair under the door handle," said the man, pointing to the chair the mother was sitting on. Liz made a mental note to ensure it was fingerprinted, and nodded for the woman to continue.

"The kiddy was screaming and she could hear someone moving about. She thought it was burglars. Anyway, she came running in to us and George came straight back here with her and managed to kick the door open."

"Let me tell it now," said the man. "I kicked the door open. She switched on the light. That window was wide open with the wind roaring in. I nipped across and looked out, but there was no sign of him. The kid was crying fit to bust, so she picked him up and then she spotted the blood and next she was yelling and screaming louder than the bleeding kid. I got my wife to phone the police and the doctor. The rest you know."

Liz walked over to the window and looked out onto a small back garden. There was a gate in the rear fence leading to a lane. Easy to get in and out without being spotted. The window had been crudely levered open, exactly the same as the other three stabbings. "Do you know if she's noticed anyone watching the house, or following her?"

"We're not on speaking terms," said Armitage. "We wouldn't be in here tonight if it wasn't an emergency. I was one of the people her old man nicked a car radio from, so we're not coming in for tea and biscuits and a chat, are we?"

Liz snapped her notebook shut. She would have to come back again tomorrow when Lily Turner had calmed down. "Well, thank you very much. Try not to touch anything. There'll be a fingerprint man here in the morning."

Mrs. Armitage walked with her to the front door. "Do you think you'll catch him?"

"We'll get him," said Liz. She wished she shared her spoken optimism. A maniac who had a thing about seeing blood on children. They had no description, no fingerprints —they didn't even know if it was a man or a woman and all of the known sex offenders she had painstakingly questioned either had cast-iron alibis or didn't fit the pattern. "We'll get him all right." The front door slammed shut behind her, but she could still hear the mother wailing.

In the car she switched her radio back on and they told her about the dead boy. She fished out the street map and tried to figure out how to get to Patriot Street.

"She had her damn radio off?" said Wells incredulously. "What does the silly cow think we give her a radio for . . . just to keep in her bloody handbag?" The phone rang. "Yes?" he snapped. It was Mullett and he sounded just the tiniest bit drunk. "My wife tells me you've been trying to reach me, Sergeant?"

Wells clapped his hand over the mouthpiece and yelled for Lambert to call back the area car. Then he told Mullett about the murdered boy.

Mike Packer stamped his feet and flapped his arms. It was damn cold. He wished he could go back on his beat and walk around to keep warm, but he had been delegated to stand with a clipboard and record details of everyone who approached the body. So far he had recorded himself, PCs Simms and Jordan, DC Burton and the two Scene of Crime officers in their white overalls who had screened off the area, plus, of course, the police surgeon who was in and out in a flash, simply confirming the boy was dead and that the circumstances were bloody suspicious. Across the road Jordan and Simms, in the warmth of the area car, were waiting to be told what to do. No sign yet of the pathologist, nor of Detective Inspector Allen, who should be in charge.

An old Ford Escort wheezed round the corner and shuddered to a halt. Simms nudged Jordan, who climbed out of the car, ready to send the newcomer away. But the man getting out of the Ford, maroon scarf streaming in the wind, was Detective Inspector Jack Frost. What was he doing here? He should be on holiday.

Burton, kneeling by the corpse, heard the car draw up and frowned. Control had told him that Detective Sergeant Liz Maud was on her way over, so this must be her. The pompous little cow would soon start taking charge, lording it over everyone and barking out her orders. But that raucous laugh that came slicing across the gloom had him hurrying out. There was only one person with a laugh like that.

Frost took a quick look round the scene. Everything seemed to be in order. The street was cordoned off and a tentlike structure erected around the shop doorway. A small generator installed by the SOC men chugged away, providing the emergency lighting. Everyone seemed to be doing what he ought to. He nodded happily to himself. DC Burton was competent enough to handle all the fiddling details.

"Right," Frost said, after lighting up one of Mullett's cigarettes for Burton, "I'd better know what we've got, just in case some nosy bastard asks."

"Dead boy, aged about eight," said Burton, leading him to the body. "Believed to be Bobby Kirby, reported missing from home. Mother separated from husband. She and her boyfriend nipped out to the pub for a couple of hours, leaving Bobby watching telly. When they got back around ten o'clock, Bobby wasn't there."

The body was still in the plastic sack. It wouldn't be removed until the pathologist, a stickler for insisting things be left exactly as found, had examined it. Frost knelt down and looked at the white face, the brown plastic masking tape round the eyes and mouth. He shook his head sadly. "Poor little sod. Have the parents been told?"

"Not yet," Burton told him. "We're waiting for Mr. Allen."

"Rather him than me," said Frost. He peered more closely, his face tight with compassion. "What dirty bastard did this to you, sonny?" He examined the tape binding the mouth, and the dribble of vomit. He sniffed. That smell. What the hell was it? He knew it from somewhere. . . . Of course, the hospital. It was always lingering around the ward when he went to visit his wife, when he sat by the bed for hours on end to watch her slowly dying. He worried away, trying to identify it, but gave up. It wasn't his case, so it wasn't his problem. "Cause of death?"

"The police doctor thinks he might have choked to death on his own vomit."

"How long dead?"

"Wouldn't commit himself. He said ask the pathologist."

"Helpful bloody bastard." Frost straightened up and squinted at his watch. Where the hell was Allen?

"He and Mr. Mullett are on their way over now, sir," Burton told him, reading his mind.

"Mullett? Don't let him see your fag, son . . . he might recognize it as a long-lost friend." Frost took one last look at the body. "I'm only the token inspector, so just carry on until smart-arse gets here." He found a dustbin to sit on while he waited.

Detective Sergeant Liz Maud skidded round the corner. She knew she was driving too fast, but she was in a state of high excitement. A murder case! Her first. And Inspector Allen unavailable. Now was the time to make her mark.

As she parked tight into the curb behind a police car, she

glanced across the road and scowled. The area was supposed to be cordoned off, but there, sitting on a dustbin, hunched up against the wind, was an old tramp dragging on a cigarette. How had the fools let him get so close? Heads would roll for this. She flung open the door of her car and sprang out. "Hey—you!" The man, who was in the process of flinging his cigarette end into the gutter, looked up briefly, then, ignoring her, rose to walk toward the canvas enclosure where the body was. Liz frowned in disbelief as the two fools in the police car in front of her just sat and watched.

She raced across the road, fumbling in her shoulder bag for her warrant card. "You in the mac—hold it!" She shoved her warrant card in his face.

Frost barely gave it a glance. "No, thanks, love—I've already got one." Then he was yelling at two uniformed men who were starting to shift the sacks of rubbish out of the way. "Leave them be! I want them checked for prints and examined." He turned to Liz. "Detective Inspector Frost. You must be new?"

She managed to keep her voice calm, but inwardly she was boiling. Her one big chance and this idiot had to come back from holiday early. "Detective Sergeant Liz Maud. I was transferred from Fenley Division last week."

Frost eyed her. In her late twenties, a bit on the thin side, her dark hair scragged back, emphasizing her sharp features. But she wouldn't be a bad looker if she took a bit of trouble and wore something different from that drab grey and black striped skirt and jacket.

"All right if I have a look at the body, Inspector?"

Frost spread his hands. "Be my guest, love. I'm only keeping it warm until Allen turns up."

Liz winced at the "love" but tried not to show her annoyance. Before she could move, a sleek black car slithered round the corner. A Rolls-Royce. The pathologist had arrived.

"Shit!" muttered Frost. "It's Doctor bleeding Death. I'd

better take over, love. He's insulted if he has to deal with
sergeants." He looked longingly up the road, hoping to see
the headlights of Allen's car roaring to the rescue, but no
such luck. Lighting another of Mullett's specials, he
mooched across to the tented area, Liz following hard on his
heels.

A man in white overalls stopped them. This was PC Reg
Evans, a Scene of Crime officer. "There's about twenty rubbish sacks there, Mr. Frost. Do you want us to fingerprint
them all?"

"Better than that, Reg. I want you to take them all back
to the station and open them up. The killer might have
dumped the kid's clothes in one of them."

Dr. Samuel Drysdale, pathologist for the Home Office,
had wasted no time. He was out of the car and kneeling by
the body before Frost returned. Drysdale studied the face
closely, watched by his female secretary, who was directing a
torch to augment the spluttering emergency lighting.
"Steady," he snapped as the beam wavered. Above him, the
canvas flapped angrily in the wind, almost drowning the
constant radio chatter from the police car in the street.

The dribble of vomit from the nostrils and the corner of
the mouth held the pathologist's attention. He lowered his
face until his nostrils were almost scraping the boy's cold
flesh, then sniffed carefully. He nodded. He was able to
place the smell which had baffled Frost. Next, he transferred
his attention to the taped mouth. Behind it, the skin round
the lips was an inflamed red and there were tiny filaments of
white fiber.

"How's it going, Doc?"

Drysdale stiffened. He didn't have to look up to identify
the speaker, and the shower of cigarette ash which floated
down confirmed it. He flapped the ash away angrily and
slowly looked up. There he was. Detective Inspector Jack
Frost in the same battered mac, a button hanging loose, and
an old scarf trailing from his neck. Drysdale glowered. "I

thought this was Mr. Allen's case . . . and kindly put that cigarette out!"

"We're trying to find Allen." Frost pinched out the cigarette and crouched down beside the pathologist. "He's attending a piss-up somewhere." He jabbed a finger at the dead boy's face. "What are those bits of white?"

"Cotton wool," said Drysdale. Before he could elaborate, there was a scurry of activity on the street. Car doors slammed and voices buzzed. Detective Inspector Allen, in evening dress, a white scarf round his neck, made a slightly unsteady entrance into the tent, bringing with him the strong reek of cigar smoke and whisky. He nodded curtly to Frost as he made his apologies to Drysdale. "Sorry for the delay, sir. I was off duty." He stared down at the body, shaking his head. "What can you tell us?"

The pathologist straightened up. "The child was anesthetized." He pointed to the lips. "Those white fibers are from the pad of cotton wool which was used to apply the anesthetic. It was clamped over his mouth and nose. When he was unconscious, a gag of cloth was inserted into the mouth, then the plastic tape was applied to keep it in place. Unfortunately, this meant that when the boy was sick, the stomach contents couldn't escape and he choked to death on his own vomit." Drysdale moved aside so Allen could examine the mouth, which the policeman did with difficulty, his eyes trying hard to focus. He nodded. "I see."

Must have been a bloody good booze-up, thought Frost.

"Any sign of sexual assault?" asked Allen.

"I haven't been able to examine him in detail. This isn't the place. Get him to the mortuary. Don't remove him from that sack and leave the plastic tape in place."

"We'll need the sack for fingrprints," said Frost.

"After I've removed it from the body. Don't worry, I'll wear gloves."

"Time of death?" asked Allen.

"It's a cold night, which tends to slow rigor down. I

would suggest he has been dead somewhere between seven or eight hours. I can be more precise once I get him to the mortuary."

Allen studied his wristwatch very carefully, holding it much closer to his eyes than he usually did. "Which makes the time of death . . ." Brow furrowed in concentration, lips moving, he did mental sums.

"About five or six o'clock this evening," offered Liz Maud.

"I can do my own sums, thank you," snapped Allen, who was a long way from calculating the answer. "Did he die here, Mr. Drysdale?"

"No," said Frost, buttoning his mac, ready to leave them to it. "He wasn't dumped here until six at the earliest."

Drysdale scowled. The question had been addressed to him. "Share your medical expertise with us, Inspector."

"You don't need medical bleeding expertise," said Frost. "The shops don't shut until six and that's when they put their rubbish sacks out."

A grudging nod from Drysdale. "Yes . . . he died elsewhere and was dumped here . . . probably four hours ago."

A burst of wind rattled the canvas and creaked the metal stays. Frost wound his scarf round his neck and lifted the canvas flap. "I'll leave you to get on with it. I'm off home."

"Hold it, Jack." Allen followed him to the street, where the wind felt like ice on his flushed, sweating face. "You couldn't do me a favor, I suppose?"

No way, thought Frost. When have you ever done anything for me? "A favor?" he asked warily.

"Flaming hell, Jack—I've been drinking—look at me. I'm in no state to take over tonight."

Hard bloody luck, thought Frost. You knew you were on call. "You sweat it out, mate, I'm on holiday and I'm off home."

"Just for tonight, Jack. I'll take over again first thing in the morning."

No way, decided Frost. You wouldn't lift a finger if it was me asking you. But he said nothing. He stared at Allen, his face impassive.

"And look at me, Jack. Evening bloody dress . . . half-drunk . . . How can I break the news to the kid's parents looking like this?"

Frost dropped his gaze. Allen had him there. A man stinking of whisky and cigars, in evening dress, swaying, speech slurred, telling you that your seven-year-old child was dead . . . murdered and probably sexaully assaulted. Bloody hell. The bastard had got him. "All right," he grunted.

Allen squeezed his arm. "You're a good 'un, Jack. I owe you one." He walked unsteadily toward the police car that had brought him from Felstead.

Frost somehow managed to reach the car before Allen and opened the driver's door. There was another passenger in the car, a man also in evening dress, sitting bolt upright in the back seat. Frost sniffed and wrinkled his nose, winking at the driver. "What a stink of cheap booze in here, driver. Get your prisoner to the drunk cell and then come straight back." He paused and reacted as if he suddenly realized who the "prisoner" was. "Mr. Mullett! Sorry, Super —didn't recognize you in the monkey suit. . . ."

Mullett kept his face expressionless, not giving Frost the satisfaction of showing his annoyance. He stared straight ahead at the back of the neck of the police driver, who was almost choking as he tried to suppress a snigger. Mullett nodded curtly to Frost as Allen clambered in and dropped heavily on the seat beside him. A few muttered words to the driver and the car sped away.

Liz Maud, seeing Allen make his exit, had renewed hopes that this would mean she would be in charge, but was disappointed to see Frost, grinning all over his face, return to the tented area where Drysdale was pulling on his leather gloves. "There's something you should see," the pathologist told them. He took the torch from his assistant, crouched by the body, and shone the light inside the bag. "Take a look."

Frost squatted down beside him. There was something white covering the boy's right hand, fastened around the wrist with yet more masking tape.

"What is it?" asked Frost.

"It looks like a small plastic bag," replied Drysdale. "I can't make anything of it at the moment, but once we get him on the table, I can take a better look." He straightened and clicked off the torch. "You can remove the body now, Inspector. I'll do a brief examination at the mortuary tonight, then a full postmortem at ten tomorrow."

"I'll let Mr. Allen know," said Frost. This was getting too complicated for him and he would be glad to dump it back in Allen's lap. He beckoned to Burton. "Whistle up the meat wagon."

As the Rolls-Royce slid away, its place was taken by the undertaker's plain, unmarked van. Frost checked that the undertaker and his assistant were wearing gloves before they touched the plastic sack and watched as it was lifted and zipped into a black body bag, then carried out to the van.

PC Evans, the SOC officer, squeezed past to take photographs, and to examine the area on which the body had been lying.

Frost drew Liz to one side. "Get back to the station and open up the Murder Incident Room. Then ask Bill Wells for a list of known child molesters."

"I've already got the list," replied Liz. "Someone's breaking into houses and stabbing toddlers in their cots."

"Good," said Frost. "Round them all up . . . any with their dicks out still warm and throbbing, treat with suspicion. . . . Burton, you come with me."

Liz hesitated. "Wouldn't it be better if I came with you

and Burton opened up the Incident Room?" If Frost was leading the inquiry, she wanted to stay with him.

"You're not missing any fun," said Frost. "We're going to break the news to the parents—a job that Mr. Allen wriggled out of. You're welcome to come if you like."

Liz shook her head. She couldn't face any more hysterical mothers tonight. "I'll get back to the station," she told Frost.

It was easy to spot the boy's house in Lacey Street: It was the only one with its lights still on. Even before Frost's Ford had scraped its tires to a stop along the curb, the front door was flung open and a woman came rushing out. "Have you found him?"

Julie Kirby, the boy's mother, eyes swollen from crying, wrenched open the car door. "Have you found him?" she repeated.

"Let's go inside, love." said Frost, lighting up the cigarette he needed to bolster his courage.

"We only went out for a quick drink. We hardly ever go out."

Frost nodded sympathetically. A man in his mid-twenties, about Julie Kirby's age, was at the door. He wore a black imitation leather zip-up jacket. "Have you found the little sod? I'll wring his bleeding neck—"

"Are you Mr. Kirby?" asked Frost.

"No, I'm damn well not. I'm her boyfriend. That kid's ruined our bloody evening."

The boyfriend! Shit, thought Frost. He'd been hoping it was the father so he would only have to break the bad news once. "Let's go inside," he said.

In the house, the mother dropped into an armchair and grabbed a table lighter. She had difficulty lighting her cigarette. Frost leant over and lit it for her. Burton stood by the door, watching, feeling superfluous.

"It's bad news, isn't it?" said the mother. "I know it's bad news."

"You're always bloody negative," said the boyfriend. "Always looking on the black side. Be bloody positive for a change."

That's right, thought Frost. Raise the poor woman's hopes so I can smash them down again. He took a deep drag, then exhaled. He couldn't put it off any longer. "Mrs. Kirby . . ." he began.

The young woman had taken a framed picture from the side table and was holding it to her chest, rocking slowly from side to side. Frost paused. "Is that Bobby?"

She nodded.

He held out his hand. "Could I see it?"

She handed it to him. A school photograph. A freckle-faced boy with light brown hair, grinning shyly at the camera. "Taken last week," she said.

Frost studied the photo, then handed it to Burton.

Burton raised his eyebrows in surprise.

It wasn't the dead boy.

CHAPTER TWO

"We haven't found your son yet, Mrs. Kirby," said Frost, "but we might have found his guy."

"Oh, bloody marvelous," said the boyfriend. "Bring the guy home, put it to bed and that's the end of it."

"Why don't you shut your mouth," said Julie Kirby. "It was *your* bloody idea we should go to the pub."

"You didn't try to talk me out of it, did you? I hadn't finished suggesting it before you had your hat and your bloody coat on and were halfway up the street."

Frost stretched out his arms like a referee parting two boxers. "Can you save the squabbling till later? We're very concerned about your son, Mrs. Kirby, and we want to find him as quickly as possible. Now, his guy—white and green plastic zip-up jacket?"

She nodded. "Bobby's old one—he'd grown out of it."

"And the mask—Guy Fawkes with a green face?"

"Yes."

"We found it in a shop doorway in Patriot Street. Would Bobby have gone there with his guy?"

"I wouldn't have thought so. No one goes through there at night. He was after money. He usually hung about around pubs and bus stops."

"Tell me exactly what happened tonight."

"We've already told it once," said the boyfriend.

"And now you are going to tell it again," snapped Frost, "and if I want you to tell it twenty bloody times, you'll tell it twenty bloody times. What's your name, by the way?"

"Green. Terry Green."

Frost waited while Burton noted this down, then turned to the mother. "What happened tonight, Mrs. Kirby?"

"Bobby had his tea at five and then he wanted to go out with his guy. I said no. It was too dark and there's been this weirdo out at night stabbing kids."

Frost nodded vaguely. This must be the case Liz Maud was rabbiting on about. "And how did Bobby take it?"

"He swore at me."

"Don't know where the little bastard gets it from," said Terry Green. "Anyway, I gave him a clout, so he swears at me—said I wasn't his bloody father and I said I was bloody glad I wasn't otherwise I'd have strangled him at birth—"

"Okay," said Frost, cutting him short, "spare us the happy families stuff. What happened then, Mrs. Kirby?"

"Bobby sat and sulked in front of the telly. Just after seven, Terry suggested we go out for a quick drink. I told Bobby that as soon as his program finished, he was to go straight to bed. Me and Terry went out and were back just after ten. I went upstairs to check if Bobby was all right—and he wasn't there."

"Little sod—just did it to spite us," said Green.

"Did the officers who came earlier do a search of the house? Sometimes kids hide, just for the fun of it."

"They turned the place upside down. He isn't here. We've been out pounding the streets, looking for him. We've been round to all his friends' houses and they haven't seen him!"

His friends. Could one of them be the dead boy? "None of his friends were missing, I suppose?"

She looked puzzled. "No . . . we spoke to them all."

"I see. And you've absolutely no idea where Bobby might be?"

"I know where he is," said Green. "He's round his bloody father's moaning about us."

"If he was there, Harry would have phoned," said the woman.

"Hold on," said Frost. "The father . . . He lives locally?"

"He lives in Dane Street with his slag Chinese girl."

"Suzie bloody Wong," added Green.

"Are you telling me the boy's father lives in Denton and you haven't checked to see if your son is with him?"

"If Bobby was with him, he'd phone me."

"And you haven't told him Bobby's missing?"

"If he knew we'd left Bobby in the house on his own while we went to the pub, Harry'd come round and cause trouble. He's already threatened to smash Terry's face in."

What better reason to go round and see Harry, thought Frost.

Outside, in the car, he radioed through to Liz Maud to tell her that the dead boy wasn't Bobby Kirby and that the search for him should continue. "If we don't find him tonight, get Bill Wells to organize a search team for the morning. We'll have to pull men in off their rest days—tell him to clear it with Mullett."

"Right," Liz said.

"Circulate all forces with a description of the dead kid. Has anyone reported him missing."

"Right."

"Anything you can't manage, let me know."

"There's nothing I can't manage," she snapped. *"Over and out."*

"What do you think of Ms. Maud?" asked Burton, as he tried to get the engine of Frost's car to cough into life.

"Maud can come into my garden any time she likes," said Frost. "Hooray!" This because the engine suddenly belched and fired and they were away. "Put your foot down, son. I can't wait to see what this Chinese girlfriend looks like."

"Oriental women are old and wizened at thirteen," said Burton.

"Then let's hope she's only eleven," said Frost.

The house looked promising. It was past midnight, but lights were on downstairs. Burton thumbed the doorbell and after a short while a woman's voice called, "Yes?"

"Police," said Burton. The door opened on a chain and he pushed his warrant card through the gap. "I wonder if we can have a word?"

The door opened. She was a stunner. A Chinese girl in her late teens, a doll's face and shiny black hair flowing loosely down her back. She had just showered and she glowed, squeaky clean and wholesome, in a white toweling bathrobe. She smelled of Johnson's baby powder. Her name was Koo Chen, she was a nurse at Denton Hospital, and she was getting ready for night duty. "How can I help you?"

Bloody easily, thought Frost, but he let Burton do the talking. "Is Bobby here?" Burton asked as Koo Chen led them through to a tiny kitchen. Here, too, everything was spotless and gleaming.

"Bobby?" A flicker of concern darkened her face. "Bobby is with his mother."

"Could we speak to his father—Mr. Harry Kirby?"

"He asleep. But I fetch."

Harry Kirby was thick-set, with fair, curly hair. Some six feet tall, he towered over the tiny nurse, who looked up at him with obvious pride. Straight from bed, he had pulled on a pair of jeans and a grey sweater. "What's this about Bobby?"

"Is he here, Mr. Kirby?" asked Burton.

"Here? Why should Bobby be here?" He glared at Frost. "What's happened?"

"He's gone missing, Mr. Kirby," said Frost.

Kirby listened, mouth agape with incredulity, anger reddening his face as Frost told him what had happened.

"That cow left my seven-year-old son alone in the house while she and that dickhead went to the pub?" He looked down at the nurse. "Shoes!" he commanded.

Her eyes widened in alarm. "Where you go?"

"Round to see that cow and her ponce of a boyfriend and smash their faces in."

She thrust out her chin. "No—you stay here."

"He's not your son—he's mine. Get those shoes!"

"Hold it," said Frost wearily, his head aching from all the squabbling. "No one's going anywhere. We're going to search the house."

Kirby stared openmouthed at Frost. "You think he's here? You think I'm hiding my own son in my girlfriend's house? Where is he—behind the attic wall like Anne flaming Frank?"

"Bobby's missing," explained Frost patiently. "We don't know where he is. He might have sneaked in without you knowing. So, for everyone's peace of mind, we're going to do a search." The father moved to follow them, but Frost jabbed a finger, directing him back to the kitchen. "Stay here, please."

Burton checked the ground floor while Frost went up the stairs. First he checked the bathroom. Nowhere a child could hide, or be hidden. Just a washbasin and a shower. A tin of Johnson's baby powder stood on the window ledge and the nurse's tiny damp footprints showed on the carpet tiles. Next to the bath was the spare bedroom, not much more than a boxroom, with a single bed and a small white-painted chest of drawers. Opposite this was the nurse's bedroom, clean, neat, and small, like the nurse herself. The room was just big enough to hold a double bed, jammed tight against the wall to save space, and a dressing table. In the corner was a built-in cupboard. Frost pulled the door open. Men and women's clothes swinging from hangers, a stack of ironing on the shelf, and two empty suitcases on the floor. He knelt and looked under the bed. Something yellow and wispy was on the floor. A very short, skimpy nightdress with a heady perfume that was not Johnson's baby powder. The thought of slipping into that double bed with the soft, compliant little nurse made Frost almost forget what he was there for and he jerked round guiltily as Burton came into the room.

"Nothing downstairs," reported Burton.

"Nor up here," said Frost. "Apart from this!" He held up the nightdress. "The naughty nurse's nightie . . . Cor, I bet her little bottom pokes out from under that like a couple of honeydew melons."

Burton grinned. The joy of working with Frost was that he never let the circumstances of the case he was working on get him down.

Downstairs in the kitchen, Harry Kirby was pulling on a thick duffle coat, anxiously watched by the nurse.

"I come with you," she announced. She had a slight lisp, which Frost was finding disconcertingly stimulating.

"No," snapped Kirby. "You get on to the hospital. You could well have two more patients in Emergency, by the time I've finished with them."

"Go to bed and save your bloody energy," said Frost. "If we don't find Bobby tonight, we'll be organizing a search party first thing in the morning and we're going to need all the help we can get, which means you *and* dickhead."

As they stepped out into the street they could hear the car radio pleading for them to answer. *"Can you get over to the mortuary, Inspector? The pathologist wants to see you urgently."*

．．．

The mortuary, a somber Victorian single-story building, was situated on the grounds of Denton Hospital. Burton parked alongside the Rolls, which gleamed and sneered at Frost's mud-stained Ford. "Looks like a bloody hearse," sniffed Frost. There were other cars, a dark blue Audi which Frost recognized as belonging to Evans, the Scene of Crime officer, and the Vauxhall belonging to Harding from Forensic.

Most of the autopsy room was in darkness, but strong lights glared down at one of the tables where a gowned Drysdale, a green waterproof apron round his waist, beckoned the inspector over. Behind Drysdale, notebook in hand, was his ever-faithful secretary. Drysdale preferred to dictate his notes rather than use cassette recorders, which had let him down on more than one occasion. Evans, also wearing a green mortuary overall, hovered in the background with his camera. Alongside Evans, similarly gowned, stood Harding from Forensic.

The tiny corpse of the boy seemed lost on the large autopsy table.

"I want you to see this," said Drysdale. He bent over and carefully lifted the boy's right hand, the hand that had been covered by the white plastic bag.

Frost stared and his mouth sagged open. Behind him, Burton gasped. Where the boy's little finger should have been was now a blooded stump. The finger had been hacked off just above the knuckle. Very gently, Frost took the cold, waxen hand from Drysdale to study it closer.

"A clean cut," said Drysdale, almost with a note of admiration at the craftsmanship. "I imagine a sharp blade was rested on the finger, then hit with something heavy. A single blow was sufficient. The wound was then doused with disinfectant, wrapped in cotton wool, and strapped with sticking plaster. The bag was put on, I imagine, in case any blood leaked out."

"Was it done before, or after, death?"

"Definitely before."

"Poor little bastard!" said Frost.

"I doubt if he knew anything about it. I imagine that was why he was chloroformed."

"Would it have required some degree of surgical skill to sever the finger?" said Burton, peering over Frost's shoulder.

"No," said Drysdale. "Just a high degree of callousness."

"So a nurse could have done it?" suggested Frost.

Drysdale frowned. "Anyone could have done it . . . a nurse, a plumber, a television repairman."

"Would there have been much blood, Doc?"

Drysdale pursed his lips. "Very little. You would get more blood cutting yourself shaving." He nodded to his secretary, who flipped open her notebook. "Let's get on." He glanced up at the clock. "Examination of the body of Robert Kirby commenced at one fifty-seven," he dictated.

"Oh!" interrupted Frost. "Sorry, Doc—should have told you. This isn't Bobby. We don't know who he is."

Drysdale glowered. "Thank you for sharing that information, Inspector. I find these little details rather important." As he turned back to the table, Frost thumbed his nose at him.

Very slowly, Drysdale inspected the body, lifting the hands to examine the fingernails, searching for cuts, abrasions, any marks of injury. He raised the head and his fingers explored the scalp.

"If you could hurry it up, Doc," urged Frost. "We don't know who the poor little sod is yet, and we want to get photographs off to the media."

Ignoring him, Drysdale dictated his findings to his secretary. "Little finger of right hand severed, but no other signs of external injuries." He bent over the face. "Vomit exuding from nose." He took samples and passed them over to Harding. "Mouth and eyes covered with brown plastic masking tape approximately fifty millimeters wide." He moved to one side. "You may remove the tape now."

Harding carefully eased it off with tweezers, first from the eyes, then the mouth. A sour smell of vomit and chloroform. The boy's mouth, distorted by the tape, had been frozen into a grotesque teeth-baring grin. The flash gun crackled and the film-winding motor whirred as Evans took pictures.

Drysdale studied the area around the lips and nostrils, pointing out where small fibers of cotton wool still adhered. He tweezered them off and passed them over to Harding. "The anesthetic was poured on a pad of cotton wool and clamped over the mouth, causing a slight burning of the flesh . . . here . . . and here." He forced open the mouth and shone a small pen torch inside. "Particles of undigested food and vomit . . . looks like ground meat . . . onion . . ." Then he tweezered out a piece of sodden cloth and held it aloft before dropping it into the large glass container Harding was holding out for him. "The gag," he announced. Then, with agonizing slowness, he extracted more samples from the mouth and nose.

"Any sign of sexual interference, Doc?" asked Frost impatiently.

"I'll tell you when I'm ready," murmured Drysdale, "and not before." He then proceeded to work even slower.

Frost sighed. The man was a bastard. He wandered off to a side room and helped himself to a mug of coffee from a thermos he found on the table. He had no wish to see the body opened and the organs removed and weighed. All he wanted was the findings. He sipped coffee and smoked and tried to think of anything he should have done, but hadn't. He poured another mug of coffee, then wandered back to the autopsy room. The pathologist had finished. He was washing his hands at the sink, while the mortuary attendant was busily suturing the gaping wounds. "Brief findings,

Doc?" He stressed the "brief." Drysdale was inclined to be long-winded.

Drysdale tugged at the automatic towel dispenser. "No sign of sexual assault. If that was the intention, it wasn't carried out."

"Good." Frost nodded, although this meant there was no way of knowing if they were looking for a sex attacker or not.

"His last meal was a fast-food hamburger—sesame-seed bread roll, ground beef, onion rings—eaten very shortly before death."

"How shortly?" Frost asked.

"Half an hour at the most."

Frost thought this over as he tried to rub some life into his cheek. It was freezing cold in the autopsy room and his scar was starting to ache. The kid had a hamburger half an hour before he died. They'd have to check all the likely places—McDonald's, Burger King—to see if someone might remember serving him among their hundreds of other customers. . . . You're bound to remember him, he bought a hamburger! A forlorn, bloody hope, he knew.

"There's a very faint mark around the hairline," said Drysdale, leading him back to the body. "You can hardly see it." He slipped a finger under the hair to lift it and showed Frost what he meant . . . a barely perceptible white mark, just under an eighth of an inch wide, running across the forehead.

"What do you make of it, Doc?"

"Something elasticated pulled over the hair. My secretary suggested a shower cap." Drysdale nodded to the woman, who blushed and went back to writing out labels for the specimen jars.

"A shower cap?"

"Doesn't make much sense, but something like that. You'll get my fuller report in the morning."

"Send it to Mr. Allen," said Frost. "Not me—it's not my

case, thank God!" Then he remembered what he meant to ask. "Chloroform. Do they still use it in hospitals?"

Drysdale shook his head. "Not for many years. It's been superseded."

"So where would you get it—a chemist?"

Another shake of the head. "Only if they've got some very old stock they haven't got around to throwing away yet. Years ago it was used in certain prescribed medicines, but not any more. Anything else?"

Frost scratched his head. "That's all I can think of, Doc."

"I'll bid you good night then." Drysdale jerked his head to his secretary, who followed him out.

Evans began to bag up the materials removed from the body—the masking tape, the cotton wool and sticking plaster. . . . The mortuary attendant came to take the body back to the storage area, but Frost held up a hand to delay him. "Take a couple of Polaroid shots of the face," he instructed Evans. "I want them faxed out to all forces in the hope someone can identify the poor little git." He moved out of the way as the flash gun fired. One last look at the body. He lifted the hand with the severed finger. "Why the hell would anyone want to do this?"

"Liz Maud has got a weirdo breaking into houses and stabbing kids," said Burton. "Could be him."

"Could be," said Frost, not sounding very convinced. "I'll have a word with her."

On the way out they passed Drysdale and his secretary in the midst of an angry exchange with the mortuary attendant, who was hotly denying helping himself to coffee from their thermos flask.

In the car Frost settled back into the passenger seat and offered his cigarettes to Burton. "I want you to check up on that little Chinese nurse. Find out where she was from four o'clock onward today."

Burton frowned. "You surely don't suspect her?"

"Sticking plaster, cotton wool, chloroform, things you'd

find in a hospital. And she'd certainly know how to lop off a finger."

"But what on earth would her motive be?"

"I don't know, son." The cigarette waggled in his mouth as he spoke and sent a shower of ash down the front of his mac. "Perhaps she was jealous of Kirby's son—perhaps he was spoiling their relationship."

"But this is a different boy."

"They all look the same to us—maybe our kids all look the same to them. Perhaps she got the wrong kid." Even as he said it, it sounded weak. Frost sighed. "Just check her out, son. It'll give us something to do. We've got no other leads at the moment."

A disgruntled Bill Wells grabbed Frost as soon as he entered the station. "If you want me to do anything for you, Jack, like organize a search party, do me the courtesy of talking to me direct. I'm not having that stuck-up cow telling me what to do."

"Sorry," said Frost, knowing how prickly Wells could be. "Have one of Mullett's fags and we'll say no more about it."

Wells took one and let the inspector light it for him. He was still not mollified.

"And where is the good lady in question?" asked Frost.

"Lording it up in the Murder Incident Room."

Frost nodded and breezed off down the corridor. "I'll give her your love," he called.

He sailed into the Incident Room. Liz had done a good job getting it organized and under way. The fax machine in the corner was chirping away, spewing out yards of messages, two uniformed men were taking calls, and another phone was ringing on an unoccupied desk. As Burton followed Frost in, Liz yelled, "Answer that phone."

Sullenly, Burton snatched it up. Like Wells, he wasn't happy taking orders from a woman.

"Be with you in a minute," Liz called to Frost, putting down her phone and galloping over to the fax machine. She skimmed through the messages, shook her head in disappointment, and dumped them in an already full wire basket. She was annoyed. "We fax all forces asking if they've had a boy answering our description reported missing and they send us details of every missing boy they've got on their books whether it fits our description or not. Some have even sent details of missing girls!"

"Anything remotely like our boy?"

She pulled a fax from the pile. "Just this seven-year-old, Duncan Ford, reported missing this afternoon from Scotland."

Frost took the fax. " 'Last seen in Montrose just after four-thirty,' " he read. "Well, unless the Concorde has changed its route, we can rule him out." He gave her the Polaroid shots taken at the mortuary. "Fax these around." Then he remembered the photograph of Bobby the mother had given him. "You'd better send this out as well."

As she busied herself at the fax machine, Frost riffled through the heap of faxes received, then pushed the tray away. His gut feeling told him that the murdered child came from Denton and they were wasting their time inquiring elsewhere. When Liz came back he asked her about her child stabber.

"We've had four cases over the past week," she told him. "He breaks into the house, usually through a window, and stabs the kids while they sleep . . . just cuts their flesh. I think he gets a sexual kick out of seeing blood."

"Do you think he'd get a bigger sexual kick cutting off a finger?" She shuddered as he told her about the dead boy and of Drysdale's findings. "Let Mr. Allen know tomorrow—and tell him his company is requested at the postmortem—ten A.M., top hat, white tie, and tails." He yawned. It was nearly three o'clock in the morning. "I'm off home." A wave to everyone. "See you next week."

As he left, she was yelling for one of the PCs to start

checking through the rubbish bags stacked in the car park to see if the dead boy's clothes had been dumped inside.

"Bossy, isn't she?" whispered Frost to Burton.

"Too bleeding bossy," muttered the DC.

"Still," added Frost, "I wouldn't kick her out of bed on a frosty night."

Burton sniffed derisively. "I wouldn't have her in my bed in the first place."

It wasn't until he got home and the front door slammed behind him that he suddenly remembered Shirley. Shirley, who had been on holiday with him and who was going away again with him in the morning. He had left her in the house while he went off to the station to nick some fags from Mullett's goody box. Bloody hell! He had told her he would only be a couple of minutes; that was nearly five hours ago.

She wasn't in the living room. He looked hopefully in the bedroom. The unmade bed was empty. Sod it! He snatched up the phone and dialed Shirley's number. The engaged tone. She had left the phone off the hook. Sod, sod, and double sod! He considered driving round to her place, but was too damn tired. What a bloody fine holiday this was turning out to be. Piddling with rain all the time he was away, a murder case, a postmortem, and a solitary bed. He undressed, letting his clothes fall on the floor by the bed, then flopped down on the mattress.

He slept soundly until seven-thirty when the insistent ringing of the phone brought him reluctantly to the surface. It could only be Shirley. But at this hour? He lifted the phone.

"Frost," he mumbled, sounding very contrite.

It wasn't Shirley. It was the station. Mullett wanted him to report there right away.

"Tell the silly sod I'm on holiday," said Frost.

"The silly sod knows that," answered Bill Wells. "But he still wants to see you and he's in a real right mood."

Frost's heart nose-dived. "He's not been counting his bloody fags, has he?"

It was ten past eight and still dark as he turned the Ford into the car park at the rear of the station. Usually half-empty at this time of the morning, it was now jam-packed with alien vehicles of all kinds. Bobby Kirby was obviously still missing and the search party was assembling. Every available officer had been called in to help, including off-duty personnel and officers who could be spared from neighboring divisions. All very efficiently organized. Frost was glad it wasn't his case. Organization and efficiency weren't his strong point. He'd have made a complete sod-up of it all.

As he bumped along, looking for somewhere to leave the Ford, a stray dog in the kennels started to bark and was answered by suppressed whining from the dog-handler's van over in the far corner of the car park. Space was at a premium, but he managed a clumsy double-park which effectively boxed in Mullett's blue Jaguar.

In the lobby, a weary-looking Sergeant Bill Wells—who should have gone off duty at six—was directing a group of constables from Thorrington Division up to the canteen where the main briefing was to take place. "Follow the smell of stewed tea and burnt bacon—you can't miss it," called Frost.

Wells beckoned Frost over, his eyes glinting as they always did when he had an item of tasty gossip to impart. "Did you hear what happened last night?"

"You got your leg over with Liz Maud?" suggested Frost.

"She should be so lucky!" snorted Wells. He leant across the desk. "That booze-up last night that Mullett and Allen attended. It was some sort of senior police do—top brass from all divisions were there."

"My invite must have been lost in the post," said Frost.

"Anyway," continued Wells, getting to the meaty bit, "my information is, they sunk a lot more booze than was good for them and they were all well·over the limit. Chief Inspector Formby from Greenford Division was giving four of them a lift back. He was in no fit state to drive, but that didn't stop him. Just outside the hotel car park there's a lamp post. Formby wraps the car round it and turns it over."

Frost beamed. "I like happy endings."

"It's even happier," continued Wells. "They're all in Felstead Hospital with broken arms and ribs—Formby's leg is broken as well."

"Serves the bastard right," said Frost. "If he had an inch of common decency, he'd have given Allen and Mullett a lift too and broken both their bloody legs."

More uniformed men swept in. Wells steered them up the stairs to the canteen, then leant over to Frost, lowering his voice. "Here's the best bit, Jack. The ambulance was called and the Traffic boys turn up anxious to breathalyse the driver—the car just stunk of malt whisky."

"Bloody hell," said Frost, "I'd give up me pension for the chance to breathalyse a sod like Formby."

"He wasn't breathalysed, Jack. Someone pulled rank."

"There's no justice," said Frost.

"Anyway, five senior officers in hospital is going to make them a bit thin on the ground for a few weeks." The internal phone rang. Mullett. "He wants you," said Wells.

"He can't have everything he wants," said Frost.

Mullett dropped the Alka-Seltzers in the glass of water and winced at the head-splitting fizzing noise. He shouldn't have drunk so much last night, but the other officers were so insistent and he didn't want to appear the odd man out. A perfunctory tap at the door and before he could say "Enter,"

Frost had shuffled in. Mullett groaned. Was that the only suit the man had? He squeezed out a thin smile and waved Frost to a chair, then swilled down the Alka-Seltzer.

"Have a good holiday?" he asked.

"Peed with rain all week," grunted Frost.

"Good," said Mullett, who wasn't listening.

"Did you get my comic postcard?" asked Frost.

Mullett frowned. Yes, he had got the card. And torn it up immediately. "It was extremely rude," he muttered.

Frost looked puzzled. "Rude? You must have spotted some double meaning I missed."

Mullett flapped a hand. "Be that as it may. Sorry to drag you in, Frost, but things happened last night. Five of our top men involved in a car accident."

"So I heard," said Frost. "The car had a fight with a lamp post."

"Yes—a patch of oil on the road. They skidded." Mullett, not a good liar, didn't sound convincing.

"Was Formby breathalysed?" asked Frost. "I understand he'd had a few."

"Oh, Chief Inspector Formby wasn't driving," said Mullett, carefully avoiding Frost's eye. "His daughter was driving and she hadn't been drinking."

Frost smiled and gave a conspiratorial wink. "Bloody clever! You're a lot of crafty sods, sir, that's all I can say."

"What do you mean?"

"It's obvious. Formby was driving. He didn't dare be breathalysed, so you brought his daughter in from home to pretend she was the driver."

Mullett tried to sound suitably shocked. "That's a libelous thing to say, Frost. His daughter was driving. We all gave statements to that effect."

"Then the witness who claims to have seen it all differently is telling lies?" said Frost. He put on his innocent expression. "What did you want to see me about?"

But Mullett was now in a high state of agitation. "What

witness? What does he claim to have seen? You must tell me."

"If what you say is true, then he couldn't have seen anything, could he, sir?" said Frost blandly. "It would be your word against his, anyway, even if he is a vicar."

Mullett stared hard and jotted a note on his pad. He would have to talk to Frost about this later, man-to-man on a friendly basis. He hadn't wanted to get involved in this wretched deception anyway, but they had pulled rank and twisted his arm. He cleared his throat. "The result of this unfortunate accident is that five senior officers are nursing broken bones in hospital."

"Then it wasn't all bad," said Frost.

Mullett ignored this. "Obviously, this has meant some temporary relocation of personnel. In our case it means that Inspector Allen has been seconded to Greenford Division as acting chief inspector until such time as Mr. Formby is fit enough to return."

"When is he going?" asked Frost.

"He's already gone. It was arranged last night."

"Do you mean to tell me," said Frost, "that Allen knew he wouldn't be here when he conned me into taking over his case on a temporary basis last night?"

"I don't know anything about that," said Mullett, again not meeting Frost's eye.

"The bastard," said Frost, banging his fist on Mullett's desk, which jolted Mullett's headache into overdrive.

"Please!" Mullett held his head. "You will take over all his cases."

"That still leaves us a man short."

"There will be a temporary replacement for Mr. Allen . . . a detective sergeant as acting inspector. We haven't finalized the details yet."

"The sooner the better—we're pushed enough as it is."

Mullett waved a hand of dismissal. "I'll leave you to it,

then. Sorry to have to cut your holiday short, but it couldn't be avoided."

"A few less drinks last night and it would have been," grumbled Frost, pushing himself out of the chair.

As the door closed, Mullett heard a startled cry from his secretary and a raucous laugh from Frost. "Caught you bending there, Ida!"

The divisional commander shook his head sadly. What could you do with a man like that?

Frost took a quick look in Allen's office on his way up to the briefing. He shuddered. The room was so neat and tidy, it almost hurt. Desktops clear, wall charts meticulously entered, and the prissy smell of lavender wax polish. A cold, heartless room, which matched its former occupant, and which made Frost itch to get back to the warm, untidy fug of his own office. He delved into Allen's in-tray and pulled out a neat stack of forms and returns which had to be completed and sent off to County by the third of the month. Trust the sod to leave them behind. He put them back and went across the corridor to the Incident Room where Liz Maud, still in her drab grey outfit, was surprised to see him.

"I thought you were on holiday, Inspector?"

He explained about Allen. Her eyes narrowed. If a detective sergeant was to be made up to acting inspector, then who better than her!

"There's a few returns and things in his office," said Frost vaguely. "Perhaps you could see if you could handle them."

"No problem," she said. "I'll move in there."

"I take it we didn't find Bobby Kirby?"

"No. The briefing for the search party is in five minutes."

"Right . . . I suppose I'd better do it."

She concealed her disappointment. In the absence of Allen, she was hoping she could take this over.

"Have we identified the dead kid?"

"No."

"Damn." Frost lit up a cigarette and stared out of the window onto the car park. "A young kid, eight years old at the most, and dead for nearly twenty hours. Why haven't his parents reported him missing?" He sucked hard at the cigarette as he had a thought. "It could be because it's his parents who killed him." He spun round to Liz. "As soon as the schools open, get on the phone to the head teachers. I want to know if there's any seven- or eight-year-old boys who haven't turned up for school today."

"Right."

"But don't tell them he's dead—not until we've traced and informed the parents."

"Of course not." Give her credit for some common sense.

"Any joy with the rubbish sacks?"

"Plenty of prints, but we're checking with the shop people today to eliminate them. And no sign of the clothing."

"Has everyone in the briefing got copies of both photographs—the dead kid and Bobby?"

"Yes."

"And the guy? People might not have noticed the kid, but they could remember the guy."

"Yes. And I've sent copies of the photograph of Bobby to the press and TV and we're having a pile of Have You Seen This Boy? posters run off. Also some extra large ones to stick on a loudspeaker van to tour the neighborhood."

"Good." Frost nodded. He had forgotten about that. "Right, let's get the search party briefed."

The canteen was packed. He snatched himself a mug of tea and a bacon sandwich and elbowed his way through to the front. "Your attention, please!"

There were murmurs of surprise. Everyone had been expecting Inspector Allen.

"First the good news—and I must ask you to promise not to laugh. Chief Inspector Formby was injured in a car crash last night and is in hospital with two broken arms and a broken leg." He paused as delighted laughter roared out. "And this will really make you laugh—he's in quite a bit of pain."

There were one or two cheers at this. Formby, with his sneering manner and sarcastic tongue, was not a popular officer.

"The bad news is that Inspector Allen has been seconded to Greenford as acting chief inspector and I'm in charge of this missing-boy inquiry. You are looking for Bobby Kirby, aged seven. You all have a photograph and a description. His parents have split up and he lives with his mother and her boyfriend. Last night the mother and the boyfriend nipped out to the pub for a quick one, leaving the kid alone in the house. When they returned just after ten, the kid wasn't there. Apparently he sneaked out with his guy to collect money. About eleven o'clock last night we found the guy behind a pile of rubbish bags stacked in a shop doorway in Patriot Street. Next to the guy was a boy's body in a rubbish sack. The boy, aged around seven or eight, had been chloroformed and gagged with plastic masking tape and had choked on his own vomit. He was naked, but there was no sign of sexual assault. The boy was not Bobby Kirby and up to now he has not been reported as missing, so we don't know who he is. We'll be checking with schools as soon as they open. So our task is twofold. To find Bobby and to find out all we can about the dead boy."

He deliberately didn't say anything about the severed finger. There'd be floods of hoax calls and fake confessions and he wanted there to be something that only the real murderer would know.

"About half an hour before he died, the boy ate a hamburger. It's going to be a bloody waste of time, but we've got to check all the fast-food joints in Denton and ask if they remember serving something as unusual as a hamburger to the boy in the photograph around between, say, four to five o'clock. I'm sure this will give us about three hundred use-less leads, but it's got to be done. Any questions?"

A duffle-coated PC from Lexton Division put up his hand. "You think there's a connection between the dead boy and Bobby Kirby?"

"The dead kid was found next to Bobby's guy. That's the only connection we've got at the moment. It could be a coincidence, but it's good enough for me. I say there's a connection." He looked around. No one else had any questions. "Right. You've been allocated your search areas, so the very best of luck."

Frost watched them file out, clutching the copies of the photographs. He was hoping for the best, but he had a nasty feeling at the pit of his stomach that they were not going to find anything.

CHAPTER THREE

Phones in the Incident Room were ringing nonstop. The TV appeal for Bobby's return made by his distraught parents, the tearstained mother with her husband's arm firmly around her, Terry Green and the Chinese nurse tactfully absent, had provoked a terrific response from people convinced they had seen Bobby. None of the leads seemed very hopeful, but all would have to be followed up.

In the same TV bulletin, a photograph of the dead boy was shown with a statement that the police were anxious to identify him. No mention was made of the fact he was dead, nor that there might be a connection with the Kirby boy.

DC Burton, his ear sore from being constantly pressed against the phone, scribbled some details and thanked the caller. He tossed the form into the main collection basket.

"Any news from Forensic?" asked Frost, dropping into the chair next to him.

"Nothing worth having. The masking tape on the boy's face is run-of-the-mill stuff and there were no prints on it. The cotton wool is a standard type. The plastic bag round his hand came from Bi-Wize Supermarket and there were no prints on the rubbish sack the body was in."

"If we didn't have a Forensic Department," said Frost,

"how would we know we had sod-all to go on? What about the prints on the other rubbish sacks?"

"The only prints found so far came from the shop staff."

"This bloke is too bloody clever to leave prints," said Frost gloomily. He glanced up at the clock. Nine-twenty-five. The kid had been dead for some eighteen hours and no one yet reported him missing. "Who's in charge of checking the schools?"

"Wonder Woman. She's in Mr. Allen's office."

"Right, son." Frost pushed himself up from the chair. "Let's go and see what she's got—if you'll pardon the expression."

Bill Wells was distributing the internal mail. From force of habit he knocked on the door of Inspector Allen's office and a red light, signaling "Wait," flashed. Dutifully, he waited. Then a green light bade him "Enter." Wells went in and stared goggle-eyed. Sitting at Inspector Allen's desk was Liz bloody Maud, looking as if she owned the bloody place. The cow! Flicking the switch to make him wait. Who the hell did she think she was?

She didn't look up, just waggled her finger at the in-tray. "In there, please." Fuming, Wells flung the mail in. As he reached the door, she called, "Sergeant!"

He turned. She was holding up a red folder and beckoning for him to come over. "Do you mind taking this to Mr. Mullett?"

"Yes, I bloody well do mind," he snapped and his slamming of the door echoed around the building.

Liz shrugged. She knew Wells resented her. Well, he'd just have to learn to start taking orders from a woman, because her immediate aim was to be promoted to acting detective inspector during Allen's absence. She had met with Superintendent Mullett and explained why she was the most suitable person for the temporary promotion. He had nodded vigorously and agreed wholeheartedly with everything she'd said. "The decision is not up to me," he had told her, "but it will receive my strongest personal recommendation." As she didn't yet know Mullett very well, she believed him.

Spluttering with indignation, Wells buttonholed Frost as he came out of the Murder Incident Room and poured out his moans about Liz Maud. "In Allen's office—and with the red light on."

"Perhaps she's turning it into a knocking shop," suggested Frost.

But Wells was too angry for jokes. "Who the hell does she think she is? She's only a flaming sergeant and she's acting like a—" He stopped openmouthed as the almost unthinkable thought struck him. "Flaming hell, Jack. You don't think she's going to be promoted to acting DI, do you?"

"Could be," said Frost. "I saw her coming out of Mullett's office with her knickers in her hand."

"I wonder she wears any!" snarled Wells, stamping off. "I bet that's how she was promoted to sergeant."

Frost went into Allen's office without knocking, although the red light was on. "What news from the schools?" he asked.

"Five boys in the right age group didn't show up for lessons today," Liz told him. "Three they know about—one to the dentist, one in hospital, and one the mother phoned through this morning to say had a cold. . . ."

"Check that one," said Frost. "The mother could be lying. What about the other two?"

"I've sent Collier round to the houses. I'll let you know as soon as he reports in."

Ten o'clock. A lull in the Murder Incident Room. The phones had stopped ringing and Frost was sitting on the corner of a desk, watching Liz, who was stretching across to stick colored pins into the wall maps, to mark the progress of the various search parties, and was showing lots of leg in the bargain.

Progress was slow. Everything up to now was negative. The five boys who were away from school had all been accounted for. The fingerprints on the rubbish bags all came from the shop staff, except for two which were too blurred to provide any positive identification but like the others probably came from a shop assistant. The little Chinese nurse was reported to be very fond of Bobby and wouldn't lift a finger to harm him. A missing boy and a dead boy and no leads to follow on either.

The phone rang. Frost looked up hopefully, but it was Mullett asking for a progress report.

"Tell him it consists of two words," grunted Frost, "and the second is 'all'!"

"Still following up leads, sir," translated Liz, into the phone. "We'll let you know as soon as we have something positive." She went back to her wall map.

Bill Wells came in, grinning. "Control have just had a phone call from a motorist. Said a naked girl tried to flag him down in Hanger Lane."

Frost brightened up. Naked girls interested him very much. "Did he pick her up?"

"No. He couldn't stop. Said he was in a hurry to keep an appointment. He phoned us on his mobile."

Frost frowned and shook his head in disbelief. "A naked girl and he didn't stop? I'd have stopped if she was only half-naked. . . . Bloody hell, I'd have stopped if she was fully dressed with one titty hanging out."

"You're all heart, Jack," said Wells.

"Some people say I'm all dick," said Frost, "but I try not to brag." A snort of disgust from Liz Maud made him pull a face at Wells.

"I've sent Jordan and Simms to pick her up," said Wells.

"Some people have all the luck," said Frost.

Another phone rang. Liz answered it. She listened and her expression changed.

"What's up?" asked Frost.

"That naked girl. It's not as funny as you thought it was. She's only fifteen. She was abducted last night by a gang of men. Her parents had to pay a twenty-five-thousand-pound ransom to get her back."

"Shit!" swore Frost. "We've got enough on our flaming plates without this. . . ." He stared at Liz thoughtfully before reaching a decision. "You can handle this one, love," he said, "if you don't mind me coming with you."

They went in Liz's car, Frost sitting next to her and Evans, the Scene of Crime officer, in the back seat. It was white-knuckle driving as she slammed the car in and out of the tight country lanes, trusting to luck there was nothing coming in the opposite direction. Frost sank down low in his seat and tried not to look at the blur of greenery flashing from side to side across the windscreen as she spun the wheel, slammed on the brakes, and skidded, narrowly avoiding catastrophe after catastrophe.

"Left here," he murmured.

"No—right," said Evans from the back seat.

She turned right. Up to now, Frost had been wrong with his directions every time and she'd had to slam on the brakes and do a reverse.

"There it is," said Evans.

Liz turned the car into a long drive leading to a large, ivy-clad Edwardian house standing alone and surrounded by fields. Frost stared at the house. He'd been here before, but couldn't remember when, or why. A police car was parked just outside the front door. Liz slowed and parked behind it. Frost and Evans staggered out. PC Jordan came from the house to brief them.

"Family of three—husband, wife, and fifteen-year-old

daughter. Husband and wife traveled up to London last night to see a show. They got back home around three in the morning. The house had been ransacked, jewelry and furs valued at fifty thousand pounds missing. They found this on the kitchen table." He gave Frost a sheet of A4 white paper which had been slipped inside a transparent folder to preserve any prints. The message had been printed on a bubble jet printer, and read:

TO MR. & MRS. STANFIELD

WE HAVE YOUR DAUGHTER. IF YOU GO TO THE POLICE WE WILL GANG-RAPE HER. ONE OF US IS HIV POSITIVE.

IF YOU WANT HER RETURNED UNHARMED YOU WILL GO TO YOUR BANK AS SOON AS IT OPENS AT 9:30 AND WITHDRAW £25,000 IN USED NOTES. YOU WILL PUT THE MONEY IN A SMALL SUITCASE. AS YOU PASS THE WHITE GATE IN CLAY LANE YOU WILL THROW THE CASE OUT OF THE CAR INTO THE DITCH. YOU WILL DRIVE STRAIGHT HOME. YOU WILL NOT LOOK BACK.

IF YOU DO ALL THIS AND THERE ARE NO TRICKS WE WILL RELEASE YOUR DAUGHTER UNHARMED. IF YOU TRY TO TRICK US SHE WON'T BE WORTH HAVING WHEN WE RETURN HER. THE ENCLOSED IS TO SHOW WE MEAN BUSINESS!

"This was with it," said Jordan, handing Frost a Polaroid photograph. It showed the girl, kneeling on the floor. A hand grabbed her hair and pulled the head back. The other hand held a knife which was pressed against the girl's throat. Her eyes were closed and her mouth sagged open.

"The family are inside with Simms," Jordan told Frost. "Do you want to see them?"

"Show me round the house first," said Frost, hoping it

might jog his memory as to when he was here before. "How did the gang get in?"

"Through the back door—I'll show you."

Jordan walked them down a side path to the rear of the property where a small patio with tubbed plants backed onto the lawn. One of the glass panels of the back door was smashed. The intruders had punched a hole in the glass, reached in and turned the key, which had been conveniently left in the lock.

Frost squinted through the smashed pane. "Stupid bastards! They install an expensive, six-lever mortise lock, then they leave the flaming key in it." He waited as Evans, his hand gloved, opened the door for them. They stepped over broken glass into the kitchen, Evans staying behind to dust the door for prints. A pine table had been laid the night before with cups and cereal bowls for a breakfast that had not been eaten. Frost picked up the cereal packet. " 'All Bran—nature's laxative.' I bet no one needed that this morning." Jordan laughed, but Liz didn't find it funny. "How many of them were there?"

"Four, we think," said Jordan, taking them through a door leading to the hall. "The first thing they did was to turn the electricity off at the mains." He opened a small cupboard under the stairs and revealed electricity and gas meters, side by side with the central-heating control box just below.

Frost frowned. "Why did they do that?"

"So the girl couldn't call the police. She had a phone in her bedroom, one of those cordless models. If the electricity is off, they don't function."

"I thought they were battery-powered," said Liz.

"The handsets are, but most base units are mains-powered—without electricity they just don't work," Jordan told her.

"I thought they only didn't work when I dropped the bleeding things on the floor," said Frost, checking the clock on the central-heating timer with his watch. It was only a few minutes slow. "It wasn't switched off for long, then?"

"Once they got the girl, they switched the power back on. They needed the electric light so they could ransack the rooms."

Evans rejoined them, shaking his head sadly. "No one leaves fingerprints anymore."

"Crooks today have no consideration for the police," said Frost. He still couldn't remember why he had been in the house. "Let's see the girl's bedroom."

A typical teenager's room. Posters on the wall advertising past pop concerts and a large one saying "Save the Whale." A wall unit held a hi-fi system with two tiny speakers and a ten-inch color TV set. The room had been turned over. Drawers gaped, their contents strewn all over the floor. Frost's nose twitched. The girl's perfume lingered. A bit sexy for a fifteen-year-old, and so were the pair of scanty briefs he bent and picked up. He showed them to Liz. "You'd have a job stuffing your hankie up the leg of these."

Jordan grinned, but Liz stared stonily. The man was an ignorant pig.

Frost flicked the briefs across the room and they butterflied delicately down to the carpet. "What was taken from here, Jordan?"

"The girl's too upset to check, but her mother doesn't think anything is missing." He pointed to a heap of chunky beads, bangles, and necklaces tipped out on the floor. "It's all junk, not worth pinching."

"I'm surprised they didn't take that little telly," said Frost. "I wouldn't mind having that myself."

"They were after bigger fish," said Jordan. "I'll show you."

The main bedroom was a bigger shambles than the girl's, with drawers dragged open and clothes strewn about apparently just for the hell of making a mess. On the big double bed the contents of a drawer had been tipped out—underwear, perfume bottles, cosmetics, in an untidy heap. "The jewel box was in that drawer," said Jordan. "They took the lot, box as well—fifty thousand quids worth they claim—including the fur coats." He nodded toward the far wall, where the sliding door of the woman's wardrobe was open, showing a jumble of coats and dresses on the floor and empty hangers swinging above.

Frost picked his way through the mess on the floor to take a closer look. "Why did they drag all these dresses off?" he asked. "They could have got to the furs without doing that."

"Some people get a kick out of leaving things in a mess," said Liz.

Frost grunted. It could be the answer. He peered through the large picture window which overlooked the garden and the fields and the winding lane which was the only access to the house. More houses in the far distance, but not a soul to be seen. He was fumbling for his cigarettes when a man's voice bellowed from downstairs.

"When you've finished sodding about up there, what about talking to us—or aren't the victims important any more?"

Frost went to the landing and looked down. An angry-looking man was glaring up at them. Robert Stanfield, early fifties, sallow complexion and a tight, thin little mouth.

Frost frowned. He'd seen Stanfield before . . . in this house, but he still couldn't recall the circumstances. He clattered down the stairs, followed by Liz and Jordan, Evans staying behind once again to photograph and check for prints. Suddenly it all came back to him. He smiled broadly. "We meet again, Mr. Stanfield."

The man's eyes crawled over Frost's face. A brief flicker of apprehension, then a thin, scornful smile. "Ah, yes—the arson attack. Let's hope you are more successful this time, Inspector. In here." He jerked his head to direct them into the lounge.

PC Dave Simms, sitting by the door, jumped up as Frost entered. It was a large and comfortable room with a recently lit log fire crackling in the grate. Wide casement windows gave a view across the garden. In the corner a large-screen television sat on a stand, beneath it a video recorder, its clock, not yet reset, flickering on and off, showing there had been a break in the current.

Stanfield hurled himself into an armchair by the fire and swilled down a glass of whisky which had been perched on the arm. Opposite him, in a settee drawn close to the fire, sat his wife and his daughter. Margie Stanfield, dark-haired, in her early forties, wearing a red and black satin housecoat, was flashily attractive. Frost couldn't remember seeing her before. But it was the girl, Carol, PC Simms's greatcoat draped around her, who held Frost's attention. Looking much older than her fifteen years, her dark brown hair was long and flowing and uncombed, giving her a wild, untamed appearance. She kept her head down, but her eyes, narrow like her father's, were watching Frost suspiciously. They reminded him of a cornered animal with nothing to lose and ready to fight back.

Somehow I don't trust you, my love, thought Frost as he gave her his warm and friendly smile.

"I want you to get these bastards," said Stanfield. "They've stolen my wife's jewelry and furs, they've subjected my daughter to hours of terror, and they've blackmailed me into giving them twenty-five thousand pounds!"

"Not your day, sir, was it?" said Frost.

Stanfield opened his mouth to reply when he noticed Liz Maud, who had followed Frost in. "Who the hell is she?"

Liz took the warrant card from her handbag and handed it to him. Stanfield looked at it and sneered contemptuously as he handed it back. "A bloody woman sergeant! I'm not being fobbed off with second-best, am I?"

"No," said Frost. "I'm second-best—she's class. And it's her case." Stanfield's snort showed what he thought of this.

He hadn't asked them to sit down, so Frost dragged the other armchair over to the fire and offered it to Liz while he sat on the arm. "Ask the gentleman your questions, Sergeant."

She opened her notebook. "Tell me everything that happened."

"I've already told that police officer." Stanfield nodded at Simms. "He wrote it all down."

"We can't read his writing," said Frost, "so tell it again."

"My wife and I went up to London to see a show—*The Phantom of the Opera*."

"Just you and your wife?" interrupted Liz. "Not your daughter?"

"As she was bloody abducted while we were away, it's obvious we didn't take her."

"I know you didn't take her," said Liz through clenched teeth, "I'm wondering why."

"If I'd booked the tickets myself, I obviously would have included Carol. Friends of ours had two tickets but found they couldn't go, so they passed them on to us. Satisfied, darling?"

She gritted her teeth at the "darling" and nodded.

"We left just after four yesterday afternoon, drove up to London, saw the show, had a meal, and came home."

"What time did you arrive back?"

"A little after three. I parked the car, Margie went upstairs to switch on the electric blanket and found the bedroom had been trashed."

"Perfume, makeup, dresses, just thrown anywhere," said his wife. "I screamed for Richard. He charged up and made for Carol's room to see if she was all right."

"The bastards had got her," said Stanfield. "My first thought was to phone the police, but I couldn't find the cordless phone—it should have been by Carol's bed."

"They threw it out of the window," said the girl. She

spoke mechanically, staring straight ahead. Her mother put an arm around her.

"Anyway," continued Stanfield, "I couldn't find it so I went to use the phone in here." He pointed to a phone next to the TV set. "A note and a photograph were propped up against it."

"We've seen them," said Liz.

"Then you know what the bastards threatened to do if I called the police. I had no choice. I did exactly what they wanted. We sat in here, staring at each other until the bank opened. It was the longest bloody night of my life. I drew out the money, chucked the case out in Clay Lane, then roared back here to wait. We were going mad with worry—and then your two officers brought her back."

"Twenty-five thousand pounds? You had that sort of money in the bank?"

"Yes. I run a used-car business. Most of my suppliers insist on hard cash."

Liz turned to the girl, who had been staring down at the floor all the time her father was talking. "Right, Carol. Can you tell me what happened to you?"

Carol drew Simms's greatcoat tighter around her and Frost realized she was naked underneath. Her voice was not much more than a whisper. She had gone to bed shortly after midnight and was just dropping off when she heard the sound of breaking glass downstairs. She thought it might be her parents back early, so she clicked on the bedside lamp. Almost immediately the lamp went out. Then she heard men's voices from inside the house. She fumbled in the dark for the cordless phone and dialed 999, but nothing happened. The phone was dead. Heavy footsteps pounded up the stairs. . . .

"I jumped out of bed and tried to wedge a chair under the door handle, but he burst in on me and there was this light in my eyes and the knife. . . ." She started to shake. Her mother held her tighter.

"Take your time, love," said Frost.

"I opened my mouth to scream, but he jabbed the knife at my throat and said if I made a sound he'd slice through my vocal cords. I must have passed out." The memory made the girl shrink back inside the greatcoat. "The next thing I remember was being bumped about. I was in the back of a van, being driven at speed. I was blindfolded and I was cold. They'd thrown a sack over me, but I was freezing. I tried to get up, but a hand pushed me down and a man's voice said 'I think she's with us again.' Then they pulled the sacking back."

"They?" queried Liz.

"There were two of them in the back with me. They pulled the sacking back and they . . . they did things."

"The bastards!" exploded her father.

"What things?" asked Liz.

The girl shook her head. "I'm not going to talk about it."

"Did they rape you?" asked Liz.

"No."

"How many of them were there?" said Frost.

Carol switched her gaze to him. "Four. Two in the back with me, the other two in the front."

"And all men?"

"I only heard men's voices."

"How old would you say they were?"

She shrugged. "I don't know—late twenties—early thirties."

"And you didn't recognize any of the voices?"

"No."

Liz waited patiently for Frost to finish. "I'd like a doctor to examine you, Carol."

"No."

"If they raped you, there are DNA tests that would help us identify them."

"They didn't rape me, I told you. . . . I'm not going to talk about it any more."

"All right," soothed Liz. "What happened then?"

"The van stopped and they changed places . . . the other two men came in. I pretended I'd passed out, so they didn't do anything much, just sat and smoked. After what seemed such a long time, someone banged on the side of the van and called 'We've got the money.' The van drove off, then it stopped and I was pushed out. By the time I'd got the blindfold off, it was out of sight. A car came . . . but it wouldn't stop . . . and then the police car picked me up." She wrapped the greatcoat around her like a cocoon.

"I really would like a doctor to take a look at you," urged Liz.

"No!" She screamed the word out. "I'm all right . . . just leave me alone." With an abrupt shrug, she shook off her mother's arm. "Just leave me alone."

"She's upset," said her mother.

"That's right," exploded Stanfield sarcastically, "explain it to them, they wouldn't bloody know otherwise." To Frost he said, "Right, Inspector, you've had a nice sit-down—now go and catch the bastards!"

"Just a few more questions," said Frost. He smiled at the girl. "You heard breaking glass. You switched on the bedside lamp and tried to dial 999. The lamp went out and the phone was dead—"

"Because they'd switched off the current," said Stanfield, as if explaining to an idiot.

"Exactly. Between the time you heard the sound of glass breaking, which was them getting into the house, and the phone going dead, how much time elapsed?"

"I don't know . . . seconds . . ."

Frost nodded. "They were bloody quick, weren't they? They knew exactly where the meter was."

"It wouldn't take a bloody mastermind to work that out," exclaimed Stanfield. "Most people have their meter cupboard under the stairs."

"Yes," agreed Frost, "but these people had to be sure.

They had to do it bloody quickly otherwise Carol would have made her phone call. There's only one way out of here —along that four-mile lane. The police would have been waiting for them. How did they know that the phone in Carol's bedroom was cordless?"

"I've had this house up for sale for the past four months," said Stanfield. "We've had estate agents in and out measuring up, we've had prospective buyers and every nosy sod imaginable poking and touching everything with their grubby fingers . . . any of them could have been casing the place."

"We'll need names," said Liz.

"Then get them from the estate agents, darling. They didn't leave flaming visiting cards, just sticky, bloody finger marks on the wallpaper."

"When did your friends offer you the tickets for the show?" asked Frost.

"The day before yesterday. He had to go to Paris on business. Why?"

"I'm wondering how the crooks knew Carol would have been alone in the house last night."

"They could have been watching the place and picked their moment. We do go out at night from time to time."

Frost pulled a face. He didn't think much of this explanation. Before he could ask another question, however, Jordan was beckoning from the doorway. "Sorry to disturb you, Inspector, but it is urgent."

Frost stood up. "What was the value of the jewelry they nicked?"

"I haven't added it up—around fifty thousand pounds," said Mrs. Stanfield.

"But you are insured?"

"It's not the money, is it? It's the sentimental value."

"Of course," said Frost.

Stanfield sprang to his feet. "And just what are you insinuating?"

Frost switched on his look of injured innocence. "Nothing, Mr. Stanfield. Nothing at all. Now if you'll excuse me . . ."

He followed Jordan into the hall, closing the door behind him. "What is it, son?"

It was a radio message from Control. A woman had just phoned in reporting her eight-year-old son had been missing since the previous afternoon. His description matched that of the dead boy.

Frost swore softly. "I suppose no one's given the poor cow any hint that he's dead?"

"No, sir," said Jordan.

"We'll go in your car," said Frost. "Sergeant Maud can stay and finish up here." He went back into the lounge and quietly explained the development to Liz. "Got to go," he told Stanfield. "Something important has come up."

Stanfield stared incredulously. "Something more important than this?"

"Yes," sighed Frost. "Something more important than this."

Jordan negotiated the car round the twists and turns of the narrow lane with much more care and skill than Liz had done. Frost sat alongside him, smoking, lost in his thoughts. If the dead boy was her son, how was he going to break it to her? Eight years old . . . God . . . He had radioed for Burton to meet him outside the house. He would have preferred to have a woman police officer with him, but they were all out helping with the search for Bobby Kirby. Still, breaking news like this was a job he had done many times before. Too many bloody times.

Jordan dragged him back from his brooding thoughts. "Who do you reckon is behind this abduction, Inspector?"

Frost took the cigarette from his mouth and dribbled

smoke down his nose. "I'm not even sure there was an abduction, son."

Jordan frowned. "What do you mean?"

"I've come across Stanfield before. He runs this second-hand car business. About four years ago the Customs and Excise were suspicious that he was working some VAT fiddle. The day before they were due to examine his books there was a mysterious and very convenient arson attack on his office. All his receipts and records were destroyed."

"And you believe he started the fire himself?"

"I bloody know he did, son, but I couldn't prove it." He wound down the window and chucked the cigarette out. "If you want my utterly biased opinion, last night's escapade was an insurance fiddle . . . hide the furs and jewels and claim the insurance."

"But if it was an insurance fiddle," protested Jordan, "the girl would have to be in on it as well."

"Ten out of ten," said Frost.

Jordan spun the wheel and turned into Hanger Lane. "This is where we found the girl . . . standing in the middle of the road, starkers."

"You're only saying that to make me jealous," said Frost. A thought hit him. "Stop the car!"

The car coasted to a halt and Jordan watched as Frost poked and prodded among the undergrowth of the grass verge, then disappeared from view as he squeezed through a gap in a hedge. Rustling sounds, then a whoop of delight, and Frost emerged carrying something grey. He climbed back into the car. "What do you reckon this is, son?"

"A blanket," said Jordan. "From a single bed."

"Exactly."

Jordan stared at it blankly. He hadn't the faintest idea what the inspector was on about.

"Listen," explained Frost. "You're a fifteen-year-old girl. You've been dumped in the road by your father to flag down a car. You're starkers and it's freezing and dawn's icy fingers are toying with your privates. So what do you do? You take a blanket with you to keep yourself warm. When you hear a car, you chuck the blanket behind a hedge, step in the middle of the road and waggle your tits. If the car doesn't stop, you retrieve the blanket and wait for the next one."

"It's possible," said Jordan, begrudgingly.

"Sniff it," said Frost.

Jordan lifted the blanket delicately to his nose. "Perfume?"

"And what's the betting that if you sniffed Simms's greatcoat where it was wrapped round her naked little body, you'd smell the same perfume?"

"But the gang could have taken the blanket from her bed and wrapped it round her."

"So why wasn't it still wrapped round her naked little figure when she was flagging cars down?" He sighed. "But that little mystery must wait, son. We're putting off the pleasure of telling a mother her son has been murdered." He tossed the blanket onto the back seat and smoked silently until they reached the address given to them by Control.

Kenton Street consisted of large, three-storied houses, converted into flats. Burton was waiting outside Number 3A. Frost steeled himself and reached for another cigarette. A few quick delaying drags before he would have to confront the mother. But like Bobby Kirby's mother the night before, the woman had seen the police car draw up and was already on the doorstep. Frost gave a deep groan and poked the cigarette back in the packet. "They can't wait for bloody bad news, can they?" He nodded at Burton. "Come on, son. Let me do the talking."

Joy Anderson, a plump, bouncy little brunette in her late twenties, anxiously watched them approach, trying to read some sign of hope from their expressions. "Have you found him?"

"Give us a chance, love," said Frost. "We've only just got your message."

They followed her up the stairs to a largish room which overlooked the street. It was basically furnished like a hotel room, with few signs of personal belongings. Two large suitcases stood beside the two-seater beige settee.

Frost parked himself in a chair by the window. "How long has Dean been missing?"

She sat opposite him, staring out of the window as she answered, leaning forward hopefully every time someone turned the corner, slumping back when it wasn't her son. "About half past two yesterday afternoon."

"But you didn't report him missing until this morning," said Burton.

She took one of Frost's cigarettes. He lit up for both of them. "It's all my bloody fault. I thought he was in bed." She held the cigarette up and watched the smoke wind up to the ceiling.

Frost didn't prompt her. He let her take her time.

"I've got this job at the Coconut Grove. It's a casino near Denton Woods."

"Yes." Frost nodded. "We know it."

"I'm one of the dealers on the blackjack tables—eight in the evening until four in the morning. Not much of a job, but you've got to grab what you can get." A cylinder of ash fell from her cigarette. She blew it off the polished tabletop. "Dean gets himself to bed. I usually look in on him when I get back, but I didn't this morning. I . . ." She hesitated, then lowered her eyes. "I brought a bloke back here." She glared at Frost defiantly. "I'm not a prostitute—just now and then. I need the money."

"Sure," said Frost. Baskin at the Coconut Grove employed plenty of girls like Joy Anderson. Punters went to the casino for a gamble, then some sex, and Baskin provided both. He probably owned this flat. Frost nodded for her to go on.

"I didn't let him know I had a kid . . . it puts some people off. They don't even know at the Coconut Grove that I've got Dean. Me and the bloke went to bed. He left just after six this morning and I was so bloody tired, I went straight off to sleep. I didn't wake up until half an hour ago. I staggered into Dean's room to see if he wanted any breakfast. His bed hadn't been slept in." She smashed the cigarette out in a heavy glass ashtray. "He's got himself lost, that's what's happened. We've only been in Denton for two days. He doesn't know his way around yet."

"When did you last see him?"

"Yesterday afternoon. He was fed up being stuck in here on his own, so I gave him money for the pictures. He went off about half past two."

The cinema! Of course, thought Frost. That would be where he bought the hamburger. Probably ate it as he watched the film. "Weren't you worried he hadn't returned home before you left for work?"

"I had to have my hair done and be fitted for my uniform. I left here just after five. He knows how to work the microwave if he wants anything to eat."

"How was Dean dressed when he left here?"

"Black trousers, Jurassic Park T-shirt, and a red and white zip-up shell jacket—and blue trainers."

Burton noted the details. Frost showed her a photograph of Bobby Kirby. "Would your son know this boy?"

She dragged her gaze from the window to look at it. "I don't think he knows anyone yet. He hasn't even started school here. Why do you ask?"

"It's not important," lied Frost, crushing out his cigarette alongside hers in the glass ashtray. He took a deep breath. Now for the moment of truth. "Do you have a recent photograph of Dean, Mrs. Anderson?"

"Miss," she corrected, "not Mrs." She reached for her handbag, which hung from the back of her chair. "Taken about three months ago. Dean's filled out a bit since then."

Frost looked at it, then passed it to Burton. Burton's eyes

flickered, but his expression didn't change as he handed it back. Not the slightest doubt about it. It was the dead boy.

"How old are you, love?" asked Frost.

"Twenty-four."

Twenty-four. She would have had the boy when she was sixteen. "Where's Dean's father?"

"With his wife back in Birmingham."

"Does he support the boy?"

"No. He claims Dean isn't his. I can't even be sure myself."

"Any friends, or family, who can help you?"

"No!" She stood up and glared down at him. "Look—I don't want any help. I just want you to find my son."

Frost stood and took her hand. "I've got some bad news for you, love," he said.

She stared at him. "How bad?"

"Bloody bad," said Frost. "As bad as it bloody well could be."

She shook her head. "No!"

"He's dead, love," said Frost. "We found him last night, but we didn't know who he was."

"No," she whispered. And then she shuddered and tears streamed down her face. "No . . ."

Frost took her and held her close to him. "You poor cow," he said. "You poor, poor cow . . ."

CHAPTER FOUR

An enlarged photograph of eight-year-old Dean Anderson, wearing a red and white zip-up shell jacket over the bright yellow Jurassic Park T-shirt he was last seen alive in, grinned down at them from the wall of the Murder Incident Room. It was a skillful combination of two photographs using Dean's face and another eight-year-old boy's body. Next to it was an enlarged school photograph of the missing Bobby Kirby.

As Frost breezed in, people swarmed around him with messages. He warded them off with a fried egg sandwich. "I'm having my dinner," he told them and found an empty desk. "Right. What have we got?"

"No luck with the missing boy yet," said Burton.

"I guessed that," said Frost, digging in his pockets for a cigarette for his dessert, "otherwise someone would have told me. What else?"

"Stacks of phone calls," said PC Lambert, offering him a heap of scribbled messages.

Frost eyed them with distaste. "You don't expect me to read them, do you? Anything positive?"

"All of them, if you want to believe the twenty-three people who claim to have seen him. Trouble is, there were a lot of kids just like Bobby out with guys last night. We've had so-called positive identifications all over Denton. We're following them all through."

Frost took another bite of his sandwich. "Right. Until something definite breaks, we've just got to pin our hopes on one of the search parties finding him. So let's concentrate on the dead kid." He stood and waved his sandwich at the photograph of Dean. "As most of you know, we've had a positive identification. Dean Anderson. His mother, Joy Anderson, is a single parent, a blackjack dealer, and, for want of a better word, a 'hostess' at the Coconut Grove. They've only lived in Denton two days. The kid knew no one here and barely knew his way around the town, although apparently he knew how to get to the cinema." He gave them the details, pausing as the phone rang and Liz answered it.

"Search party three covering sector two," she reported. "Nothing found. Now moving to sector three. Denton Woods." She shifted a colored pin to a new position on the wall map.

Frost went cold, remembering an earlier occasion when they were combing the woods, then in deep snow, for a missing girl, eight years old, who was dead when they found her. He uttered a silent prayer that the pattern wouldn't repeat itself with Bobby . . . surely one dead kid was enough? But his prayers were seldom answered these days. He turned back to the photograph. "The first thing to do is see if the mother's story checks out. In the absence of anyone else, she's our sole suspect."

"What possible motive would she have for killing her own son?" queried Liz.

"He could have been getting in the way when she brought men home," said Frost. "Nothing puts a man off more when he's halfway up her leg and the kid comes in for an ice lolly."

You callous bastard, thought Liz.

"It may not be very probable," continued Frost, "but let's

check Joy Anderson out. Did anyone see the boy leave the house at the time she claims? Did anyone see her leave for the Coconut Grove? What time did she get there . . . what time did she leave? And we'll need to question her client."

"They don't usually leave their name and address," Liz pointed out.

"The Coconut Grove is a gambling club—you've got to be a member. And knowing the way they work, the punter probably paid for Joy's services by credit card so he could clock up some Air Miles. There'll be no difficulty getting his name and address." He shuffled through his notes. "Someone was going to check with the cinema."

Jordan elbowed his way through. "I did it. They think they remember seeing Dean yesterday afternoon. They often get kids in the afternoon who have sneaked off from school. The ticket seller thinks she sold him a ticket about three-ish. The woman in the hamburger kiosk says Dean could have been one of the kids who bought food . . . but all kids look alike to her."

"Right." Frost took a last bite of his sandwich before hurling the crust into the bin. He wiped his fingers on his jacket and lit up the cigarette before sitting down again. "Let's assume he went to the cinema around three and saw the film through. What time would he leave?"

"Between half past five and six."

"By which time it was dark, most of the shops shut, and the town looking like a morgue. I reckon he would want to go straight home." He swung his chair round so he was facing the large street map of Denton on the wall. "He doesn't know the area too well, so he takes the main road, not the back doubles."

"But that wouldn't take him anywhere near Patriot Street where we found the body," said Burton.

Frost nodded. "You're right, son. So let's try this for a working hypothesis. He's walking home. Some bastard in a car toots his horn and says 'Do you want a lift, sonny?' He gets him in the car, gives him chloroform, kills him, panics, and dumps the body. So . . ." He jabbed the wall map. "Let's set up a roadblock here tonight. Stop all cars. 'Were you here this time last night, sir? Did you see anyone give a lift to a kid?' You know the form."

"I'll lay it on," said Burton, scribbling on a pad.

"Hold it!" said Frost, spotting a snag. "It's not as simple as that, is it? The kid has only just moved to Denton. He could have been going the wrong bloody way. He stops a bloke. 'Excuse me, kind sir, can you tell me how to get to Kenton Street?' 'You're miles out of your way, sonny. Hop in, I'll give you a lift—mind that bottle of chloroform and the knife.' "

"I'll get Traffic to cover all roads in all directions," said Burton. "It'll mean more overtime. Mr. Mullett won't like that."

Frost flapped a dismissive hand. "Don't worry. I'll sort old rough-chops out. Let's put out an appeal over the media. Anyone who was in the Curzon Cinema between, say, two and seven, we want to hear from you. . . . All calls treated in the utmost secrecy just in case kids playing truant might not want to come forward. . . . And say we'll accept reverse-charge calls if they don't want to phone from their parents' home." He rubbed some life into his scar. "Anything I haven't thought of, do it anyway."

"Do we still need to check out all the hamburger outlets?"

"I think so, son. Forensic are comparing Dean's stomach contents with a sample from the cinema, but until they confirm it's the same we'd better check them out." He stifled a yawn. He hadn't got to bed until the early hours, then he'd been dragged in at the crack of dawn by flaming Mullett. Quite a few of the team looked as if an early night wouldn't go amiss, and they were only into the first few hours of the murder investigation. "Split up into two groups—half of you snatch a few hours sleep, then relieve the others. I don't want you stumbling around like bloody zombies—there's enough useless people in this station as it is." He looked up as Mullett entered and, without changing his expression, said: "Hello, sir, we were just talking about you."

Mullett smiled and nodded to the team, wondering why some of them seemed to have difficulty in keeping their faces straight. He peeked surreptitiously to check that his zip wasn't open, then said: "A quick word, Inspector."

"Be with you in a tick, sir." Back to the team. "One last thing. On no account must we let anyone know that the poor little sod had his finger hacked off. We'll soon be swamped with phone calls from weirdos and cranks confessing they killed him. Most of them will be time-wasters, but if anyone mentions a missing finger we jump on the bastard."

They clattered out. Liz answered another phone call from a search party reporting negative results. She resited a yellow pin on the wall map. Mullett took Frost's arm and moved away from her. This was to be confidential. "Any progress?"

"Everyone's sweating their guts out, but nothing definite achieved so far," grunted Frost.

"It would be helpful if we could get this tied up very quickly, Frost. With all the overtime involved, the cost of these searches is astronomical. I take it we do need all these men from other divisions? The cost goes on our account, you know, not theirs."

"Tough!" said Frost. "And yes, we do need them all. If we want to find him alive, we need to find him quickly. It's bleeding cold out there—you probably noticed it as you staggered out of the boozer last night."

Mullett's face reddened. That was something he didn't want to be reminded about. "Do you think you will find the boy today?"

"I'm not a bleeding fortune-teller."

"I can cover the overtime from our budget for another eight hours. After that, I'll have to go to County, cap in hand."

You can go with your dick in your hand for all I care, thought Frost, but aloud, he said: "It'll take as long as it takes. I can't hurry it." He felt this was not a good moment to tell the superintendent about the extra overtime needed for Traffic tonight. He yawned again as another wave of tiredness washed over him. "And when are we going to get a replacement for Inspector Allen?"

Liz Maud, hovering in the background, pricked up her ears. This was what she was anxious to know. As Mullett turned his head in her direction, she pretended to be engrossed in the contents of a folder.

Mullett lowered his voice. "I'll have news on a replacement for Mr. Allen very shortly. I'm only waiting for confirmation from County." He gave Liz a thin smile as he went out. She beamed back, reading the secret message in his smile. She knew that the temporary promotion was hers. Frost had come over to her. She closed the folder. "Yes, Inspector?"

"Your abduction case. It might be a good idea to chat up the girl again." He told her about finding the blanket by the roadside.

"And you're suggesting it was all a fake? She wasn't abducted? There was no robbery?"

He nodded. "The bad guys knew too much . . . where the meter cupboard was, that there was only a cordless phone upstairs. They knew the parents would be away and they knew they wouldn't be back until well after midnight."

Liz shrugged. "There are ways they could have found that out."

"The ransom was twenty-five thousand pounds. Do you know how much Stanfield had in his current account? I phoned the bank and they told me: twenty-five thousand pounds, give or take a few quid. If the abductors had asked for more, he couldn't have paid it."

"It still doesn't prove anything," Liz said stubbornly. "What father would put his daughter through all that for an insurance scam?"

"A father called Richard Stanfield," said Frost. "Get tidied up here and we'll go and pay the Stanfields another visit."

He was on his way to his office to see what junk Mullett had dumped in his in-tray when Bill Wells called him. "Lady to see you, Inspector." Wells nodded in the direction of a small woman in her mid-seventies in a faded brown coat, who rose wearily from the hard bench in the waiting area and shuffled over. "It's me again, Mr. Frost," she began apologetically.

"Who the hell is she?" whispered Frost to Wells, always worried when people asked for him by name. He rarely forgot a criminal face, but members of the public were just not recorded in his mental filing system. But before Wells could reply, she had shuffled across to him. "Have you managed to get them back yet?"

Then he remembered. The robberies—the con man who wangled his way into people's houses by pretending to work for the Water Company. This old dear had had her jewelry stolen, plus her late husband's war medals. Her husband had been an RAF pilot during the Battle of Britain and had been awarded the Distinguished Flying Medal, among other decorations. Frost tried not to meet her eye as he shook his head. "No luck yet, love—but we're still trying." Why was he lying to the poor old girl? He'd dropped her case months ago.

She looked as if all hope had been drained out of her. "I don't care too much about the jewelry. It's the medals. He was so proud of them. . . ."

"I know," said Frost. The last decoration had been

awarded posthumously. A tracer bullet had penetrated the fuel tank and the heat-warped canopy had jammed. The man had screamed to his death in the blast furnace of a burning Spitfire, crashing to merciful oblivion in a field in Kent on a blazing hot summer's day in August 1940.

"How long before you catch the man who stole it?"

"Can't really say, love. We're following several leads." More lies. He didn't have a bleeding clue! "I'll be in touch as soon as we have anything." Which would probably be bloody never! "Sorry I haven't better news."

"I'm sure you're doing your best," she said.

He walked her to the door and watched her hobble across the road, fumbling for her bus pass. She realized she was being watched and turned to give him a wave.

Frost slouched back to his office and crumpled the two niggling memos from Mullett he found lurking in his in-tray. Staring through the dirty grime of his window, he wished it would hail or snow or pee with rain, anything to match his mood. But the sun glinted off the grime. He couldn't even get that right.

Liz poked her head around the door. "Ready, Inspector?"

"Yes." He nodded. "I'm ready."

They took Frost's car and he cowered down in the passenger seat as Liz did her Monaco Grand Prix stuff. The sun zipped backward and forward across the windscreen like a typewriter carriage as she hurled the car down the zigzagging lanes. Away to the left, flying past, he could see the distant figures of one of the search parties spread out across a field. Liz screamed the car round a tight corner, shooting him forward as she abruptly slammed on the brakes. "Stupid, stupid, stupid!" she snarled. She had almost run into a cluster of cars parked in the lane. Over on the right another search party was clambering up a steep hill.

"Half a mo!" Frost fumbled to get his seat belt off and

slipped out of the car. Just ahead, on the grass verge, Detective Sergeant Arthur Hanlon, in charge of the search team, was bending to tie up his shoelace. His back was to Frost, his tight trousers providing a target the inspector was never able to resist. Frost's stubby finger shot forward, hitting its target with unerring accuracy. "How's that for center, Arthur?" he cried triumphantly.

With a yelp of outrage, Hanlon sprang up, his indignation instantly evaporating as he recognized Frost. "You sod, Jack! No matter where I am, I've only got to bend over and you appear!"

"Fatal attraction, Arthur. The moving finger pokes, and when it pokes, moves on." Frost squinted up at the men, now disappearing over the crest of the hill. "Where are you going to search now?"

"Those old bungalows behind the hill." The huddle of decaying, prewar jerry-built shacks were now mainly roofless and little more than shells. The area should have been cleared and flattened years ago when the last residents were rehoused, but the Council had better ways to spend its money. "What's your gut feeling about our chances of finding him alive?"

"Don't ask, Arthur. It would only depress you." He took one last look at the straggle of men disappearing over the top of the hill. "If we don't find him by tonight we'll start dragging the river and the canal tomorrow." A brief nod to Hanlon and he returned to the car.

Carol Stanfield was now dressed in tight jeans and an even tighter grey woolen sweater. Her hair had been brushed back over her shoulders and as the teenager passed close to Frost she smelled just like the blanket. Her mother and father were still sitting on opposite sides of the fire. Stanfield looked up with irritation. "More questions? We've told you everything. Now go out and catch the bastards."

Frost plonked himself down on the settee and loosened his scarf. The heat in the room was oppressive. "We've found something." He pulled the grey blanket from the plastic carrier bag he was holding and offered it to Mrs. Stanfield. "Did this come from here?"

She examined it with a frown. "It could be ours."

"It *is* ours," said the girl from the far side of the room. She was staring out of the window, her back to them. "They took it from the bed."

"You never mentioned it," said Frost.

She shrugged. "They wrapped it round me in the van."

"Bloody nice of them," said Frost.

"It was freezing in there. I was naked."

"It was a darn sight colder outside the van, but they took it off when they booted you out."

"I expect it fell off."

"Then it would have been in the road. We found it on the grass verge."

"Then they probably chucked it out as they were driving off."

"You must have seen it," said Frost.

Her father's head snapped up. "If she had seen it, she would have wrapped it around her, instead of standing there, starkers, freezing to death."

"But how could you miss it?" insisted Frost. "It was lying there in the open." He was hoping to catch her out. Hoping she would say "It wasn't in the open, I hid it behind the hedge," but before the girl could answer, her mother had chimed in. "It couldn't have been all that obvious. Your policemen didn't see it this morning."

"Silly me!" said Frost, forcing a smile as he pushed himself up out of the settee. He stuffed the blanket back into the carrier bag. "We'll hang on to this for a while—let our Forensic people give it a going-over."

He held his feelings in check until he and Liz were back

in the car. "The scheming bastards! They went back to re-cover the blanket and realized we had found it."

"There's always the possibility they're telling the truth," said Liz, spinning the car into a reverse turn.

"No way." Frost winced at the thought of the rubber they were leaving in the road. "There was no robbery and no abduction. I want it tied up quickly. We've got more important things to do than sod about with this."

They were passing a small isolated house when, suddenly, Liz slammed on the brakes again. His head hit the wind-screen. He had forgotten to put the seat belt on. "What the hell . . . ?"

"Sorry," she said, getting out of the car. "That house. There was no reply this morning when I knocked to ask about the van. Someone's in now."

"Oh—the nonexistent bleeding van loaded up with na-ked teen," said Frost, rubbing the bump on his forehead. "Well, make it quick." He watched Liz walk up the path and knock on the door. An elderly man answered.

"Control to Mr. Frost."

He picked up the handset. "Frost." He listened. It wasn't good news.

Liz was scribbling down the details the old man was giv-ing her when the car horn blasted out repeatedly. She tried to ignore it, but it went on and on. Frost was waving franti-cally and yelling for her to return. Muttering apologies to the old man, she raced back to the car. What was up now?

Frost, now in the driving seat, had the passenger door open for her. "Get in!" he yelled, and the car was away even before she had the door shut.

"Why did you drag me away?" she protested. "I was getting details. He saw the nonexistent van going toward the Stanfield house late last night. Even gave me the color—light brown."

Frost skidded the car round a tight bend and removed several inches of hedge in the process. "I've had Control on the radio. Arthur Hanlon's search party—those old bungalows. They've found a body."

Liz went cold. "The boy?"

"Life's not that bleeding simple," snorted Frost. "It's not a boy—it's a man, probably a dosser. It never rains flaming bodies, it pours!"

The car wheezed its way up the steep gradient of Denton Hills, its engine making unhappy noises and giving off the smell of burning oil. They were behind the woods in a barren section of the district. Years ago a sprawl of prewar bungalows and weekend shanties occupied the area, their dwellers living in primitive conditions without main drainage or electricity. These substandard dwellings were deemed unfit for human occupation and some twenty years earlier the Council had rehoused the occupants and compulsorily acquired the land for a building project for which it had long since given up trying to raise the money. The empty properties were quickly vandalized and opened up to the weather and were now of no interest, even to the local tearaways. Roofless, windows smashed, doors torn off their hinges, the flimsy buildings cowered under the wind and weather. The whole area was overgrown with vegetation and stank of damp, rot, and decay.

Arthur Hanlon and a uniformed man were waiting for them, hands in pockets, stamping their feet for warmth. The sun was a watery yellow in a clear sky. It was going to be a freezing cold night.

Hanlon led them across what was once a front garden, overgrown grass slapping at their legs. The garden fronted the shell of an asbestos-walled bungalow, painted in now-faded pink. Frost peeked in through the glassless windows onto strewn rubbish and charred floorboards where someone, years ago, had tried to start a fire, but the wood had been too damp to burn. "I wish my place was as tidy as this," he muttered.

They trudged round the side to the rear. Other overgrown gardens could be seen, many of them with ram-shackle wooden structures like sentry boxes. "Outdoor privies," explained Hanlon. "The old bucket and wooden seat—there was no mains sewerage."

"The body's not in one of them?" asked Frost apprehensively.

Hanlon shook his head.

A sigh of relief from Frost. "If he'd known I was going to be on the case he'd have died headfirst down an unemptied privy bucket."

Hanlon grinned. Frost had an affinity for mucky cases. "He's in a bunker, Jack."

"A bunker? It's not bloody Hitler, is it?"

"A coal bunker. Over there." Hanlon pointed to where a uniformed officer stood guarding a taped-off section. The undergrowth there was almost waist-high, but had been trampled down to form a path leading to an almost-concealed brick coal bunker, four feet long, three feet high. A rusted sheet of corrugated iron that had once covered the open top was propped to one side. A strong smell of putrification drifted out to greet them.

Frost wrinkled his nose. "Bloody hell, Arthur, what have I told you about changing your socks?"

Hanlon giggled. "We reckon it's probably a dosser . . . crept in there to sleep and got hypothermia."

Frost took a deep breath, then looked inside. "Bloody hell!" Moving back, he sucked in great gulps of clean, cold air. He passed his cigarettes around and moved a few steps back, but the smell seemed to be following him. Liz pushed forward to take a look, but Frost held out a restraining hand. "Best if you don't, love."

Angrily she shook his hand off. "I've seen bodies before." She took a breath and looked down. Huddled at the bottom of the bunker, in inches of soupy rainwater, were the remains of a man. The body was in an advanced state of decomposition and the face, covered with black mold, was unrecognizable. Liz moved back, exhaled slowly, then took some deep breaths. She fought back the urge to be sick.

"Are you all right?" asked Frost.

"Yes," she snapped. "Perfectly all right."

"Remind me to tell you of that dead tramp I found in a heat wave," he told her. "You could have poured him away. It made this one smell like Chanel No. 5 in comparison. . . ."

"Don't let him tell you that story, Liz," said Arthur Hanlon. "Not on a full stomach—I was sick for three days after I heard it."

"You're thinking of the other one," said Frost. "The bloke who drank the contents of the spittoon for a bet."

Hanlon went white. "I'd forgotten all about that one. If you value your stomach, Liz, don't let him tell you that story either."

A short tubby figure carrying a medical bag came puffing toward them. Frost waved. "Over here, Doctor."

Dr. Maltby beamed when he saw the inspector. "I thought you were on holiday."

"They couldn't do without me, Doc." Frost jerked a thumb at the bunker. "There's your patient."

Maltby took a quick look. "I confirm life is extinct."

"Is that all we get for our bloody money? How long has he been dead?"

The doctor shrugged. "No idea, Jack. Weeks . . . probably months. Was that corrugated iron sheeting on the top when you found him?"

"Yes," confirmed Hanlon.

"Sun beating down on that would make it like an oven—and there's a good two inches of water down there to speed things up. Decomposition would start in hours."

"Cause of death?"

"No idea. If you drag him out I'll take a further look, but if you think I'm going to climb down inside . . ."

"Sod it!" sighed Frost. He pulled Hanlon to one side.

"Pathologist, Forensic, SOC's, the works, Arthur. You know the drill."

"You think it might be murder?"

"There's water and broken bricks at the bottom of that bunker, Arthur. A dosser would have to be pretty hard up for a bed to sleep on that."

"I'm off, then," said Maltby, backing away.

"Thanks, Doc," said Frost. "If you hadn't told us he was dead we'd still be pushing aspirins down the poor sod's throat." He waved the doctor off, then turned to Hanlon. "You'd better handle this one, Arthur. It was your team who found him, you can suffer the consequences." He took one last look at the bunker and shuddered. "I'd hate to be one of the blokes who have to lift him out. Don't pull him up by his arms, they might come off in your hand . . . and for the same reason, don't lift him by his dick."

Liz screwed up her face in distaste. She didn't find death the least bit funny.

"We're going to need some more help, Jack," Hanlon said.

"Our beloved divisional commander has it all in hand," said Frost. "We're getting another detective inspector."

As they climbed back into the car, Liz had an awful thought and consulted Frost for reassurance. "You don't think Mr. Mullett is going to upgrade Sergeant Hanlon to acting DI?"

"No," said Frost, wriggling down into the passenger seat. "Arthur's a lovely bloke, but, like me, he hasn't got the makings of an inspector and Mullett knows it."

"Oh," said Liz. She smiled to herself. Then it would definitely be her.

Bill Wells sipped his mug of tea and took a sly drag at his cigarette. His first chance to relax all afternoon. Mullett had been flapping in and out, wanting to know if anyone had been asking for him, but not explaining who he was expecting. A blast of wind gusted in as the main doors opened. With practiced skill, he pinched out the cigarette and slid his mug of tea under the countertop. "Can I help you, sir?"

The man, carrying a suitcase, walked across to the desk. Fair-haired and thick-set, he gave a curt nod.

A cry of recognition from Wells. "Jim Cassidy! What are you doing back in Denton?"

Cassidy put down the suitcase and twitched a wan smile. His manner was far less enthusiastic than the sergeant's. "Hello, Bill."

"I've heard you've been in the wars—some bastard stabbed you?"

Cassidy nodded, his expression making it clear this was something he didn't want to discuss. "I'm here to see Mr. Mullett."

So this was why Mullett had been flapping. And not a word to a flaming soul! "May I ask what about?" said Wells, picking up the internal phone and dialing Mullett's number.

Cassidy frowned. Surely the news should have been out by now? "I'm back in the division for a while. I'm going to be your acting detective inspector."

Wells's jaw dropped. Cassidy! Acting detective inspector! Cassidy, who was a trainee constable while Wells was already a sergeant. Some people, if their faces fitted, would always rise in the ranks, while others who flogged their guts out, worked all the hours God sent, were bunged on the rota every bloody Christmas. . . . He realized Mullett had answered and was barking angrily in his ear. "Detective Sergeant Cassidy to see you, sir. . . . Yes, sir." He put the phone down. "Go straight through, Jim. You know the way."

Cassidy nodded and slid his suitcase across the counter for safekeeping. At the swing doors, he paused. "Important point, Sergeant. While I'm acting inspector, I want to be treated as such. Call me 'Inspector,' or 'sir'—not 'Jim.' "

Forcing a smile, Wells seethed inwardly. You bastard! Pulling rank on me! "Very good . . . *sir*," he said, through clenched teeth. "By the way . . . sir. I saw your wife— sorry—your ex-wife in town the other day."

Cassidy stiffened. He wouldn't turn round. He had no intention of letting the sod know how deeply that shaft had hit home. "Did you, Sergeant? How was she?"

"She looked great. Her new husband was with her. They both looked very happy."

The swing doors closed shut behind him and Wells chortled with wicked delight. "Game, set, and match." He beamed, retrieving his mug of tea.

"What was that all about, Sarge?"

Wells turned his head. PC Collier, on his way up to his meal break, had seen the little drama enacted.

Normally Wells would have told him to mind his own business, but basking in the warm glow of his little victory, he was only too pleased to explain. "That big-headed git you just saw go through is Jim Cassidy. He was a detective constable here some four years ago—before your time. Career-mad . . . nothing was going to stop him getting on—and he didn't give a toss who he stepped on to get there. Grabbed all the credit, even when it wasn't his, and worked all the hours going without claiming overtime, which made him Mullett's blue-eyed boy. Anyway, one night he'd promised to take his teen-aged daughter out to see a film she'd been dying to see, but a job came up so he cried off. The kid went out on her own and got knocked down and killed by a hit-and-run driver. He went to pieces and his marriage broke up. Started criticizing everyone here because we couldn't trace the hit-and-run driver and became impossible to work with. So he was transferred to Lexford, at which point we stopped hating him and they started."

"And now we've got him back as acting detective inspector?"

Wells nodded grimly. "And that will put the cat among

the pigeons, I promise you." There was a bit more to the story, but Wells was keeping it to himself. He couldn't wait to see Jack Frost's face when he told him Cassidy was back. The internal phone rang. Mullett. Demanding two coffees.

Wells looked round, but Collier had gone. "Sorry, sir, I've got no one to send."

"And some biscuits," added Mullett, disconnecting the phone.

"Come in, Jim, come in," said Mullett warmly, hand outstretched. "Good to have you back in the division."

Cassidy shook the offered hand and noted with relief that there was a hard-seated chair in front of the polished mahogany desk. He could lower himself in it all right, but the effort of hauling himself from its depths would trigger off the pain again. He gritted his teeth and sat. No one must know he was still suffering from the aftereffects of the stabbing, not if his promotion to inspector was to go through this time. He turned a grimace into a smile of thanks as a ripple of pain sizzled across his stomach. The seat was lower than he thought and there was no support and it was pulling on his wound.

Mullett took the other armchair, concerned to see Cassidy looking so drawn. "Sorry to hear about the stabbing. Are you all right now?"

"I'm fine," lied Cassidy. He was learning to mask the pain. He had fooled the police doctor; he should have little difficulty in fooling Mullett and his pack of dummies. "I'm anxious to get started, sir. I understand Inspector Allen was handling a murdered-boy inquiry. When can I take over?"

"One dead boy, one missing boy," corrected Mullett. He paused as a sullen-looking Sergeant Wells came in with the coffees and banged them down on the desk, spilling some into the saucers. Mullett waited until Wells had departed before continuing. "You'll be working with Mr. Frost on this one."

Cassidy's head snapped up. "Frost! Jack Frost?"

Mullett saw something very interesting to look at through the window—the blank wall on the other side of the road. "Er . . . quite so."

"My understanding was—"

"Circumstances have changed," interrupted Mullett. "I had intended you would be taking complete charge of Mr. Allen's cases and working on your own—"

"That was the only reason I agreed to come back here," cut in Cassidy. "You will appreciate that Denton has many unhappy memories for me."

"I understand that, but nevertheless you will be working under Mr. Frost."

"*Under?* I'm an acting detective inspector. I didn't come all the way back here just to stay a sergeant."

"The chief constable is a little concerned as to your fitness—"

"I'm perfectly fit."

"—and he has a much higher opinion of Frost than, perhaps, those who have to work with him have. The chief constable wants you to work under Frost's authority, as he considers this a case requiring the leadership of an experienced officer."

With difficulty Cassidy pushed himself out of the chair, his anger overcoming the pain. "I am sorry, sir. I would find it impossible to work with Frost. The way he mismanaged the investigation into the death of my daughter . . ."

Mullett gave a deep sigh. "I know you weren't happy at the way he handled the case. I agree he's unorthodox—"

"Unorthodox!" exploded Cassidy. "He's more than unorthodox. He's sloppy, lazy, inefficient, devious—"

"That will do!" An angry Mullett pounded his fist on the desk. It was not that he disagreed with the views expressed —he, himself, might have gone further—but he wasn't having this sort of talk from a sergeant, especially one from another division, who could well carry a report of the conversation back. He was concerned that Frost's deficiencies should not be too widely known, otherwise his chances of dumping the man on another, unsuspecting division, would be minimal. "Whatever your feelings, Cassidy, you will put them to one side. The chief constable has decreed that you will work with Mr. Frost and that he will be the senior officer."

"I am not happy with this, sir."

"I take note of your unhappiness," said Mullett, "but would advise you to take full advantage of this opportunity." He smiled his crocodile smile. "Any successes that you achieve will be duly noted and, should the time come for Inspector Frost to be replaced . . ." He spread his palms significantly and let the option hang. "However, if you decide you cannot work with him, I am sure County can find some other sergeant who would be only too pleased to improve his promotional chances by acting as inspector."

Cassidy grunted. "I'll work with him."

"Good man." Mullett beamed. "Well, I expect you will want to get started. You'll be in Mr. Allen's office. You know where it is." He stood up to indicate the interview was over. "I'm glad we've had this little chat."

A stab of pain caught Cassidy by surprise as he reached for the door. He winced and gritted his teeth.

"You all right?" Mullett asked.

"Leg a bit stiff after the journey," explained Cassidy, forcing himself not to limp as he crossed the threshold.

"Oh—one other thing," said Mullett, making his carefully rehearsed speech sound like an afterthought. "That business with your daughter . . ."

Cassidy turned slowly to face the divisional commander. "Yes?"

"Over and done with—all in the past." Mullett gave Cassidy's arm a "man-to-man" squeeze.

"Yes," said Cassidy tersely. "All in the past." There was no one in the passage outside so he was able to allow himself the luxury of a limp back to Allen's office.

Thomas Arnold, assistant branch manager at Benningtons Bank, blinked nervously at Frost through thick-lensed glasses. By his side stood the cashier who had attended to Stanfield when he withdrew the £25,000 that morning. Arnold waited for his secretary to give Frost and Liz cups of lukewarm instant coffee, then nodded for the cashier to proceed.

"Mr. Stanfield was waiting outside the bank when we opened at nine-thirty," the cashier told them. "He handed me his withdrawal request; I raised my eyebrows and said 'Rather a large sum!' And he said 'Just get it!' I obviously didn't have that amount of money in my till and it was more than I like to count out over the counter, so I took him round to Mr. Arnold's office to wait while we fetched the money from the vault."

"That's correct," said Arnold. "I offered him coffee, but he refused."

Frost pushed his half-empty cup away from him. "I'm not surprised."

"How did he seem?" asked Liz.

"In what way?"

"She means," said Frost, "did he look as if his daughter was going to be raped if he didn't cough up the cash, or did he behave normally?"

"He seemed very impatient—but then he usually is," replied the manager. "It only took eight minutes to provide the cash."

"I brought it in, but before I could hand it over he snatched it from me," said the cashier. "He didn't bother to count it, just stuffed it in his suitcase and left."

"You didn't think it strange he should withdraw such a large sum in cash?"

"To be quite honest," said Arnold, "I thought he was going to do a runner . . . you know, leave the country. I believe the Customs and Excise and the Inland Revenue are breathing very hard down his neck . . . but that is strictly off the record, of course."

They nodded their thanks and left.

"Well," smirked Liz when they got back in the car. "He was agitated and impatient—it's starting to sound genuine."

"Of course he looked agitated. You'd hardly expect him to be whistling 'Happy Days Are Here Again.' He knew we'd check."

"Then what about my witness who saw the van?"

"I don't care if he saw a hundred bloody vans. I still reckon this is a tax and insurance fiddle."

"We'll see." She smiled, determined to prove him wrong.

He dropped her off at her digs. "Get a few hours sleep. I'll see you back at the station later."

He drove to his house for a quick cup of tea and flopped wearily in an armchair to drink it. He was dead tired. He leant his head back on the cushion and closed his eyes for a second. He woke with a start. His untouched tea was stone-cold. Outside it was already dark. The phone was ringing.

"Frost," he mumbled.

It was Johnnie Johnson, who had taken over from Bill Wells as station sergeant. "You'd better get over here, Jack. Another child's gone missing."

"On my way," said Frost.

CHAPTER FIVE

He slouched into the Incident Room rubbing sleep from his eye. "What's all this about another missing kid?" He yawned.

"Judy Gleeson, fourteen years old," said Burton.

Frost collapsed into a chair, relieved that it wasn't another eight-year-old boy. "Tell me about it."

"Mother goes to work. She came home at five. No sign of her daughter and no table laid, which the daughter usually did. Mother assumed the kid was with her mate. Half past six, still no Judy, so the mother gets worried, phones around and learns that Judy hadn't been at school all day."

Frost chewed this over. "I can't see it tying in with our missing boy. Sounds like your average girl doing a runner to me."

"Probably, but we can't take chances. Detective Sergeant Maud has gone round to the house to get details. Should be back soon."

"Right," said Frost. "And how are things going with the search for Bobby?"

Burton told him the position. The search parties had plodded on until it was too dark to see properly. All the more likely areas had been covered and they were now moving on to the less likely ones. "I've laid on the frogmen team for tomorrow morning."

Frost nodded his approval. "What about our appeals to the Great British Public?"

Lambert replied, "Thirty-five more positive sightings. Eight of them were kids with men."

"Probably fathers taking their sons home. What about the dead kid? Did anyone see him?"

"There's a snag," Burton told him. "Both kids left home wearing similar clothes. People are reporting seeing kids in zip-up jackets and it could be either of them."

"Or neither," said Frost. "The cinema?"

"Three kids playing truant from school are pretty certain they saw Dean in the Curzon yesterday afternoon. He was sitting on his own. They didn't pay much attention to him and didn't see him leave."

Liz stuck her head round the door. "That missing girl. I've circulated details, but it looks as if she's just run away from home. I spoke to one of her friends, who reckoned there had been some friction between Judy and her parents, but the mother denies it."

Frost waved a hand in acknowledgment. Kids running away from home were all too common these days.

Liz went back to Allen's office to check the in-tray and was irritated to find someone had been in and removed all her stuff from Allen's desk and dumped it back on the small desk in the corner. Probably moaning Bill Wells up to his bloody tricks again. Seething with annoyance, she moved it all back and was just reaching for the phone to ask Wells what the hell he was playing at when the door crashed open and a thickset man in his early forties barged in.

"Do you mind knocking before coming into my office?" snapped Liz.

The man glowered at her. "And do you mind getting out of my bloody desk?" he roared.

· · ·

Cassidy had dumped his suitcase at his digs, then had taken a drive round Denton to see how much the place had changed since he was here last. He drove past his old house, the house he'd had to make over to his wife as part of the divorce settlement. The downstairs blazed with light and the front lawn looked immaculate. Very different from when he lived there, when there was never any time for gardening. He stopped the car and stared at the small upstairs window, his daughter's bedroom. Today would have been Becky's eighteenth birthday, not that anyone else would have remembered.

He passed a florist's that was just closing and, on impulse, stopped and bought a small bunch of flowers. Becky loved flowers.

It was getting dark, but he managed to find the grave without much difficulty. A small white headstone. *Rebecca Cassidy—aged 14 years.* To his annoyance there was already a large, ostentatious bouquet of pink carnations by the headstone. The attached card read: *"On your birthday, darling, from Mummy and Geoff."* Geoff! The new bloody husband! Cassidy shook with rage. How dare that swine give my daughter flowers! He never even bloody knew her! Cassidy snatched up the bouquet and tore the card to shreds, then gently laid his own small offering in its place. Fourteen! Fourteen years old, all her life in front of her, and some bastard, probably drunk, had mowed her down and didn't bother to stop to see if she was alive or dead. And then Frost had sodded up the investigation.

He walked away, clutching the carnations, looking for a bin where he could dump them. He passed another grave, overgrown and neglected. He stopped. Talk of the devil! It was the grave of Frost's wife, the grass overgrown, long dead stalks of flowers in a vase. The callous bastard hadn't been back to tend it since the day she was buried. As he tore up some of the grass to make room for the carnations, Cassidy winced. The cold night air was getting to his wound, triggering off the hurt. He set down the bouquet and hurried back to the warmth of his car.

Mullett marched into the Incident Room and headed straight for Frost. "Another missing child?" he barked, making it sound as if it were all Frost's fault.

"Yes, sorry about that, Super. I'll try and see it doesn't happen again." Frost scooped up some papers and headed for the door, but was called back.

"Traffic are talking about extra overtime. I haven't authorized it. Do you know anything about it?"

"Ah, yes," said Frost, who had forgotten all about it. "I was going to come in and see you about that." But he was saved by the bell. Liz Maud came in, not looking at all happy, and behind her was—flaming hell! Jim bloody Cassidy. Where did he spring from?

"Ah," said Mullett. "In case you don't know, our old colleague Mr. Cassidy is taking over as acting detective inspector—only until Mr. Allen gets back. I'm sure we're all delighted to have such a worthy addition to our team."

The news was greeted with stunned silence. It was finally broken by Liz. "If I could have a word, sir," she said, her eyes smoldering with resentment. Mullett had as good as offered the promotion to her and she wanted to know why he had gone back on his word.

"Later, later," said Mullett, backing hurriedly to the door. "Make an appointment with my secretary . . . I'm a bit tied up just now." He scuttled back to his office and quickly switched on the red Engaged—Do Not Enter light. Cassidy might be trouble, but there was no way he was having a woman detective inspector in his division, even if the promotion was only temporary.

· · ·

"Good to see you, Jim," said Frost. He didn't hold out his hand. He knew Cassidy wouldn't take it. He introduced him around. One or two people knew Cassidy from his previous time in Denton, but did their best to hide their dismay. "And, of course, you've met Detective Sergeant Maud?"

Cassidy flicked her a brisk nod. "I'd like an office on my own. Perhaps she could move in with you."

"Of course," agreed Frost. This wasn't the time or place to start a row.

"And I'd like someone assigned to me to do my filing and odd jobs and things." Cassidy pointed to Burton. "He looks a likely chap."

"We all do our own filing and odd jobs and things," said Frost. "I can't spare anyone—we've got too much on."

Cassidy's expression did not change. "I see. Well, perhaps you had better brief me on just what you do have on."

He sat at a desk and listened, without comment, making neat, copious notes, as Frost gave him the details of the two boys, the dubious abduction, the weirdo who was stabbing sleeping kids, and the body in the bunker. When Frost had finished, Cassidy capped his fountain pen and smiled sourly. "You don't seem to have made much progress with any of them."

Before Frost could answer, however, the phone rang. It was Arthur Hanlon, calling from the mortuary, where the postmortem on the body in the bunker was taking place. "You'd better get down here right away, Jack. There's something odd about the body."

"Two dicks?" asked Frost. "I'll send Liz."

"The tops of three of his fingers have been chopped off. After death, the pathologist says."

"I'll be there," Frost said.

• • •

Frost backed into the parking space outside the mortuary, squeezing in between Drysdale's Rolls-Royce and a hearse. The mortuary attendant, busy writing up records in his cubbyhole, waved him through. Inspector Frost was a frequent visitor.

At the far end of the darkened autopsy room, under the splash of overhead lights, a cluster of men stood at a discreet distance from the postmortem table where a green-gowned Drysdale was bent over, cutting carefully with a scalpel. The atmosphere was oppressive; it worsened rapidly when the pathologist opened up the dead man's stomach. Overhead the extractor fans whirred, fighting a losing battle. Drysdale's gloved hands removed something from the corpse.

"Got any pieces for the cat, Doc?"

Drysdale stiffened. That damn Frost again, making his tasteless jokes. He affected not to hear and carried on with his task.

Frost's scruffy figure emerged from the gloom. "Bloody hell. He doesn't improve with keeping, does he?" The match rasped as he lit a cigarette.

"Please don't smoke," snapped Drysdale. "There are things I need to smell."

"Whatever turns you on, Doc," said Frost, shaking out the match, but keeping the unlit cigarette in his mouth. "So what's the verdict?"

"I have already given my preliminary findings to the sergeant," said Drysdale. "I am not in the habit of repeating myself."

A white-faced Arthur Hanlon came round the table to Frost. The postmortem was making him decidedly queasy. "Dead for some time, Jack—two, maybe even three months. Died as the result of a heavy blow to the back of the head which fractured the skull. Killed elsewhere. The body was dumped in the bunker shortly after death."

"He died about an hour after consuming his last meal," added Drysdale, transferring something horrible to a jar and handing it to his secretary for labeling. "A substantial meal —dinner or lunch." He stepped back and peeled off his rubber gloves. "I've finished with him. Sew him up, please."

"Give us a minute, please." Frost waved the mortuary technician back with a hand holding a match, ready to light his cigarette. "What's this about fingers cut off, Arthur?"

Hanlon panted. He wasn't going to touch that puffed, squashy flesh. "His right hand, Jack."

Frost stared, then bent over to study the hand. The thumb and little finger were intact, but the tops of the corpse's three middle fingers had been hacked off at the upper joint. "This couldn't have been an accident, Doc—shut his hand in a door, or something?"

"No," said Drysdale, bridling as always at being called "Doc." "No. These injuries occurred after death and were deliberate. A knife, or something sharp, laid across the joints, then struck with a hammer or something heavy. Whoever did it had to have a couple of tries—just below the joint there's the marks of an attempt that failed." He pointed to a bloodied indentation running parallel to the severed ends.

Frost straightened up. "I suppose the missing bits of finger weren't dumped in the coal bunker? You have looked, Arthur?"

Hanlon hadn't, but he fished out his radio and gave instructions for this to be done.

The body was of a man in his mid-forties, a little over six feet tall, overweight, with long, lank, water-blackened hair. "Biggish bastard, isn't he?" mused Frost aloud as he studied the bloated face with its purple lips, the eyes little more than wet swimming slits in the puffed and mold-stained flesh. A buzzer sounded at the back of his brain and tried to stir his memory. Frost stared at the face, trying to imagine how it might have looked in life. "I know this sod from somewhere. Any identification on him?"

"Nothing, Jack. He was wearing a jacket over a boiler suit, but the pockets were empty. I'll get Forensic to give it the once-over."

Frost signaled to Evans, who was keeping as far from the body as possible and answered Frost's summons reluctantly. "I'm afraid you're going to have to touch it, son. Fingerprint the fingers that are left and check with Records to see if we've got him on our books." He stubbed out his cigarette. The smoke was tasting of the body. "Let's get out of here, Arthur."

As they moved away, the mortuary technician, whistling tunelessly to himself, began sewing up the incisions made during the postmortem, leaning to one side in mid-stitch so Evans could gingerly take fingerprints.

Outside the night air had a clean, fresh smell. But it was cold. Bitterly cold. And they still hadn't found the boy. "We're not going to break our necks on this one, Arthur," said Frost, pausing as Drysdale, followed by his secretary lugging a metal specimens case that seemed far too heavy for her, strode past to the Rolls with only a curt nod to the two detectives. "He's been dead for weeks," continued Frost, "so another couple of days won't make any difference. We'll keep it ticking over and look busy if ever Mullett comes sniffing around, but we'll concentrate our efforts on trying to find Bobby Kirby and the bastard who killed the other boy." He shivered. The cold was beginning to get to him. "Let's hope that poor little sod isn't out in this."

All they had for him in the Incident Room were more negative reports. The few sightings they had been able to check had all turned out to be false leads.

"What about the dead kid's mother? The blackjack dealer. Have we checked her out?"

"I saw Harry Baskin, this afternoon—" began Burton.

"Harry Baskin?" said Cassidy, who had been sitting at a corner desk, listening and scribbling notes. "Is he still running The Coconut Grove?"

Burton nodded. "Baskin says she started work at the club at eight, worked through her meal break, and finished around three in the morning. She left with one of their clients."

"By eight o'clock her son was dead," said Frost. "She could have killed him before she went to work. I want to interview her client to see if he noticed anything in the flat when he went back with her, like the smell of chloroform or a severed finger on the breadboard."

"Baskin refuses to give the bloke's name. Says he respects people's rights to privacy."

Frost stood up and grabbed his scarf. "This is a murder case. He'll give me the punter's name or I'll run him in for living on immoral earnings."

"Hold it!" called Cassidy, rising to join him. "I'm coming with you."

"Sure." Frost nodded. "Glad to have your help." But he wasn't happy. This could open old wounds. It was just outside the Coconut Grove where Cassidy's daughter had been run down and killed.

They traveled in Cassidy's car and it was a silent, uncomfortable ride with Cassidy making it tacitly clear he was only tolerating Frost's company. The Coconut Grove was busy. The car park was three-quarters full. They brushed past the bouncer who wanted to know if they were members and ignored the leggy blonde who tried to take their hats and coats, making straight for Harry Baskin's office. A sign on the door said Private—Do Not Enter. They went straight in without knocking.

Harry Baskin, dark and swarthy, looked up from his desk with a frown. "Can't you bloody well read?" Then he saw who it was and gave a deep sigh. "What the hell do you want?"

Frost dragged out a chair and sat down. He pointed a thumb to his companion. "You remember Mr. Cassidy?"

For a moment Baskin looked startled, but quickly composed himself. "Mr. Cassidy! I heard you were back in Denton!" He waved a hand. "Sit down."

But Cassidy had moved to the window behind Baskin, a window that overlooked the road running past the club. He stared out at the cars that sped past, on to the straight section of the road before it curved toward Denton. He spoke, almost to himself. "That's where it happened. That's where that bastard killed my daughter."

Baskin shot a glance across to Frost, whose face remained impassive. "It was a long time ago, Mr. Cassidy."

"Was it one of the drunken bastards from your club who was at the wheel, Harry?"

"We've had all this out before, Mr. Cassidy. The driver didn't stop. We don't know who he was." Baskin swiveled his chair to face Frost. "Is this what you've come to talk to me, about—ancient bloody history?"

"We're here to talk about Joy Anderson," said Frost.

"The new girl! If I had known she had a bloody son, I never would have employed her."

"She hasn't got a son anymore, Harry," said Frost. "He's dead."

Baskin spread his palms, the chunky gold cuff links on his wrists clanking as he did so. "Tell me about it!" he moaned. "Bloody fine advert for the club, isn't it . . . have your blackjack cards dealt by a girl whose son was murdered. It puts a damper on the bloody place. I'm not a hard man, Mr. Frost, but I'm getting rid of her."

"No you're not, Harry," snapped Frost. "The poor thing has suffered enough without losing her job as well."

"All right." He tried to sound reasonable. "She can stay away for a few days—I might even pay her—but when she comes back she'd better not go around with a long bloody face. We need to keep the punters happy."

"Of course you do, Harry—so we want to know the name of the gambler she kept happy last night."

"As I told the other copper, people who come to this club have a right to privacy. Whatever arrangement the gentleman made with Joy Anderson after she left the club is a matter entirely for him."

Frost gave a sweet smile. "Let me put it plainly, Harry. People come to your club for a gamble and a bit of the other and you are happy to provide both so long as they pay. Most of the girls who work for you are known prostitutes. You take at least half of what they earn on the side, probably more, if the client pays by credit card. You also provide the girls' flats at exorbitant rents. So what say I nominate you as Pimp of the Year and charge you with living off immoral earnings?"

Baskin's face flushed a dark red. "This is a respectable club. I could have you up for defamation of character . . . but if it will help you catch the boy's killer . . ." He scribbled something on a pad and tore off the sheet. "There's his name and address. Now piss off!"

Frost glanced at the note, then stuffed it into his mac pocket. "Thanks, Harry. I knew I could appeal to your better nature." He looked over to Cassidy. "Ready?"

Cassidy was still staring out of the window. He seemed to have taken no interest in Frost's conversation with Baskin. He frowned as if dragged out of a reverie. "What?"

"Let's go."

"Sure." One last look out of the window. "Sure."

Joy Anderson's client lived in Lexington. Frost radioed through to Lexington Division to send someone round to question him. They had barely got inside the station when Arthur Hanlon came running up to them, beaming all over his face and falsely raising Frost's hopes that the Kirby boy had been found. "You were right about the body in the bunker, Jack. We've matched his prints—we know who he is."

"Are you going to tell me his name, Arthur, or do I get three guesses?"

"He's Lemmy Hoxton."

Hanlon offered the form sheet to Frost. Frost didn't take it. He stared at Hanlon openmouthed. Lemmy! The bloated balloon of the putrefying face swirled in front of him as he struggled to compare it with the living Lemmy Hoxton, a vicious and habitual petty criminal he had arrested many times. "We won't try too hard on this one," said Frost. "Whoever killed him deserves a medal." He fumbled for a cigarette.

"He's been dead over two months and his wife hasn't reported him missing?" observed Cassidy.

"Probably couldn't believe her bloody luck," said Frost. He sighed. "But you're right. She's got a hell of a lot of explaining to do. Let's pay her a visit."

The house was a semidetached, two-story dwelling, its front garden asphalted over to provide parking space for Lemmy's metallic bronze Toyota, which was still parked there. The place was in darkness and all the curtains were drawn. It looked empty, but Frost thumbed the doorbell anyway and waited. Nothing. He tried again, egged on by Cassidy's impatient shuffling, implying that if he rang it, the door would open. Still no reply. Frost lifted the letter-box flap and squinted through. All dark inside. Then he stiffened. He could have sworn he heard a door at the back of the house quietly click shut.

"Let's take a look round the back."

They moved to the rear garden. Frost stopped abruptly and flapped his hand at Cassidy for silence. He pointed.

Cassidy peered into the darkness. Movement. There was someone clambering over the rear wall into the garden, someone who didn't want to be seen. They watched as the figure darted across the lawn, then darkness swallowed it. The sound of a sash window being cautiously raised and closed.

Frost moaned. "A flaming burglar! Just what we bloody need!" He sent Cassidy round to the front door to guard that escape route while he tiptoed across the straggling grass of the lawn, probably last cut by Lemmy some three months ago. A small patio of checkerboard paving stones led to the back door, which he tried but it was locked. Farther along was a small window. The curtains were only partially drawn and he was able to flash his torch beam through to reveal a small utility room with a washing machine and a dish-washer.

To Frost's relief, the window slid up easily. He squeezed through, closing it carefully behind him and turning the catch to prevent the intruder from getting out again that way. A door to the right took him into the darkened hall. A rustling sound. He froze. The sound was coming from a door to his left. He tiptoed over and pressed his ear tight against it. More rustling. Someone moving stealthily. He padded across to the front door to let Cassidy in, his finger to his lips as he pointed to the room. Cassidy nodded, eyes aglow, all eager for action. Frost reached for the handle, turned it silently, and gingerly inched the door open. The room was in pitch-darkness but the radiator was going full blast and it was hot and stuffy and . . . Frost's nose twitched. Sweat. The strong smell of male sweat.

His hand slid down the wall trying to locate the light switch. Got it. He shifted his grip on the torch to use it as a club, if necesary. A sudden cry. A woman in pain. He pressed the switch.

.   .   .

A large, candy-striped settee was in the middle of the room, and on it, two naked figures, blinking at the light, were frantically trying to disentangle themselves. The woman, reddish hair, freckle-flecked body, all buttocks and floppy breasts, was in her early fifties. The man . . . no, not a man . . . a youth, fifteen, sixteen at the most, probably younger, had pushed himself free of the woman and charged at Frost with a knife.

All confusion. The woman screaming "No, Wayne!" and Cassidy yelling "Police!" while seeming to be rooted to the spot, and Frost belting the extended knife arm with his heavy torch and the youth shouting obscenities.

Cassidy froze. It was the knife. The cold steel of the knife that jabbed and jabbed. He suddenly realized he was terrified of being stabbed again . . . or was it that he wanted to see Frost get hurt . . . Frost, the bastard who had fouled up the investigation into his daughter's death. He gritted his teeth and forced himself to move, but before he could do anything Frost's knee came up sharply and with a scream of pain the youth dropped the knife and fell to the ground, clutching his groin.

Quickly, Frost pocketed the knife, then turned to the woman, who was struggling to cover her nakedness with a dressing gown. She scowled at him. "Don't look, you dirty bastard!"

"Dirty bastard!" echoed Cassidy. "That's rich, coming from you, Maggie. We've just caught you having sex with an underage kid."

"He's not underage. He's sixteen!"

"Inches perhaps, but not years," said Frost, looking down at the speechless youth, who was still rocking in agony. "Cover yourself up, son, you're making me feel inadequate."

The boy crawled over to the settee and began to pull on a pair of faded jeans whimpering as he did so.

"You've no right to come barging in here," said Maggie Hoxton.

"We rang your bell, but got no reply," explained Frost calmly. "We saw superdick climbing through your back window and thought you had burglars."

"We've got nosy flaming neighbors. Tongues would start wagging if he came in the front door."

"And his dick started wagging when he came in through the back." Frost turned to the youth, who was now dragging a red T-shirt over his head. "So what was the idea of the knife, sonny boy—protecting your gran?"

"She's not me gran," mumbled the boy.

"She's bloody old enough to be."

"I thought you were her husband. He's supposed to be a mad sod."

Frost nodded. "Lemmy'd have broken you in two, sonny. You wouldn't have left here with all the bits you came in with." He told Cassidy to take the boy into the next room and question him. He wanted to talk to the woman on her own. "Well, Maggie?"

"I've done nothing wrong. He's my toy-boy." She looked worried.

"I know," said Frost. "I saw you toying with his dick." He parked himself in the armchair and loosened his scarf. "I didn't come about him. It's about Lemmy."

"Oh?" She tried to sound unconcerned, but her nervousness showed. She wouldn't look at Frost as she dug down in the dressing-gown pocket and found a cigarette, then crossed to the mantelpiece for her lighter, keeping her back to him.

Frost was watching her every movement. He wished he could see her face. "Lemmy's dead, Maggie."

Her back stiffened. For a brief second the lighter paused an inch from her cigarette then, hand shaking, she lit up and turned slowly to face him. "Dead?"

He nodded. "He's been dead for three months."

She sat in the other chair, facing him, and inhaled deeply on her cigarette. "How did it happen?"

"Someone smashed his skull in."

She gave the tiniest twitch of a shrug. "Oh, dear."

"I must say, you're bearing up bravely to your sad loss, Maggie."

She snorted a sarcastic laugh. "If you're waiting for me to break down and cry, don't hold your bloody breath. Lemmy was a bastard—a vicious, sadistic bastard—and if he's dead, I'm glad . . . I'm over the moon."

"When did you see him last?"

Her brow furrowed in thought. "Beginning of August. We had a row and he walked out." She flicked cigarette ash toward the fireplace and seemed unconcerned when it fell short onto the carpet. A woman after my own heart, thought Frost.

"Lemmy walked out . . . just like that? Leaving his house . . . his car?"

"Yes."

"I find that very hard to believe, Maggie. What was this row about—theological matters?"

"He'd been seeing another woman."

"What's her name?"

"I don't know her name . . . Lily, I think."

Behind Frost the door opened and closed as Cassidy came back in.

"Where does Lily live?"

"I don't know her address. Someone told me he'd been knocking about with another woman. I questioned him about it, we had a row, and he walked out."

"I've got a better suggestion," said Cassidy, crossing the room and standing over her. "Lemmy couldn't satisfy you so you started paying young kids to have it away. Lemmy came home early one day and caught you at it. There was a fight and you killed him."

Maggie was up on her feet, screeching at him. "That's a bloody lie!"

"Is it?" smirked Cassidy. "I've been talking to your toy-boy in the other room. All the kids round here know about you and your depraved habits, Maggie. You pay them ten quid a time, don't you? It's been going on for months—even when Lemmy was still alive."

She glared at him. "If—and I'm not admitting anything—if I had it off with kids, they were all overage."

"Did they come with their dick in one hand and their birth certificate in the other?" inquired Frost mildly.

Cassidy scowled. This was a serious murder inquiry and he could do without Frost's infantile jokes. "He caught you at it once, didn't he, Maggie? The kid only just got out of the house in time. Lemmy beat the living daylights out of you."

"All right—so he caught me at it. So bloody what?"

"He finds you with a kid and he beats you up, but when you tell Lemmy you've heard he's having it off with another woman, he meekly legs it away, not even bothering to take his motor?"

"Yes." She thrust her chin out defiantly at Cassidy. "That's exactly what happened."

"Get some drawers on, Maggie," said Frost. "We'll continue this down at the nick." When she went upstairs to dress, he asked Cassidy, "Is he underage?"

"He says he's sixteen."

"We'll check him out when we get to the station."

"I'll do the questioning," said Cassidy. It was a statement, not a request.

"This is Arthur Hanlon's case," said Frost.

"Hanlon is only a sergeant."

Frost shrugged. . . . What the hell. . . . Arthur would be only too pleased to get rid of it. "Sure . . . take the case over."

Cassidy smiled his satisfaction. Maggie Hoxton's story was so weak, he was sure he could get a confession out of her without any trouble. Nice to be able to go into Mullett and say, with the right touch of diffidence, "I've cleared this one up, sir."

"We'd better get a team here to search the house," said Frost. "If she killed Lemmy there might be the odd drop of blood or bits of finger knocking about she forgot to wipe up."

He had just finished radioing instructions through to Control when Bill Wells took over the microphone. "Jack—you're just round the corner from the old Rook Street housing estate?"

"Is that so," grunted Frost. "I was wondering where I was."

"That missing girl—Judy Gleeson. Just had a phone call. Bloke wouldn't give his name, but reckons he saw a man dragging a young girl into one of those derelict houses in Rook Street."

"Which house? The street's full of them."

"That's all he told us, then he hung up."

"Bless his bleeding heart," said Frost. "It won't take us more than four or five hours to search through the lot. I'll need help."

"Wonder Woman and Burton are on the way."

"I'll meet them on the corner," said Frost.

The Rook Street estate had been built in the early fifties using a new French method of construction which involved preformed concrete slabs and metal binding rods. The building was cheap and quick. The finished estate looked like a prison block, but people desperate for housing were pleased to have anything. Over the years, serious faults began to develop.

It transpired that the wrong mix of cement had been used in the construction. The concrete slabs started disintegrating and the metal binding rods corroded and crumbled, making the structures highly dangerous. Experts said there was no economical cure, so the properties were condemned and the tenants rehoused.

The street was now a double row of decaying properties with damp-blackened concrete and boarded-up doors and windows. It was an empty, miserable street, exuding the damp, musty aroma of desolation.

Slowly, Burton drove down the road with Frost and Liz flashing torches on the houses as they passed them, looking for signs of forced entry. Nothing. All doors and windows appeared firmly sealed. "I suppose we checked this place when we were looking for the boy?" Frost asked.

"One of the first places we looked," replied Burton. "But I think they only checked that the doors and windows were still boarded up."

"Better do it thoroughly tomorrow," Frost told him. "Let's take a look round the back—that's where I'd break in."

As they climbed out of the car, the wind kicked ancient sheets of newspapers across the road in front of them and dribbled an empty tin can along the curb.

A high wooden fence protected the rear area. Frost clambered over it, hissing with annoyance as his mac caught on a nail and tore. He leant over to help Liz, but she ignored him, insisting on climbing over on her own and then offering her hand to Burton, who was making heavy weather of it. They thudded down into a junk-littered jungle that once was a garden. The harsh moonlight shone on a row of boarded-up windows and doors, all looking secure and untouched. Scrambling over dividing fences, they checked each house carefully. None of them had been breached.

"Right," grunted Frost. "Let's try the other side of the road."

They found the point of entry in the third house they examined. Here the boarding had been newly wrenched away from a downstairs window. Frost signaled for Burton to go round to the front of the house in case anyone attempted to escape that way, then swung over the sill and dropped inside. Liz followed. The intense darkness of the abandoned house seemed to swallow up the light from Liz's torch as they padded across bare floorboards. A door swung ajar. Frost pushed it gently, then flapped his hand for the torch to be extinguished. Floorboards creaked above. Someone was moving about upstairs.

A muffled voice. Then a scream. A chilling, unhuman scream of pain.

"Come on!" yelled Frost.

They charged up the stairs, taking them two at a time. At the top of the landing, a crack of orange seeped out weakly from under a door. They charged through it, into a room, its windows boarded, the darkness eased only by a candle stuck on the mantelpiece. In the flickering light they could just make out the back of a man bending over someone on the floor. A girl. A young girl. The room still echoed from her scream.

At their entry, the man swung round. Candlelight glinted off the knife in his hand.

Shit! thought Frost, not another bloody knife!

He advanced gingerly, jerking back as the knife blade slashed the air, just missing him. The man's eyes were wild. "Keep back or I'll rip you open—"

"Drop it!" Liz had managed to work her way behind him and had grabbed the knife arm. Furiously, the man tried to shake her off, but she hung on with bulldog tenacity. "Drop the knife or I'll break your arm!" With a howl of rage, he again tried to shake her off. A sickening cracking sound and a shriek of pain, then a clatter as the knife dropped to the ground. Frost, for the second time that day, scooped the weapon up.

"Leave him alone, you bitch!" screamed the girl from the floor.

"Police," announced Frost, flashing his warrant card. "Are you all right, love?"

The girl was lying on the floor beneath a couple of coats. Her face was glistening with sweat and her lip was bleeding where she had bitten it.

A yelp of pain from the man as Liz snapped handcuffs on his wrists. "You've broken my bloody arm!"

Frost ignored him. He was more concerned with the girl. "What did he do to you, love?"

Her bloody lips moved as if she were going to answer, then her eyes widened and she opened her mouth and shrieked, arching her back, almost shaking off the coats that covered her.

Frost yelled to Liz: "Get an ambulance!" As she radioed through, he bent over and pulled the coats from the girl. His jaw sagged. "Shit!! She's having a bloody baby!"

Liz stood frozen to the spot, still gripping her handcuffed prisoner. The girl was now in convulsions, sweating and shaking from the pain and the terror at what was happening to her young body. Her head thrashed from side to side as convulsion after convulsion racked her.

Frost moved back. He felt helpless. He didn't know what to do. He didn't even want to stay in the room. He beckoned to Liz. "Help her!"

Liz's face drained of color. She went as white as Frost. "I don't know anything about having babies."

Frost buzzed Burton on the radio. "She's having a baby. Can you help?"

"Yes," said Burton, to Frost's immense relief.

"Then bloody get up here—and quick." The airless room was becoming suffocating, smelling of blood and sweat and burning candle. Liz looked ready to pass out.

"Take him to the car," yelled Frost, indicating her prisoner. The cold should revive her. He didn't want another patient on his hands. He turned back to the girl, who was gripping his wrist, her nails digging into his flesh. Pain forced another scream out of her. "Come on, Burton," pleaded Frost aloud. "Come on . . . !"

The sound of the baby crying coincided with the approaching siren of the ambulance as it turned into the street.

CHAPTER SIX

"Any joy?" Wells asked as Frost mooched in.

"They had the bleeding joy nine months ago," said Frost. He filled Wells in on what had happened. "Fourteen years old. Too young to buy a packet of fags, but not too young to have a baby." He shook his head sadly and dug in his pockets for his own cigarettes. Only three left. Another forage into the superintendent's office was called for. "Is Hornrim Harry in?"

His question was answered by the booming voice of Mullett, who came striding through the swing doors, beaming. "I understand Cassidy has cracked the Lemmy Hoxton killing. That's what I like to see, Frost, quick results . . . something that is sadly lacking in other officers." He gave the inspector his meaningful stare, which Frost pretended not to understand.

"Are you telling me Maggie Hoxton has confessed to killing her old man?" asked Frost.

"Not confessed as such, but it's just a matter of time. Mr. Cassidy tells me it's an open-and-shut case. She never reported him missing, she's been forging his name on checks, and if that wasn't bad enough, she's been buying young boys for immoral purposes. Even without a confession we've got the strongest possible case."

"I never knew she'd been forging his checks," said Frost.

Mullett gave his thin, sour smile. "Sergeant Hanlon found evidence of it in the house. You really should keep yourself up to date, Inspector. You are supposed to be in charge." He spun on his heel to return to the old log cabin, tightening his lips and pretending not to hear what sounded suspiciously like a moist raspberry.

Frost hurtled down the corridor to the Incident Room to find Arthur Hanlon sitting at one of the desks making a list of the contents of a large cardboard box which contained items found during the search of Lemmy's house. "Arthur, who's been crawling round Mullett telling him things I don't know?"

"The forged checks, you mean? I've only just found them, Jack. I haven't even had a chance to let Acting Inspector Cassidy know yet." He stressed the word "acting." "Look at this."

He showed Frost a sheet of lined notepaper on which someone had been writing the signature *Lemmy Hoxton* over and over again, getting more like the real thing each time. Then he produced a white envelope and tipped out the contents: a wad of canceled checks returned by the bank. Frost riffled through them. They were all dated later than the date of Lemmy's death. "Here's an old check," said Hanlon, pushing it across. "That is a genuine Lemmy. These later ones are forgeries."

Frost studied them and nodded. "Maggie must have been bloody sure Lemmy wasn't coming back to have tried this lark. What else have you got in the box? If it's worth having, we share it fifty-fifty."

Hanlon grinned and dragged a carrier bag from the box. He tipped it on the desk. "We found this poked behind the cold-water tank. I'm going to check it against the stolen-property list."

Frost poked through the pile of assorted bric-a-brac—necklaces, silver-plated and gold compacts, dubious-looking strings of pearls, wads of family photographs, letters tied with ribbon. There was a gold cigarette lighter, which Frost flicked a couple of times, dropping it back when it refused to work. "Nothing worth pinching here. Hello—what's this?" A small black stippled rexine-covered case bearing the letters DFM in gold on the lid. He pressed the catch. Nestling inside on a bed of blue plush was a medallion on a white and maroon ribbon. The Distinguished Flying Medal. Frost took it from its case and examined it. Awarded to Flight Sergeant J. V. Miller. Miller! The old dear who was conned by the fake Water Board man. Lemmy must have been involved in that scam somehow, but he certainly didn't match the description of the man given by Mrs. Miller. The man she described was small and thin with a moustache. He put the medal back and pushed the case across to Hanlon. "Let Mrs. Miller know we've got it. It'll cheer the poor woman up no end. Where's Mr. Cassidy?"

"Still questioning Maggie in number two Interview Room."

"I think I'll stick my nose in—if only to irritate him."

Cassidy had just left the Interview Room and PC Collier was about to take Maggie Hoxton back to her cell.

Frost beckoned Collier outside. "How is it going?"

"She hasn't cracked yet, but Mr. Cassidy is sure she will."

"Let's see if I have any luck," said Frost. He went back into the Interview Room with Collier. Maggie Hoxton, seated at the table, arms folded, looked up at him defiantly as he flopped into the chair opposite her and treated her to his disarming smile, which immediately put her on her guard. He pushed across a cigarette and lit up for them both. "Things don't look too good for you, Mag."

She smirked. "If they look so bloody bad, why haven't I

been charged? You've nothing on me, not a damn thing. Like I told that other git, we had a row, Lemmy walked out, and I haven't seen him since."

"When he walked out on you, Mag, did he say 'Maggie, dearest, I'm never coming back, not ever'?"

"No. He slammed the door and went."

"He didn't even do a typical, lovable Lemmy thing, like putting your hand in the door frame as he slammed it shut?"

"No."

"Didn't it strike you as strange that he left his home, his clothes, his change of underpants, and his bronze Toyota?"

Maggie shrugged. "Perhaps he didn't need them. Perhaps his new lady friend has lots of money."

Frost beamed. "Funny thing that, Mag. I was going to ask you about money. Did he leave you anything for the housekeeping?"

"No."

"Did he send you a check from time to time?"

"No. He didn't give a sod about me."

"Oh come, Maggie. You do that noble man an injustice. Lemmy was so concerned about your welfare that even though he was dead, rotting away and stinking the place out, he still insisted on signing checks so you could entertain your toy-boys." He produced the canceled checks from his pocket and dumped them on the table. "He's been dead for three months, yet there's one here dated last week."

She stared at the checks, her mind whirring trying to find an explanation that just wouldn't come. "All right. So I forged his name. How was I supposed to live? The sod had walked out on me."

"If you believed Lemmy was still alive, you wouldn't have dared forge his name to his checks. He'd have broken every bone in your body if he found out. You did it because you knew he was dead. You knew because you killed him, you and young superdick." He gave her a sweet smile. "So I'm going to charge you both with murder."

She snatched the cigarette from her mouth and leant across the table. "You're not pinning this on me. I never killed him."

"Then who did, Maggie?"

"I don't know!" She leant back and took a long drag at her cigarette. "All right, I'll tell you the truth. We didn't have a row. He went out one day and never came back. Well, you don't look a gift horse in the mouth. He'd been a bastard to me, knocked me about and kept me short of money. I didn't give a damn what had happened to him. I was just thankful he'd gone."

"What did you think might have happened to him?"

"At first I thought he'd been arrested. I knew he'd gone out that day to do a job."

"Nicking stuff from old-age pensioners?" suggested Frost.

"Sounds his bleeding mark, but I don't know what it was. Anyway, he never came back—end of story."

"So you started forging his checks?"

"After a week. I had to live, didn't I?"

"Didn't it occur to you that Lemmy might be dead?"

"Occur to me? I was bloody *banking* on it."

"So why didn't you tell the police? If you and young rent-a-dick didn't kill him, you had nothing to lose."

"If I told the police and they found his body, Lemmy's flaming wife would have copped the house and all his money."

Frost gaped. "His wife? I thought you were his wife!"

Maggie shook her head. "Lemmy walked out on his real wife over ten years ago. The greedy, grasping cow—she'd have had me out of the house and on the street before the ropes came off the coffin handles."

"So he went out, never came back, and you did sod-all about it?"

She glared at him defiantly. "There's no law against that."

"There's a law against forging checks," said Frost.

"I was his common-law wife. I had no money. I don't think any jury's going to convict me on that, do you?"

Frost tapped his empty cigarette packet on the table. "You might be telling the truth, Mag. Trouble is, you still fit nicely into our frame. We reckon Lemmy came home unexpectedly, found you and little Wayne having it away. There was a fight, you killed him and disposed of the body. You then proceeded to lead a life of unlimited dick and luxury."

She snapped her finger at PC Collier. "Give me my handbag." She opened it and took out a window envelope which she gave to Frost. "Have a look at that!"

He unfolded the printed sheet inside. It was a Visa credit card statement made out to Lemmy Hoxton. The amount outstanding was £699.99 covering a purchase from Supertek Discount Warehouses, Denton. Frost looked at it, then back at her. "So?"

"Lemmy never let his credit card out of his sight. It was in his wallet, which he always kept on him. If he was dead in August, how come he spent nearly seven hundred quid in October?"

Frost looked again at the statement. The date of the purchase was October 12. "Are you saying you didn't buy this?"

"I didn't have his bloody credit card, so how could I? I reckon whoever killed him took his wallet. Check with the store—they ought to remember who they sold seven hundred quid's worth of stuff to."

Frost refolded the statement and popped it back into the envelope. "Okay, Maggie. I'll check it out."

He ambled back to the Incident Room where Arthur Hanlon was putting the finishing touches to a sheaf of schedules which he waved at Frost.

"Do you want to okay the arrangements for dragging the lakes and canals tomorrow, Jack?"

Frost shook his head. "No, thanks, Arthur. If you did it, I'm sure it's impeccable." He yawned. "I'm going to put my head down for a couple of hours. If any more bodies turn up with limbs or dicks cut off, let Mr. Cassidy handle them."

He drifted into his office on his way out. Liz Maud's things, following her expulsion from Allen's office, were neatly stacked on the spare desk. He took a cursory glance through his in-tray. More piddling little memos from Mullett and a wad of returns demanding to be filled in. In the middle of his desk Liz had left a list of the jewelry and furs allegedly stolen from Stanfield's house, together with a copy of their claim to the insurance company which suggested they had been robbed of the Crown Jewels. He skimmed through it and put it back on her desk. There were more important things to think about than that at the moment.

He almost made it to his car. As he was unlocking it, Wells charged out, yelling his name and waving a message sheet. "Another kiddy stabbed in his cot, Jack!"

"Give it to Liz Maud," said Frost. "It's her case."

"She's off-duty. Mr. Mullett wants you to deal with it."

"Me? Why?"

"You're an inspector. The kid's father is a friend of his."

"Any friend of Mullett's is an enemy of mine. Tell him you just missed me."

But as he spoke he could see the divisional commander watching them both from his office window. He heaved a sigh of resignation, took the message sheet from Wells, and climbed into his car.

The address was an expensive-looking bungalow with a large garden whose rear boundary backed onto Denton Golf Course. A police car was parked outside. As Frost slid in behind it another car skidded to a stop behind him and Liz Maud got out, her hair all over the place. She had heard the call over the radio and driven straight over.

PC Jordan let them in. They could hear angry voices. "That's the father," explained Jordan. "He's throwing his weight about . . . a real right bastard."

"Of course he is," agreed Frost. "He's a friend of Mr. Mullett's." Not feeling an immediate desire to go inside to be shouted at, he asked Jordan to tell him what had happened.

Jordan flipped open his notebook. "Family name is Wilkes. Him and his wife were down at the golf club—the annual dinner and dance or something—leaving the nanny to put their four-year-old daughter to bed. Around half past eleven the nanny hears the kiddy screaming. She tried to get into the nursery, but the door was jammed. Anyway, she managed to give it a kick and burst in. The nursery window was wide open, the kiddy screaming, with blood all over her pyjamas. Nanny looked out of the window and saw someone scrambling over the garden fence onto the golf course."

"How's the little girl?" asked Liz.

"No real damage, thank God. She's gone back to sleep now, I think." Jordan frowned his disapproval at the angry shouting still coming from the other room. "Assuming she can sleep through that damn row."

"Show me where he got in," said Frost. Jordan led them round the back of the bungalow, past the patio windows of the lounge, where they could see the father striding up and down and yelling at PC Simms. He glared at them as they quickly scuttled past.

The end casement window was wide open and outside it the SOC man was closing up his case of equipment. He shook his head at Frost. "No prints other than the mother's and the nanny's."

"You're bloody useless," said Frost, looking inside at the nursery, which was decorated in pink and white. A pink and white wooden chair lay on its side in front of the open door. The matching pink and white bed by the wall was empty. "Where's the kiddy now?"

"In the nanny's room."

Frost turned to look across the garden to the golf course. "She saw him clambering over that rear fence?" It wasn't a very high fence.

He swung his leg over the sill and dropped into the nursery. Liz and Jordan followed. "He wouldn't have to be much of an athlete to get in here, would he?" muttered Frost as he padded over to the bed. He looked at the counterpane, which was decorated with circus images. One of the grinning faces of a clown was freckled with tiny drops of blood. Frost looked at it closely, then nodded. He had seen enough. "I can't put it off any longer—let's go and talk to Mr. Mullett's mate."

The mother, an ash blonde in her mid-thirties, wearing a low-cut emerald-green evening dress, was sitting hunched by the electric wall fire. Her husband, dark-haired, with a trim black moustache, wore a white dinner jacket and a black bow tie. He spun round angrily as they entered. "It's too damn late now. He's miles away. If you'd have got here sooner instead of sitting on your fat arses doing nothing, you might have stood a chance of catching him."

Frost dropped uninvited into a vacant chair and beamed up at him. "I would hardly describe my lady colleague as having a fat arse, sir—it's smaller than yours."

The man's face darkened. "Don't use that tone with me, Inspector. Some perverted maniac has broken into my house and stabbed my daughter. Instead of sending twenty men to surround and search the place, we get two men in a car. It's pathetic . . . bloody pathetic."

"We couldn't send twenty men even if we wanted to, sir," replied Frost evenly. "At the moment, all we have got is eight men covering the whole of Denton. The rest have been out all day from early this morning, searching for a missing boy. They only stopped when it was too dark to continue. They are now getting some sleep and will be out again early tomorrow morning."

The man wasn't interested in facts and figures. "Someone's going around stabbing babies!" he yelled. "Get some more police in!"

Frost held up his hands in mock surrender. "Let's calm it down, shall we, sir? You want him caught, we want to catch him. We won't achieve that by yelling at each other. You and your wife were out when it happened, so let's have a word with the nanny. She, at least, saw him."

Frost had imagined the nanny to be a grey-haired little old lady in a nurse's uniform, reeking of wintergreen. He was pleasantly surprised when a strapping Swedish blonde in her late teens came in carrying the sleeping child wrapped in a blanket.

"Flaming hell," he whispered to Liz. "She can breast-feed me any time she likes!"

Liz pretended not to hear and hoped the family hadn't heard either. Frost had a genius for tasteless jokes at the wrong time.

"Helga's English is not too good," said the man.

I bet she knows how to say "Yes, please," thought Frost. He smiled encouragingly. "So you heard a noise, Helga, and you ran to the nursery?"

She nodded, eyes glowing at the chance to recount her adventure. "I hear baby cry. I run to nursery, but door is jammed. I kick and it opens. There is blood on baby. I look out of window and there is man climbing fence into golf field."

"Can you describe him?" asked Liz, pen poised.

"No. Too dark. Too far. I phone Mr. Wilkes at golf place."

"That's right." Wilkes nodded. "I called the police from there and we came straight over."

"If it was too dark and too far, could it have been a woman?" asked Frost.

Helga's eyes widened in astonishment at such a question. "Would a woman do such a thing to a little baby?"

"Women want equality with men," said Frost. "How bad was Julie hurt? Did you call a doctor?"

"Three little stab marks on her bottom," said Helga. "I put on sticking plaster." She pulled down the child's pyjama trousers to show them the plastered wound. It didn't look too serious and the sleeping child hardly stirred.

"I shudder to think what that pervert might have done if Helga hadn't disturbed him," said Wilkes. He turned to his wife. "First thing tomorrow—security bars on all these windows."

"It will make it look like a prison," she objected.

"I don't give a damn. Until these plods catch him I'm taking no chances."

Frost ignored the "plod" jibe. "These aren't the pyjamas she was wearing in bed?"

"No. They had blood. I changed."

"Perhaps you'd get them for me," smiled Frost.

The nanny returned in a few minutes, after putting the child back to bed. She held a small bundle of Care Bear pyjamas. Her breasts bounced delightfully as she crossed the room and Frost wished he could think of more things for her to bring back. He took them and held them up. There were blobs of blood on the bottoms corresponding to the trio of stab wounds. He examined them closer. The cloth was intact—no sign of tear marks made by the knife point. "When he got into the bedroom, were these trousers pulled down?"

Helga shook her head and her blond hair shimmered from side to side. "No. Bedclothes pulled back. Baby lying on her face, but pyjamas not pulled down."

Frost smiled his thanks. "I see." He passed the pyjamas to Liz. "We'll take these with us, if you don't mind." He stood up. "We'll see ourselves out."

"And that is it?" demanded Wilkes. "You're not going to search the area?"

"For what, sir?" asked Frost. "For a man whose description we haven't got?"

"So what *are* you going to do?"

"We've got a few promising leads, sir. We'll follow them up and let you know."

"I'd like to remind you that I'm a personal friend of Police Superintendent Mullett's," said Wilkes.

"Don't worry, sir," said Frost. "We won't hold that against you."

Outside the house he said to Liz: "Those other kids that were stabbed . . . were their wounds the same as this one —little jab marks?"

"Yes," replied Liz.

"I thought they were stabbed—slashed."

"No. It's all in my report—on your desk."

"You know I don't read bloody reports," said Frost. "Were any of the others stabbed in the buttocks?"

"Two in the buttocks, one on the upper leg, and three on the upper arm."

Frost opened his car door and slid into the driver's seat. "And did he ever stab them through their clothes?"

She thought for a while. "No. He pulled the nightdress or the pyjamas away and jabbed their bare flesh."

"This little girl tonight . . ." He was riffling through the dashboard compartments hoping to find the treasure trove of a cigarette end. "The bloke must have pulled down the elasticated bottom of those pyjamas while he stabbed her, then let it zip back." To his delight he found a sizable butt, which he poked into his mouth, frowning at the heavy nicotine staining of his fingers.

"Is all this significant?" demanded Liz.

"It could be," said Frost. "Follow me back to the station as quick as you can."

.   .   .

A fuming Acting Detective Inspector Cassidy was hovering in the corridor outside his office when they returned. "A word, please, Inspector," he snapped, marching into Allen's office and waiting for Frost to follow.

"Sure," called Frost, going into his own office and waiting for Cassidy to join him there. After a couple of minutes of waiting, Cassidy twigged what had happened and barged in. "You will excuse us please, Sergeant," he barked at Liz.

"Chase Bill Wells up on those files, would you, love," smiled Frost. When she had gone he spun his chair round. "What's up now?"

"I was in the middle of questioning Maggie Hoxton about the death of her husband. I take a break, and when I come back, what do I find? I find that you have had the nerve to carry on questioning her on evidence that was not made available to me."

"You weren't there," replied Frost.

"But that doesn't give you the right to take over my case, to question my suspect, to use my evidence."

"Sorry, son," said Frost. "I never seem to have time for the niceties. You're right. It is your case and I won't interfere again."

Cassidy sank down into the spare chair. He had expected Frost to bluster and had intended hauling him before Mullett, but the man's contrite apology had thrown him completely off balance. "It's not good enough," he said weakly.

"Quite right, son—in fact, it's bloody diabolical," said Frost, warming to his theme.

Cassidy's mouth opened and closed. He couldn't think of anything else to say; he was glad of the distraction when Liz Maud returned, followed by Bill Wells. Each bore a stack of dusty folders which they dumped on Frost's desk.

"They should be in alphabetical order," explained Wells, "but they got mixed up when we had the burst tank and the flooding in the old Records Room."

"You've always got a bloody excuse," said Frost. "If you

had any respect for the job, you'd come in on Christmas day and sort them out."

"I'm already due to come in on Christmas day," said Wells, taking the bait. "Every bleeding Christmas I'm on that rota."

"So you are," said Frost. "I forgot . . . you should have mentioned it." He split the files into four piles and handed them around. "We're looking for Sidney Snell's file."

Cassidy's head came up. "Who?" The name rang a bell.

"Sidney Snell—Slimy Sid—child molester. Used to pretend he was a doctor."

Cassidy snapped his fingers. Now he placed him. "He called at the house and told the mother he was from the Health Department . . . said the kids had to be vaccinated."

"Vaccinated?" asked Liz.

"Yes, Sergeant. Our Sidney was a pervert. Liked sticking needles in little bottoms or little plump arms. It gave him a kick to see them bleed, to hear them cry."

"He injected the arms and buttocks?" said Liz, still not taking it in.

"He only had a water syringe," said Frost. "The object was to make them bleed. He did it to about six or seven kids before we caught him. Prior to that he used to expose himself to mothers with kids in pushchairs."

"We had a couple of complaints this morning," said Wells, "about a bloke exposing himself to women in the park."

Liz leant back and snatched up a sheet of typescript from her desk. She waved it angrily at Wells. "I asked you for a list of all known sex offenders against children. This is what you gave me. Why isn't Snell's name on it?"

"Because he's ancient history," retorted Wells. "This all happened some ten . . . eleven years ago—"

"Even so," Liz cut in.

"If you would kindly let me finish." Wells sniffed. "Snell

doesn't live in Denton any more. When he came out of prison about five years ago, he moved up north. Too many parents in Denton had threatened to do him over if they ever saw him back here."

"Oh!" said Liz, crestfallen. She really thought Frost was on to something. She transferred her annoyance to him. "Then why are we wasting our time looking for his file?"

"I've an idea the sod might have sneaked back to Denton," Frost told her. "I think I saw him yesterday."

"And you didn't think it worth mentioning to anyone?" asked Cassidy sarcastically.

"I wasn't sure," said Frost, shuffling through his stack of files. "It's been ten years since I last saw him." He looked up as Wells cried, "Bingo!" He held aloft a file and flipped it over to Frost. Frost blew off the dust, then turned the cover so he could see the photograph affixed inside. The photograph showed a podgy-faced man in his early thirties scowling at the camera. Frost jabbed it with a nicotine-stained finger. "I was right. It was Snell I saw."

"Are you sure?" asked Liz, getting excited at the thought of an arrest.

"I'm positive," said Frost. "It's been ten years, but he's still got the same little piggy eyes."

"He used to live with his mother," Wells said. "Proper little mummy's boy." He leant over Frost's shoulder and pointed to the address on the file. "Ten years ago it was thirty-nine Parnell Terrace. I don't know if she's still there."

Liz picked up her handbag and checked that the street map was inside. "I'll go and find out."

"Hold it!" Now Cassidy sounded excited. He was staring at a typed sheet in the folder. "You've overlooked something, Inspector." He held out the arrest sheet.

"What's that?" asked Frost, quickly skimming through it.

"Snell used to carry a genuine medical bag around with him when he posed as a doctor."

"I know," said Frost.

"Do you remember what was in it?"

Frost shrugged. "Syringes, bandages, iodine . . ."

"And a bottle of chloroform," said Cassidy with a smug smirk. He pointed out the entry on the arrest sheet.

Frost whistled softly. "Bloody hell! You're right. I'd forgotten about that."

"Chloroform?" asked Liz.

Frost nodded. "No evidence that he used it at the time. Apparently he had an uncle who was a doctor. The uncle died and Slimy Sid pinched his bag." He chewed at his thumb as he thought this over. "Chloroform! I can't see our luck running that way, but it would be bloody handy if it was Sidney who stabbed the kids and killed Dean Anderson." He got to his feet. "I'll drive."

"Hold on!" Cassidy was buttoning up his jacket. "I'm coming with you." There was no way he was going to miss out on this. "Two more cases solved," he would tell Mullett with studied modesty. "I spotted the reference to chloroform and put two and two together. . . ."

"It doesn't need three of us," Frost pointed out.

"Detective Maud can stay here and look after the administration," said Cassidy.

Liz was indignant. "This is my case!"

"The murder of the boy takes precedence," said Cassidy. "You'll be more useful here, helping Sergeant Wells put these files in alphabetical order."

Liz looked in mute appeal to Frost, who shrugged and went out, followed by Cassidy. Picking up a file, she hurled it with all her strength against the wall, where it fluttered papers all over the place. She looked to Wells for support. Wells's delight at the smug cow's frustration fought with his hatred for Cassidy. His hatred won. "The bastard!" he said.

Cassidy swung the car into Parnell Terrace, pointedly fanning his hand to drive away the smoke from the stale cigarette Frost had found in the torn lining of his jacket. The car crept between a double row of identical and ugly terraced buildings made of preformed concrete. Not a light showed anywhere. The houses stood sullenly silent and an unnatural stillness hovered over the street. Cassidy's heart sank. The street was derelict. Every house was empty and boarded up with contractors' chalked notices saying "Gas Off . . . Electricity Off . . . Water Off . . ."

"All that's missing is 'Piss Off,'" said Frost gloomily.

"What the hell . . ." began Cassidy.

"Concrete cancer," explained Frost. "The same as the houses in Rook Street where the fourteen-year-old had her baby." He now remembered the article about it in the local paper. "They've rehoused everybody."

Muttering audibly about the complete and utter waste of time, Cassidy drove to the end of the road where he could reverse and head back to the station.

If Frost hadn't been looking up at that precise moment, he would have missed it. A flicker of light from one of the houses as a curtain was twitched back and quickly closed. A brief glimpse of a pale face looking down at them.

"What light from yonder window breaks!" whooped Frost, nudging Cassidy and pointing. "There's someone in that house."

It was the only house in the street where the doors and windows were not boarded up. It was number 39.

Four empty milk bottles stood in a line on the doorstep, waiting in vain for a milkman who no longer called. Frost jammed his thumb in the bell push and leant his weight on it. A bell inside shrilled. He gave the door a couple of kicks, then yelled, "Open up—Police!"

A light clicked on inside and showed dimly through the grimed fanlight over the front door. They heard someone stumbling down the stairs.

"Who is it?"

"The Avon Lady," said Frost. "Come on, Sidney, open up . . . you know damn well who it is."

A chain clinked and the door opened a fraction so a bleary eye could study the warrant card held out by Cassidy. Then the chain was unhitched and the door opened wide. A meek-looking man in his early forties, wearing a dressing gown over red-striped pyjamas, thinning brown hair falling over his eyes, blinked at them. "What is this all about?"

"Hello, Sidney," beamed Frost. "Long time, no see."

Snell peered at the inspector. "Sergeant Frost!" He shivered and drew his dressing gown more tightly around him. "I'd hoped I'd never meet up with you again."

Frost pulled a face. "I don't seem to endear myself to people, do I?" He stepped into the hall and kicked the door shut behind them. "Can we come in?"

There was a musty smell to the house. Snell led them to the lounge, a cold room with old, worn furniture. Two battered suitcases and a pile of bulging carrier bags stood on the floor. A picture of Snell as a young boy, in the garden with his mother, stood in the center of the sideboard. He switched on a two-bar electric heater and motioned them to chairs. "I'm sure, if I wait long enough, you'll tell me what this is all about."

"We were passing, we saw your light, and we knew we'd get a friendly welcome and a fairy cake," said Frost. "But I'm forgetting my manners. How's your mother?"

Snell's lip quivered. "My mother is dead."

"My sincere condolences," said Frost, remembering that this was the old bitch who used to provide Sidney with watertight alibis all those years ago.

Snell knuckled his eyes. "On the generous assumption that you are being sincere, I thank you." He sighed. "It's hard coming to terms with it."

"Sudden, was it?" asked Frost.

Snell shook his head. "She'd been in hospital for nearly two months. Three weeks ago they phoned me to say she was dying. I came straightaway. She died half an hour before I got there." He covered his face with his hands. "We never said goodbye."

"Three weeks ago? And you've been in Denton ever since?"

He nodded. "Don't worry. I'm not staying. I couldn't, even if I wanted to. The Council are tearing this entire street down."

"That's a bit drastic, just to make you move on," said Frost.

Snell ignored him. "Mother was the stumbling block. She wouldn't leave. As soon as they heard she was dead— she wasn't even buried—the Council slapped a demolition order on the place. I'm disposing of her effects—not that she had much—and I go back to Newcastle tomorrow." He nodded toward the suitcases. "So you needn't concern yourself with what I might do."

"It's not a question of what you *might* do," said Cassidy, deciding it was about time to make his presence felt. "It's a question of what you've already done."

Snell stared at Cassidy, his eyes blinking in puzzlement. "Perhaps you'd kindly explain yourself."

"The day after you returned to Denton, we had complaints of a man exposing himself to mothers and children. Isn't that what you used to do?"

"Coincidence."

"Coincidence has a long arm, but a very short dick," chipped in Frost. "Two of the mothers said it was the smallest they had ever seen, which immediately made us think of you."

Snell flushed brick-red. "Now you are being insulting."

"And then," continued Cassidy, raising his voice to let Frost know *he* was doing the questioning, "we had instances of children being stabbed in the arms and buttocks, just as you did when you pretended to be a doctor."

Slowy Snell stood up, trembling with outrage. "I committed my crime ten years ago. I was caught and I was punished. I've learnt my lesson." He turned to Frost. "They don't like child molesters in prison."

"Not too keen on them myself," said Frost.

"I got beaten up—buckets of filth thrown over me. I'm not going to risk that again."

"Where were you this morning around half-past eight?" asked Cassidy.

"In here, sorting out Mother's things."

"And where were you earlier tonight—from about ten o'clock onward?"

"In here. I never went out."

"Got a girlfriend, have you?" asked Frost.

"No."

"Boyfriend?"

"No."

"So if you're not sticking pins in little kids, hearing them cry, watching the blood spurt out of chubby little arms and bottoms, what do you do for kicks?"

With a disdainful smile, Snell opened the sideboard drawer. He took out a Bible, which he waved in the inspector's face. "Nothing you would understand, Mr. Frost, but I get my *kicks*, as you call them, from the Good Book. I'm a born-again Christian."

"It wasn't your Bible you were waggling at those women this morning," said Frost. "It was your little winkle."

"How many times do I have to tell you—I never went out this morning . . . I'll swear to it on the Bible if you like."

"I bet you would, you bastard!" snarled Cassidy.

Snell glowered. "I don't have to put up with this harassment. You haven't got anyone for these crimes, so you're trying to fit me up, even though I've gone straight for the past ten years."

Cassidy pulled two photographs from his inside pocket.

The first was of the missing boy. He handed it to Snell. "Where did you pick him up?"

As Snell studied it, Frost watched him closely, noting an expression of puzzlement followed by relief. If you're acting, you're bloody good, he thought.

"I've never seen him before."

"Then what about him?" Snell took the photograph of the dead boy, but his eyes were on Frost, who had got up from the chair and was now mooching about the room, pulling open drawers, rummaging inside. "Do you have a search warrant?" he called.

Frost flashed a beaming smile. "Of course not, Sidney. This is just a courtesy call."

"The photograph," snapped Cassidy, tapping it with his finger.

Snell gave it hardly a glance before returning it. "Never seen him before."

"He was chloroformed," said Cassidy.

"So?"

"There was chloroform in the medical bag you used to carry around with you."

"Was there? If there was, I never used it and that was ten years ago. I've taken my punishment and I've turned to the Lord. If He can forgive me, why can't you?"

"Perhaps the Lord didn't know you had these in your drawer," called Frost from the sideboard. He was holding up a colored photograph he had found in the drawer: two young children, aged about five, hand in hand and crying. They were both naked. He thrust it at Snell's face. "Given it up, have you, Sidney?"

Looking disgusted at the suggestion, Snell snatched the photograph from Frost. "A perfectly innocent snapshot of two sweet young children. What sort of a mind have you got to see something dirty in that?"

"The sort of mind," replied Frost, "that looks at a born-again Christian and sees a dirty lying bastard!"

Snell moved forward indignantly. "I don't have to put up with this!" He spat out the words. "This is sheer harassment."

"Shut up!" barked Frost, poking him in the chest. "And sit down!" Snell flopped in the chair. "Now listen and listen carefully. You are a hypocritical bastard, trying to hide behind the Bible. But you've been up to your old tricks again, haven't you, Sidney?"

"No, I—"

"Yes, you bloody have! Exposing yourself, stabbing little kiddies. Sadly for us, Sidney, this is your lucky day. At the moment we are so flaming busy we haven't got time to put trash like you away. When are you going back to Newcastle?"

"Tomorrow."

"Then make it first bloody thing in the morning, because if one more kid is molested, one more mother sees a man with a microscopic dick exposing himself, I am going to throw the bloody book at you, whether you did it or not. Do I make myself clear?"

"Now hold on a minute!" roared Cassidy.

"Shut up!" Frost waved him to silence. "Well, Sidney?"

"I swear on the Bible that I have committed no crimes since I've been in Denton, but as you wrongly and unjustly suspect me, I shall return to Newcastle first thing tomorow. I hope *that* satisfies you."

A curt nod from Frost. "Okay. We'll show ourselves out."

Cassidy hurled himself into the driver's seat and punched the dashboard in rage and frustration. Why did Frost always interfere at the critical time? "I was questioning him—"

"He had nothing to do with the boys," said Frost. "They were far too old for him. Anyone over six is old and wrinkly to Sidney."

"How can you be so damn sure?"

"I was watching his face when you showed him the pho-

tographs. He looked so relieved that you were veering away
from the stabbings. He did the stabbings all right, but he
knows nothing about the two boys."

"So why don't we arrest him?"

"We've got no proof."

"We can find proof."

"We haven't got the time, son. We're struggling with a
missing boy, two murders, and an alleged robbery with violence."

"We can get him for exposing himself," insisted Cassidy.
"The woman should identify him."

"It's too bloody petty to worry about."

"Like the hit-and-run killing of my daughter was too
bloody petty to worry about?"

Frost ignored this. "Tomorrow morning he'll be gone and
he won't be our problem any more."

"And the minute he gets back he'll be up to his filthy
larks again."

"Don't worry. I'll tip Newcastle CID the wink. They can
do all the work and when they nab him he'll confess to our
crimes as well."

"And they'll get the credit."

Frost shrugged. Credit didn't interest him.

"I'd like to put on record that I disagree utterly with
what you have done."

Frost shrugged. "If you like, son. It's a free country." He
yawned. "Take me home, would you?"

Cassidy drove in frigid silence to Frost's house.

Frost yawned again. "I shall go off to sleep the minute
my head hits the pillow. You're in charge. Don't wake me
unless it's bloody urgent."

He was woken up at three o'clock in the morning by the
insistent ringing of his phone and someone banging at his
front door.

It was bloody urgent.

CHAPTER SEVEN

Two o'clock in the morning and cold. Bitter cold. The moon glared down from a cloudless sky onto a frost-rimed landscape where a raw, cutting wind moaned and punched the side of the dark green Ford transit van as it turned the corner into Cresswell Street and drew up outside a small bungalow. The man sitting next to the driver climbed out and went to the back of the van. Mark Grover was twenty-six years old, married with three children, a fourth on the way. He opened the rear doors and took out his metal tool-box. Closing the doors, he banged on the side of the van. Without looking back, the driver acknowledged with a grunt and a curt wave as he drove off. Grover watched the van's rear lights disappear as it rounded the corner, then, humping the heavy toolbox, he turned toward the house.

He shivered. It wasn't just the cold. He had the uneasy feeling that someone was watching him. He stared up and down the street. Moon shadows rippled across the pavement as the wind shook the trees, but no sign of anyone.

The front gate was swinging back and forth, creaking in the wind. He frowned, trying to remember. He was sure he had closed it when he had left earlier that night to go to work. He hurried up the path, tugging the front-door key from his trouser pocket. But he didn't have to use it. The front door also was swinging ajar. Something was wrong. Something was very wrong.

He stepped into the dark of the hall, and was fumbling for the light switch when a loud crash made him drop the tool case and spin round. The door had slammed shut behind him. A strong blast of wind hit him in the face. A window or door at the back of the house somewhere must be open. He hurried along the passage to the kitchen. There it was. The door to the rear garden was wide open. He looked outside. Crystals of frost on bushes glinted in the moonlight. The gate in the wall leading to the path running along the rear of the properties seemed to be firmly closed. He closed the back door and turned the key in the lock. Then he saw that the piece of plywood he had nailed over the broken door pane was loose. The nails had been wrenched out of the woodwork. Someone had broken into the house.

Mark Grover ran into the passage and called his wife's name. He flung open their bedroom door. She wasn't there. Across the passage to the children's room. He opened the door, he listened. . . . Silence. An awful silence. Steeling himself, he clicked on the light.

The woman in the house opposite couldn't sleep. Another one of her blinding migraine headaches. She lay in bed, biting her lip against the pain, then flung back the bedclothes and went to the window where she stared out into the empty street, almost as bright as day under the moon. Headlights. Then the transit van pulled up. The woman watched Mark Grover get out and walk to his front door while her mind debated whether to take a second sleeping tablet. Lights came on in the bungalow. She had often watched the Grover children playing on their front lawn.

Beautiful children, but noisy. Their mother didn't seem able to control them.

She checked the time. Five past two. Another six hours of tossing and turning. She went to the bedside cabinet and shook out two more sleeping tablets, swilling them down with a glass of water.

A piercing wail of agony, like the cry of an animal, drew her back to the window. A man came stumbling from the bungalow. He was carrying something in his arms. Good God! It was a child, its arms flopping limply. He must have taken leave of his senses to bring it out in the bitter cold.

Grover was yelling and shouting. She couldn't make out what he was saying, it was incoherent and he seemed to be crying. Lights came on in other houses and windows were raised. The woman in number 25 shouted angrily for Grover to stop that bloody row before he woke up her kids.

Someone phoned the police and complained about the noise. A yawning Bill Wells sent a car out to investigate.

Frost staggered down to the phone and yelled to the police motorcyclist who was banging at the front door that he would be there in a minute.

Bill Wells was on the phone. He sounded grim. "Nasty one for you, Jack. Three kids strangled and the mother's gone missing."

Frost slumped down in the chair by the phone. "How old were the kids?"

"The eldest was three, the youngest a few months."

"Bloody hell," murmured Frost. "Bloody, bloody hell."

Most of the houses on Cresswell Street now had lights show-ing and curtains were twitching back as curious neighbors watched the comings and goings. A few, wearing dressing gowns, were clustered at front gates, talking in hushed, disbelieving voices and shaking their heads sadly. One neighbor who ventured across the road was abruptly turned back by the police. "Please keep to the other side, madam. Nothing to see here."

The line of vehicles parked opposite the bungalow were filled with duffle-coated reporters and photographers with flashy Japanese cameras fitted with enormous telescopic lenses. Standing apart from the representatives of the big London dailies was Sandy Lane, chief reporter of *The Denton Echo,* his ears tuned to what the big boys were saying, but hoping to use his local knowledge to talk to the people who mattered. This was a big story which Sandy could sell to London with a byline, although it would be too late for the morning editions.

The man in the BBC Television van, an early arrival on the scene and therefore able to park almost directly opposite the murder house, drained his cup of thermos coffee and mounted his video camera on his shoulder to film the arrival of Detective Inspector Frost. He panned the approach of the Ford as it coughed exhaust and jerked to a halt behind the police cars. He focused sharply on the figure at the wheel, who wore a none-too-clean mac with a maroon scarf, then zoomed in to show him climbing wearily out and surveying the murder house, which had lights blazing from every room.

Outside the front door Mike Packer, the young PC who had found the body of eight-year-old Dean Anderson, moved to one side to let the inspector pass. "Sergeant Hanlon is inside, sir."

Frost looked back at the knots of people outside the other

houses. "Don't waste time here, son. Go and knock on doors . . . talk to people. . . . Most of the street are up anyway. It'll save time in the morning." Relieved to be doing something useful, Packer hurried off.

The duty police doctor, anxious to get away, was waiting for Frost in the hall, which had its grey carpeting covered with plastic sheeting. From a far door came the heartrending moan of a man in the depths of despair. "The father," explained the doctor. "He's in shock. I've given him a mild sedative but he needs to go to hospital. The ambulance should be here shortly."

"Can I talk to him?"

"I don't advise it. He'll be out cold soon, anyway."

Frost nodded as if he accepted this, but he intended to question the father as soon as the doctor had departed. "The children?"

"Asphyxiated, probably by a pillow being held over their faces. They've been dead two to three hours. You'll need a pathologist."

"Drysdale's on his way," said Frost.

The doctor snatched his bag and reached for the doorknob. "Then you can manage without me." Like Frost, he was not overfond of the Home Office pathologist.

"Hello, Jack." Detective Sergeant Arthur Hanlon emerged from the door where all the wailing was coming from. Usually perky whatever the circumstances, at the moment he looked shattered. "It's a mess, Jack. Three little kids dead and the mother's gone missing."

Frost rested against the wall and fished out his cigarettes. He hated this type of case. "She killed the kids and did a runner? I wonder what drove the poor bitch to do that. We're looking for her, I hope?"

"Yes," said Hanlon. "I've circulated her description."

Frost rubbed his hands together to restore the circulation.

The pervasive breath of death made the house seem very cold. "How was she dressed? Was she wearing a coat?"

"No idea, Jack. Haven't been able to find anyone yet who saw her leave."

A row of clothes were hanging neatly from hooks in the hall: a man's raincoat and anorak, lots of brightly colored children's coats and hats, and, at the far end, a woman's thick red woolen coat with chunky black buttons. Frost patted the pockets and took out a small suede leather purse which contained about nineteen pounds. "I reckon this is the coat she would have worn, Arthur. So it looks like no coat and no money—probably just wearing a dress or nightgown. If we don't find her soon, she'll freeze to death. Has she got any friends or relatives living nearby she might have gone to?"

Hanlon shrugged helplessly. "We can't get any sense from the husband and none of the neighbors have come up with anything yet, except to say she kept to herself and she loved the kids."

"Never mind," said Frost. "I doubt if she's gone to anyone. I can't see her saying 'Can you put me up for a few days, I've done in the kids.' "

"I'll show you the bodies," said Hanlon.

Frost took another deep drag at his cigarette. "There's no hurry—they're not going anywhere." He coughed as the smoke irritated his lungs. "Fill me in on the facts, first."

"Married couple. Mark Grover, aged twenty-six—"

"He's the one making that bleeding row?"

Hanlon nodded. "The father—he found them. The missing wife is Nancy Grover, aged twenty-one. They had three kids, two boys and a girl, the eldest is three, the youngest— that's the girl—eleven months. Difficult to get details, but from what I can piece together, the husband is a self-employed carpet-fitter. He had to go out at eight last night on a rush job."

"Funny bleeding time to lay carpets!"

"That's what I thought. Anyway, Grover came home just after two this morning and found the front door wide open. The back door was open as well. He dashed upstairs to the kids' room . . ." Hanlon cleared his throat. "I'll show you what he found."

Frost took one last, long drag at his cigarette and pitched it out into the street. "Let's go."

Upstairs, Hanlon opened the nearest door, which was painted a nursery blue. Frost followed him into the small children's bedroom with its nursery wallpaper and heavy-duty orange and brown carpeting. The room held two single beds and a cot. Frost found himself tiptoeing across and holding his breath as if afraid to wake the tiny children lying in them. At the nearest bed he touched the cold, slightly swollen face of a boy who could not have been more than three. He was lying on top of the bedclothes and wore white knitted cotton pyjamas with Dennis the Menace figures printed on them.

"His name was Dennis," said Hanlon in a soft voice.

"Was he found like this—on top of the bedclothes?"

"No, Jack. When we arrived the father was cradling the dead kid in his arms. We had a job getting the boy away from him. We put him back here."

Frost nodded. The room had a lingering smell of Johnson's baby powder, which reminded him of the little Chinese nurse. God, was that only last night?

They moved across to the other bed, by the window. Another boy, fair-haired and slightly chubbier than his brother. His eyes were wide open and there were small dots of blood in his ears and nose. The bedclothes were drawn up to his chin.

"Jimmy, aged two," murmured Hanlon.

Frost shuddered. "Poor little bleeder!"

A crumpled pillow lay on top of the bedclothes at the foot of the bed. There was a slight discoloration in the center. It had been used to smother the three children.

A car pulled up outside. Frost looked through the window to see if it was the pathologist, but it was a black Vauxhall which he didn't instantly recognize. He turned back and went over to the cot.

Sandy Lane, stamping his numbed feet on the pavement, looked up as a black Vauxhall pulled in behind Frost's car. The man who got out and scowled at the press looked familiar. Cassidy! Detective Sergeant Cassidy, who'd been transferred from Denton some four years back after his young daughter was killed in a hit-and-run. So what was he doing back here? Sandy made a mental note to ask around.

The baby in the cot, so still and small, looked like a child's doll. Her arms, covered by the sleeves of a pink nightdress, lay on top of the bedclothes.

"Linda . . . eleven months," Hanlon said.

Very gently, Frost touched the pale cheeks. They were ice-cold. He felt he couldn't take much more and found something interesting to study out in the street, his eyes misting. Why the hell did he become a copper? "Poor little bastards!" he muttered.

Angry voices from the hall. Frost frowned and went to look. Cassidy was snarling away at young PC Packer.

"He was supposed to be guarding the front door," growled Cassidy. "Any Tom, Dick, or Harry could have walked in."

"Then we'd tell the bastards to walk out again," replied Frost. "I asked him to get statements from the neighbors."

"Well, I've told him to come back on the door."

Frost exchanged a sympathetic glance with Packer, but said nothing. He wasn't going to row over trivialities with three dead children in the house. He could have done without flaming Laughing Boy tonight. If he had known Cassidy had wanted to come he would cheerfully have let him handle the case.

Cassidy was out of sorts, annoyed that Frost had managed to get here before him. He went with Hanlon into the children's room, then emerged, tight-lipped, and they all went into the parents' bedroom with its large double bed and scarlet duvet. The bed, neatly made, its matching scarlet pillows plumped with nightdress and pyjamas folded on top, hadn't been slept in.

Frost wandered across to the window and parted the velour curtains to look out onto the rear garden, which was lit up from the lights streaming from the bungalow. Beyond it there seemed to be fields and woodlands stretching to the horizon. At first he couldn't orient himself, then he realized he was looking at the golf course. On the far side was the bungalow of Mullett's golfing friend where the little girl was stabbed. "Get someone to search that golf course. The mother might have wandered out there."

"Doing it now," said Hanlon, pointing to little pinpricks of bobbing lights from distant torches.

They went back through the hall to the dining room where the father was sitting by the table, staring straight ahead. Quieter now that the sedative had started to work, but from time to time he shook convulsively. He seemed to have no control over his hand, which was drumming a tattoo on the tabletop. His zip-up suede jacket was grease-marked and scruffy. There was the tiniest smear of blood across the front.

"From when he carried the body of his son out to the street," whispered Hanlon.

"Someone make some tea," said Frost, drawing up a chair to sit opposite the man. "Mr. Grover. My name is Frost. I'm a police officer."

Grover stared straight through him, his lips moving, but saying nothing.

"Mr. Grover . . ."

Grover's head came up slowly; his face was wet with tears. "My kids. She killed them."

Someone must have given him whisky. Frost could smell it on his breath. "Who killed them, Mr. Grover?"

"That bitch . . . that lousy bitch." His fingers flexed and clawed as if squeezing someone's throat.

"Do you mean your wife?"

Grover suddenly stared at Frost as if seeing him for the first time. "Who are you?" Then he slumped forward, buried his head in his hands, and started to sob.

Frost wriggled uncomfortably and fished out a cigarette stub. Grover wasn't going to be of any use to anyone. Where was that flaming ambulance?

More commotion from outside, then a tap at the door. PC Packer looked in and said, "Ambulance is here, Inspector. And there's a bloke outside who says he's able to help us. His name is Phil Collard. He was working with Mr. Grover tonight. He drove him back here this morning."

Frost took an instant dislike to Collard the minute the man waddled in. Balding and in his late twenties, Collard was running to fat, had a beer gut and an air of oily concern. "Mark! It's not bloody true, is it? God—tell me it's not true!"

Grover looked up at him and gave a chilling, mirthless smile. "They're dead," he said simply. "They're all dead." Then he saw the ambulance man and stood up. "I've got to go to the hospital." Without another glance at any of them, he walked out of the room with the ambulance man. The passage crackled with blue flashes as the waiting pressmen snatched the opportunity to take their photographs of the bereaved.

Frost waved Collard into the chair vacated by Grover. "How do you fit into this, Mr. Collard?"

"Mark's my best mate. We went to school together and now we work together."

"Carpet fitting?"

"Yes."

"So what can you tell us about tonight?"

"Not much. We usually go to the pub, but just after seven we had this phone call from Denton Shopfitters asking if we could help out with a rush job."

"What rush job?"

"Fitting a new carpet in the restaurant at Bonleys Department Store. It's been completely refurbished. Tomorrow is the grand opening—David Jason's cutting the ribbon—but the special carpeting got held up by Customs at the docks. It wouldn't reach the store until well after ten tonight. They wanted us to work all night and lay it—two hundred quid each, no tax—so we jumped at it."

A tap at the door and a rattle of cups. Packer with the tea. He handed it out in the mugs he had found in the kitchen and put a bag of sugar on the table. "Thanks," grunted Frost, nodding for Collard to continue.

"I called round with the van just after eight to pick Mark up. Nancy had the hump. Sat there sulking, not saying a word . . . the kids screaming and shouting."

"Why did she have the hump?"

"She said she was frightened—she didn't like being left on her own all night. She was always moaning about being left on her own, even if we only went to the pub for a couple of hours. Anyway, we got to Bonleys about a quarter past eight and fitted all the grippers and underlay. At five past ten the delivery van turns up with the carpeting. We worked like the clappers to get the job done and finished about ten to two. I drove Mark back, dropped him off outside here, then went off home. Later I hear all the police sirens so I goes out to take a look and someone tells me Nancy's done the kids in. I couldn't believe it."

"Did she ever threaten anything like this?"

"She threatened to do herself in—we had all the bleeding dramatics—but never the kids."

Frost showed him the red coat from the hall. "Is this the coat she usually wore?"

Collard nodded. "Mark bought it for her last Christmas."

"Any idea where we might find her?"

He pursed his lips and shook his head. "I heard she'd legged it, but she's got nowhere to go."

"Friends . . . relatives . . . ?"

"Nancy didn't make friends. She was a funny one, very moody. Relatives?" He shrugged. "Not as far as I know. When she was a kid, her mother's boyfriend started getting fruity so she ran away from home and never went back."

Frost took a sip of his tea. "Just for the record, Mr. Collard, is there anyone at Bonleys who can confirm you were there all night?"

"The night security guard—he's on duty until six." Then he realized the implication. "You're not suggesting . . . ?"

Frost smiled. "Just for the record, Mr. Collard. We have to check everything and everybody, innocent or guilty." He thanked him and let him go, then lit another cigarette. "I'm beginning to feel a lot of sympathy for the poor thing," he told Hanlon. "Three kids, no friends, a husband who's either round the pub or out all night . . ."

"I can't feel sorry for her," said Hanlon. "They had all their lives in front of them, and she killed them."

"Something must have snapped, Arthur." He lifted the mug of tea to his lips when he saw it was a child's mug. It bore the name "Dennis." He put it down and pushed it away. He didn't feel like tea any more.

Frost told PC Collier to phone Bonleys and listened to PC Jordan, who had been knocking on doors and talking to the neighbors. "The mother didn't mix with anyone, Inspector. She and her husband were always rowing—someone heard them quarreling tonight just after seven. Another witness thought she heard raised voices just before midnight, but couldn't be sure if it was coming from this bungalow or not. Oh—the woman at number twenty-two said she was getting undressed a couple of nights ago when she saw a man staring in at her through the window."

"Did she report it to the police?" asked Cassidy.

"No—she didn't think we'd do anything about it."

"How well she knows us," grunted Frost. "Any description?"

"No. She screamed and he legged it."

Frost nodded. "Thank you, Constable. You've been sod-all help." He looked up as Collier returned to report he had tried to phone Bonleys but could only get the answerphone.

"Send a car round," ordered Frost. "I want to know what time Collard and Grover arrived and what time they left—and check that they were there all the time."

"You're surely not suggesting they've got anything to do with this?" asked Hanlon.

"Just being thorough," replied Frost. "Mr. Mullett suggested I give it a try in case the novelty appealed to me."

Cassidy finished his tea in silence, staying aloof from the others, then went back into the children's bedroom. He wanted to take a thorough look around. He was bending over the body of Dennis when he spotted something that Frost, in his usual slapdash manner, had missed. On the upper arm of the boy's pyjama jacket, there was a small stain. A bloodstain. Cassidy's eyes glinted. Very gently, he lifted the arm and tugged back the sleeve until he could see a small blob of blood from a recent wound on the upper arm. It looked as if Dennis Grover had been jabbed with something sharp, exactly the same as the little girl in the other bungalow.

He pulled the pyjama sleeve down and lowered the tiny arm. What to do about it? He smiled grimly and decided he would keep this tidbit to himself for the time being. For the first time since he arrived in Denton, Cassidy began feeling happy.

•   •   •

Cassidy walked back to the dining room, where Frost was staring moodily up at the ceiling. "I'll take over now," he said.

"Thanks," said Frost, trying not to sound too grateful. This was the sort of case he was only too happy to give up. Not much satisfaction in arresting a poor bitch of a mother who just couldn't take any more and getting her locked away in a mental institution.

In the hall, he bumped into Liz Maud. "Sorry I'm late getting here," she told him. "I lost my way. I couldn't find Cresswell Street on my map."

"Apologize to the bloke who kicked you out of your office," Frost told her. "He's in charge now."

He walked back to his car, deaf to the volley of questions from the waiting reporters. Then everyone's attention was diverted by the arrival of a gleaming black Rolls-Royce. Flash guns fired as Drysdale and his secretary walked into the bungalow. They flashed again when the bodies were brought out, bodies so tiny the undertaker was able to accommodate all three in a single coffin.

Frost drove back past the golf course, all silver and black in the moonlight. The flag on the clubhouse was whipped out stiff and straight by the wind. No longer any sign of police with torches looking for Nancy Grover. The search had proved fruitless.

He detoured to skirt Denton Woods, a place where the mother might make for. His headlights picked out an occasional small animal furtively crossing the road, but no sign of the woman. He shivered and turned up the heater. Something white caught his eye, something moving behind one of the bushes. He braked sharply, but it was only a plastic carrier bag blown by the wind.

As he turned into Bath Street he caught sight of the blue lamp outside the police station. He reversed and drove into the car park. It would be warmer there than in his cold, empty house. He found the station a relaxing place to be in the wee, small hours when the phones were quiet, the offices empty, and he could prowl around and read the contents of other people's in-trays to see what was going on. And best of all there was no Mullett to keep finding fault with everything he did. He parked and went inside.

"Nasty business with those kids," said Wells, taking the offered cigarette.

"Yes," grunted Frost. "Any tea on the go?" He was munching away at the tuna-fish sandwich Wells had brought in for his own consumption. The canteen wouldn't open until five so the night shift had to fend for themselves.

Wells clicked on the wall switch with his foot. The kettle was already plugged in. "Did I tell you that Mullett's got me working here on Christmas day again?"

"Yes, I believe you did mention it," said Frost. It was Wells's sole flaming topic of conversation these days. Frost was not really sympathetic. He always got the Christmas day shift. He didn't mind. It was just like any other day to him, with the added bonus of the absence of the divisional commander.

"I'm going to have it out with him," continued Wells. "I can be pushed just so far." He picked up a written message. "We've had two more sightings of the missing boy—one in Manchester and one in Sunderland."

"Thanks," grunted Frost gloomily, stuffing the message into his pocket. "In a couple of hours we start dragging the canals and the lakes. God knows how many dead dogs and horses we're going to turn up." He watched Wells drop a tea bag in each of two mugs and fill them with hot water, and his mind drifted back to the bungalow. "That place was spotless. The nippers were well nourished . . . clean . . . bags of toys." He sighed. "Poor cow. Better if we do find her dead. How can you carry on living knowing you've killed your own kids?"

Wells nodded sympathetically as he brought out the carton of milk. Then he stiffened. He had heard something. A car door slamming in the car park. "That sounds like Mullett's car."

"You're just trying to frighten me," said Frost.

But it was Mullett, shiny and polished in his uniform, chin pink and smooth and freshly shaved. "I've just come from Cresswell Street," he said.

"Ah!" Frost gave a knowing nod. Cassidy must have told the publicity-hungry Mullett that the press and TV boys were there in force with half a million quid's worth of Japanese cameras. "Get your photograph taken, did you, Super?"

Mullett smoothed his moustache. "I thought it advisable to take advantage of the TV cameras to appeal for help in tracing the mother." He flashed a smug smile. "I think it went very well. It'll be shown on breakfast television."

That should put people off their cornflakes, thought Frost.

"Ah, tea!" beamed Mullett. "You must have known I was coming, Sergeant." He picked up the mug Wells had poured for himself. "I'll take it with me." His smile clicked off abruptly. "And I'd like a word in my office, Frost . . . now!" He spun on his heels and marched up the corridor.

"He's found out about the fags," said Frost, horrified.

"Don't implicate me," called Wells. "I had nothing to do with it." He glanced at the cigarette smoking in his hand and quickly stubbed it out.

But it wasn't about the cigarettes. "Sit down," began Mullett, but he was too late, as usual. Frost had already slumped into one of the visitor's chairs, putting his mug of hot tea on the polished top of Mullett's desk. Mullett hastily slipped a sheet of blotting paper under it.

"Cassidy seems to think these unfortunate children might not have been killed by their mother."

"Oh?" said Frost. "First I've heard about it."

"He detects strong similarities between these kills and the spate of child stabbings we've had over the past weeks."

"Stabbings?" said Frost. "The kids were asphyxiated."

"There was a stab wound on the elder boy's upper arm."

Frost frowned. "I never spotted it."

"But Cassidy did. We're fortunate in having him, Frost, otherwise goodness knows what vital clues might be missed."

"Kids always get knocks and scratches," said Frost.

"This was definitely a stabbing wound . . . and the Home Office pathologist says it was inflicted after death."

That bastard Cassidy, thought Frost. He's deliberately kept this from me. "No doubt when we find the mother she'll tell us what happened."

"*If* the mother was responsible. Cassidy is beginning to suspect Sidney Snell."

"Snell? Rubbish!"

"Consider the coincidences, Frost. Snell likes jabbing very young children on the arms or buttocks. This boy was jabbed in the arm. Snell likes staring in windows, watching women undress. There was a report of a man doing just that in the same street. The previous stabbing was in a bungalow by the golf course. . . . This also was a bungalow by the golf course. Too many coincidences to be ignored."

"Snell gets his kicks from seeing little drops of blood on chubby arms and legs. He doesn't kill with pillows."

"There's always a first time for everything," retorted Mullet. "Something could have gone wrong tonight. The children woke up and started crying. He panicked and tried to silence them with a pillow."

"And the mother?"

"Mr. Cassidy thinks she could have heard the commotion and come running in, so he had to kill her as well."

"And then he took her body away in case someone tripped over it?"

Mullett flapped away the awkward question. "We don't know the exact details."

"The mother killed her kids and did a runner," said Frost firmly. "Snell had nothing to do with it."

"I hope, for your sake, you are right," said Mullett, sounding insincere. "I understand Cassidy wanted you to arrest Snell, but you were content to warn him off. Might I ask why?"

"We've got too much on at the moment to sod about with Snell. Let Newcastle handle him."

Mullett took a sip of his tea. "If we find that the man you couldn't be bothered to arrest then goes out and murders three innocent children, I will personally throw the book at you, Frost."

Frost gave him a sweet smile and stood up, ready to go. "I wouldn't expect anything else of you, sir."

Bill Wells could hear raised voices rolling down the corridor and was deciding whether to take a stroll past Mullett's office in the hope he could overhear what was going on when a sudden blast of cold air that ruffled the papers on his desk made him look up. A little old woman had toddled in from the street. Frail-looking, in her eighties, she clutched a large empty shopping bag. Her feet flip-flopped across the lobby. She was wearing pink bedroom slippers with large red pom-poms.

"What's happening with the buses?" she demanded in a shrill voice. "I've been waiting ages at that bus stop for a number six and nothing has turned up—nothing! I've got to get to the shops before they close."

Wells sighed and shook his head sadly. "It's four o'clock in the morning, Ada. The buses stopped running long ago and the shops are all shut. Everyone's in bed—and that's where you should be."

The old woman blinked at him in confusion. "But I've got to get dinner ready for my husband. He . . ." Her voice trailed off. Her husband had been dead for more than sixteen years.

The phone rang. "Yes," said Wells, answering it, "she's just walked in here. I'll get someone to drive her back." He put down the phone and went over to the woman. "That was your daughter, Ada. She's worried about you."

"Did you tell her I'd gone shopping?"

"I think she knows," said Wells, taking her arm and sitting her down on the bench.

Frost came charging through, still seething after his bout with Mullett, but he brightened up when he saw the woman. "Hello, Ada. What are you doing here?" He gave her his mug of tea.

"I'm doing my shopping."

"Shopping? Not the sex aids shop again—you cleaned them out of mechanical dicks last time."

She giggled and slurped her tea. She liked Frost. He made her laugh.

"Any chance of giving her a lift home?" whispered Wells.

"I've still got things to do here," replied Frost.

A brisk clatter of feet as Mullett bustled through. Frost called him over and spoke quietly. Mullett frowned and looked across to the old woman sipping noisily from Frost's mug of tea. "It's on your way, sir," wheedled Frost.

"Very well." Mullett wasn't too happy about it. It would take him well out of his way, but one had to do one's duty to the public. He walked over to the woman and shouted in her ear: "If you'll come with me, madam, I'll drive you home."

"I'm not deaf," Ada snapped, gathering up her shopping bag. "Can we stop at the shops on the way?"

"They're closed, madam," said Mullett, ushering her out.

As the swing doors closed behind them, Wells turned in agitation to Frost. "Did you warn him, Jack?"

Frost frowned. "About what?"

"About Ada—she's incontinent."

"Is she?" Frost sounded surprised.

"You know damn well she is. The last time you took her home she piddled all over your front seat."

"I thought that was Mrs. Mullett," said Frost innocently. Then he snapped his fingers as if he had just remembered. "No, you're right . . . it was Ada." He smiled. "I suppose I shouldn't have let her drink my mug of tea."

Wells's jaw sagged. "You gave her tea? Bloody hell, it'll go straight through her."

"Let's hope he drives fast," said Frost. "Them blue velvet seats don't half stain, and Ada's output always seems to exceed her input."

Feeling considerably bucked, Frost wandered into the Incident Room where Burton, the only occupant, was sitting by the phone, reading a paperback, as he munched on a sandwich. He looked up guiltily as Frost entered. "It's all right, son." Frost dropped into the seat beside him. "Anything happened? Has the kid been found, but it slipped your mind to tell me?"

Burton grinned and pointed to a filing basket brimming over with the night's phone messages. "Sightings galore, most of them worthless, but we're following them up. No joy from the roadblocks. Too many kids out with guys for anyone to recall one specific boy." He tugged out a message from under the stapler. "This bloke phoned a couple of hours ago. Wouldn't give his name, but was most insistent we should follow it up. He said he and his girlfriend were having it away under the canal bridge off Union Street when they heard a car draw up overhead. He heard some grunting and groaning as if something heavy was being lifted from the car, then something was chucked into the canal. It sunk right away. He reckons it could have been a body."

"Grunting and groaning?" said Frost. "I reckon him and his girlfriend were doing all the grunting and groaning." He took the message and skimmed through it. "We've got the frogmen arriving tomorrow, they can start off looking by the bridge." He poked a cigarette in his mouth. "Having it away under the canal bridge? Some people pick the most romantic spots—it's cold, it's damp, and it stinks. I'm not fussy, but even I would think twice." He stood up and stretched. "Let's go home, son. Early start tomorrow. The briefing is at eight." He consulted his wristwatch. "Just over four hours' time."

CHAPTER EIGHT

The early morning TV news showed pictures of the "sad bungalow of death" and of the undertakers carrying out the bodies in a single coffin. Interviewed neighbors said how shocked and saddened they were and what a loving family it was and how everyone was shattered. A photograph of the mother filled the screen and a grim-faced Superintendent Mullett explained that the police were concerned for her safety and appealed to members of the public to look out for her.

Mullett clicked off the set with a nod of approval. An impressive performance, he thought. He picked up his gloves and patted his pocket to make sure he had his car keys. A final check in the hall mirror, a slight repositioning of the knot of his tie to dead center, and he was out to the car. As he opened the driver's door, he frowned and turned his head away, his nose wrinkling. The blue velvet seat cover on the passenger's side had been removed and was in soak with lots of disinfectant, but the smell still lingered. Mullett vigorously squirted the interior with air freshener and drove to the station with the window open in spite of the cold. That damn woman! And Frost! Frost would have known all about her. He had set this up deliberately. Mullett smiled grimly. Well, Detective Inspector Jack Frost was due for the biggest dressing-down he had ever received.

His car purred down Bath Hill and glided into Cork Street. A young uniformed officer spotted it and gave a smart salute, which Mullett acknowledged with a smile and a wave, delighted to see that the officer was in uniform. He had noticed two officers entering the station in their street clothes: He would have a few sharp words with Sergeant Wells about that.

The car park was crowded with vehicles of all types, most belonging to members of the search party. It was still dark and they would be having breakfast in the canteen before the morning's main briefing. In the far corner of the car park two men were off-loading Aqua-lung cylinders from a van. The frogmen team had arrived. Mullett had difficulty maneuvering into his own parking space. As he locked the doors and tested the handle he was almost run down by a dirt-streaked Ford which squealed to a halt within inches of his heels. His face darkened when he saw the driver, a cigarette dangling insolently from his mouth, climb out.

"Frost!"

Frost looked up, startled. He hadn't expected to see Mullett in so early. A quick check confirmed that Hornrim Harry's seat cover was missing. A warm glow started up inside him. God bless incontinent old ladies. "Good morning, Super!" he called cheerily.

"That woman you induced me to take home—" spluttered Mullett.

"Yes, very kind of you, sir," interrupted Frost. He smacked a palm to his forehead as if the thought had just struck him. "Meant to warn you about Ada, although I'm sure it isn't necessary in your case. I was going to warn you, don't get sexy with her. If you rub your knee against hers, tickle her groin, or anything like that, she'll pee all over your front seat."

Mullett's mouth opened and closed. He never quite knew how to take Frost.

"What was it you wanted to say to me, sir?" asked Frost innocently.

"Nothing," snapped Mullett. "Nothing." He spun on his heel and stamped off into the building.

In the Incident Room, PC Jordan was waiting to report to Frost. He had got the information from the discount warehouse on the posthumous purchase made with Lemmy Hoxton's credit card. "That was flaming quick," said Frost. "I thought they didn't open until nine."

"Mr. Cassidy said I should drag the manager and his staff from their homes," said Jordan. "He reckoned a murder inquiry shouldn't have to wait for the store to open up."

"Quite right," said Frost, wishing Cassidy wouldn't poke his nose in. Lemmy had been dead for months, so what was the point of dragging people out of bed to save a few minutes? "So what have you found out?"

"The item purchased was a twenty-eight-inch Nicam Stereo Panasonic TV set. But after two weeks no one at the discount warehouse had any recollection of the purchaser or what he looked like."

"They wouldn't have known what he looked like after two flaming minutes," said Frost. "All they look at is your credit card. . . . You could walk in those places with your dick hanging out and they wouldn't spot it."

Jordan had asked the credit card company to fax a copy of the actual Visa docket and it was clipped to his report. Frost compared it with a genuine Lemmy signature. It was an all too obvious forgery. "You'd think the store would have queried the different signatures," he muttered. "I suppose there's no chance the set was delivered and we've got an address?"

"No, it was collected."

Frost swung from side to side in his chair, sucking at his fourth cigarette of the day. Someone had used Lemmy's credit card to buy an expensive large-screen TV. So was Lemmy killed for his credit card? Hardly likely. The card was only used once and that was months after his death. More likely that someone with a motive had done Lemmy in and the credit card was a bonus. Or perhaps the killer had thrown the card away and someone else had used it? He flapped the Visa docket to shake off cigarette ash. He couldn't work up much enthusiasm in finding Lemmy's killer. The wife was right: The sod deserved to die. A thought struck him. "Check with Panasonic. See if the guarantee's been registered."

"He'd be a bloody fool to do that," said Jordan.

"It's the sort of stupid thing I'd do," said Frost. "Check it."

Burton stuck his head round the door. "Time for the briefing, Inspector."

A fair-sized crowd waited for him in the canteen, not quite so many as the day before, when hopes were high that the boy would be found alive. Frost noticed that Liz Maud was there, alone at a corner table, snatching a hurried breakfast, even though she must have been up until the small hours with the tragedy in Cresswell Street. He bought himself a hot sausage sandwich, its melted butter making the bread soggy, and took it, with a mug of tea, to the raised section at the end. He yelled for silence. As the burble of conversation died down he let his eyes drift around the room, checking who was present. He couldn't see Detective Sergeant Hanlon.

"He's in the toilet," someone told him. Almost on cue there was the rumble of a cistern emptying and Arthur Hanlon, looking a mite bedraggled, stumbled into the canteen, doing a mock bow to the applause that greeted his entrance. "Sorry I'm late, Inspector," he apologized.

"Flaming hell, Arthur," said Frost. "You always come out of the toilet looking as if you've just gone twelve rounds with Mike Tyson. Which reminds me . . . did you hear about the constipated mathematician? He had to work everything out with a pencil and a piece of paper." A roar of laughter, the loudest coming from Frost himself, who then almost choked on a lump of sausage sandwich. Mullett, who had just come in and was standing at the back, scowled. This was not the time or place for poor-taste jokes.

"Okay," continued Frost as the laughter subsided. "That's probably the last laugh any of us will have today." He jabbed his sandwich at the photograph of Bobby Kirby on the wall. "We didn't find the poor little sod yesterday. My gut feeling is that he is either dead, or he's being held captive somewhere. As you all know, another boy, Dean Anderson, was found dead near where Bobby went missing. Dean's naked body was stuffed into a black plastic dustbin sack and we've got to consider that the same fate might have overtaken Bobby. This means that some of you are going to have to go down to the Council Refuse Depot and start examining the hundreds of filled rubbish sacks collected by the Council yesterday." He gave a nod to Burton. "DC Burton will tell you which of you lucky lads and lassies have drawn the short straw." He took another sip of his tea. "But let's hope Bobby is still alive, in which case we've got to find him bloody quickly, so the sooner you get started the better."

Mullett moved forward and indicated to Frost that he would like to say a few words.

"Bit of hush for Mr. Mullett," called Frost. "You've seen him on the telly, now hear him in the flesh."

The thinnest smiles from Mullett. "Inspector Frost forgot to mention that we are also looking for this woman." He waited as Liz Maud rose from her table and pinned up a large photograph on the wall by that of the boy. "A tragic case. Her three children dead and she has gone missing. You have other priorities, I know, but please keep an eye out for her." A brisk nod to Frost and the superintendent strode back to his office.

Frost sat on the corner of a table, legs swinging, watching the main group file out. He wiped the front of his jacket where the melted butter from the sandwich had dripped, then wandered over to the table where Liz was doing her crossword puzzle. He leant over her and pretended to read a clue. "Four down—'Little Richard that ladies love big'?— that must be Dick!" She found herself looking at four down before she realized it was another of his childish jokes. Too tired even to fake a laugh, she knuckled her eyes and took another sip from her mug of black coffee.

"Did you get any sleep last night?" Frost asked.

She shook her head. "I was questioning neighbors until six and the postmortems are at half past eight." She took the offered cigarette. "Mr. Cassidy suggested I attend it."

Frost clicked his lighter. "The kids? I'll get someone else to go, if you like."

Her eyes blazed. "Do you think I'll faint? I've been to postmortems before."

"I've been to the dentist before," said Frost, "but that don't make me anxious to go again. It's worse when it's children, love. Wild horses wouldn't drag me if I didn't have to."

"Very kind of you to be so concerned for me, but I'm going," she said firmly.

He drained his tea, then dumped the crust from his sandwich in the mug. "Any developments after I left last night?"

"Nothing particularly helpful. Mark Grover is still in hospital, heavily sedated, so we haven't been able to question him. I've found two more neighbors who say they heard raised voices from the bungalow just before midnight. They thought it was the husband and wife having one of their frequent rows."

Frost frowned. "The husband? Could it have been him?"

She shook her head. "Mark Grover never left the department store until just before two."

"Are we sure about that?"

"I've spoken to the night security guard. He confirms that the two men were there until a little before two o'clock in the morning."

"Could they have got out without his knowledge?"

"No. All the main doors are security locked and he would have to operate the release switch."

"Damn," said Frost. The wife rowing with another man around midnight was a complication he would have preferred to be without.

"And I've spoken to the owner of Denton Shopfitters," continued Liz. "He phoned the store just before midnight to check on their progress and spoke to Grover."

"You're very thorough," said Frost ruefully.

"Mr. Cassidy is suggesting that the man the neighbors heard could have been Sidney Snell."

Frost treated this with scorn. "You don't have a row with a man who breaks into your house . . . you scream and shout at the bastard. Did the neighbors think she sounded frightened?"

"No. They said it was a heated row."

"Well, then . . ." He shook his head. "Sidney Snell is not a killer. Don't waste your time going down that road." He glanced up at the clock, then flicked his scarf over his shoulder and stood up. "Frogman time . . . If anyone wants me I'll be paddling in the canal." At the door he paused, trying to remember what it was he intended asking Liz to do. Oh, yes. He wanted her to check with the Council to find out who used to live in the derelict houses where Lemmy's body was found. But Liz looked ready to drop and she had a three-body postmortem to attend. He'd get someone else to do it.

·   ·   ·

PC John Collier pulled at the oars and winced as his blistered hands throbbed. He wished he hadn't volunteered for this. He thought it would have been pleasant, scudding the boat across the water, watching the frogmen plunge in with a kick of their flippers. But it was hard, back-breaking work. There was a strong wind blowing the boat in the opposite direction to which he wanted it to go.

"Steady as she goes, number one." PC Ken Ridley, systematically prodding the murky bottom of the canal with a long pole, was doing his captain-of-the-battleship act, which got progressively less funny with constant repetition. Ahead of them, a line of bubbles marked the progress of one of the police frogmen.

Frost sat on the bank, moodily surveying the proceedings and sucking at a cigarette while tossing small stones into the water. It was cold and windy and he had the strong feeling this would be a waste of time. The canal at this juncture was crossed by the road bridge, which made it the ideal point from which to hump junk out of a car boot and chuck it into the black soup of the stagnant water. Much of this had already been retrieved by the frogmen and the towpath was cluttered with foul-smelling heaps. There were sodden mattresses, a couple of bundles of carpeting that looked almost new, but which would never lose the ripe canal smell, a black plastic bag which turned out to be full of offal from a butcher's shop and the bloated carcass of a long-dead goat. Particularly revolting was a soggy cardboard box crammed full with maggoty chickens' heads and feet. "All we want now is a few spuds and we've got ourselves our dinner," he commented bitterly, grimacing as the wind changed and drove the smell of putrefaction straight at him. Many years ago, when he was a small child, he had sat on this same towpath, probably not far from this same spot, and fished for tiddlers. But there was nothing living in the water nowadays. Denton Union Canal, long since abandoned by the once-thriving barge trade, was now a choked, evil-smelling backwater.

A frogman's head broke the surface. He had been tying a rope to something enveloped in mud at the bottom and was signaling for Collier and Ridley to haul it up. A bulging black plastic dustbin sack was dragged into the boat. Frost's heart sank. It was the right size and shape for a young boy's body.

The boat bumped against the side of the towpath and the two policemen lifted out the sack, which streamed water from holes, apparently punched in it to make it sink. They laid the sodden mass alongside Frost, who regarded it gloomily, dreading to think what was inside. He stood up, chucked his cigarette into the canal, then gave the sack a tentative prod with his foot. Something soft and yielding, like flesh. He crouched down, sliced through the string tying the neck of the sack with his penknife, then peered inside. A sodden mass of water-blackened human hair. He looked up at Ridley and nodded grimly. "It's the boy." He pulled the neck of the sack open wider, then the cold sweat of relief flooded through him. He looked up again at Ridley. "I'm a prize twot!" he said. It wasn't human hair. Reaching inside the sack, he pulled out a heavy, sodden fur coat. Frost had no idea what a mink coat looked like, but this, even dripping with filthy canal water, looked expensive. As did the silver fox cape which was under it. At the bottom of the sack was a grey plastic bag tied tightly with clumsily knotted string. The bag held something heavy. Frost's penknife sawed through this, leaving the knot intact so Forensic could submit it to their scrupulous examination and come up with sod-all. Inside was a brick, put there to ensure the sack sank, and a jumble of jewelry. The haul from Richard Stanfield's house.

Frost stared at it. Why had it been stolen, then dumped? It suggested an insurance scam, although the furs and jewelry looked genuine enough. He put everything back inside the sack. "Trot it down to the station. We'll get old mother Stanfield in to identify it."

Ridley's pole had prodded something that belched up large, rancid-looking bubbles which burst to exude a stomach-churning smell. He signaled to the frogmen, but before they could respond, Frost's radio squawked. Control calling him urgently. *"Can you get back here at once, Inspector? We've received a ransom demand for the missing boy."*

"What's the betting it's a bleeding hoax," muttered Frost, clicking the radio off.

He took one last look at Collier and Ridley, who were hauling up something slimy and phosphorescent that broke in half as they tried to get it into the boat, then made for his car.

There was quite a crowd waiting for him in the Incident Room, including Cassidy, Hanlon, Burton, and Harding from Forensic. All looked grim. "So where's this ransom demand?" asked Frost.

Cassidy pointed to a padded envelope lying on the desk. "This came in this morning's post." The typed label was addressed to "The Missing Boy Officer, Denton Police Station." The postmark, date-stamped the previous evening, was that of the main Denton Post Office. "This was inside." Cassidy handed Frost a sheet of white A4 paper which had been slipped inside a transparent cover for protection.

The message was printed out on a dot matrix printer in draft mode. Frost read it aloud.

"To the officer in charge:
    I have the missing boy—the enclosed should enable you to convince Sir Richard Cordwell, managing director of the Savalot Supermarket chain, that this is genuine."

Frost paused. "What was enclosed?"

Cassidy shook out a matchbox from the padded envelope and, holding it carefully by the corners, mutely passed it to Frost. Frost pushed open the box and stared in horrified disbelief. "No!" On a bed of blood-flecked cotton wool lay a severed human finger. He looked away, then back again in the hope it wouldn't still be there. A tiny finger, the flesh waxen, grime under the nail, dried blood caking the severed end. It almost looked too small to be real, but Forensic had confirmed it was from a child of seven or eight years old.

Frost stared at nothing, lost for words. Then, very carefully, he closed the matchbox and handed it back to Cassidy.

He poked a cigarette in his mouth to compose himself before he resumed reading the letter.

> I am sorry about the first boy. That was an accident, but if Bobby Kirby is to die, that will not be an accident. It will be because you have failed to carry out my instructions.
>
> 1) For the safe return of the boy, I require to be paid the sum of £250,000. This money is to be paid to me by Sir Richard Cordwell, managing director of the Savalot Supermarket chain. This money will be a fleabite to him.
>
> 2) I have also written to Sir Richard Cordwell explaining how the money is to be paid. If he refuses to pay, the boy will die and his company's name will be mud.
>
> 3) Your job is to convince Sir Richard he must pay and then to stay out of it. You will take no further part in the proceedings if the boy is not to be harmed further. Any sign of the police when the money is handed over to me—even if a police car

should accidentally pass by—then the boy will die. I will be monitoring all police radio calls to ensure you keep out of it.

4) Any attempt at stalling for time and the boy will lose another finger.

5) The boy is well, but in some pain. He is hidden where you will never find him. Do what I request and I will tell you where he is. Ignore my requests and you will never see him again.

6) I am sending a copy of this letter and a cassette tape to *The Denton Echo* so the public are aware that it is up to Savalot whether Bobby lives or dies.

"Give credit where credit's due," muttered Frost, "he's a cold, calculating, businesslike bastard." He read it through again, then tossed it on the desk. "He forgot to sign it."

"There were no prints on it," said Harding from Forensic.

"Never mind," said Frost. "It's not entirely your fault." He pinched the scar on his face as he thought things over. "Someone get on the phone to Sandy Lane at *The Denton Echo*. I want that letter. He's not to open it or play the cassette—he's to bring it straight over here."

"Already done," said Cassidy. "He should be on his way over now."

Frost tapped the matchbox. "Have we checked that this is Bobby Kirby's finger and not the dead boy's . . . or even some other boy we don't know about yet?"

"I've sent someone over to the mother's house to get prints from Bobby's room," said Harding. "We're also checking the prints of the dead boy in the morgue."

"For Pete's sake don't tell the mother about the ransom demand," said Frost.

"Of course not," said Harding.

Frost spun his chair round and looked at the wall map which charted the progress of the search parties. He said, "Call off the search."

"We haven't checked if this is the boy's finger yet," Cassidy protested. "It could be some medical student's hoax."

"A hoax? We should be so bloody lucky," said Frost. "It's genuine, I promise you. Call it off, Arthur. What about the letter he's sent to Sir Richard Cordwell, Cassidy?"

"I've been on to Savalot's main office. They're going through all their post now. I've also spoken to Cordwell's private secretary. She's going through his personal mail."

The internal phone buzzed. Sandy Lane from *The Denton Echo* had arrived.

Bill Wells ushered him in. Lane was carrying a padded envelope, identical to the one in front of Frost. He handed it over. It had been opened.

"We asked you not to open it," said Cassidy.

"I didn't get the message until I'd just slit the flap," lied Sandy.

"Did it photostat all right?" Frost asked.

"Perfectly," grinned the reporter.

The postmark was the same. The envelope was addressed to "The Chief Crime Reporter, The Denton Echo."

"Chief Crime Reporter?" queried Frost.

"That's me, Jack—Chief Crime Reporter, Chief Sports Reporter, Jumble Sales and Church Fêtes."

"I expect your bleeding fingerprints are all over it," said Frost, letting Harding extract the contents and slip them into transparent folders. There were two letters and a cassette tape. The first letter read:

To the Chief Crime Reporter:
  I have the boy Bobby Kirby. The police will confirm this. I require £250,000 from Sir Richard Cordwell, Managing Director, Savalot Supermarkets.

His company can well afford this sum. If he refuses to pay, the boy will die and I am sure it will make an interesting story for your newspaper.

Let the police have the tape after you have listened to it. Copy of my letter to the police enclosed.

"I suppose you've played the tape too?" said Frost.

"I might have accidentally listened to it," affirmed Sandy.

Burton took the tape and poked it into a cassette player. Everyone quietened down.

For a second or so, nothing, just the hiss of raw tape and the rumble of the recorder motor, then a boy's voice. There were lots of pauses and clicks. The recorder had been switched on and off a few times while the man obviously told the boy what to say. Bobby was clearly distressed and it made harrowing listening.

"My name is Bobby Kirby. I'm tied up and blindfolded. The man says if you do what he tells you, he will let me go home. He says you know what will happen if you don't do what he says. I want to go home. Please . . . I want to go home. . . ." A click and the sound of raw tape without the recorder motor noise. Burton switched the machine off.

Harding leant across and fast-forwarded the rest of the tape on cue and review. There was nothing else on it. He removed the cassette and carefully examined it. "I think that was the first recording on a brand-new tape, but I'll get it checked in case we can pick anything else up."

"Any idea what sort of machine it was recorded on?" asked Cassidy.

"Judging by the sound quality, certainly not a state-of-the-art hi-fi. I'd guess at a cheap portable model with a built-in microphone—that's why it's picking up the sound of the motor."

"Are they rare?" asked Frost.

Harding shook his head. "There's millions of them," he said.

"What about the cassette? Could we trace the shop where he bought it?"

Again Harding shook his head. "One of the commonest types . . . sold in the thousands. I'll replay it back at the lab and boost up the background. It might give us a clue as to where it was recorded."

"Get a copy made," said Cassidy, "and take it to Mrs. Kirby—see if she can identify the voice."

"No!" said Frost. "Why upset her? If the fingerprint matches, we'll know it's genuine."

Cassidy scowled. He resented being contradicted in front of everyone. He resented even more the fact that on this occasion Frost was right.

"What's this about the boy losing another finger?" asked Sandy.

Frost filled him in. "But I don't want it reported. We've got to keep that up our sleeve. In fact, I don't want any of this reported until we've got the boy back safe."

"Bloody hell, Jack," the reporter protested, "this is the biggest scoop I've ever had. I could make a bomb selling it to the London papers!"

"It'll still be a scoop when we get the boy back. You can have it as an exclusive."

Sandy sighed. "All right. I'll make do with that."

"How do you know you can trust him?" demanded Cassidy when Lane had left.

"I can trust him," said Frost firmly. He read through the letters again. "The bastard's on to a winner here. Kidnap someone—anyone. It doesn't matter if the parents have got any money because you then blackmail some large corporation into coughing up the cash, knowing the public will think them shit if they refuse and let the kid die." He groaned inwardly as Mullett came bustling in. He could do without another dose of Hornrim Harry this morning.

"I've just come from your office, Frost," said Mullett. "There's a terrible smell in there."

"You don't have to apologize, Super," said Frost, pretending to misunderstand. "We all have the odd accident." Mullett glared and Frost snapped his fingers. "Oh—sorry . . . You mean the stuff we fished from the canal. It's the loot from the Standish robbery. I'm getting the insurance assessor over to have a look at it."

"I understand there's been a ransom demand?" Mullett was trying not to reveal his irritation at the suppressed giggles from some of the others in the room.

Frost pushed the letter across, then showed Mullett the contents of the matchbox. Mullett's face creased with concern, which grew as he listened to the tape. He took his glasses off and pinched his nose. "I do hope Savalot agree to cooperate."

"They'll cooperate," said Frost. "They daren't risk the bad publicity."

"Bad publicity?"

"When the papers print the story that they've refused to come up with money they can well afford and the kid dies."

"That's blackmail," said Mullett.

"All ransom demands are blackmail," retorted Frost.

Burton, the phone pressed to his ear, called him over. "Savalot," he murmured. "Sir Richard Cordwell's private secretary. She's been through all his private mail—nothing. The main office has opened up all the general mail and there's nothing there either."

"It's got to be!" Frost frowned. "It's bloody well got to be." He scrubbed his face with his hands, trying to think. "Wait a minute. He must have sent it to Cordwell's house. Get the number."

The number was unlisted and the secretary refused to pass it on, but she did condescend to phone the house herself. She called back within minutes. The letter, marked

"Strictly Personal and Confidential," was waiting for Cordwell, who was still in bed.

"Tell him not to touch it, we're on our way over," said Frost. The secretary started to suggest he make an appointment, but Frost had slammed the phone down.

The internal phone rang. "There's a Mr. Hicks here to see you," said Bill Wells.

"Send the sod away," said Frost. "We're too busy."

"He says you asked him to come," insisted Wells. "He's the claims assessor from Cityrock Insurers."

Frost snatched his mind away from the kidnapping and on to the furs and jewels dredged from the canal. "Send him to my office. Tell him to follow his nose—he can't miss it."

Hicks, a jolly little man wearing heavy horn-rimmed glasses, beamed as Frost tipped out the contents of the plastic bag. He held the furs at arm's length, his nose screwing up at the smell, nodded, then let them drop to the floor, more interested in the jewelry. His smile widened as he compared each item with his typewritten list. "Looks as if it is all here, Inspector."

"Is it worth what they're claiming?"

A firm shake of the head. "They're claiming seventy-five thousand pounds. I'd put it at thirty-five to forty thousand top whack."

"An insurance fiddle?"

Hicks pursed his lips. "Not a very clever one, if it was. We'd have knocked the claim down to something nearer thirty-five thousand pounds, which is what the items are worth. They could have sold them for that and there'd have been no need to chuck them in a canal." He zipped up his briefcase. "As far as my company is concerned, the stolen items have been recovered and we don't have to pay out. Mr. Stanfield can carry on paying the premiums for his own inflated valuation, but should they be 'stolen' again, we'll settle on the basis of my own figure."

"What about the money he claims he handed over to get his daughter returned?"

Hicks shrugged. "If he was insured for such a loss then it wasn't with my company, but I don't think any insurers give cover for money held in a bank."

Frost drummed the desk with his fingers. He still wasn't convinced this was a genuine robbery and abduction. If it was genuine, why steal stuff then dump it? He thanked Hicks, and steered him in the direction of the street.

Back in the Incident Room, Burton was on the phone. He put his hand over the mouthpiece as Frost entered. "Forensic were on. The prints check. The finger is from Bobby Kirby."

Frost grunted his acknowledgment.

"And I've got PC Ridley on the phone. He wants to know what I should do with all the stuff we pulled out of the canal."

"He shouldn't have to ask," replied Frost. "There's a 'Keep Britain Tidy' campaign in force this week. Tell him to chuck it back in the canal."

Burton relayed the message and hung up. "All search parties are disbanded," he reported.

Frost nodded and walked over to study the photographs of the two boys. "He intended Dean to be the kidnap victim. He chloroformed him, but the kid died. This didn't put the bastard off, he just looked for someone else—and he found Bobby."

"What made him pick Dean Anderson in the first place?"

Frost took a deep drag at his cigarette. "Any kid would have done—that's the clever part. The money is coming from a rich supermarket chain—pay up or your customers will know you let a kid die. This bloke is a clever bastard and he's on to a flaming winner." He dropped his cigarette on the floor and crushed it with his foot. "Come on, son, let's find out how the rich people live. We're off to see the Supermarket King."

Mullett stopped them on their way out. He had been told the result of the fingerprinting, but not by Frost as he should have expected.

"Can't stop, Super," grunted Frost, edging past. "We're on our way to see Tricky Dicky."

A concerned frown from Mullett. With someone as important as Sir Richard Cordwell involved, he was wondering if the uncouth Frost was the right person to handle the interview. "He's a very influential man, Frost, and I understand he can be quite nasty when he likes, so handle him with kid gloves."

"Don't worry, Super," said Frost, sidling past him toward the door to the car park. "I shall treat him with my usual tact."

Mullett's smile tightened to the vanishing point. This was exactly what he feared. "I think I'd better come with you," the superintendent said.

The manor house was an imposing edifice, stolidly Victorian, forests of chimney pots, standing in extensive grounds and enclosed by a high stone wall thickly coated with ivy. The black cast-iron gates were firmly closed and a video security camera scrutinized them closely as Burton announced who they were into a microphone. Their credentials established, the gates swung back, closing again as soon as they were inside. They coasted up to the main entrance behind a gleaming pearl-grey Rolls-Royce. Frost checked its tax disc and seemed disappointed to find it was current. Up stone steps to the front door where a secretary hovered. She led them directly to Cordwell's study, a large, high-ceilinged room with tall French windows opening out onto a billiard-table lawn, a rose garden, and a fish pool with a weathered stone fountain in the shape of a boy with a dolphin.

Cordwell, a thickset, coarse-featured man in his early fifties, sat at an antique mahogany desk, its green leather top scarred with cigarette burns. As they entered he was bawling into a white and gold phone and didn't give them a second glance. "If he's not measuring up, then chuck him out—you can find a reason. I'm not carrying bloody passengers." He banged the phone down, grabbed an enormous cigar from a silver box and lit up with a lighter fashioned from a genuine flintlock pistol, then flapped a hand for Frost and Mullett to sit. Cordwell had started in business selling broken biscuits from a barrow in street markets and, by cheating, scheming, and doing down his associates, had worked his way up to owning one of the largest cut-price grocery chains in Britain. A grunt and a snap of his fingers signaled the hovering secretary to place a folder in front of him. He slid it across to the two policemen. "The letter."

Frost opened the folder. The envelope had been slit open and the letter was fastened to it with a paper clip.

"We asked you not to open it," Frost said.

Cordwell gave him a sweet smile. "Nobody tells me what to do."

While Frost read the letter, Cordwell was back on the phone tearing some other poor devil off a strip. "Cancel the bloody order!" he barked. "I don't care if they have got a binding agreement—there's bound to be a bloody loophole somewhere, so cancel it." As he slammed the phone down he shouted across to his secretary. "What's that prat's name?" She told him. He scribbled the name on his pad. "Next lot of redundancies, he's got pole position."

Frost shut his ears to this as he and Mullett skimmed through the letter. Similar to the others, it read:

Dear Sir Richard Cordwell:
   I have the boy Bobby Kirby. The police will
confirm this is genuine. For his safe return I require
from your company the sum of £250,000 in used

notes—no marked money or the boy dies. Be near
the public telephone kiosks in the shopping mall
outside your Denton store at 8 o'clock tonight with
the money and I will phone you with instructions
for the handover. Just you—no police—I'll be
checking to make sure. If you do not comply, the
boy will die. The press have been informed and the
public will know the consequences.

"We'll keep this," said Frost, closing the folder and daring Cordwell to refuse, but this was agreed to with a wave of
the hand.

"Is it genuine?"

"We believe so," said Mullett.

"*Believe* so? I'm not sodding about with it if it's a fake."

"It's genuine," said Frost. "He sent us a tape of the boy."

Cordwell flicked a long cylinder of ash from his cigar
onto the carpet. "And you reckon he'll carry out his threat
to kill him?"

"Yes," said Frost.

Cordwell beamed. "Good. You got a photograph of the
kid?" Frost slid one across the desk. Cordwell studied it
through a fog of cigar smoke and nodded his approval.
"Nice-looking kid—I was afraid he'd be an ugly little bastard with a squint and bad teeth." He flipped the switch on
his intercom. "Roberts—come in!"

A tap on the door and a lean, mean-looking man in a
sharp silver-grey suit entered. Cordwell showed him the
photograph. "The kidnapped kid," he grunted.

Roberts looked at it and nodded. "Nice-looking kid . . .
and a good photograph. Should come up well in half-
tone. . . . I think we should go ahead."

"So do I," said Cordwell. "This is what I want you to
do. . . ." He barked his orders: "Check with the parents
and see if there are any more photographs—the kid as a
baby would be nice. Then a press release for tomorrow to all

the London dailies—'Supermarket Chief to the Rescue'—
you know the sort of thing. And get me some television
interviews—me and the boy." He dismissed Roberts, then
turned back to Frost. "If you give a press conference you can
quote me as saying that to save the boy I'm giving the police
my unstinted, wholehearted cooperation."

"You're too good for this world," said Frost. "Can you
get the money together in time?"

"No problem."

"How soon can you get it over to us?"

Cordwell frowned. "Why should I let you have it?"

"We've got to mark the notes and record as many of the
numbers as we can. We also need to put a small radio transmitter inside the case."

"No!" Mullett winced as Cordwell's fist thumped down
on his desktop, making the silver cigar case rattle. "The
object of the exercise is to save the kid, so no tricks, no
marked notes, and no transmitters." He reached over and
clicked on the intercom again. "Roberts! You can add this to
the press release. 'The police wanted the notes to be marked,
but Supermarket Chief Sir Richard Cordwell said no. Even
though the ransom money is being paid by Sir Richard, his
first and only consideration is for the safe return of the
boy.' " He clicked Roberts off in mid-acknowledgment.

"Now, listen to me—" began Frost.

"No!" snapped Cordwell. "You listen to me. I'm not doing this for the love of humanity. This bastard has grabbed a
kid and is on my back for the money. He thinks he's blackmailing me, but he's not—I'm doing this of my own voli-
tion, because it suits me to do so."

"Hardly," smirked Mullett. "What would the public say
if you refused?"

"Sod the public. They wouldn't desert Savalot. Knock
tuppence off a tin of baked beans and they'd be fighting to
come in, whether the kid's dead or not. I don't usually give

in to blackmail, but I can get some publicity out of this. For a lousy two hundred and fifty thousand quid I can get a million quid's worth of publicity and that's the sort of bargain I like. So you either do it my way, or I'm out!"

Frost said reluctantly, "All right. We do it your way."

"No police involvement in any shape or form until the kid is safely returned?"

"No police involvement," agreed Frost.

"Do I have your word?"

"You have my word."

Cordwell jabbed a stubby finger at Frost. "Cross me and I'll crucify you—do you read me, buster?"

Frost put on his hurt look. "I've given you my word," he said.

They were curtly dismissed and ushered out to the car by the secretary. As Frost settled himself down in the seat, Mullett turned to him angrily. "You had no business giving him your word, Frost."

"Don't worry, Super," said Frost. "I have no intention of keeping it."

Mullett's eyebrows soared. "What?"

Frost gave the same sort of sweet smile that Cordwell had given him. "No one tells me what to do," he said. As the black gates closed behind them, he dug down in his pocket and produced three cigars. He stuck one in his mouth and offered the others to Mullett and Burton.

Mullett hesitated, but they were excellent cigars, probably costing something like nine quid each. He accepted a light from Frost and inhaled with deep satisfaction. Soon the interior of the Ford was hazy blue and redolent with the rich Havana aroma. The superintendent thought wryly of the smell in his own car from that wretched woman last night. He took another drag and beamed with well-being. There was something about a good cigar . . . Maybe it wasn't Frost's fault. Perhaps, at times, he was too hard on the man.

He took the cigar from his mouth and contemplated the glowing end. "An excellent smoke, Frost. Where did you get them?"

"I pinched them from Cordwell's box when he wasn't looking," said Frost.

CHAPTER NINE

When he got back to his office he nearly tripped over the fur coats the insurance assessor had dropped on the floor. Mullett was right, the office did stink. Frost opened the window a fraction to let in some fresh air, while he made a few phone calls. Liz was still attending the postmortems where, no doubt, Drysdale was being his usual thorough self with all three tiny bodies. Bill Wells confirmed there was still no sign of the missing mother. Frost drummed the desk in thought—had he called off the dragging of the canal too soon?

The jewelry was still on his desk. He'd have to get Margie Stanfield down for a formal identification of her property. The sooner she took back her skunk-smelling furs, the better. Margie! She must be Stanfield's second wife. He seemed to remember an entirely different woman when he was at the house all those years ago for the arson case.

He stared at the jewelry. Damn, this phony abduction case was irritating him. He wanted to get it out of the way, but he couldn't wait for Liz to come back from her autopsy treat, so he collared Burton from the Incident Room.

"Where are we going?" asked the DC, sliding behind the steering wheel.

"Benningtons Bank," Frost told him. "I want to take a look at their security video for when Stanfield was drawing out all that cash." The car slowed for a traffic light. "How are you getting on with Sergeant Liz?"

"She tore me off a strip today," said Burton, moving forward as the lights changed. "I put the wrong date down on a report." He grinned. "I think I'm starting to fancy her."

"She wouldn't be a bad looker if she tarted herself up," mused Frost. "Reminds me of those old Hollywood films where the heroine is a schoolmistress with no makeup, thick glasses, her hair in a bun, and a flat chest. When she has her first kiss from the hero, she takes off her glasses, lets her hair down, and her tits swell up to twice their previous size." He started unbuckling his seat belt as the bank loomed into view. "The same thing could happen to our Liz."

Burton grinned again as he turned the car into the "Staff Only" car park behind the bank. "I wouldn't mind being the bloke who makes it happen," he told Frost.

The bank manager brought in the videotape and fed it into the player for them. "I'm rather busy, so I'll leave you to it, Inspector."

"Yes, you go and foreclose on some poor sod," answered Frost. "We'll manage." He pressed the play button.

On the monitor was a black-and-white picture of the customer area of the bank. It was a minute to opening time so there were no customers. A running clock superimposed on the corner of the picture showed the seconds zipping on to 9:30 A.M. A cashier walked across the customer area, checked the time with the wall clock, then opened the doors. He was shoved to one side as an impatient Stanfield, barging his way through other customers, managed to reach the cashier's window before anyone else. He was carrying a large briefcase.

It was a wide-angle shot taken from behind the counters. Other customers went to different cashiers, but the two detectives kept their eyes on Stanfield, who pushed across a withdrawal slip, drumming his fingers impatiently on the counter as the cashier read it through. Stanfield snapped some angry remark and then moved to the end of the counter. The cashier came out and led Stanfield to the assistant manager's office and out of camera range. "He's waiting in there while they're getting the money out of the vaults," explained Frost.

More people came into the bank. Queues shuffled forward, cashing checks or depositing money.

"What are we looking for?" asked Burton.

"I haven't the faintest bloody idea," admitted Frost.

Ten more minutes of watching people come and go and Frost's attention was starting to wander. He began to read a confidential letter on the manager's desk. "There he is!" said Burton. Frost was all attention again.

Stanfield moved back into the picture. The briefcase bulged and seemed heavier. He snarled at someone who dared to get in his way as he barged his way through the crowded customer area. The doors closed behind him and he was gone.

Frost let the tape run for a couple of minutes, then fished out his cigarette packet. "There's something there, son, something screaming at me . . . but I don't know what it is." He wound the tape back to the start and played it through again, only half watching as he dribbled smoke from his nose. Suddenly, he stiffened. "Yes I do!" His finger jabbed the freeze-frame button, making the picture quiver and stop. "In the corner, there—at the automatic cash machine." The frozen picture was quite blurred and Burton couldn't make out who Frost meant. Then he saw a figure in the corner of the screen drawing money from the service till. The person's back was to the camera. He could just make out light-colored trousers and a dark duffle coat with the hood up.

"So?" asked Burton.

Frost pressed the play button again. The figure, not much more than an out-of-focus blur, seemed to be getting money from the machine, then a swirl of customers hid him from view. Frost fast-forwarded the tape. The superimposed clock had moved on another six or seven minutes. The crowd suddenly thinned. "Look!" cried Frost. "The bastard is still there. . . . What's he doing now?"

The figure had now moved away from the service till and was by the automatic deposit machine, where he seemed to be finding difficulty in filling in one of the bank forms, crumpling up the current effort and starting on a new one. He was still there as Stanfield emerged from the assistant manager's office carrying his briefcase. Stanfield left. The man crumpled up his form, tossed it in a bin, and sauntered out of the bank.

"He followed Stanfield in," said Frost. "He was here all the time Stanfield was in the bank. When Stanfield left, so did he." He zipped back the tape, replaying some of it, freeze-framing from time to time.

"Assuming he was involved," said Burton, "the picture's nowhere near good enough to identify him."

"There's more than one way of skinning a banana," Frost said. He called the manager back into the office and pointed at the shape on the screen. "I want to know who he is."

The manager gave a shrug. "I've no idea."

"Yes you have," said Frost. "Look—he's using his cash card to draw money from your cash machine. You can see the clock—that gives the exact time he took out the money. You've got to have a timed record of all money withdrawn from that machine."

The manager went to a computer terminal on a small table by his desk and rattled away at the keyboard. "Yes. Nine thirty-four. Five pounds withdrawn." He peered at the screen. "That's strange. At nine thirty-nine it was paid back in again."

"He was stalling for time," said Frost. "I want his name, address, and inside leg size."

The manager twitched an apologetic smile. "I can't give you information about our customers. You will have to go through the proper channels."

"Tell me that next time you come whining to me because you've got a parking ticket," said Frost.

The manager clicked away at a few more keys and the screen display changed. He stood up. "I have to go out for a few minutes. Please do not look at this screen. It contains classified customer information."

Frost beamed his thanks and was at the computer even as the door was closing behind the manager. His eyebrows raised in surprise. The customer was a girl. Tracey Neal, 6 Dean Court, Denton. She had a balance of £25 in her account. Her date of birth was shown. She was fifteen, the same age as Carol Stanfield. Burton scribbled down the details.

"Mullett banks here," Frost told Burton, sitting down in the chair by the computer. "I wonder how much he's got in his account. What's the betting he's in the red? Let's see if he's made any checks out to ladies of ill-repute." He pulled the keyboard toward him.

Burton looked nervously toward the door, expecting the manager to return any minute. "Do you really think you should . . . ?"

Frost ignored his concern. "Do you reckon we just type in his name?" He pressed a key and the words "ACCOUNT NAME?" appeared on the screen. Frost started to peck out M-U-L when the computer let out a high-pitched buzz, the screen display kept flashing on and off, and an electronic voice bawled: *"Unauthorized input . . . unauthorized input . . ."*

"Flaming hell!" Frost leapt from the keyboard to the vacant visitor's chair on the far side of the room. As the manager came running in, looking angry, Frost gave a puzzled frown toward the computer. "What the hell is up with that?" he asked with all the innocence he could muster.

Liz was sitting at the spare desk when Frost got back. She looked shaken, but was busying herself with heaps of papers. She accepted the cigarette he tossed over to her.

"How did it go?"

Her hand was unsteady as she put the cigarette in her mouth, but she tried to sound calm. It had been a harrowing experience. Drysdale was always thorough, even when the cause of death was obvious, and to watch him being thorough three times, and on the bodies of tiny children, was almost too much. Even Cassidy had been affected and had mumbled some excuse about a phone call, leaving her to see it through, and she had managed a smug smile as she watched him leave, but now she felt shattered. "Asphyxiated with a pillow, probably while they were sleeping. They wouldn't have cried out and they wouldn't have known anything about it."

"Poor little sods." He saw she was having trouble striking a match, so leant across with his lighter. "What about the stab marks on the boy's arm?"

"Not serious and made after death. That's all he could say."

"Time of death?"

"Between eleven P.M. and midnight. Drysdale will be able to pin it down closer when he knows the time they had their last meal. I'm seeing the father later on, he should be able to tell us what time she usually fed them." Liz shuddered as she thought of the mother preparing their food, cooking it ever so carefully, the last meal they would ever have. "They all died within minutes of each other."

"And still no sign of the mother?"

"No."

"Let's hope she's killed herself. It'll save everyone a lot of sodding about."

Liz winced at Frost's apparent callousness, but she knew what he meant.

"What about that row people heard? Has anyone owned up to it?"

She shook her head. "I questioned our witnesses again and they still say they thought it was the wife and husband quarreling, but as we know, the husband wasn't there."

Frost scratched his chin. "The man who never was. Ah well . . . one of life's little mysteries." He switched to the Stanfield case. "I've got a job for you." He told her about the girl hovering about in the bank when Stanfield drew out the alleged ransom money. "Check her out."

Glad of anything that would take her mind off the memory of those three small bodies on Drysdale's autopsy table, Liz tucked her papers in a folder and grabbed her handbag. She had to squeeze past Burton.

"You enjoyed that, didn't you, son?" grunted Frost, when she'd left.

"Never thought I'd fancy a sergeant," replied Burton, pulling Liz's chair up to Frost's desk and sitting down.

"Is it still warm from her lovely bottom?"

"Red hot!" Burton grinned. "Right. The phone booths at the supermarket. I've had them all bugged, as you asked, ready for when the kidnapper makes contact. Every phone call in and out is now being recorded."

"What about bugging the money case so we can track it?"

Burton took a padded envelope from his pocket and carefully tipped out a small grey plastic object, not much bigger than a fifty-pence piece, and put it on Frost's desk. "Self-powered . . . range up to two hundred yards."

Frost prodded it with a nicotine-stained finger. "Doesn't look like much—you sure it works?"

"Positive. I tested it on the way over. But how will we get it in the suitcase with the money if Cordwell refuses to cooperate?"

"Leave that to me, son. One of Savalot's security guards is going to slip it in for me."

"Which one?"

"A bloke called Tommy Dunn. He used to be a copper—took early retirement under pressure from Mullett—he'd been taking back-handers."

"Can you trust him?"

"No—but Tommy'll do anything for a bottle of whisky. He's done a bit of nosing around. The accounts manager is going to make the ransom money up from today's takings at the store. It will be put into an overnight case ready for Cordwell to collect. Tommy reckons he can slip the homing device under the lining so no one will notice it." He returned the tiny transmitter to its padded envelope and handed it back to Burton. "Get over to Savalot, and ask for Tommy Dunn. . . . Drop this in his pocket and leave."

As Burton went out, the internal phone rang. Bill Wells from the front desk. Mrs. Stanfield was here to identify the furs and jewelry fished out of the canal. "Right," said Frost, but as he spoke, panic set in. His eyes began a swift search of the office. Liz had picked up the sodden furs from the floor and hooked them over the hat stand, but where was the flaming jewelry? "Hold on a tick, Bill." He put the phone down and started to ransack the place, looking everywhere, even where he was sure he hadn't put it. Forty thousand pounds' worth of jewelry and he'd left it lying on his desk in full view where anyone could see it and the door open. . . . Don't say some bastard has nicked it, he silently pleaded. A sudden thought. The insurance assessor. Hicks must have taken it.

A quick phone call. "No, Inspector," Hicks said firmly. "It was still on your desk in a black plastic bag when I left."

"Oh, yes—of course," said Frost, trying to sound as if he

had just spotted it. He lit up a cigarette for inspiration, then realized angry noises were coming from his internal phone. Bill Wells was still hanging on. "Tell her to wait, Bill. I'll call back." He banged the phone down and again searched everywhere he had searched before, hoping that, in some magical way, the bag of jewelry would suddenly appear.

His internal phone rang again. Mrs. Stanfield was getting impatient. "She'll have to come back later," said Frost. "Tell her the insurance assessor has got to check the stuff first."

"But I thought—" began Wells.

"Just tell her!" snapped Frost.

"Okay," said Wells, miffed by Frost's manner. "By the way, Mr. Mullett wants to see you."

"He wasn't carrying a black plastic bag by any chance?" Frost asked.

"As a matter of fact, he was."

Frost put the phone down, relief mingled with irritation. It was his own stupid fault, but if you couldn't leave stuff unattended in a police station, where the hell could you leave it? He was trying to work out his ploy with Mullett when Cassidy stormed in. Flaming heck, thought Frost dolefully. Not more bloody moans?

Cassidy jerked a thumb at the spare desk. "Where's the girl?"

"Doing a job for me," said Frost. "Why?"

"Call from the track inspector at Denton Railway Station. There's a body on the track. It could be the missing mother."

"Let's hope it is," said Frost. "We haven't got time to keep looking for her. Why don't you follow up?" Cassidy could handle this on his own.

The phone rang. This time it was an angry Mullett demanding the inspector report immediately to his office. Frost put his hand over the mouthpiece. "Hold on—I'm coming with you," he called to Cassidy. Back to the phone. "Sorry, Super—urgent call." He hung up quickly.

· · ·

As they drove down the road which ran parallel with the railway track all signals were at red. There was a stationary passenger train, its windows studded with the heads of angry passengers trying to make out what the hold-up was. Cassidy parked the car on the stone-walled bridge which continued the road over the tunnel and the two detectives slithered down the embankment to the mouth of the tunnel where two railway track inspectors in fluorescent yellow jackets were waiting for them. Cassidy looked nervously at the gleaming rails. "Is the current off?"

The senior track inspector nodded. "Yes—and it would help if you could be as quick as possible. This is playing havoc with our train schedules."

Emergency lights were on in the tunnel, but did little to dispel the gloom. A strong wind roared noisily past their ears and they had to shout to be heard. Frost wrapped his scarf tighter around his neck and squinted his eyes against the dust and grit which the wind was hurling through the tunnel like bullets.

"There!" The railwayman stopped and pointed, turning his head away. He had seen it before and that was more than enough. He squeezed against the tunnel wall so they could get past him.

She was some thirty yards into the tunnel, a crumpled heap, one arm lying across the rail and partly severed. As Frost bent to examine her he realized that she had been decapitated and the head was a few feet forward in the middle of the track. So cleanly was it cut, it could almost have been done with a very sharp knife. The high-speed train would have barely quivered as it sliced its way over her. Frost pulled his eyes away from the blooded stump of the neck and gingerly touched the flesh of her arm. Hard and cold. She was lying lengthways along the rail and wore a black acrylic jumper and green slacks. He forced himself to look at the severed head. The eyes were vacant, the face bruised and battered, light brown hair snarled and matted with blood. No doubt about it. She was Nancy Grover.

"Could she have been hit by a train as she walked through the tunnel?" asked Cassidy.

"No way. If a train had hit her while she walked, she'd have been sent flying and would probably have been cut in half as it went over her," replied one of the railwaymen. "My guess is she jumped from the bridge. I can't tell you the number of suicides we've had to bag up from here. It's all flaming copycat. One does it, the others read about it in the paper, then they all do it."

"They used to jump from the top floor of the multistory car park," said the other track inspector. "Sod that for a way to die, strawberry jam all over the concrete."

"This is worse," put in the other railwayman. "You could end up with your arms and legs cut off by the train and still be alive."

"So if your bum itched you couldn't bloody scratch it," added Frost. "So come on . . . how would she have got halfway up the tunnel?"

"They go to the bridge, climb onto the wall, and wait for a train, then jump down in front of it. Only I reckon this poor woman misjudged it. She left her jump too late, fell on top of a carriage, and was whooshed into the tunnel. As the train took the bend, she was thrown off and smashed against the tunnel wall. Then she slid down, her head fell over the rail, and the wheels sliced it off."

"Wouldn't the train driver or any of the passengers have heard her crash on the roof?"

"Not over the noise of the train."

Frost shuffled forward to take another look at the head. The eyes were wide open and staring, the face looked strained and in torment. "You silly bitch," he whispered. "You've properly sodded this up."

The senior of the track inspectors was muttering into a

mobile phone. He beckoned Frost over. "There's a logjam of trains going right back to four stations. We'd like to get her shifted out of here so we can get things moving again."

"I bet you would," said Frost. He scratched his chin, working out the distance from the tunnel to the woman's home. Nancy Grover couldn't have walked here in less than half an hour. The kids were killed around midnight, which meant she must have done her diving act at half past midnight at the earliest. "So what train did this to her?"

"There's one at five past midnight."

"Too early," said Frost.

"Then it would have to be the twelve thirty-five. That's the last through train until five twenty-two this morning."

A yell from the mouth of the tunnel where a disgruntled passenger, fed up with waiting in a stationary train, had walked along the line to complain. "How much bloody longer? We've been here nearly an hour already!"

"Get back in the train," shouted the track inspector.

"I'm going to report you!" called the passenger.

"And I'll bloody report you—it's an offense to walk on the track—now get back!" snarled the track inspector. He turned to Frost. "Can't we move her?"

"Not until the police surgeon has certified she's dead."

"Dead? Her bloody head is off!"

"If it was a man and all we had left was his dick, we'd still have to wait for the doctor to certify he was dead." Frost shouted down to the mouth of the tunnel where Cassidy was in contact with Control on his radio. "How long's the doctor going to be?"

"He's on his way," called back Cassidy.

"Can't we cover her up and let the trains go through?" pleaded the senior track inspector. "This is causing one hell of a disruption."

"All right," said Frost. "But shift her head off the track first."

The man shuddered. "I'm not touching her head."

"Then we wait," said Frost.

They didn't have to wait long. Dr. Slomon, the on-call police surgeon, scowling because this was miles out of his way and he had slipped on the mud coming down the embankment, smearing his light brown camel-hair overcoat, looked anxiously at the rails. "Is the current off?"

"Should be safe as long as you don't pee on the live rail," Frost replied, moving back so Slomon could see the body.

Slomon shuddered as he eyed the trunk, then the head. Why did Frost always have to be involved with the messy ones? He remembered only too well the tramp in a toilet swimming with urine. He bent down and briefly touched the hardened flesh. "Been dead some time—nine, ten hours."

"Did the decapitation kill her?" asked Cassidy.

"Well, it certainly didn't help," sniffed Slomon. "You'll need a postmortem to find the exact cause." He scribbled on a pad and tore off a sheet. "She's dead. You can move her." He scrambled back up the embankment, glad to be away from the macabre scene. Cassidy was radioing to Control to get them to contact an undertaker to remove the body and to arrange an autopsy.

Frost wandered off, happy to let Cassidy attend to all the details. The suicide tied up the case nicely. He clambered up the embankment, then realized he had traveled in Cassidy's car and would have to wait for him to get a lift back to the station. Damn. Down to his left he could see clusters of angry passengers arguing with the guard on the halted train. The sound of a car approaching. A bit too soon for the undertaker, surely? He hoped Control had warned them there was a severed head to collect as well. Some of them were a bit fussy about the state of the corpses they transported. But it wasn't the undertaker. It was Liz Maud. The sergeant braked to a sliding halt alongside him.

"We've found the mother?" she asked.

Frost opened the passenger door and slid in beside her. "Yes, love. Parts one and two—she jumped in front of a train." Liz moved to get out, but he restrained her. "You don't want to see her."

She shook off his hand. "Why not?"

"She's in two bloody halves."

"But if Mr. Cassidy is down there—"

"Sod Mr. Cassidy. The case is all tied up. It's the fiddling, messy tying up the ends now and Cassidy's quite capable of doing that on his own." He heard footsteps echoing from the tunnel below. "Let's get out of here . . . I think he's coming."

Liz drove off, swerving to avoid a battered black van that lumbered toward them. The undertakers didn't use their shiny black Rolls-Royces for messy jobs like this.

Frost lit up. "Have you seen that girl—Tracey what's-her-name?"

"Not yet. I called at her house, but she's at school— Denton Grammar—the same school as Carol Stanfield."

Frost pulled the cigarette from his mouth. "Same school, same age—they must be in the same class. Interesting."

"It's probably a coincidence. Half the girls of her age in Denton go to the same school."

Frost's eyes gleamed. A school full of pubescent, busty teenage girls had the edge on following a maimed corpse to the mortuary. "Let's visit the school and question her there. I want to get this lousy case tied up so we can concentrate on more important matters."

The head teacher, Ms. Quincey, was not too pleased. This scruffy man, who appeared to be a detective inspector, seemed more interested in watching the fifth-form girls playing handball in the gym through the glass partition of her office, than listening to what she was saying. She cleared her throat noisily. "It's just as a witness you wish to talk to her, Inspector Frost?"

Frost nodded. "Tracey might have seen something that would help us."

Ms. Quincey was still doubtful, but was relieved there was a woman police officer with him. She would have preferred to have sat in on the questioning, but she had to take 4B for Social Studies while their normal teacher was away having an abortion. "Ah—here comes Tracey now."

Tracey Neal pushed through the swing doors into the gym and hurried past the excited, squealing, flush-faced handball players. She was wearing her school uniform, a light brown jacket over a white blouse with a black skirt. She looked a lot younger than the figure on the bank security video.

"Come in, Tracey," said the head teacher.

Frost flashed both his warrant card and his frank and innocent smile. "Won't take more than a couple of minutes, Tracey. You might have seen something that could help us." The girl sat down and crossed her legs, with an almost too studied expression of unconcern. Frost squinted up at the wall clock where the minute hand was quivering on the hour. He was itching for the bell to signal the start of the next period so Ms. bloody Quincey would leave them alone. "Better just take your name and address for our records." He tried not to show his delight as the bell jangled.

"I'll have to leave you now," said Ms. Quincey, gathering up some books from her desk. "Perhaps you could see yourselves out."

"Of course." Frost nodded, disappointed to note that the bell also signaled the end of the handball game and the girls had all disappeared into the dressing rooms where . . . God! . . . they'd be having showers! All those sweaty little nubile fifteen-year-olds, stark naked. . . . Then he realized the girl was talking to him. "Sorry—what was that?"

"You wanted my name: Tracey Neal, six Deans Court, Denton."

He scribbled it down, although it was unnecessary. They already had her details from the bank. "You were in Benningtons Bank just after nine-thirty yesterday morning?"

"That's right." She flicked away a strand of chestnut hair that had fallen over her face and tried to look bored.

"You know Carol Stanfield, don't you?"

"Yes."

"And you heard about the robbery at her house?"

"It was on the radio. They kidnapped her and stripped her—" Her eyes widened as if she had just realized. "Her father—when I saw him in the bank—was he picking up the ransom money?"

"So you saw him?"

"Only briefly. I don't know him that well. I sort of gave him a smile, but I don't think he noticed me."

"You're being a great help, Tracey," said Frost. "Did you notice anything suspicious—anyone hanging about—apart from yourself, of course."

She screwed up her face to show she was trying hard to remember. "There were lots of people there. I didn't notice anyone especially."

"When you left the bank, did you spot anyone hanging about outside, or in a car . . . ?"

She shook her head. "Sorry."

Frost beamed his deceptively reassuring smile. "Not your fault, love. Oh—just for the record. What were you doing in the bank?"

She frowned. "Why? What has that got to do with it?"

Frost spread his hands vaguely. "Just routine. We have to check out everyone who was in the bank at that time, even if it is obvious they weren't involved. So what were you doing there—getting money out?"

"Yes."

"You weren't at school yesterday?"

"No."

Frost noticed she was starting to wriggle and look uneasy. He fished out his cigarettes and pretended to be preoccupied. Actually, he was looking through the glass to the doors of the dressing room where the first of the damp-haired, squeaky-clean girls was scampering out. "Why didn't you go to school?"

Tracey shrugged and looked up at the ceiling. "Didn't feel like it."

A sympathetic smile. "As good a reason as any. So what did you do with yourself all day—read the Bible—take soup to the sick?"

"I went round to a boy's house and we played records."

"That's terrific," said Frost enthusiastically. "Then he can vouch for you—save us doing a lot of checking. What's his name?"

"Ian Grafton."

"Address?"

"Twenty-three Fairfield Road."

"Right." Frost scribbled this down on the back of a supermarket till receipt, then suddenly seemed to think of something else. "This may sound silly. You took five pounds out. What did you want the money for?"

"I was going to the disco at Goyas. It's a big night."

"The disco was in the evening. Why did you draw the money out in the morning?"

"Why not?" she said defiantly. "It was as good a time as any."

"I suppose so," said Frost grudgingly. He worried away for a while at his scar. "After you drew it out, you waited a few minutes, then paid it back. Why was that?"

"I suddenly realized I had a standing order coming up and if I withdrew the money it couldn't be met."

"So you had to give the disco a miss?"

"No. Ian lent me the money."

"Good old Ian. Did you go straight to the bank from your house?"

"Yes."

"Your mother seemed surprised when we told her you were at the bank. She thought you would have been at school."

"I don't tell my mother everything."

An understanding smile. "I bet you don't. Did you go straight from your house to the bank?"

"Yes."

"Right." He started to scribble this down, then paused. "Wait a minute. Your mother said you left the house at your usual time for school and you were wearing your school uniform."

"Yes—well, I wanted her to think I was going to school, didn't I?"

"And you went straight to the bank."

"That's right." She wasn't so quick with her answers now.

"We've got a witness . . ." Frost shuffled through some pieces of paper and pretended to read from one. "Ah, yes . . . An old dear. Not very reliable, I'm afraid . . . half-blind and didn't have her glasses with her. She says she could have sworn you were wearing jeans and a dirty old duffle coat . . . not your nice smart uniform."

"Then she was mistaken."

"So you were in school uniform—the one you are wearing now?"

"Yes."

Frost turned to Liz Maud as he scratched out what he had just written down. "You see, Sergeant. That silly old dear got it all wrong." He patted the papers together and stuffed them in his pocket, then swung the chair round to face the girl and smiled with a nod as if that was all he wanted her for. As she got up to go he suddenly snapped his fingers. "I'm a stupid git—I'm getting all confused. It wasn't the old lady who said you were in casual clothes, it was the bank security video . . . black duffle coat with the hood up and light trousers." He beamed at her. "So either you— or the bank video camera—are telling me porkies."

She stared at him, her lips moving silently as she tried out various answers. At last she said: "I took different clothes with me and changed in the public toilets."

"So what did you do with your school clothes—flush them down the pan? They weren't with you while you were in the bank."

"All right, all right!" She was almost shouting. "Ian met me round the corner from my house in his van. My mother doesn't like me going out with him. I changed in the back of his van while he drove me to the bank. He waited for me, then took me to his place. Satisfied?"

"Perfectly," said Frost, standing up. "I just wanted to get the inconsistencies straightened out. Thanks for your time." He gave the girl a brisk nod, then he and Liz left the school.

In the car, Liz said, "She was lying."

"Of course she was," said Frost. "So let's nip round and see Ian what's-his-name and find out what sort of lies he's going to tell us."

There was a van parked outside the house, a battered, rust-riddled light brown Ford with the name of the previous trader crudely erased with black paint.

"Your witness said the van he saw was light brown," said Frost.

"I thought you didn't believe him," sniffed Liz.

"I can be flexible when it suits me," smirked Frost. "Sometimes I'm flexible when it doesn't suit me." He pressed the doorbell.

Ian Grafton was eighteen, tall and wiry, wearing his black greasy hair in a thick pigtail. He took them to his upstairs flat.

"I expect Tracey's phoned you about us, Ian," said Frost,

who had noted the pay phone on the landing. "Just wanted to confirm a couple of things."

Grafton occupied a bed-sit. He was unemployed. Social Security paid the rent. His last job was doing deliveries for a local furniture shop, but the job collapsed when the firm went bust some five months ago. He hadn't worked since. They sat on the bed in his tiny room with its pop posters and the Midi hi-fi unit and went through the motions of scribbling down his confirmation of Tracey Neal's story. Ian agreed to every word of it and Frost was sure he too was lying.

"You waited outside the bank for her?" he asked. "Now, thinking back on it, did you notice anything suspicious . . . any weirdos hanging about?"

"The only weirdo was a fat bitch of a traffic warden who gave me a flaming ticket for parking on a double yellow line." He snatched it from a shelf and waved it at Frost, who squinted at the date and time. It tallied.

"Thank you, Ian. We might want to speak to you again."

Frost took another look at the van as they left. The same color as the one the witness saw, but if it received a parking ticket at 9:35, then it couldn't have been the van the naked Carol Stanfield was held in. He worried away at this, but the pieces refused to fit.

He didn't have time to brood. As soon as Liz opened the car door, there was a radio message. Would Frost get over to the mortuary right away? Nancy Grover hadn't committed suicide. She had been murdered.

"Murdered?" said Frost.

The hospital pathologist, who had thought he was going to carry out a routine autopsy, nodded. "Come and see."

The body was on the autopsy table. Much of the blood had now been washed off and her clothes had been removed and the head had been put in place, ready to be sutured back on the torso to make her presentable for relatives. The junior technician who had been summoned to perform this task was hovering in the background.

Frost and Liz looked down at the corpse. With the clothes removed, the pathologist had no need to explain. There were stab marks all over the abdomen and the area of the heart. The lower incisions were encrusted with dried blood. Frost did a quick count. She had been stabbed eleven times.

"Shit!" This was a complication he could well have done without.

"The incision through the heart would have been enough to kill her," said the pathologist. "She was dead before she went over that railway bridge."

Frost gave a deep sigh. "Any chance the wounds were self-inflicted, Doc?" He knew it was a stupid question, but he wanted to cling to his suicide theory.

The pathologist shook his head. "Look at her hands."

Frost knew he should have checked before he asked. The back of the hands showed slashes and stab wounds. They were inflicted as the woman tried to defend herself.

"This is outside my league," said the pathologist. "You'll have to get Mr. Drysdale to do the autopsy."

"All right," said Frost. "Put her back in the fridge until he gets here."

The junior technician helped the mortuary assistant slide the torso onto a trolley then, with a look of distaste, carefully picked up the head and dropped it into a large polyethylene bag which he also placed on the trolley.

They met Cassidy as they were walking back to the car. "Stabbed," reported Frost tersely. "About eleven times. Dead before she was chucked in front of the train."

Cassidy barely concealed a smirk. "I knew this case wasn't as straightforward as you tried to make out."

"Nothing I touch turns out to be bloody straightforward," said Frost ruefully.

"Have they done the autopsy?"

"They've sent for Drysdale. If it's anything more complicated than an ingrown toenail, this bloke doesn't want to know."

"I'm going to pull Snell in," announced Cassidy.

"Don't be a prat," said Frost. "You need to start putting pressure on the husband."

"The husband couldn't have done it. Snell broke in, started to stab the kid, when they all woke up and started screaming. He panics and silences them with the pillow. The mother runs in and he has to kill her as well."

"Then why didn't he leg it and leave her? Why try to make out her death was suicide?"

"I don't know, but I'm going to find out."

"I'll give you a better scenario. The husband comes back from work to find his wife smirking at him. She tells him she's killed his kids to pay him back for leaving her on her own, night after night. He takes it amiss and goes berserk, stabbing her again and again. He realizes suspicion must fall on him, so he carts the body away and tries to make her death look like suicide."

"He couldn't have done it," repeated Cassidy stubbornly. "He's got a watertight alibi. Three people can confirm he was in that store until nearly two o'clock in the morning."

"Then recheck his alibi . . . see if we can break it." Frost turned to Liz. "Is he still in hospital?"

"Yes. They should be releasing him tomorrow."

"Good. He was taken there straight from the house, so he was still wearing the clothes he had on that night. Get those clothes. I want Forensic to do a proper job for a change and go over every inch of them for bloodstains . . . there must have been one hell of a lot of blood. You'd better hang on for the autopsy, Cassidy. Drysdale should be here any minute. I'll make my way back to the house and wait for Forensic and the Scene of Crime boys."

Cassidy wasn't happy at the way he was being ordered

about. After all, he was, if only temporarily, the same rank as Frost. But he decided to swallow it. It looked as if there could well be some embarrassing foul-ups with this case so it would be better if Frost was in charge. "Right." He went through the doors of the mortuary to wait for the Home Office pathologist.

Liz dropped Frost off at the house in Cresswell Street and drove on to the hospital. The constable on duty, young PC Packer, handed over the front door key. "Go and get yourself a cup of tea or something," Frost told him. "I'll be here for at least an hour." Packer nodded gratefully. It was boring standing on guard, nothing to do, no one to talk to except when he was fending off questions from the inquisitive. There was a burger bar in the main road. He'd nip off there for a bite to eat in the warm.

Frost let himself in and closed the door behind him. In the oppressive silence, small sounds seemed to be exaggerated. The lounge door creaked as he pushed it open. The curtains had been drawn to stop people peering in and the room was in darkness. He clicked on the light. Was the woman killed here and taken away? If so, there should be blood, but he couldn't see any.

He clicked off the light and went along the passage to the kitchen where there were still unwashed mugs on the small table. He should have got someone to tidy up after they left. Polyethylene sheeting had been laid over the floor to protect it from the feet of everyone tramping in and out. He hitched a section back and peered down onto blue and white vinyl. Blood would have screamed. There was none. The white surface of the tall fridge freezer gleamed coldly. He took a look inside. Near the top, an opened tin of Heinz baby food.

Over to the back door. At some stage one of its glass panes had been broken and a makeshift repair of a sheet of plywood nailed over the gap. The bottom of the ply was loose where the nails had been wrenched out, making it possible for anyone outside to squeeze a hand through and reach the key. This had been noted the night before, but not much attention was paid to it, as the case then seemed uncomplicated.

He left the kitchen and mounted the stairs, the soft padded creak of his footsteps following him. The children's bedroom still breathed Johnson's baby powder. The beds, stripped of their sheets, were icy to the touch. Across the room, on a shelf, a row of soft toys, animals, golliwogs, dolls, stared reproachfully at him. As he turned to leave, his heart froze. A child's voice cried, "Mummy!"

It was a doll. A bloody doll on the floor and he had trodden on it. He picked it up and put it on the shelf with the others.

Shaken, he hurried downstairs and sat in the darkened lounge and smoked. The heavy curtains insulated the room from outside noises, but kept in the stifling silence of the house. It was chilly and he shivered. At one stage he was jolted from his thoughts by a sound like a child giggling, but when he listened hard there was nothing.

Someone was knocking at the door. The Forensic team. "Not today, thank you," Frost said. "I never buy at the door."

After letting them in, he went back to the lounge and left them to it. Painstaking, methodical work was not his forte and he got impatient with people who had to work this way. Young Packer reported back and was sent to check with the neighbors about what they saw or heard the previous night. If the mother was killed in the house she would have had to be driven to the railway bridge, so did anyone see or hear a car?

A tap at the door. "We'd like to do this room, Inspector." He was getting the distinct impression he was in the bloody way.

He moved on to the kitchen. Harding from Forensic was

out in the garden examining the door in the wall that led to the outside lane. He saw Frost and hurried over. "Something to show you." It was the back door. With rubber-gloved hands Harding eased back the plywood panel and pointed to its jagged bottom edge. Dots of red and flecks of skin. "Someone forced back the wood to get a hand through so they could turn the key from the inside. The edge of the ply grazed the back of his wrist, drawing blood. Whoever did it would have a nasty scratch on the back of the hand."

"It could have been the father . . . or even the mother," said Frost. "Forgot their front-door key one day, so came in through the back."

"Possible," said Harding. "We should be able to do some DNA testing on the skin fragments. Find a suspect and we could match him to this. You wouldn't need a confession."

Frost grunted. "Science is wonderful. It's making the rubber truncheon obsolete."

Two men from the Forensic team in their gleaming white boiler suits came in. "We'd like to do the kitchen now, Inspector."

Nowhere could he sit and think and be undisturbed. He let them get on with it and caught a bus back to the station.

Cassidy was waiting for him in the Murder Incident Room. He had the results of the postmortem on Nancy Grover. "Numerous stab wounds to the abdomen and heart. The wound to the heart killed her and she would have died almost instantly. Stab marks on her hands where she fought off her attacker."

"What sort of knife?"

"Single edge, sharp pointed. Could have been a kitchen knife."

"Time of death?"

"Between eleven and one o'clock last night."

Frost told Cassidy about the back door panel. Cassidy's eyes glinted with satisfaction. "I want to bring Snell in . . . now."

"He should be back at Newcastle," said Frost. He hoped and prayed Snell would be there, sitting in his flat, reading his Bible, the backs of his hands entirely without a scratch.

"He isn't," said Cassidy. "The Newcastle police have checked."

Frost stared out of the window. Heavy black rain clouds had swept in and it was already dark outside. "All right. Let's try and find him."

CHAPTER TEN

Thunder rumbled ominously in the distance as Cassidy pulled up outside Snell's house in Parnell Terrace a few minutes past four o'clock in the afternoon. Only one of the streetlights was on; the other had been vandalized, its metal cover forced off and the spaghetti of colored wires wrenched out. No lights shone from the house and there was no reply to Cassidy's pounding at the door. Outside the front door five bulging dustbin sacks lolled against the wall.

Frost crouched to take a peek through the letter box into more darkness. "We'd better take a look round inside."

"Do you have a key?" sneered Cassidy.

"Don't need one, son. What's that?" He pointed into the darkened street. As Cassidy's head jerked to look, there was the sound of breaking glass. When he turned back Frost seemed to be replacing an empty milk bottle on the step and the glass pane of the front door was shattered. "Looks as if someone has tried to break in here," said Frost. "We'd better check." He stuck his hand through the broken pane and unlocked the door from the inside.

Cassidy didn't want to get involved with any of Frost's corner-cutting, but there seemed to be no chance of anyone finding out, so he followed him inside.

The hall light came on when Frost tried it. There were two preprinted postcards on the door mat, one from the Electricity Board, the other from the gas company. Both were dated that day and each said that their service engineer had called at nine A.M . . . "as requested by you for the purpose of taking the final meter reading and cutting off the supply. He could obtain no answer. Please contact our office to make a fresh appointment."

They moved through to the living room. On the table were six carrier bags packed with the dead Mrs. Snell's personal effects. There was food in the fridge in the kitchen, a Marks and Spencer chilled meal, and an unopened carton of milk. The bed was made, with folded pyjamas on the pillow.

Frost poked around a few drawers, but they had been emptied. "He hasn't been here since last night," he decided. "The bed hasn't been slept in."

"He could have made it after he got up," objected Cassidy.

"No, son. He was going back to Newcastle today. He was all packed up, ready to go. He might make the bed after he got up, but he wouldn't fold his pyjamas and bung them on the pillow. And he'd have opened up the milk for a cup of tea." He chewed his thumb knuckle thoughtfully. "He went out last night, but didn't come back. Why?"

"I'd have thought that was obvious," snapped Cassidy. "He killed the kids, then the mother, and he's now on the run."

"I can't buy that, son. Why should he try to make her death look like suicide? It doesn't make sense."

"You're looking for a rational explanation. The man's a nut-case."

"If Slimy Sid chucked her in front of the train to make it look like suicide, why has he done a bunk?"

"Perhaps he saw the train hadn't gone over her. He wanted the body all mangled up so we wouldn't spot the knife wounds. When that didn't happen, he ran."

Frost chewed this over. It was as plausible as some of his own stupid theories, but it would mean that Snell, who up to now had been content to draw pinpricks of blood, was suddenly a frantic mass murderer. He poked in one of the carrier bags on the kitchen table. On the top was a silver-framed photograph of the eight-year-old Sidney Snell in a sailor suit, hair combed, face washed for the camera, clutching the hand of his young mother. A sweet and innocent child . . . who grew up to be a pervert. "Okay." He sighed. "Get on to Newcastle. Ask them to keep an eye on his place and if he shows up to arrest him on suspicion of murder. Tell Control to radio all patrols—if they see him, arrest him on sight." He took one last look round the room. "And get someone to check this place from time to time in case he comes back for his milk."

The front door slammed behind them, echoing in an empty street. As their car turned the corner, a furtive figure emerged from the shadows of a derelict house on the opposite side of the road. Sidney Snell, shaking with fear. He had come back to the house to retrieve his belongings when some sixth sense warned him to wait. He watched from the old house and sweat had broken out from every pore of his body when he saw Frost and Cassidy forcing their way in. He couldn't hear their car any more, but he hesitated, racked with indecision. Should he risk it and dash over to the house, or were they lurking round the corner waiting for him to do something stupid like that? Sidney was tired and he was hungry. He'd had no sleep at all last night. The back of his hand was bleeding again. He sucked it and wound the dirty handkerchief tighter. What to do? God, what to do . . . ?

•   •   •

The old woman was waiting for Frost as he pushed through the doors to the lobby. She hurried toward him, eyes glowing. "You've got them back! The sergeant says you've got them back."

He smiled, but she had wrong-footed him. Who the hell was she? Then he placed her. Of course . . . the old dear who'd had her husband's medals pinched. Bloody hell. He hadn't had time to sort out half the stuff they'd found stacked behind the cistern in Lemmy Hoxton's house. "Your medal—yes, love . . . If you'd like to formally identify it . . ."

He took her into the main Interview Room and they waited for Burton to lug in the large cardboard box. The medal, in its black case, was near the top. It deserved more respect than being piled on top of the other junk. Frost gave it to her.

She beamed her delight. "I never thought I'd see this again," she sobbed. She took the DFM out and held it close to her cheek. "He wanted our son to have it. There was going to be a baby, but I lost it when our house was bombed and I had a miscarriage. The doctor said it would have been a boy."

Frost nodded in sympathy and explained they would have to hang on to the medal for a little while. "Don't worry, love, it'll be quite safe here. I'll look after it." Look after it! He grinned wryly to himself. As well as I looked after forty grand's worth of jewelry from the Stanfield robbery? Which reminded him of the treat to come . . . He was going to have to face Mullett about that.

"And you've found the photographs. That's such a relief!"

Photographs? Now what was she babbling about?

There was a wad of small photograph holders held together with a rubber band in the box. Frost had only skimmed through them briefly. Most looked like family

snaps. It seemed Lemmy had scooped up everything he
could lay his hands on, whether it was of value or not..

She had pulled out the top holder and was shuffling
through the photographs. "I'd hate to think of these falling
into the wrong hands." She gave Frost a conspiratorial wink
and nodded toward Burton. "Do you think he's old enough
to see these?" She handed them over.

Frost stifled a yawn as he took the photographs. More
black-and-white family snaps. Then he sat up straight.
"Bloody hell!"

Black-and-white postcard-sized prints, but not for family
viewing. They showed a young, pert, dark-haired girl in a
bedroom. Completely nude. "Bloody hell!" he said again as
the girl in the photograph cupped her breasts with wide-
spread fingers to reveal rosebudlike nipples, or turned her
back, peeping over her shoulder and showing a lovely tight
bottom. Then his jaw dropped. He recognized her. He
pointed to Mrs. Miller. "It's you!"

She nodded roguishly. "My husband did his own devel-
oping. He used to get his chemicals and paper from the RAF
photographic section. It was hard to come by during the
war."

"Bloody hell!" repeated Frost for the third time. "You
were a little cracker." He showed them to Burton, who
grinned his approval. Reluctantly, Frost stuffed them into
the album. "You'd better take these with you, love. They'll
get us all too excited if you leave them here."

She dropped them in her handbag and snapped it shut.
"I wasn't always old, you see," she said wistfully.

"Good job I wasn't around then," Frost told her. "Your
husband wouldn't have got a look in." He showed her out.
When he returned to the Interview Room, Burton was
packing the stuff back in the box.

"Hold on, son," said Frost. "Let's see what other goodies
Lemmy had stashed away."

In an old chocolate box they found more pornographic

photographs, some involving children. There was a set of photographs of a man dressed in women's underwear. Frost showed them to Burton. "I like his frilly knickers, but the beard puts me off." There were letters. Frost read through one and whistled softly. "This is a blow-by-blow description of what this couple got up to while her old man was away," he told Burton. "And I use the word 'blow' advisedly."

"This one's a bit naughty too," said Burton, showing him a deckle-edge sheet of light green notepaper.

Frost found another letter, still in its envelope, which gave the name of the recipient. An address Frost recognized. Inside was a letter and a Polaroid color print of a woman bending over an armchair. A big, hefty woman. Her skirt was up and her knickers were round her ankles. A man in a mortarboard and gown was standing over her, wielding a long leather strap. Frost skimmed through the letter. The writer, a man, was arranging to call round the following evening and was detailing the punishment he meted out to naughty girls. His name and address were not included. Stapled to the letter was the carbon of a letter to him from the woman explaining how naughty she had been. "So me old tom!" sniffed Burton.

"Not an old tom as it happens," corrected Frost. "She's a retired civil servant . . . lives in one of those posh houses in Charter Street."

"You know her?"

"Not as a client. You know her too, son. She's a friend of Mullett's wife—they both serve on the same hospital committee or something. She reported some money stolen from her bedroom after a man from the Water Board called—"

"I remember now," interrupted Burton. "The very next day she claimed she was mistaken and nothing was pinched after all."

"That's her." Frost nodded. "We never suspected it at the time, but I reckon she must have received a blackmail threat—pay up or we send the photos to the vicar, that sort of thing." He pulled the photograph toward him and studied it. Behind him the door creaked open.

"Inspector Frost!"

Frost groaned. Flaming Hornrim Harry, ready to give him a bollacking for leaving the loot unattended. He turned with a surprised smile. "I was just on my way in to see you, Super." He held up the photograph. "Just for the purposes of elimination, the man in the mortar board isn't you by any chance?"

Mullett took one look at the photograph and flushed angrily. "You know damn well it isn't. My office—*now*!"

Mullett's voice droned on and on as Frost sat in the chair, on his face a look of rapt attention, his mind miles away, trying to filter out Mullett's drivel as he turned over the day's events in his mind. If Mullett's wife's mate was being blackmailed, it was a near certainty that Lemmy had been putting the squeeze on others for stuff pinched from bedrooms during his Water Board scam. Which meant Lemmy was a blackmailer as well as a thief and blackmail was a strong motive for murder. Perhaps one of his victims had decided that enough was enough. Mullett still hadn't finished.

". . . not the sort of behavior I expect from an officer under my command . . ."

Frost clicked the sound off again. The first thing to do would be to call on this woman and see if she could throw any light on Lemmy's death. Come on, Mullett, hurry up and finish . . . I've got work to do. Frost became aware of a welcome silence. Mullett had stopped at last and was looking at him questioningly.

"You've finished, sir? Good—sorry and all that. Won't happen again." Frost snatched up the bag of jewelry and made for the door before the superintendent could think of any more of his shortcomings to moan about.

"Wait!"

It was a tone that could not be ignored, even by Frost. He turned slowly. "Sir?

"That photograph you showed me . . . there was something familiar about it."

"Don't worry, Super . . . I'll try and keep you out of it."

Mullett tightened his lips and stretched out a hand for the Polaroid print. "Let me see it again." He studied it, then took off his glasses and polished them slowly. "It's Mrs. Roberts."

"Top marks!" cried Frost. "I would never have recognized her just from her bare behind . . . although, of course, I've never seen her behind. . . ."

Mullett reddened. "I recognized the room," he snapped.

"Of course, sir," agreed Frost. "Whatever you say."

Mullett glowered. "My wife and I have been there many times . . . those pictures . . . that bookcase . . ."

"Oh, I see, sir," said Frost, leaving a lingering tinge of doubt in his voice to annoy Mullett further. "You probably sat in that self-same chair she's bending over."

Mullett wiped his eyes wearily and replaced his glasses. "Look, Frost, this is all extremely embarrassing. Mrs. Roberts is a friend of mine and she's very big in the town."

"She's even bigger round the buttocks," said Frost.

Mullett ignored this. He gestured at the photo. "What do you intend doing with this?"

"I'm going round to her house to show it to her."

Mullett stared hard at the surface of his desk and moved his fountain pen a fraction of an inch. "I think it would be better if I handled that, Inspector. Mrs. Roberts is a good friend, but she could also be a very bad enemy. If I could return the photograph and let her know we were keeping her name out of it, it would make things go a lot smoother in our later dealings."

"Sorry, Super," said Frost. "You're too late. I think she's been blackmailed already. In fact, it could be the reason

Lemmy Hoxton was killed." As he filled Mullett in, the superintendent became more and more agitated.

"I'd prefer it if you would drop it, Frost. I'm sure the woman's not involved in murder. Dammit, she's a family friend!"

Frost adopted his air of puzzled incomprehension. "Is this a bit of the judges' rules that I've missed, sir—that I shouldn't question any murder suspect who happens to be a friend of yours?"

Mullett leant forward, his face creased with anger. "You know damn well that's not what I meant. Of course you must question her. If, by some remote chance, she is involved, then you have my full permission. But if this goes wrong, if it blows up in our faces, I'll come down on you like a ton of bricks."

Frost retrieved the photograph and slipped it into his pocket. Mullett, as usual, had covered himself both ways and couldn't lose. He said, "I knew I could rely on your full support, Super."

He looked in the Murder Incident Room and yelled for Burton to accompany him. Mrs. Roberts was a big woman: He didn't fancy tackling her on his own.

Mrs. Emily Roberts lived in a semidetached house at the end of the road. A neat front garden fronted by a trimmed hedge led to a porch and a front door with colored leaded lights. The bell push surround was polished brass which Frost smeared by jamming his finger on it. After a pause, the door opened suspiciously on a length of chain and even his warrant card wasn't enough to gain admittance. Mrs. Roberts snatched it from him and went off to phone the station to make sure they were not imposters. She still remembered the fake Water Board official, but at least he looked the part, while this scruffy individual who thrust a dog-eared warrant card at her looked nothing like a policeman.

She had demanded to speak to her friend Stanley Mullett, the divisional commander. Mullett, who had sounded a trifle edgy on the phone, confirmed that Frost was one of his officers, although he wasn't exactly sure what case the inspector was on at the moment.

They were ordered to wipe their feet, which Frost did very perfunctorily, and were marched into the living room where a cheery coal fire blazed. She meant for them to sit in the hard chairs, but the scruffy one immediately made for one of her large leather armchairs. "Lovely chair," remarked Frost, sinking down. "Feels brand spanking new."

Her heart skipped a beat. Was it her imagination, or did he stress the word "spanking." She smiled bleakly. "How can I help you?"

The room looked exactly as it did in the photograph, but the woman, large, almost mannish, in her tweed trouser suit, seemed light-years away from the baby-talking writer of the letter imploring "teacher" to correct her errors. "You reported a robbery some months ago, Mrs. Roberts," said Frost. He wished she would sit down. She was standing, towering over him, making him crick his neck as he talked to her.

With an airy wave of the hand she dismissed the nonsense about the robbery. "All a mistake, as I told your officer at the time."

"We're wondering if it was a mistake."

She frowned. "What do you mean?"

"We think there was a robbery, which you reported, but then you realized the robber had taken certain items you didn't wish the police to know about."

She drew herself up to her full height, towering over him even more. "There was no robbery. Nothing was taken. I can't help you."

"Why don't you sit down," said Frost. "Or is your little botsy-wotsy sore?"

She stared, mouth gaping. At first she thought she hadn't

heard him correctly and then her eyes widened in stunned shock as he produced the envelope and the photograph.

"Not exactly full face," said Frost, "but we're pretty certain this is you."

She tried to snatch it from him, but he drew his hand back. "How dare you!" she hissed. "How dare you!" Her mouth opened and closed, but that was all she could think of to say.

"Sorry about this," said Frost, sounding as if he meant it, "but when you lift stones, all sorts of nasty things come crawling out. I'd just like to get a couple of things sorted out to help with our inquiries."

"I'm not saying another word." Emily Roberts dropped down in the armchair opposite him and folded her arms defiantly.

"Fair enough," smiled Frost. "Bank down the fire and get your hat and coat. We can continue this down at the station. It's not very private there, I'm afraid, but if you're not ashamed of what you've been up to, then what the hell. . . ."

She said nothing, but the defiant look withered.

Frost took a folder from Burton and flipped it open. "On the fifth of August you telephoned your personal friend Mr. Mullett to report a burglary. A man posing as a Water Board engineer gained entrance to your house and after he had left you discovered valuables missing from your bedroom. Within twenty minutes of your phone call you received a visit from Detective Sergeant Hanlon. You gave him a list of stolen items—brooches, pearl necklace, gold powder compact, silver bangle—total value nearly two thousand pounds."

He tugged out the list. "This is what you said were stolen." He held it in front of her. She stared straight ahead as if it weren't there.

"Your very good friend Mr. Mullett then called me in and ordered me to pull out all stops to apprehend the criminal. But the very next day you phoned, and subsequently signed a statement . . . *this* statement"—another sheet of paper was waved in front of her—"which states that it was all a mistake and nothing was taken . . . you had misplaced the articles and had then found them in another drawer. Mr. Mullett instructed me to take no further action and I immediately complied." He replaced the papers in the folder. "My fault. I don't look for work, but I should have followed it up. I should have asked to see the items you now claim to have found." He beamed at her. "If I asked nicely, could you show them to me now?"

She stared at him, then lowered her gaze to the floor. "No."

"The stuff was stolen?"

"Yes."

"So what happened to make you tell us it wasn't?"

She stood up and went over to a small coffee table where she took a cigarette from a black-and-gold lacquered box, lighting it with an onyx cigarette lighter. Before she turned round again, Frost had lit up one of his own. She said, "That night I received a telephone call. A man. He read me a part of that letter and described the photograph. He said he was thinking of sending them to the press, but perhaps I would like to buy them back." She dragged deeply at the cigarette. "I asked how much. He wanted five hundred pounds in used notes. I said I would pay." She crushed the cigarette out.

"And . . . ?" prompted Frost.

"He said there was a litter bin next to the bus stop in Stacey Street. I was to hide the envelope containing the money between the bin and the wall. If I returned there the next day, in its place would be the letter and photograph."

"And?"

"I did what he said. I left the money. But when I returned the next day, the money was still there. It hadn't been picked up. The following day the same. So I retrieved the money and waited for him to phone again. I never heard another word from him."

"And what did you do with the money?"

"I paid it back into my bank account."

"Do you have copies of your bank statement?"

She glared and went over to an oak-veneered bureau where she took some papers from the top drawer. These she handed to Frost who passed them to Burton.

"Do you think I am a liar, Inspector?" she asked icily.

"People do lie to us," said Frost mildly. "They tell us robberies haven't taken place when they have." He looked across to Burton, who nodded. The payments in and out were recorded exactly as she said.

Frost showed her Lemmy's mug shot. "Was this the man who robbed you?"

She studied it carefully. "I think so . . . I can't be sure. I didn't pay a lot of attention to him at the time . . . one doesn't when it's workmen."

"And the last time you saw him was when he left your house on the . . ."—he consulted the file—"the fifth of August, the day you reported the robbery, and the day before you then reported it never took place?"

"Yes."

"We think he might have come back here the next day," said Frost. "We think he demanded money and threatened to send the photograph and the letter to the press if you didn't pay."

"I've already told you what happened."

"But are you telling me the truth?" queried Frost.

"I'm not used to having my word questioned and I'm not going to say another word unless you have the common courtesy to tell me what this is all about," she snapped.

Frost smiled his reasonable smile. "Of course. The man I asked you to identify is Lemmy Hoxton, a known criminal. We found your letter and the photo with other stolen goods, hidden in his house. We also found some jewelry that might be yours were it not for the fact that you had told us it hadn't been stolen."

"My reason for silence no longer applies, Inspector. Yes, I was robbed. As I have admitted."

"What I didn't tell you," said Frost, as if suddenly remembering something not too important, "was the reason we went to Lemmy's house in the first place. Would you like to know why?"

"Not particularly, but I imagine you are going to tell me anyway." Her face was stony.

Frost took a long drag at his cigarette. "It was because we had found his decomposing body feeding the maggots in someone's back yard. Someone—perhaps to avoid being blackmailed—had murdered him."

She stared at him, openmouthed, the color seeping from her face. "Murdered? You surely don't think that I . . . ?"

"Why not?" asked Frost. "If I was in your position I would cheerfully have murdered the bastard, especially if I thought I could get away with it."

She picked up the poker and began belaboring the coals on the fire as if it was Frost's skull she was smashing. "I've told you what happened. I've nothing more to say. You have property of mine. I'd like it back."

"All in good time, Mrs. Roberts." He studied her through narrowed eyes. A hefty woman, as strong as an ox. One blow from that poker would certainly make Lemmy's eyes water and she wouldn't have too much difficulty humping the body out to her car. But it might not have been so easy to carry Lemmy from her car to the coal bunker on her own. She might have needed help. Then what about her bottom-smacking chum in the mortar board?

"I'd like you to give me the name and address of your gentleman friend in the photograph."

"No!" She was firm on this. "I'm not having him involved."

Frost considered insisting, but decided against it. He

thought about getting Forensic in to give the place a going-over, but decided against that also. Too much time had gone by and, in any case, she wasn't denying that Lemmy had been here. Forensic had plenty of better things to do. He decided just to let her sweat for a while.

"What size television set have you got, Mrs. Roberts?"

"Television set?" She gaped at him as if he was mad. "I haven't got a television set. I wouldn't have one in the house."

"Then you won't mind if my colleague takes a look." Frost nodded to Burton who left the room. He stood up. "I'll want you to go down to the station some time today and give us a full statement about the robbery and the blackmail attempt."

She colored a deep crimson and pulverized another piece of coal with the poker. "A statement? Is that really necessary?"

"You needn't be specific—some of our young officers are easily shocked. You can just refer to a letter and certain activities it mentions you would prefer were not made public."

Burton returned, shaking his head. No TV set of any size in the house. They showed themselves out, leaving her looking decidedly uneasy.

At the station Mullett was flapping about in a state of high agitation awaiting their return. He grabbed Frost and hustled him into his office. "Well?"

"She could be involved," said Frost. "But I haven't got any hard evidence yet." He filled Mullett in on the details.

"There were other compromising letters and photographs —have you checked to see if those people were being blackmailed by Hoxton?"

"It's on my long list of things to do," replied Frost, who hadn't got round to thinking of that aspect.

"The sooner we can clear Emily Roberts—"

"As I am sure you would wish, sir, clearing Mrs. Roberts is right at the bottom of my list of priorities," said Frost.

"Of course, of course. The letter and the photograph—you didn't tell her I'd seen them?"

"She never asked."

"Good." Mullett dabbed at his brow with his handkerchief. "It would be extremely embarrassing if she thought I knew." He rearranged the blotter on his desk to show he was changing the subject. "What's the procedure for the ransom hand-over tonight?"

"We've got all the public telephone kiosks in the shopping mall bugged, so whichever one the kidnapper calls we'll be able to hear everything. I've also arranged for a homing device to be slipped inside the suitcase with the money."

"How did you manage that?"

"Remember Tommy Dunn—used to be with us in CID?"

Mullett pulled a face. He did indeed remember Dunn, an inefficient officer with a drinking problem and the strongest of suspicions that he took bribes. Dunn had been arrested on a charge of driving while well over the limit, but Mullett had managed to get the charge dropped in exchange for Dunn's resignation. A pity, he thought wistfully, he couldn't do something similar with Frost. He also recalled that Dunn was one of the investigating officers four years ago when Cassidy's daughter was killed and there were vague whispers he'd been bribed by the hit-and-run driver. "I remember Dunn. What about him?"

"Tommy works for Savalot as a security guard. He's going to slip the homing device in the suitcase for us."

"Why should he do that? He owes us no favors."

"He's doing it for three bottles of Johnny Walker and the cancellation of a couple of parking tickets." It was six parking tickets actually, but Frost wasn't telling the superintendent this.

"I don't want to know," said Mullett hurriedly.

"I'll bung the cost of the whisky on my petrol expenses," said Frost blithely, "so don't query it if it looks a bit high." He was also going to sneak in the cost of petrol bought while he was on holiday, which would make it higher still.

Mullett flapped a hand. "Spare me the details. I'm not happy that Dunn is involved in this, Frost. You can't rely on him."

"He's all we've got," said Frost. But he shared Mullett's concern. Tommy sounded half-drunk when he'd agreed to do it.

"So," continued Mullett, "if things go as you hope and Dunn runs contrary to past form, we will have a homing device hidden in the ransom money?"

"Yes. We'll be able to track Cordwell to the hand-over point and then keep tabs on the kidnapper after he's picked it up."

"What about his claim he can monitor police radios?"

"I don't believe him, but just in case he does we'll be scrambling all our radio messages."

"The safety of the boy is paramount," insisted Mullett.

"We won't make a move until we know where Bobby is and are assured he's safe."

Mullett scratched his chin thoughtfully. It sounded foolproof, but when Frost organized things, nothing was foolproof. "Well, I'll leave the details to you," he said, so he could deny any knowledge of them should things blow up in their faces. "The only stipulation I make is that things must not go wrong."

"That's a bloody good stipulation!" said Frost in mock admiration as he walked to the door. "I'll bear it in mind, sir."

While Mullett was trying to determine if there was a tinge of sarcasm in this, he heard an indignant squeal from Miss Smith, his secretary, then a cry of "How's that for center?" and a guffaw from Frost. He shook his head sadly.

How could you work with a man like that? He looked up in sympathy at the scarlet face of Miss Smith as she burst in to complain.

Liz was waiting in Frost's office. She pushed a pile of reports over to him. Without looking at them, he pushed them back. "Just tell me what they say, love. My lips get tired when I read."

She took them and gave him a précis of each. "I saw Mark Grover in hospital and broke the news of his wife's death."

"Shit!" said Frost. "I should have done that! Sorry to dump it on you, love—how did he take it?"

"He took it very well. He said it served the bitch right."

"You didn't tell him we suspect it was murder?"

"No. I just said it looked as if she had fallen in front of a train. He told me she had kept threatening to kill herself—the doctor had prescribed her pills for depression."

"They don't seem to have worked all that bloody well," sniffed Frost. "I'll check it out with her doctor." He scribbled a reminder on his pad. "What else?"

"You told me to take his clothes to the lab. They're still doing tests, but if there's any blood, they haven't found it yet."

"Did you ask him about the row the neighbors heard?"

"He swears it wasn't him. He never left the store until nearly two o'clock. I've spoken to his workmate who again confirms this. Then I checked with the security man at the store. No one can get in or out until he operates the electronic locking system and he's definite that he didn't operate it at all that night. And their boss at the shopfitting firm confirms he phoned and spoke to Mark Grover at twenty past midnight."

Frost chewed this over. There was not a lot of support for his theory that Grover murdered his wife. But he was only giving Liz half his attention. His mind was still on the ransom hand-over. He didn't want another of his usual cock-ups on this one.

"Which means," Liz continued, "that we can concentrate on our number one suspect, Sidney Snell, who seems to have done a runner."

"I just can't see Sidney killing anyone," said Frost. "That woman was killed in a frenzied attack. Sidney might stamp his foot and say 'knickers' but he wouldn't get into a frenzy."

"Three children, all in one room—that could have worked him up to a sexual state where he'd do anything."

"A bit of bare thigh does the same for me," sighed Frost. He saw there was more to come.

"We've got a key witness. An old boy walking his dog who swears he saw someone running from the house and driving off in a blue car."

Frost's head jerked up. "What time was this?"

"About ten minutes before two o'clock."

"In the morning? What was the silly sod doing walking his dog at that time?"

"He used to be on shift work before he retired and old habits die hard."

Frost tugged the man's statement toward him and read it. The old boy seemed pretty definite as to what he saw. "He's sure the man he saw came out of the Grovers' house?"

"He's positive . . . And remember, Mark Grover says that when he came home last night the front door was wide open."

Frost dug in his pocket and found a half-smoked cigarette hidden in the lining. It was stale, but better than nothing. He lit up. "And Snell's got a blue car—there could be a clue there somewhere." He sucked in smoke and coughed, shaking ash all over a memo from Mullett complaining about the inadequacy of Frost's daily call reports. He heaved himself up and snatched his scarf from the hatstand. Something was nagging away at him, something just out of reach, something he knew he should have picked up, but the more he tried to remember, the more it crept back to cower in the dark, inaccessible recesses of his mind. He had to get out of the office and think. "I'm off to see her doctor. Let's find out if he agrees with the husband about her suicidal tendencies."

The waiting room was crowded, people hunched up coughing, snuffling, and groaning in counterpoint to children running around, screaming unchecked. If you weren't ill when you went in, you certainly would be after a few minutes of this.

The receptionist was flustered. Patients were annoyed with her because the doctor was running late, the phone was ringing nonstop, and this scruffy man, claiming to be a detective, wanted to nip in in front of people who had been waiting for nearly an hour. "I don't know when he will be able to see you. We're very, very busy," she said.

"That makes two of us," said Frost.

A patient emerged from the surgery clutching a prescription form and the receptionist was about to ask the next patient to go in when the scruffy man scooted in before the surgery door closed and before she could warn the doctor.

"I thought I was next," said one of the women indignantly. "I'm writing to the General Medical Council about this."

The doctor, a plump young man with bad skin, was at his desk, scribbling something in a register. He didn't look up as Frost entered. "Please sit down, Mrs. Jenkins. What's the trouble?"

"The sex-change operation didn't work," said Frost, sitting as requested.

The doctor looked up. "I thought—"

"I'm not a patient," said Frost, sliding a warrant card across. "Police!"

The doctor stared at the warrant card as if Frost had just dumped a hand grenade with the pin removed on his desk. "Look, Officer. I think my solicitor had better be present. I never touched that girl. She stripped to the waist, I gave her a normal examination. I know she was only fifteen—"

"Hold it," interrupted Frost. "This has nothing to do with that . . . I wish it did, it sounds quite juicy. I'm inquiring about another patient of yours—Mrs. Nancy Grover, Cresswell Street."

In his relief, the doctor couldn't have been more helpful. He pulled a file from his filing cabinet and opened it up. "Yes—those poor children. I had no idea she would do anything like that."

"What were you treating her for?"

"Depression—paranoia. Nancy imagined people were following her everywhere she went, watching her, staring at her through the windows of her bungalow at night when her husband wasn't there."

"And the bastard rarely was there, was he? Shouldn't she have had specialized help?"

"Yes. I wanted to send her to a consultant psychiatrist, but she wouldn't go. I prescribed tranquilizers, but I don't think she took them."

"You say she was imagining she was being watched . . . that a man was looking through her window. Could this really have happened?"

"It's possible. It's difficult to be certain with patients like her. They are convinced that things that only happen in their own minds are actually occurring. She was so upset because her husband didn't believe her."

"What do you think brought it all on?"

The doctor gave a sad smile. "Three children, another on the way. A husband who worked most of the day and was out drinking most of the night. No relatives or close friends she could confide in. It was all getting too much for her."

Frost stared at the desk in silence. He felt so sorry for the poor thing. He stood up. "Thanks, Doc."

Angry faces sped him on his way out of the waiting room. Outside in the darkened street, the first heavy drops of rain were splattering the pavement.

"Penny for the guy, mister?"

He froze. The small boy standing in front of him with his palm outstretched, a misshapen Guy Fawkes dummy propped up in a pushchair at his side, was the spitting image of Bobby Kirby. But it wasn't Bobby, of course.

"You didn't ought to be out," said Frost.

"You tightfisted old sod," snarled the boy, trundling off with the pushchair.

Frost watched him go and wondered if parents should be warned of the dangers. He'd have a word with Mullett when he got back.

As he turned the key in the ignition and his engine tried to cough itself into life, the radio called him. Burton, sounding excited. Frost's mind was still on that poor woman and her kids, terrified because someone had been staring in her house. Her husband didn't believe her and had left her all alone. Could the face at the window, the face that everyone thought was only in her mind, have been the face of Sidney Snell? He shuddered, then realized Burton was still talking.

"Sorry, son—I didn't catch that."

Burton told him again, slowly and clearly, as if the poor old sod was going deaf. This time Frost was able to share the DC's delight. It was the first stroke of luck they'd had in the Lemmy Hoxton case.

CHAPTER ELEVEN

"We have a name and an address!" said Burton triumphantly. The television set bought posthumously with
Lemmy's credit card had been registered for the guarantee.
"Douglas Cooper, two-A Merchant Street, Denton. And
he's got a record." He handed the inspector a photostat of
the record sheet.

Frost didn't need to read it. "I know Duggie Cooper,
son. I've nicked him a couple of times . . . breaking and
entering, handling stolen goods, obtaining money under
false pretenses."

He looked at his watch. Ten past two. He shook his wrist
with annoyance. He must have forgotten to wind the damn
thing last night. "Have we got time to give Duggie a tug
before the ransom caper?"

Burton checked his own watch. Six thirty-five. The ransom call was due to be made at eight. "Not really," he said.

"Let's do it anyway," said Frost.

Merchant Street, a narrow side road to the north of
Denton, was jam-packed with parked cars, most of them
without a current tax disc. Burton had to double-park at the
end of the street and they walked back to the house. A dark
grey Ford transit van stood outside Duggie's house. This

reminded Frost that he should get someone to keep an eye on the boyfriend of Tracey Neal with the light brown van.

Cooper answered their ring. A thin-faced, shifty-eyed man, he had a little toothbrush moustache with dark, greasy hair brushed straight back. His face fell when he saw who his visitors were. "Mr. Frost!"

"Just passing," said Frost. "Knew you'd never forgive us if we didn't drop in and say hello." He pushed past Cooper and went straight into the lounge. There it was, in the corner, gleaming and dominating the room, a large-screen Panasonic television set. Frost plonked himself down on the settee and pulled out his cigarettes.

Cooper hurried in after them looking very agitated. "What do you want, Mr. Frost?"

Frost tutted reproachfully. "Since when do friends have to have a reason for calling on each other?"

"I ain't done nothing," insisted Cooper.

Frost cupped a hand to his ear as if he had difficulty in hearing what Cooper was saying. "You give us permission to search your house, did you say? That's damn decent of you, Duggie. It saves all that sodding about getting a warrant." He nodded to Burton, who scuttled up the stairs before Cooper could stop him.

A woman bounded into the room. Duggie's wife, Jean, hadn't started out as a redhead and the various color changes she had gone through before reaching her present shade had left their mark on the final result. "There's a bloke going up our stairs," she shouted, stopping abruptly in mid-protest when she saw Frost. She screwed up her face in annoyance. "Oh, no—just what we bloody need!" Hands on hips, Jean glowered at her husband, then spun back to Frost. "Don't try and tell me he's done something, because he never does damn all. He sits on his arse in the house all day and never does a bloody stroke." The thudding of Burton's feet across the ceiling made her look up. "What's he looking for? There's nothing in the house that shouldn't be here. . . ."

And then she saw the expression on Duggie's face. "At least, there bloody well had better *not* be!"

"Nice telly," commented Frost, nodding at the set in the corner. "Must have cost a bomb."

"It's all legitimate," she snapped. "We've got the receipt." She darted across to the sideboard and pulled open a drawer. "It's in here—"

Duggie sprang across and pushed the drawer shut. "No it isn't," he said.

She frowned. "What are you talking about? I saw it there this morning."

"No you didn't," he hissed. "I lost it . . . weeks ago."

"But I saw—" And then the penny dropped. With an icy glare at her husband which said "I'll sort this out with you later," Jean Cooper turned to Frost, smiling sweetly. "Duggie's right. We lost it."

"Then it's lucky I called in," said Frost. "Because I've got a copy of the receipt here." Humming to himself, he unfolded the photostat and pretended to check the details. "Panasonic . . . Model number TXT2228 . . . serial number . . . call out the serial number, would you, Duggie—it's on the back." He waited as Duggie moved the heavy set with difficulty and read it out. "Number TXT2822311Y."

"Check," beamed Frost, folding the receipt and returning it to his inside jacket pocket. He stood up. "Sorry I troubled you, Lemmy. . . ." He frowned. "Why did I call you Lemmy? Your name isn't Lemmy . . . I must be going bloody mad." He took the receipt from his pocket again as if to check the name.

"All right, all right," said Duggie. "It was bought with Lemmy Hoxton's credit card. He owes me, so he let me use it." He fumbled for a cigarette and lit up with a none too steady hand.

"Ah," said Frost, sitting down again. "I knew there was a rational explanation. When did Lemmy give you his card?"

"The same day I bought the telly."

"You bought the telly and gave the card back to him?"

"Of course."

"What deodorant does Lemmy use?" asked Frost.

"Eh?" Duggie frowned. "What's that got to do with it?"

"It must be bloody strong stuff, because the day he lent you the card Lemmy would have been stinking the place out—he'd been dead for two months."

"Dead?" Duggie's mouth gaped open, the lighted cigarette dangling.

Frost nodded cheerfully. "Dead—the way Domestos kills ninety-nine percent of known germs. You killed him and took his credit card."

"Killed him?" echoed Duggie, his face now a chalky white.

"Him? Kill Lemmy?" screeched his wife. "Don't make me laugh. He wouldn't kill a bloody fly."

"A bloody fly hasn't got a credit card, has it?" asked Frost. He looked up as Burton returned carrying a drawer from a dressing table.

"Found this upstairs," said Burton. The drawer was crammed with cheap jewelry, silver-plated photo frames, trinket boxes, tawdry stuff, most of which Frost recognized from the list of articles stolen by the phony Water Board inspector.

"Dear, dear," said Frost. "I might have overlooked you murdering Lemmy, but stealing from old ladies. . . . Douglas Cooper, I'm arresting you on suspicion of murder and robbery. Anything you say, et cetera, you know the rest by heart."

"I never damn well killed him!" cried Duggie.

"On being charged, the prisoner said 'It's a fair cop, guv'nor, you've got me to right,' " chanted Frost. "Come on Duggie . . . we're off to the nick."

Duggie's wife was boiling with rage. "That bloody telly!

You had to be clever and buy it. There was nothing wrong with the old one."

"You said you wanted a big one," answered Duggie meekly.

"She didn't mean the telly," said Frost, hustling him out. "Come on—I'm running late."

There was a sour, stale smell in the Interview Room. Someone had been sick in it recently and the lingering aroma was proving its superiority over the cheap pine disinfectant used to swab it out.

Burton fed a cassette into the recorder and announced who was present while Frost lowered himself carefully into the chair opposite Douglas Cooper.

"Right, Duggie," said Frost. "Time to make a clean breast of all your naughtiness. We found a quantity of items believed to be stolen in your house today. Would you like to tell us about them?"

"No comment," said Duggie.

"We also found a television set known to have been purchased with Lemmy Hoxton's credit card some two months after his death. Would you like to tell us about that?"

"No comment."

"Are you going to say 'No comment' to everything I ask you?"

"No comment," repeated Duggie stubbornly.

"Switch the bleeding tape off," said Frost. "Interview terminated at whatever time it is." He rammed a cigarette in his mouth. "You're a prat, Duggie. We don't need your statement. I've got enough evidence to convict you without it. I don't think you killed Lemmy—you haven't got the balls, but I need an arrest and you are tailor-made. As long as I get a conviction, I score the brownie points and the fact that you didn't do it is neither here nor there." He jerked a thumb at Burton. "Take him back to his cell."

He wandered back to his office, where Liz Maud was working diligently through a pile of returns, too busy to look up. He sat at his desk, trying to work out where he was with the cases they were handling. The dead Dean Anderson was connected with the Bobby Kirby kidnapping and, hopefully, this would be resolved tonight when they nabbed the kidnapper picking up the ransom. A message on his desk from Newcastle Police stated there was no sign of Sidney Snell back at his flat, but they were keeping a close watch. So that case was in abeyance until they found him. Another sheet of paper on his desk detailed the findings of the lab, which had analyzed the contents of Lemmy Hoxton's stomach and were able to report that Lemmy had died within two hours of consuming a meal consisting of salmon fish cakes, chips and peas, washed down with a carbonated cola drink.

He interrupted Liz and told her to check with Lemmy's wife and see if she served up such a meal to Lemmy, remarking, "The fizzy drink sounds more like a meal she'd serve to her toy-boy." He thought about it and liked the sound of it. "You know, that could be it. She has the meal all ready for her toy-boy when Lemmy arrives home unexpectedly, so she has to pretend it was for him. After dinner, he spots the kid hiding behind the curtains, his dick dragging on the floor. There's a fight and they split his skull open."

"Then why did they cut the tops of his fingers off?" asked Liz.

"It could have happened during the fight," said Frost lamely. He sighed. "I don't know." He pushed himself back from the desk, his chair scraping the brown lino with a teeth-setting squeal. "All this talk of stomach contents is making me hungry. I'm off to the canteen."

Arthur Hanlon spotted Frost in the canteen and waddled over carrying his tray of food. He sat down opposite him and dolloped sauce on his egg and chips. "Everything set for tonight, Jack?"

"I hope so, Arthur. The phones are tapped and the suitcase should be bugged."

"How many men will you need?"

"Don't confuse me with numbers, Arthur," said Frost, forking a chip from Hanlon's plate. "One man watching the phone booths, one keeping an eye on Cordwell and tailing his car in case the homing device conks out, two area cars on call, the SAS, the United States Cavalry . . . two or three hundred should do it at a pinch. How many can I have?"

"Twelve, if you're lucky."

"As long as one of them is Arnold Schwarzenegger, we should manage." He dipped one of his own chips in Hanlon's egg, then had to leave when the Tannoy called him to the phone. Duggie Cooper had decided to make a statement.

On his way down to the Interview Room Frost spotted Cassidy and Mullett in cosy conversation. Both frowned and nodded curtly to him as he passed. Cassidy had handed the superintendent a wad of completed progress reports and Mullett was beaming all over his face. "You haven't done them already, Cassidy!" he exclaimed delightedly. "Good man!"

"You wanted them, so I did them," said Cassidy.

Frost squinted at the returns. They were the ones he had seen Liz Maud filling in earlier. Liz had done the work and Cassidy was unashamedly taking the praise. The man hadn't changed since he was last in the division.

Duggie Cooper was already in the Interview Room, waiting for him. "I hope you're not going to waste my time, Duggie." Frost grunted, settling down wearily in the same uncomfortable chair. "I've got important things to do . . . I can always frame you later."

"Look, Mr. Frost. I didn't kill Lemmy. I'll cough for a

few bits of nicking if it makes you happy, but I haven't killed anyone."

Frost signaled for Burton to bung in a tape. "You're on the air, Duggie, so sing."

"Me and Lemmy Hoxton were working together. Lemmy was the brains. He had this idea about conning our way into people's houses, and while they were busy downstairs, nicking their stuff upstairs. Sometimes we got rubbish, but now and again we hit the jackpot."

"So how did it work?" asked Frost.

"We'd pretend to be men from the Water Board. We'd case some likely places—mainly old dears living on their own—then one of us would put on overalls and pedal up to the house on an old bike. We had various scams. One was to turn the water off at the hydrant outside, then knock and say we'd had complaints about the water supply, and would they check their taps. So they'd do it and the tap would run dry. 'Never mind,' we'd say, 'I'll fix it for you.' We'd turn the hydrant back on again and give them another knock. 'Try it now.' And of course, now it works fine. 'You watch the tap,' we'd say, 'and I'll go upstairs and flush the toilet . . . let me know if it makes any difference to the flow.' They were tickled pink to help. While we were upstairs, we'd nip in the bedroom for a quick rummage. You'd be surprised at the stuff people stow in their dressing tables . . . some of them had hundreds of pounds in cash. Anyway, we stick the loot in our tool bag, toddle off downstairs, refuse the cup of tea the grateful old dear would offer, and get the hell out of there on the bike. One of us would be waiting in the van. We'd stick the bike inside and rip off the overalls. If the cops are on the lookout, they're after a man on a bike in overalls, not two men in a van in suits."

"Speed it up, Duggie," said Frost. "I want to get to the bit where you kill him."

"I never killed him," insisted Duggie, "though the sod was swindling me left, right, and center. Everything I found we'd split fifty-fifty. If Lemmy found anything good, he'd pocket it and say there was nothing there."

Frost shook his head sadly. "You should have complained to the police. That's what we're here for. All right, fast-forward to the bit where you nick his credit card."

"The last job we did together was back in August . . . August sixth, I think. We had a few jobs lined up for that afternoon. The first was a cottage near Alderney Cross . . . two women living alone. Lemmy reckoned it was ideal—remote and it looked as if there would be rich pickings. Before the job we had lunch in a pub."

"What pub?"

"Forget its name—little country pub just off the main road."

"What did you have to eat?"

"Bloody hell, Mr. Frost, this was months ago. I can't even remember what I had for dinner last night."

"Did Lemmy have anything to drink in the pub?"

"Nothing alcoholic. We made a point of it . . . these old dears get suspicious of workmen with beery breaths. We stuck to soft drinks."

Frost exchanged glances with Burton. This tied in with the analysis of the stomach contents. "Then what?"

"I parked down a side lane. Lemmy changed into his overalls and pedaled off. I read the paper, smoked a fag, and waited . . . and bloody waited. He never came back. I waited over an hour, then thought, bloody hell, he's been nicked, so I roared off back home and sat indoors in fear and bloody trembling expecting the old Bill to knock any minute. But nothing. Nor the next day. I phoned his house, but his old lady said he'd gone away for a few days and she didn't know when he was coming back."

"And . . . ?" asked Frost.

"That's it. I never saw him again."

"You must have seen him to nick his credit card."

"His suit jacket was in the van. He'd gone off in his

overalls. I stuck the jacket in my wardrobe for when he came back, but he never did."

"What did you think had happened to him?"

"I reckoned he'd probably struck bloody gold at the cottage he did over that day."

"What do you mean by that?"

"I reckoned he'd found the old girl's life savings in the bedroom—a few thousand quid—and decided he wasn't going to share it, so he did a runner. So I thought to myself, 'You lousy bastard, Lemmy!' and I took the wallet from his jacket, helped myself to the few quid in it, and bought myself a telly with his credit card."

"You didn't buy anything else with it?"

"I wasn't going to push my luck any more. I chucked it away after that."

Frost leant back and puffed a salvo of smoke rings up to the ceiling. "Not a bad story, Duggie, but I prefer my version . . . that you quarreled over the split-up of the loot and you killed him."

"On my life, Mr. Frost . . ."

"What was the address of that cottage he was going to do?"

"It was called Primrose Cottage—you can't miss it, it was painted yellow like custard."

Frost flipped open his burglary file and checked. No one had reported a robbery or an attempted robbery at that address. He snapped the file shut. "I don't believe a word you've said, Duggie, but you know me—heart of gold—so I'll tell you what I'm going to do and you can abase yourself in gratitude later. I'll try and check out your story. But first, I want you to put your hand up to all the jobs you and Lemmy did—all of them."

"Right, Mr. Frost." Duggie couldn't pour out the details quickly enough. "First there was—"

Frost quickly restrained him. "No—not to me, Duggie, I haven't got time. Hold on a minute . . ." He was out of his seat and looking up and down the passage. The unlucky passerby was Arthur Hanlon.

"Congratulations, Arthur!" called Frost, grabbing him by the arm. "You've just solved a whole batch of burglaries . . . Mr. Mullett will pee himself with pleasure when you tell him."

"Eh?" said Hanlon as Frost steered him firmly into the Interview Room.

"You know how I hate paperwork, Arthur. You can have all the credit and be Mr. Mullett's blue-eyed boy." He jabbed a finger at the prisoner. "Okay, Duggie—cough!"

PC Collier, wearing plain clothes, drove slowly to the end of the road where he parked silently and switched off the lights. Rain was bucketing down and visibility was limited, but the floodlit drive to Sir Richard Cordwell's front door made it easy to keep tabs on what was going on. As soon as Cordwell drove out, Collier would radio to let Frost know, then, at a discreet distance, follow.

In the crowded shopping mall leading to the Savalot Supermarket, Burton jostled his way to a wooden bench that gave him an unrestricted view of the clump of four public telephone boxes. Syrupy music oozed from overhead speakers, interrupted from time to time by a chirpy voice advising shoppers of the latest bargains to be had in the store. The four kiosks all had Out of Order notices on their doors and the phones had been fixed so no outgoing calls could be made. This had been done by Cordwell's security officers to ensure the phones were not being used by the public when the kidnapper tried to make contact.

Burton eased the radio from the inside pocket of his jacket and made a call to the Incident Room to test that the scrambler was working as it should.

.   .   .

"I can hear you, and that bloody music, loud and clear," Frost told Burton. He checked his watch. Coming up to a quarter to eight. Cordwell should be leaving the house any second.

"Can I have a word, Inspector?"

Hopalong flaming Cassidy! And the edge to his voice meant he was going to have a moan about something. "What is it, my son?"

"I'm not your son, I'm an inspector, if you don't mind," corrected Cassidy stiffly. "Could we go outside?"

"Call me if anything happens," said Frost to Lambert as he followed Cassidy out to the corridor. "So how can I help you, Inspector?" He kept his eye on the door, ready to dash back any minute.

"You can help me by letting me handle my own cases," snapped Cassidy. "Lemmy Hoxton. Am I handling it or not!"

Oh shit! thought Frost. He's found out about Duggie Cooper . . . and I never told him about Mullett's mate, Mrs. Roberts. "Do you mean Cooper?"

"Yes, I damn well do. Not only have you questioned the man without bringing me in on it, you've let that fat sergeant take all the credit for clearing up the robberies."

"Sorry, son," said Frost, "but I knew you wouldn't want to take the credit for things you weren't entitled to." Cassidy's eyes flickered at the shaft. "Anyway, it's your case from now on." Cassidy still wasn't satisfied and was ready with the next moan, but Frost was spared this by the door opening. "Radio message, Inspector," called Lambert.

He dashed back inside. PC Collier was on the radio reporting that Cordwell had left the house.

"Which car was he in?" asked Frost, hoping it wasn't the inconspicuous pearl-grey Rolls-Royce with the personalized number plate. They'd have half of Fleet Street following if it was.

"It's a dark green Nissan," reported Collier. He gave the registration number. *"Shall I follow?"*

"Yes, but keep well back. We know he's coming to the store, so you needn't hug his tail. Once he's in the store, park in a side street off the Market Square. We'll contact you when he comes out." He radioed through to Burton to let him know Cordwell was on his way. "Should be with you in five minutes."

"Right," acknowledged Burton.

Frost was lighting up when Liz came in. "We've located the pub where Cooper says he and Lemmy went to. It's the Green Dragon. They serve pub lunches. The menu changes every day, but every Friday it's salmon fish cakes, and August the sixth was a Friday."

"I used to like salmon fish cakes," said Frost, "but not since I saw them swimming around inside Lemmy's stomach. Funny how little things like that can put you off." He spun his chair round as the radio speaker crackled, but it was only static. "Did you check out Custard Cottage?"

"Primrose Cottage. Two sisters, one around forty, the other in her mid-thirties. I haven't spoken to them yet, though."

"Good—we'll do it together—tomorrow morning—remind me." His smile died when he saw Bill Wells making his way over to him. The sergeant's face shouted "trouble." Something had gone wrong.

"Were you going to get Tommy Dunn to plant that homing device, Jack?" Wells asked.

"Yes—why?"

"I wouldn't count on him doing it."

"Why not?" asked Frost, very concerned.

"Tommy's got himself arrested."

Frost's stomach screwed into a tight ball. "Arrested?"

"PC Simms is bringing him in. Tommy was caught nicking two bottles of whisky from Savalot's liquor store."

Frost stared at Wells, hoping and praying he had misheard. "Stealing?"

"Savalot want him charged. And they want his flat searched. They think he's been making a habit of taking their stock home and they'd like some of it back."

Frost stared at the ceiling and swore softly. "Bloody, bloody hell." He punched his palm with his fist and thought quickly. "All right—change of plan. Tell all cars engaged in the exercise that due to circumstances beyond our bleeding control, we won't have the homing signal, so it's vital we don't lose track of Cordwell's car. Circulate the description and registration number to all mobiles. If they sight it, let me know. And tell all mobiles not in the exercise to stand by. We might have to call them in as well if we lose him." He groaned audibly as Mullett marched in. "Oh, no!" The bleeding vultures were descending.

"What's this I'm hearing about Tommy Dunn, Frost?"

He obviously knew all about it, so Frost was terse. "He's been arrested for theft. We won't have the homing device."

Mullett's eyes glinted and he smirked in self-justification. "I warned you about using rubbish like him, but you wouldn't listen and now you must pay the consequences. Can we still go ahead with this without alerting the kidnapper? If that child is harmed because of your incompetence—"

"We can still do it. What I've done is—"

Mullett's hand shot up. He didn't want the details. Hearing them could imply his seal of approval and this would only be forthcoming if everything went off without a hitch. "Just make sure nothing goes wrong."

He turned on his heel and marched to the door, spurred on his way with a V sign behind his back from Frost, who then tapped his desk to get everyone's attention. "Just thought you'd like to know that Mr. Mullett is one hundred percent behind us, providing we pull it off. But if we fail, then God help us!" He drummed his fingers impatiently and looked pleadingly at the speaker, waiting for the next radio report.

"Subject car in car park," radioed Collier. "Cordwell getting out and entering the mall by the side entrance."

A few minutes later Burton called in. "I have Cordwell in sight. He's waiting outside the four phone kiosks."

"Check the phone-bugging devices again," called Frost. If they were going to go wrong, then now was the time.

The officer with the earphones did a quick check and gave the thumbs-up signal. "All working perfectly."

"Right." Frost kept the radio channel to Burton open. They could hear the bustle of shoppers in the mall. The Muzak had stopped, no doubt by Cordwell's orders so he could hear the phone ring. The wall clock in the Incident Room clunked away another minute. The kidnapper was already five minutes late.

"I don't think he's going to phone," said Liz.

"Don't be a bloody pessimist," said Frost. "He's probably in the middle of a long wee-wee. You don't pick up ransom money with a full bladder." Still, only crowd noises emerged from the monitor speaker.

Burton's voice suddenly made everyone sit up. But it was only to report that nothing was happening.

"For Pete's flaming sake!" yelled Frost. He hated people reporting there was nothing to report.

Cassidy came in and stood behind Frost. "What's happening?"

"Sod-all," grunted Frost.

"Did I understand you were going to use Tommy Dunn?" Cassidy asked.

"Yes," said Frost.

"I'd like to talk to you about it," hissed Cassidy.

"Some other bloody time!" snarled Frost. Cassidy was really getting on his nerves tonight. He was relieved when the acting inspector left the room.

Twenty past eight.

"Are you sure the bloody phones in the kiosks are work-ing?" asked Frost. "What if Savalot's security men acciden-tally cut off incoming calls when they cut off the outgoing?"

"You could always try ringing one," suggested Liz.

Frost dragged a phone toward him and dialed.

A yell over the speaker from Burton. *"Cordwell's moving toward a kiosk! The phone's ringing!"*

Frost hastily banged the receiver down. "I know—it was me . . . just testing." This is turning into a flaming farce, he told himself.

Almost immediately Burton was back on the radio. *"Something's happening. A manager from Savalot is running toward Cordwell . . . talking to him. Cordwell's leaving the kiosks . . . they're both running back toward the store."*

"Follow him," hissed Frost. "Don't let the sod out of your sight."

Lots of rustling and roars from the radio as Burton barged his way through the crowd. *"Lost him . . . no, I see him. He's going to the Customer Service Desk. He's picking up their phone. . . . I can't get too near, he'll spot me. . . . He's listening, he's put the phone . . . Now he's going through a* Staff only *door. Do I follow?"*

"No!" snapped Frost. "He's probably gone to get the money. Has he got to come past you again to get to his car?"

"I don't know."

Frost's mind raced. "Right—get down to the car park. Locate his car and let me know when he leaves." He clicked to Collier. "Collier, go to the car park exit and get ready to follow when he leaves. . . . All other units, stand by."

"What's happening?" Sensing that something was going wrong and anxious to witness Frost's discomfiture when it did, Cassidy had returned.

"The sod's put one over on us," Frost told him. "He never intended using the kiosks—must have guessed we'd bug them. He phoned direct to the store."

"So what are you going to do?"

"I'm hoping we can follow without him or the kidnapper spotting us. We might have to anticipate where he's making for and try to get there before him. We play it by ear."

Cassidy smirked to himself. It seemed as if this whole operation could blow up in Frost's face. He was pleased he had expressed his doubts to Mullett when his views were sought. "I foresee trouble, sir," he'd said. "It's too slap-dash." And Mullett had nodded grimly in agreement.

A muffled roar and some fragments of speech, totally incomprehensible, from the loudspeaker. "Say again!" yelled Frost. "Say again!" More gibberish. "What's going on?"

PC Lambert jiggled some switches. "It's the underground car park—the radio can't work down there."

"Tell him to move outside," ordered Frost.

Lambert spoke into the mike, then shook his head. "It's no use. We can't hear him and he can't hear us."

Frost snatched up his radio. "Collier! Cordwell should be coming out any second. Get ready to follow."

"Burton to Control—receiving? Over."

A collective sigh of relief. Burton had moved to an area of better reception. *"Cordwell has put a canvas travel bag on the front seat of his car. He's got a couple of his security men with him, so it must be the money. He's getting in the car . . ."*

"On his own or with the security men?"

"On his own . . . He's driving out now."

Frost clicked on the other radio. "Did you hear that, Collier?"

"Yes . . . I see him. . . . I'm following."

"Don't get too close," pleaded Frost, "but for God's sake, don't lose him."

"I'll try."

"Collier's not up to it," said Cassidy.

"Neither am I," said Frost, "but we've got to use what we've got." He could murder Tommy bloody Dunn. He'd been pinning all his hopes on being able to sit back and follow the homing device.

"Subject turning into Bath Road," reported Collier.

Frost glanced across to Lambert, who was marking up a map. Too soon yet to work out where Cordwell was making for.

"He's turning left . . . he's slowing down . . . I'm not sure, but I think he's spotted me."

"Drive straight past him," ordered Frost. "Don't look at him as you do." He ran across to consult Lambert's map. "He can't turn off until he reaches Hilton Road, so go and wait for him there. Tell me when he passes you."

He lit a cigarette before noticing he already had one smoldering away in the ashtray. He called Burton and told him to get ready to take over the tail from Collier.

The monitor speaker hummed softly to itself, now and again giving a little crackle as if it were going to speak, but nothing. Impatiently Frost snatched up the radio and jabbed the transmit button. "He should have bloody reached you by now, Collier."

"But he hasn't. I'm looking straight down Bath Road . . . visibility's a bit hairy in this rain, but I should be able to see him. There's a couple of lorries, but that's all."

"Damn!" Frost scrubbed his face with his hands, trying to work out what had happened. "The bastard must have done a U-turn! Collier—drive back. If you see him, swing round and follow . . . report to me when you reach where you last saw him."

He stood up and paced around the room, swinging round abruptly as Collier's voice came over the radio.

"I've gone right back to the Bath Road turnoff. No sign of him."

"Shit!" Frost pounded the desk in frustration. "All units, you heard that. Look for the bugger. . . . Report as soon as you get a sniff of him."

The door clicked open and Mullett marched in. He had a genius for turning up at precisely the wrong time. "How's it going?"

"The inspector seems to have lost him," said Cassidy, barely concealing his delight, just as Frost was about to lie and say all was going to plan.

Mullett's face hardened. "Is this correct?"

"Temporary setback," Frost assured. "We'll find him."

"You'd better," snapped Mullett. "You'd damn well better." He marched out.

"He's got a foul tongue, hasn't he?" observed Frost. He suddenly felt he couldn't bear to be cooped up in the claustrophobic Incident Room any longer, just listening and not being a part of things. He grabbed his scarf. "I'm going to join in the hunt. The more cars looking for him, the better." He looked at Cassidy. "Want to come?" He only asked because he was sure the acting inspector intended coming anyway.

Cassidy hesitated. If it all went wrong he wanted no part of it, but if Frost was successful, if he arrested the kidnapper and got the boy back, then Cassidy wanted to be there to share the glory. The thought of glory won. He snatched up his coat and followed Frost out.

They dashed, bent double through the rain, to the Ford. Frost slipped behind the steering wheel and persuaded the engine to start at the third attempt. The car splashed through deep puddles as he maneuvered out of the car park.

"Where are we going?" asked Cassidy.

"I'm heading toward Denton Woods. If I was arranging a cash handover, that's where I'd choose."

"That area is bloody big," said Cassidy.

"So's my dick," grunted Frost, "but I usually manage to find the bit I want." He radioed through to Lambert to ascertain the current position of all mobiles. Lambert reported straight back. As many cars as possible were scouring the town, but there were too many roads which Cordwell could have used and not enough vehicles to cover them. Again Frost cursed Tommy Dunn. With the homing device it would have been a doddle. Without it they were flying blind in the thickest of fogs. Sod Tommy Blood Dunn.

"Tommy Dunn." A voice sliced through his thoughts as if it could read his mind.

"Eh?" Frost's head swiveled round. Cassidy was staring hard at him, waiting for an answer. "Sorry, son, I was miles away."

"I'm not your damn son and I asked you for Tommy Dunn's address."

"I don't know it," muttered Frost, squinting through the windscreen at an approaching car that could have been green. But it wasn't.

"You're a bloody liar," said Cassidy.

Frost didn't reply. Yes, he was lying. He knew Tommy's address but he wasn't going to let Cassidy go round there stirring everything up again. "It happened a long time ago, son. Let the wounds heal."

"You and Tommy made a great team, didn't you? One damned incompetent and the other always on the take."

"I did my best to find that hit-and-run driver, son. We all did. We worked bloody hard, but we failed."

"I don't doubt you did your best, Inspector, but your best is inadequate and bloody pathetic."

Frost shrugged. Cassidy had idolized his daughter and his bitterness at the failure of the investigation, even after all these years, was understandable, if not excusable.

"That bastard hit my daughter at speed, flung her forward, then ran over her and roared off without bothering to see if she was alive or dead. She was smashed to pieces. Fourteen years old. She hadn't lived. She hadn't bloody *lived*!"

"I know, son. I know."

"You know much more than you're damn well saying."

"What do you mean?"

"You let me down four years ago, so I've been making my own inquiries. I've found a witness."

"Oh?" A green car roared passed them, but it was a hand-painted VW Beetle.

"He was in the car park at the Coconut Grove when he saw this car speeding past. Then he heard it pumping its horn, and the smash as it hit my daughter."

"He didn't actually see the accident?"

"No. He went running out to the road and there was a crowd of people and they were looking down at my daughter's body."

"We know all this, son." Frost would never forget that night . . . the flashing blue light as the ambulance was leaving, reflected in the long, untidy smear and the shiny pools of blood inside the chalked outline marked out by the traffic police. He had viewed the broken body in the morgue, the small fourteen-year-old body that had spilt so much blood on the road. The car that hit Becky Cassidy must have been doing close on to a hundred. He had tried to stop Cassidy from seeing her, not until they had tidied her up, but had been pushed aside. The memory of the man's grief and anger still hurt, a mental wound that would never heal. "We know all this," he repeated.

"Then here's something you apparently don't know. There was a BMW parked in the road outside the club that night. The driver was in it. Tommy Dunn was talking to him."

"I've no knowledge of Tommy talking to anyone, son. If he had, there would have been a witness statement."

"Depends on how much Tommy was paid to keep his mouth shut."

Frost lit a cigarette. "It depends on how reliable your witness is. Funny he never told anyone about this at the time."

"He says he told you," said Cassidy.

Frost slowed down. He was driving much too fast. "He's mistaken." Headlights of an approaching car dazzled the windscreen. A white Mercedes. "Look, son, let's drop it for now. We're not concentrating on the job in hand."

"I'd like to see the file on your investigation of Rebecca's death," said Cassidy stubbornly.

"I'll dig it out and let you have it," replied Frost. As soon as he got back to the station he would hide it where no one could find it. There was no way he would let Cassidy see it. And he'd get Tommy Dunn to have a word with this mouthy witness. He knew who he was. He offered a cigarette to Cassidy. It was curtly refused.

"What was Dunn doing at the Coconut Grove that night —collecting bribes?"

"Checking on stolen credit cards," said Frost, twisting his neck as another car sped past. "I never realized there were so many damn green cars in Denton." He sank back gloomily in his seat, squinting at the road ahead through the solid curtain of rain which his squealing windscreen wipers were making pathetic efforts to clear.

"Burton to Inspector Frost. I've found him. Back on the Bath Road, heading north. I'm following."

"Exactly where on the Bath Road?" yelled Frost into the handset as he swung the car around, shooting up a shower of rainwater.

"Just passing Sandown Road."

"Right—Frost to all mobiles. I want two of you to get ahead of him. Charlie Baker—you get to the motorway turnoff, and when he approaches, you take over from Burton. Charlie Abel—tail them both. If it looks as if he's spotted Charlie Baker, then you take over." Frost began to whistle cheerfully. Action: This was more like it.

"Subject turning north into Forest Row," reported Burton.

Frost nodded resignedly. It looked as if Cordwell was heading for Denton Woods, where it would be bloody difficult to keep track of him once he left his car. It now needed lots more men than he had available. And yet again that evening he bitterly cursed Tommy Dunn for dropping him in it like this.

"He's slowing . . . he's slowing," reported Burton. *"He's stopped!"*

"Where?" yelled Frost. "Just in case we might want to know."

"Sorry. By the public call box, corner of Forest View. He's getting out of the car . . . making for the call box. He's waiting and checking his watch. The phone's ringing . . . he's answered it. Now he's hung up and he's dashing back to the Nissan."

"It must be the final instructions for the drop," said Frost. "Don't lose him . . . we'll be with you soon."

Burton braked. He was getting too close. A short way back he had lost sight of the Nissan and had jammed down on the accelerator, only to have to slam on the brakes to avoid shooting up its backside. Luckily Cordwell had other things on his mind and did not seem to notice.

The road wriggled into another sharp bend and again the rear lights of Cordwell's car slipped out of sight. Burton accelerated as much as he dared. The weather conditions were making the road surface treacherous. As he negotiated the bend, he cursed. The Nissan had stopped. Had Cordwell seen him? Was he, perhaps, checking to see if he was being followed? Burton drove straight past, avoiding turning his head as he passed the Nissan, but at the very next bend, he slowed and bumped the car up onto the grass verge. Quickly, he stuffed the radio into the pocket of his raincoat, slung the night glasses round his neck, and stepped out into torrential rain.

Running back toward the oak tree, he reported to Frost. *"He's stopped."*

"Where?" asked Frost.

"The big oak alongside Forest Common."

"What's he doing now?"

Burton didn't know. He couldn't see a flaming thing. He couldn't even see the car. Cordwell had switched off the lights and the rain was making visibility very limited. *"Wait,"* he panted, dropping the radio back in his pocket and getting out the night glasses.

He located the oak tree, then moved down to the car. It was empty. He panned the common. Bushes . . . trees . . . He'd lost him . . . he'd damn well lost him. He began swinging the glasses wildly from left to right, hoping to pick up something. What was that? Something white. He held the glasses steady on Cordwell in his white mac. Thank goodness it was a white raincoat, otherwise he might never have spotted him. He adjusted the focus. Cordwell was carrying something. The money bag.

He became aware of squawkings from his pocket. The radio. Frost pleading for some news. He fished it out and reported breathlessly, *"Have subject in sight. Will report back."* He raised the night glasses again. Damn. Bushes, trees . . . but no sign of Cordwell. He panned quickly from left to right. Nothing. Where the hell was he? He almost shook with relief when he again picked up a blur of white. Cordwell emerging from a line of bushes and bramble. He was coming back. Returning to his car. Had he made the drop? At first Burton wasn't sure. Cordwell was at the wrong angle. But when he turned toward the oak, Burton could see that the supermarket chief no longer had the travel bag.

He pulled out the radio and brought the anxious Frost up to date. *"He's made the drop."*

A sigh of relief from Frost. "Good boy. What's he doing now?"

The night glasses followed him. *"He's going back to his car."*

The sound of the Nissan's engine could just be heard

over the drumming of the rain. *"He's reversing. He's heading back to Denton."*

Frost ducked his head as approaching headlights flared in the windscreen and Cordwell roared past them. He radioed Charlie Baker, the area car, to wait by Sandown Road and, as soon as Cordwell passed, to follow him at a discreet distance. "If he goes anywhere but straight home, I want to know." The kidnapper was such a wily bastard, all that had happened could have been a feint and the money could still be with Cordwell to be dumped elsewhere.

Looming ahead of them, creaking in the wind, was the large oak tree where Cordwell had parked. Frost slowed, squinting through the windscreen for Burton's car. He spotted it just round the next bend and bumped up on the grass verge to park behind it. He and Cassidy climbed out and peered into rain and darkness. No sign of Burton. "Where are you, son?" Frost whispered into his radio. Burton blinked his torch a few times and they homed in on his signal.

It was an uncomfortable walk in the dark over bumpy and puddle-ridden ground, fighting against the wind and the rain, and it was making Cassidy's stomach hurt like hell. Was this why Frost had asked him along—to show up his damn weakness? If so, and he winced as a flame of pain rippled across his stomach, if so, Frost was going to be disappointed.

Burton was crouched behind the trunk of a stunted tree. Not much of a place to hide, but better than nothing. He pointed to a dark mass ahead and handed Frost the night glasses. "The money is behind there somewhere."

Frost shook off the rain and raised them to his eyes. "I can't see a bleeding thing." He tried again. "Ah—got it."

Cassidy took the glasses. "Those bushes?" he exclaimed. "They're seventy yards away. Can't we get any closer?"

"It's all open ground," said Burton. "We'd be seen."

"So where's the money?"

"Round the back somewhere," Burton told him.

"Somewhere? Can't you be more precise?"

"I saw him go behind with the money and come back without it."

"So it could be any of those flaming bushes and we're on the wrong side seventy yards away."

Burton indicated the sprawling terrain. "There's nowhere on the other side to hide. We'd be seen miles away."

"What about those bushes there?" Cassidy pointed.

Frost gave them a glance, then shook his head. There was too much open ground between them. "We couldn't get to them without being seen." He jabbed a finger at the mass of trees in the background, the start of Denton Woods. "For all we know he's in among those trees, so even if you go over there, he'd spot you. This is as good a place as any."

The call light on the receiver flashed. Burton turned the volume down and listened. Charlie Baker reporting in. Cordwell had made one stop on the way back—at a phone box. As he approached it, it rang. He spoke briefly, then drove straight home.

"The kidnapper wanting confirmation the drop had been made," said Frost. "He must have phoned from a call box. Where's the nearest one from here?"

"The one in Forest Row," said Burton.

"If that was the one he used, he should be here in less than ten minutes," said Frost to Burton. "Get back to your car and wait and be ready to tail him after he collects the money."

"He might not have used that one," objected Cassidy. "He might have a mobile phone. For all we know he could be standing in those trees over there, watching."

"If he had a mobile phone and was standing in those trees," said Frost, "he'd have seen Cordwell drop the money and wouldn't have needed to make the phone call." He nodded Burton on his way.

Burton hurried off while Frost panned the area through the night glasses to see if he could spot anyone watching them. A radio call came from Burton. He was back in his car awaiting further instructions.

Frost consulted his wristwatch. Nine forty-six. His clothes were sodden and rain was beating down on them. Too wet to smoke and nothing to do but to wait.

They waited.

CHAPTER TWELVE

Cassidy wriggled and tried to make himself comfortable on the soaking wet grass. "How long do you think we'll have to wait?" he whispered to Frost, shivering as the cold wind roared across the open ground, driving rain straight into them.

"Not too long," muttered Frost, scanning the far ground through the night glasses. "There's too much money just lying around. He won't want to risk anyone else finding it."

"Car coming," reported Burton over the radio.

They held their breath and waited. But the car sped past. And so did the next.

A lull in the traffic and Frost went back to his surveillance of the bleak-looking area. It was tricky using the night glasses and he hadn't got the hang of them. Every now and then his view would be completely obscured as a large bush or tree trunk took up the entire field of vision. He swung back to the bushes where the ransom was hidden. He wasn't happy with their situation. The money bag was on the other side of the bushes and they couldn't see it. He scoured the area with the glasses, looking for somewhere where they could at least see the travel bag, but there was nowhere. Back to those trees where—

A clap of thunder and the heavens opened. Rain drummed on the ground. They had to shout to hear each other. Cassidy wiped stinging rain from his eyes and brushed back dripping wet hair. "Bloody weather!" he snarled.

"It's perfect," said Frost. "No one but kidnappers and prats of policemen would be out in this. Whoever turns up has got to be our man." Again he raised the glasses and focused on some trees eighty yards or so away. Just before the downpour, he thought he had seen something move. The stair-rods of rain were making it difficult to see anything and he was just convincing himself he was mistaken when . . . Yes, there it was. He nudged Cassidy. "I spy, with my little eye, something that looks like a motor."

"Where?" hissed Cassidy, straining his eyes into the blurred darkness.

Frost handed him the glasses and pointed. "Behind the trees."

Cassidy panned carefully. He located the tree and . . . yes, Frost was right. Half-hidden . . . a car. He locked onto it, holding his breath and bracing himself to steady the field glasses. A Ford Escort. The night glasses gave everything a green tinge, but it was a light color . . . cream, brown, or grey, perhaps. "I see it. Its lights are out."

Frost grunted. "Most of the cars that come down here turn their lights out. They only turn them on if the girl can't find her knickers afterward. Can you see anyone inside?"

Cassidy stared hard, trying to penetrate the curtain of blurring rain. "No."

"Let me have a go." Frost took the glasses.

"Shall we pick him up?"

"No," said Frost. "Until he collects the money, we've nothing on him. . . . Hello . . ." He steadied the glasses and started to chuckle. . . .

"What is it?" hissed Cassidy.

"You'd better see this."

Cassidy snatched the glasses, then he snorted with disgust. The car was bouncing up and down on its springs and the windows were well steamed up.

"Not our kidnapper, I'm afraid," said Frost ruefully. Then he remembered a poem he'd seen on a lavatory wall once and began to recite:

> "You could tell he was a master,
>   In the art of love.
>   First the slight withdrawal
>   Then the mighty shove."

Cassidy snorted his disgust. Hadn't Frost got any damn taste? They were trying to catch the killer of a child, for Christ's sake!

The car gave a sudden lurch. "Flaming heck," said Frost with admiration. "I bet that brought the color to her cheeks."

"Bloody animals!" snarled Cassidy.

But Frost was lost in recollection. "I used to come here and behave like a bloody animal. . . . Long time ago of course . . ."–It was when he was in his teens, young and lusty. Who was that dark girl . . . ? What was her name . . . ? And then he remembered. Flaming heck, how could he have forgotten! It was his wife. Long before they were married. She was a little doll in those days . . . bouncy little figure, jet-black hair, snub nose, and she thought the world of him . . . that showed how long ago it was! A time, before all the rows, when everything marvelous was going to happen. When they made plans about getting married, about him joining the police force and rising in the ranks to chief superintendent. It all came back . . . that night . . . that summer night when it was so hot you could have trampled through the grass in the nude at midnight and not feel cold. That was when it happened for the first time . . . when he undressed her and—

Someone was shaking his arm. "Frost!"

"Eh?" It wasn't a summer night any more. It was peeing with rain and he was wet and cold. Cassidy was shaking his arm and pointing back to the road. "What did you say?"

"Another car coming!"

All they could see at first were the headlights shining blearily through the rain. Then the car. A dark blue Austin Metro.

"He's slowing down," said Cassidy in excitement. "He's stopped . . . the bugger's stopped!"

Frost squinted through the glasses. He could just about make out the figure at the wheel. There didn't appear to be anyone else in the car, which splashed to a stop, almost dead in line with the clump of bushes hiding the ransom money.

"It's him!" hissed Frost. "It's bloody got to be him."

For some minutes the car just stood there, engine ticking, lights on. Then the lights went out, the engine was switched off, and the only sound was the drumming rain.

"Keep down," hissed Frost, tugging at Cassidy, who was raising his head to get a better view.

They waited. Frost was able to wriggle through the long glass and pick out the Austin's registration number through the binoculars. Cassidy whispered it into the radio for Control to check. The reply came back in seconds. The registered owner was a Henry Finch, 2 Lincoln Road, Denton. The car hadn't been reported stolen and nothing was known about the owner.

Frost grabbed the radio. "The kidnapper would be a prat driving his own car. The owner may not have realized his motor's gone. Phone Finch and ask where his car is. If he says it's parked in the street outside, then we know this one's been nicked. If there's no answer, send an area car round to his house to nose around. If Finch is the kidnapper the kid might be in the house. Get cracking!"

"Will do," acknowledged Control. *"Don't switch off—Mr. Mullett wants a word."*

"Over and out," said Frost, dropping the radio back in his pocket.

Cassidy nudged him. "Someone's getting out of the car."

The driver's door had swung open and a man in a dark blue raincoat, shortish and plump, got out, snapping open an umbrella before stepping gingerly over a puddle. For a while he stood still, head turning from side to side, like an animal checking for signs of danger. It was difficult to make out his features as rain streamed off the umbrella and curtained down to the ground. Frost guessed he would be somewhere in his late fifties.

There seemed to be no one else in the car. Frost nodded his satisfaction. "Not a courting couple and this is definitely not the weather for a peeping tom. . . . This could be our bloke!" Then he frowned. "Bloody hell . . . what's he doing now?" The man had turned and was leaning back inside the car. He seemed to be taking something from the glove compartment and stuffing it into his pocket.

"Did you see what it was?" asked Cassidy. "Could it have been a gun?"

"I flaming hope not," said Frost. "It looked too small for a gun." He had the glasses firmly fixed on the man, who was now opening the rear passenger door and looked as if he was talking to someone inside. His mouth was moving but the wind tore the words to shreds before they reached them.

"There's someone else in there!" said Cassidy.

"They must be bleeding small, then," said Frost, "because I can't see anyone."

The man, huddling under the umbrella, took a few steps, then turned and called out something. A small white and brown Jack Russell terrier, its tail docked far too short, jumped from the back seat, yapping excitedly. The man closed the car door, then took the object from his mac pocket, a well-chewed tennis ball which he hurled across the waste ground, urging the dog to fetch it. Undeterred by the rain, the little dog raced after it while the man stood by the car and watched.

Cassidy snorted his disappointment. "He's exercising his damn dog. He's not our bloke after all."

"Worse than that," said Frost glumly. "Him and bloody Rin-Tin-Tin bloody dog could drive the real kidnapper away."

The radio in his pocket called him. Control reporting. As ordered they had rung Finch's number. No reply. An area car had been dispatched and was at the house now. The house was in darkness and no one answered their knocking. A neighbor said she had seen Mr. Finch drive off with his dog about half an hour ago.

Frost grunted resignedly. It was just telling them what they already knew. This flaming clown had stumbled on the very spot the ransom money was to be collected from and was going to play ball with Fido all flaming night.

The cigarette he tugged from the packet was sodden before he could get his lighter to it. He shoved it into his top pocket to dry out for later. That damn man, seemingly oblivious to the belting rain, was huddled under the umbrella, calmly hurling the ball, and no sooner had the dog retrieved it, than he would take it and fling it again. Bite the bastard, Frost silently urged the animal. A cold trickle of rain ran down the inside of his upturned collar. He was wet, and uncomfortable, and was getting that all-too-familiar feeling that, bad as things were, they were going to get a bloody sight worse. He could sense the smirk of satisfaction at his discomfiture on Cassidy's face.

Then, in a flash, his despair evaporated. The dog had returned with the ball, which he dumped proudly at the man's feet, its stump of a tail wagging wildly. Scooping up the ball, the man suddenly turned at right angles and hurled it straight into the midst of the clump of bushes where the money was hidden, apparently unobserved by the dog, which was still sniffing around in the grass. They could hear the man saying "Fetch, fetch!" and pointing to the bushes, but the dog just yapped its puzzlement and jumped up at him for the ball to be thrown again.

Finch bent down and picked up the dog, then carried it back to the car. With the waggle of a finger, telling the dog to "Be good!" he turned and walked back toward the bushes, disappearing from view behind them.

"It was him all the time!" breathed Frost. "He's putting on a bloody good act, but it's him!" He radioed through to Burton. "Get ready to tail him, son. He's collecting the money now." There was no denying the simple brilliance of Finch's ploy. If the police pounced, he could feign innocence—he was simply looking for his dog's ball—and if he had already collected the money, he could claim he found it by accident. And there'd be no way we could prove otherwise, thought Frost . . . unless the bastard has got the kid in the boot of his car. He swung the binoculars over to the Austin. All he could see was the brown and white head of the Jack Russell, paws up at the window, waiting for its master.

Control radioed through. A further report from the area car at Finch's house. They had nosed around as much as they could without actually breaking in. Nothing obviously suspicious could be seen from the outside.

"Tell them to stay put," said Frost. If Finch was arrested they could help search the premises. He clicked off and returned to his surveillance of the thicket. "Hasn't he come out yet?"

Cassidy shook his head.

Frost wiped the rain from his eyes and raised the glasses again. He stared at the thicket until his eyes hurt. No movement. Nothing. "He's taking his damn time." Worry started gnawing. "Could he have come out and we didn't see him?"

"We'd see him going for his car," said Cassidy. Then a thought struck him. "Unless he's letting us watch the Austin and he's got another car parked further up the road for his getaway."

"Shit!" Frost hadn't thought of this. He turned and looked again at the Austin. The dog was still staring out of the window. It seemed to be whimpering. "I can't see him abandoning his dog," said Frost. "The bastard might kill a kid, but he'd never leave his dog." He hoped and prayed he was right and that the dog wasn't some poor stray Finch had collected from the gutter on the way over.

Cassidy came up with another depressing theory. "We're not even certain this man is Finch. He could have pinched Finch's car and his dog and left Finch tied up somewhere."

Frost checked his watch. "How long has he been behind there?" It seemed like hours, but was only six minutes. Finch might have grabbed the money and they were sitting here like a couple of wallys, staring at a lousy bush. On the other hand, if they charged across now, they might find Finch doing a long pee and the real kidnapper could spot them and jag it in. He sighed. Whatever he did could be wrong. But he always believed that doing something was much better than doing nothing. He jerked his head at Cassidy and stood up. "Come on—let's take a look."

"I think we should wait," said Cassidy, just to get it on record that he had his doubts. But Frost was already lumbering over the soggy, uneven ground. Cassidy pushed himself up, hissing in agony at the damp-aggravated pain from his scar. He hobbled along behind Frost, moving as quickly as he could while stamping his foot and muttering about "Damn cramp."

They split and went around each side of the thicket, Cassidy praying that Finch wouldn't break away in a run. There was no way he could run after him.

At first it seemed that Finch had managed to take the ransom and make off without being seen. Their torches slashed through the darkness, the beams steaming in the rain. There was no one there. A noise. "What was that?" They listened. Just the drumming of the rain, then . . . There it was again. A groan. Frost directed his torch downward. Someone sprawled on the ground. It was Finch.

He was lying facedown in the long grass and as they turned him over the dog's ball rolled from the pocket of his raincoat. His eyes were closed and the blood trickling from a swelling lump on his forehead was diluted to a watery pink and spread over his face by the rain. He felt cold. As Cassidy radioed for an ambulance Frost looked everywhere, beating the grass flat, kicking aside the thick carpet of fallen leaves, looking for the travel bag. It had gone.

"The Ford Escort!" exclaimed Frost. "The bloody Ford Escort!" He turned the glasses toward the trees. No sign of the damn thing. He fumbled for the radio and called up Control. "Message for all mobiles. I'm anxious to interview the occupants of a Ford Escort, lightish color, last seen on the outskirts of Denton Woods by Forest Row. Believe man and woman inside. Any vehicles answering this description to be stopped and held."

"Do you have details of the registration number?" asked Control.

"If I had, I would have bloody-well told you!" shouted Frost.

"It's not much to go on," said Control.

"It had four wheels and two red lights at the back," snarled Frost. "Does that help?"

"Thank you," said Lambert, his mildness tacitly rebuking Frost's outburst. *"Mr. Mullett wants a word."*

"How did it go?" asked Mullett eagerly.

Frost stared at the radio, trying to think of a pithy reply that would shut Mullett up for all time. The bugger never asked how things had gone when they had gone off brilliantly. "Couple of minor snags, Super," he said. "I'll fill you in when I get back."

"Snags?" roared Mullett. *"What snags?"*
But Frost had switched off.

The junior house doctor, looking dead tired, came into the waiting room. "Inspector Frost?"

Frost stood up, pinching out the cigarette and dropping it into his mac pocket. "How is he?"

"He's had a nasty knock. Mild concussion, nothing serious. We'll keep an eye on him tonight, but he can go home tomorrow."

"Is he conscious?"

"Yes, but I'd prefer it if you didn't question him tonight."

"Your preference noted, Doc, but I've got a missing seven-year-old kid. . . ."

The doctor shrugged and pointed to the end bed where a young nurse was twitching back the curtains. He yawned again. He was too tired to argue.

Frost shuffled over to the bed. He too was tired. It had been a long day and the adrenaline that had kept him hyped up while they were waiting for the ransom to be collected was now drained by failure. He felt ready to drop. The little nurse smiled. She recognized him. The number of visits he had made at night to the hospital. The times they had called him in because they hadn't thought his wife would last out until the morning, but she had hung on. There was an empty bed in the center of the row, its clean white sheets folded back. Frost wished he could just climb in and go straight off to sleep. But Mullett was waiting for him back at the station. There was a bollocking to be got through before he could enjoy the luxury of sleep.

The clipboard at the foot of the bed read: "Henry Alan Finch, aged 66." There were figures for temperature and blood pressure and a scribbled prescription for painkillers.

Finch looked older than when he had climbed out of his

car. Plumpish, with thinning ginger hair and a clipped ginger moustache. He had the appearance of a retired army officer. His face was grey, his eyes were closed, and his breathing heavy, almost a snore. A rectangle of plaster covered the wound on his forehead.

Frost dragged a chair up to the bed and dropped down into it. He loosened his scarf and unbuttoned his mac. The ward was hot and he had to fight off the urge to close his own eyes and drift off to sleep. "Mr. Finch?"

The eyes fluttered open and the man winced as he swiveled his head to look at Frost. "Who are you?" he said softly.

Frost held up his warrant card. Finch blinked at it. "Where's my dog?"

"At the station. He's being looked after. How do you feel?"

"I'm all right. I want to go home." He squinted down the darkened ward. "Where's the nurse?"

"A couple of questions first. What were you doing on the common at that time of night?"

"Taking the dog for a run."

"In the peeing rain?"

"I do it every night. There's no law against it, is there?"

"Do you always go to the common?"

"Yes." His eyes were still focused down the ward. "Nurse!"

"What happened tonight?"

"Some bastard attacked me—knocked me out."

"Let's take it step by step. We saw you pull up in your car."

Finch's eyes narrowed. "What were you doing there?"

"Never mind why we were there. You're lucky we were. You could have been lying unconscious all night and ended up with pneumonia. You pulled up in the car. You took your time getting out—why?"

"The rain suddenly came down heavily. I was wondering whether to give it a miss."

"But you didn't?"

"Czar was all excited. I didn't want to disappoint him."

"Did you see anyone else about?"

"No."

"There was another car parked under the trees. Did you see that?"

"No." Finch gritted his teeth as he wriggled his back and tried to make himself comfortable. "Do you want me to tell you what happened?"

"Please."

"I was throwing the ball for Czar when it went into those bushes. I tried to get him to fetch it, but he wasn't interested, so I put him in the car and went off to look for it."

"In all that rain? A lot of trouble for a ball." Frost fished the well-chewed, almost bald tennis ball from his pocket and placed it on the bedside locker.

"Have you got a dog?"

"No," admitted Frost.

"Then you don't bloody know! It was Czar's favorite ball. If you had a dog, you'd understand."

"Okay. You went behind the clump of bushes . . ."

"I was looking for the ball when I saw this travel bag. It looked new and felt heavy. It was still fairly dry so I guessed it hadn't been there long. I decided to lug it back to the car and hand it in to the police station in the morning."

"Very commendable," said Frost. "You weren't at all curious as to what might have been inside?"

Finch sighed. "All right. I was going to take it home and force the lock. If it was full of drugs, I'd take it to the police, but if it was money . . ." He twitched his shoulders. "Well, I don't know. But I never had the chance to find out how honest I was. Suddenly this lout is there. He says 'Ah, you've found my bag . . . thanks very much,' and tries to get it off me."

"Did you give it to him?"

"No, I damn well didn't. So he threatened me. He said,

'If you don't want to get hurt, granddad, just hand it over,'
and he balls his fists as if he's going to hit me. Me—I was in
the war. I fought for bastards like him. 'Just you try it,
sonny,' I said. So he shrugs as if to say 'You win' and makes
to go. Like a silly sod I turned my back on him and, wham!,
he's belted me with a brick or something. I hit the ground
with a thud. The next thing I knew I was in the ambulance."

"Can you describe him?"

"About five feet nine, clean-shaven, and a sneer on his
bloody face."

"How old, do you reckon?"

"I don't know—mid-twenties, I suppose."

"Color of hair?"

"Couldn't see—he wore one of those anorak things with
the hood up."

"What color anorak?"

"Dark blue, red lining, and sort of rabbit's fur round the
hood."

"Trousers?"

"Dark—darkish . . . didn't pay much attention to
them. But I'll tell you something. I'd recognize him anywhere. Let me get near him when he hasn't got a brick in his
hand, I'll show the little swine."

Frost was now beaming. "You'd recognize him?"

"Like a bloody shot!"

Frost jumped up. He wasn't tired now. "Nurse—get this
gentleman his clothes. He's coming with me."

The dog, sensing its master was in the station, was yapping
almost hysterically. Sergeant Wells let it into the Interview
Room where it went mad, jumping up at Finch, its stumpy
tail a blur. Finch was settled down at the table with a cup of
tea from the vending machine and the books of photographs

placed in front of him. "Take your time," said Frost. "If you're not sure, just say so."

"If he's in your books, I'll spot him," said Finch firmly. He took a swig at the tea, patted the dog, which was now stretched out on the floor at his feet, and turned the first page. Frost left him with Burton and went into his office.

Another batch of paperwork had been heaped in his in-tray, most of it nagging rubbish from Mullett. Didn't the sod have anything better to do? He flopped heavily into his chair, lit up a cigarette, and pulled the tray toward him, at the same time dragging the wastepaper basket over with his foot. The first three were Mullett memos beginning "When may I expect . . . ?" "You can expect whenever you flaming well like," Frost muttered, "but you're not going to get." He screwed them into a ball and flipped them into the bin. The fourth was again from Mullett: ". . . I have repeatedly asked for . . ." It joined the others.

"Ah, Frost, there you are! I've been waiting for you in my office."

Heck! Hornrim flaming Harry! He had been putting off attending the old log cabin for his bollocking until he had some good news from Finch to take the edge off it.

"I was just coming, Super."

Mullett eyed the screwed-up balls of paper in the waste-paper bin. They looked suspiciously like the memos he had dictated earlier. "I sent you some memos," he said.

"Did you?" said Frost, all wide-eyed and innocent. "I haven't come across them yet." He jumped from his chair and footed the waste bin under his desk. "What was it you wanted to see me about?" He followed Mullett to his office.

Mullett went on and on. Frost managed to shut most of it out, but the words "fiasco," "ill-conceived," "sloppy," and "utter disgrace" kept filtering through. The old log cabin, like the hospital, was overheated and that, plus Mullett's droning, was sending him to sleep. His head began to droop, then snapped up as his autopilot told him Mullett was expecting an answer.

"Sorry, Super . . . won't happen again," Frost muttered, hoping it was the right response.

"Sorry! Sorry isn't good enough," said Mullett, getting his second wind.

Isn't it, thought Frost, then what about "balls!"? How was this helping? He was just working himself up to the point where he was going to tell Mullett to stuff his flaming job when he was saved by the bell. The phone.

Annoyed at being interrupted, Mullett snatched at it. "Mullett," he barked. A look of alarm crossed his face. He clapped a hand over the mouthpiece. "It's Sir Richard Cordwell," he hissed. Back to the phone. "Hello, Sir Richard . . . Yes, I've just got into the office and I believe that what you say is correct. I know he gave his word. I shall look into it. . . . I don't know the details. . . . I wasn't involved, of course. . . . No, disappointingly, the man got away. . . . No, regretfully, we have no idea who he is. . . ." He eased the phone away from his ear and the buzzing of angry invective crackled round the room. At a pause for breath from the other end, Mullett smiled ingratiatingly into the mouthpiece and asked, "I suppose the kidnapper hasn't contacted *you* with news of the boy's release?" He winced and pulled the phone away again as another molten lava of abuse erupted from the earpiece. "No contact from the kidnapper," he hissed superfluously to Frost. Back to the phone. "Yes, Sir Richard, but I don't really think you can blame us. . . . Oh, come . . . that's hardly fair. . . ." His feeble interjections were receiving short shrift.

The internal phone buzzed and, at Mullett's signaling, Frost, who was wondering if this might not be a good opportunity to slip out, answered it. It was an excited Burton.

"Mr. Finch has made an identification. We're checking it out now."

"Is he sure?" said Frost, waving down Mullett, who was signaling for him to be quiet.

"He says he's bloody positive."

Frost put the phone down and waved to Mullett, who again slapped his hand over the mouthpiece. "We could have an identification. If so, we could make the arrest tonight."

Mullett hesitated. "Is he definite?"

"He says he's positive. I'm checking on it now."

A deep sigh of relief from Mullett, who conveyed this information to Cordwell. "I'll be back to you very shortly," the superintendent assured him. "You'll be the first to know, Sir Richard." He replaced the phone and gave it a little satisfied pat. "I'll come with you," he told Frost.

Mullett followed him back to the Interview Room where a smugly self-satisfied Finch was leaning back in his chair, his hand ruffling the neck of his dog. "Definitely him," he told Frost proudly. "I'd know him anywhere. I never forget a face."

Mullett beamed and gave the dog a couple of tentative pats while Frost studied the details under a photograph of a scowling youth. Richard Francis Hartley, aged twenty-four. Lots of petty offenses, scaling up to robbery with violence for which he had served a two-year stretch. Not one of Frost's arrests, so he couldn't place him, but from his mug shot, Hartley looked a real right charmer.

The door opened and Burton looked in. He caught Frost's eye and beckoned, at the same time giving the thumbs-down sign to signal it was not good news. A dismayed Frost moved to sidle out but Mullett wanted to hear the good news firsthand and called Burton in.

Burton cleared his throat. "A slight complication," he said. "The man Mr. Finch positively identified is in the remand center at Bister. He's been there for the past two weeks."

Mullet glared at Frost, whose fault this clearly was. "Typical," he snapped. "Damn typical!"

"I could have sworn it was him," said Finch, completely unabashed. "If it wasn't him, it was someone very much like him."

"The courts don't go much on look-alikes," said Frost. "They insist on the real thing."

"Sorry." Finch shrugged, taking the dog's lead.

"Never mind," smiled Frost through clenched teeth. "We'll catch him."

"When you do," said Finch, "just give me a shout. I'll identify him."

"Or someone very much like him," added Frost as the door closed. "Stupid old sod." He dropped into the chair vacated by Finch. The tiredness was back.

"Tonight's stupidity was not confined to him," said Mullett significantly.

Frost was too tired to come up with an answer. He could barely make the V sign as Mullett left. From outside he could hear Finch's dog yapping. Bloody dog. It had the chance to bite Mullett and didn't do so. He took another look at the photograph Finch had identified. "I suppose he hasn't got a twin brother who's done time for kidnapping?"

Burton grinned and shook his head. "A sister on the game, that's all."

A match flared as Frost scratched it down the side of the table and lit up. "Not one of my better days, son. We don't know who the kidnapper is, we've lost the money, and the kid isn't back. On the credit side, Mullett isn't very happy, but even that doesn't entirely cheer me up." The Interview Room door opened and Cassidy came in. Frost forced a smile of welcome. "You've heard about Finch's identification?"

"Yes, rotten luck," said Cassidy, in a tone completely devoid of sympathy. "We've got Snell."

"Good," said Frost. He was too bloody tired to care. "Where was he?"

"PC Jordan spotted him driving away from his mother's place. He went back again to collect his things. They're bringing him in now."

"Terrific!"

"I'd like to do the questioning."

"Sure." He wasn't going to fight over the questioning. All he wanted to do was go to bed. In any event, he wasn't sold on the idea that Snell had killed the woman and the kids. He stood up and wound his scarf round his neck. "See you in the morning."

"Yes," agreed Cassidy. "In the morning."

A tap at the door. "Do you want Snell in here?" asked Wells.

Cassidy nodded. He decided to ignore the lack of a "sir" or "inspector." "Yes, Sergeant. Bring him in." He quickly sat down in the chair vacated by Frost in case the inspector decided to stay after all, then smiled in anticipation as Jordan and Simms ushered in Snell. The man looked frightened. None of his cockiness from the previous day remained. It was Frost he turned to.

"I didn't do it, Mr. Frost. I never touched them."

Frost pointed to Cassidy. "This is the gentleman you tell your lies to tonight, Sidney."

Cassidy indicated the chair opposite him. "Sit down."

As Snell dragged out the chair, his coat sleeve rode up, showing the edge of the bandage round his wrist. Frost grabbed his arm and pulled the sleeve back further. "Hurt yourself, Sidney?"

Snell snatched his arm away. "Cut myself," he muttered.

"What with—the edge of a sharp Bible?"

Cassidy showed concern as Frost started to unwind his scarf as if he had decided to stay. There was no way he was going to let Frost elbow his way in for a share of the lime-light. "I'll see you in the morning, then, Inspector."

Frost took the hint and, with a brief nod, wandered out to the car park. He heard hurrying footsteps clattering down the corridor behind him. A grim-faced Mullett in his tailored overcoat was determined to get out of the station before Cordwell rang back to ask about the promised arrest of the kidnapper.

"Mr. Mullett!"

Mullett's brow creased with annoyance as Wells hurried after him. "Sir Richard Cordwell on the phone. Wants to know if we've made the arrest."

"Tell him I've left," said Mullett, pushing open the doors to the car park. "Tell him you can't contact me."

Wells stood by Frost, staring at the undignified sight of the divisional commander, overcoat flapping, running to his car. "Then he wants to speak to you, Jack."

"Tell him I'm with Mr. Mullett," said Frost.

Now that there was no need to lie in the open on wet grass, the rain had eased off. He didn't drive straight home. For some reason he detoured and took the road by the golf course, finding himself coasting down Cresswell Street where he stopped outside the house and switched off the engine. The murder house, dark and silent like the other houses in the street, but a different dark, a different silence. A creaking sound. The front gate swinging in the wind, the way it was swinging when Mark Grover came home in the early hours of the morning. Frost climbed out of the car to click it shut, then decided to take a quick look around.

His footsteps crunched up the path. The evening paper was poking from the letter box. No one had stopped delivery. The uncollected newspapers signaled that the house was empty, an open invitation to burglars. Frost pushed it through and heard it plop on the doormat. On impulse he

took the key from his pocket and let himself in. Still the
lingering smell of Johnson's baby powder. Still that terrible
silence. Not a rustle, not a creak. He dug down deep in his
mac pocket for a torch and let the beam creep along the
passage. He glanced up the stairs. But he didn't want to go
into that empty bedroom with its row of sad-faced dolls.

On to the kitchen. All the mugs the police had used had
now been washed up and the place looked neat and tidy.
Crossing to the back door, he undid the bolts and stepped
outside to the garden. The sheet of plywood covering the
broken glass panel had been removed by Forensic for tests
on the traces of blood and skin tissue. A new square of ply
had been nailed securely in place. Was he standing where
Snell had stood, where Snell had poked his hand through
and let himself in? The same Snell he could have arrested,
but had let off with a caution because he was too damn lazy
and wanted someone else to do all the paperwork.

He stepped back into the kitchen and bolted the door.
An involuntary shiver shook his body, so strong was the aura
of tragedy that pervaded the house. What the hell was he
doing here? He pocketed the torch and hurried back to his
car where Cassidy, oozing smugness, was calling on the radio, anxious to impart his news.

*"Thought you'd like to know, Inspector. Forensic have done
a quick test. Every indication that the blood and skin on the
plywood panel definitely came from Snell. They also found
small splinters of plywood on his wrist. So we've got our killer."*

"Terrific!" said Frost, trying to sound pleased.

*"I've phoned Mr. Mullett. He's over the moon, although he
feels it's a great pity Snell wasn't arrested yesterday. He says he
would like to have a word with you about it tomorrow."*

"I can't wait," said Frost. He clicked off and chucked the
radio down on the passenger seat alongside him. Three little
kids and their mother. Would they still be alive if he had
locked Snell up? He had never felt more guilt-ridden, more
inadequate, and more bloody useless as a policeman than he

did right now. He reached into the glove compartment for the duty-frees Shirley had given him.

He shouldn't have drunk the whisky. He tried to work out how long it had been since he had had anything substantial to eat, but gave it up. It was too far back. Too much spirit on an empty stomach. He yawned, but fought off sleep, although the urge to close his eyes just for a few minutes was almost irresistible. He would drive home and go straight to bed. It required a lot of concentration to start up the engine. Very, very carefully he eased the car from the curb and turned back toward the town. It was so hot inside the car. He loosened his scarf as he turned onto the ring road.

At first he drove slowly, but gradually, so gradually he was hardly aware of it, the Ford gathered speed. Huddles of trees and houses swished past and then he was racing down the main road to the town.

Not another car in sight. Ahead of him he could see, in diminishing dots of color, approaching traffic lights pin-pricking into the distance like a string of tiny fairy lamps. He wound down the window and let the cold slap of the slipstream cool his head. That whisky was a mistake, a bloody mistake. He was feeling light-headed. He fought off the urge to drive straight round to Mullett's house, throw stones at his bedroom window, and demand, "If you've anything to say to me, bloody say it now."

At the junction of Bath Road the traffic lights had changed to red, but he took a chance. As the car floated across the junction there was the vibrating clang of a sudden hammer blow. It made him jerk forward, snapping against the restraint of the seat belt. Then a splintering and a shattering of glass and the furious blasting of a horn. He slammed on his brakes and stared through the windscreen in dismay. He had smacked into a dirty great expensive-looking motor that had suddenly appeared out of nowhere.

He climbed out of his car, leaning against it for support.

The other driver, an indignant woman in her late fifties wearing a full-length mink coat, came striding over to confront him. The coat looked as expensive as her car, a Bentley, all gleaming paintwork and stainless steel. It couldn't have been more than a few months old, but now the front wing was crumpled and the headlight smashed.

She looked ready to scratch his eyes out before getting down to more savage violence. "You stupid, silly bastard! What's your flaming game? Are you blind or something—didn't you see the bleeding traffic lights?"

The woman and the Bentley blurred out of focus, suddenly clicking back sharp and clear, with every detail of the damage screaming at him. The cold air and the shock of what he had done served to sober him up. "I'm sorry, love," Frost mumbled. "All my fault."

"You bet it's all your fault. You could have killed me!" Her nose quivered. She leant forward and sniffed. "You're drunk! You're bloody drunk! No wonder you drove straight past the red light. I'm calling the police." She fished a mobile phone from inside the Bentley. "Bastards like you ought to be locked up."

His dejection was complete. As if he wasn't in enough trouble! His medal wasn't going to get him out of this mess. Mullett would have a field day. But why was the woman studying him, staring at his face? He stared back. Something about her pressed a buzzer, but not loudly enough.

She poked an accusing finger at him. "I know you, don't I? You're a cop. A bloody cop!" She snapped her fingers. "Frost . . . . Sergeant Jack Frost."

"You'll never believe this, madam," he said, leaning heavily against his car because his legs didn't seem to want to support him, "but it's now Detective Inspector Jack Frost." He focused his eyes on her and felt a faint ripple of recollection. "Do I know you?"

"You ought to, you old sod, the number of times you've run me in for soliciting."

"Soliciting?" It was difficult to say the word without slurring. He closed his eyes. A mental picture of a thinner, much younger version of the woman, this time wearing a cheap, imitation leopard-skin coat. He opened his eyes as the filing index of his mind obliged with a name. "Kitty—Kitty Reynolds. And you haven't changed a bit. Are you still on the game?"

She grinned. "A different branch of the business. I'm in management now. I run a little specialized house—four girls. I won't tell you where, though."

"I don't want to know, love," said Frost, holding up his hand. "I can't even cope with the cases I've got." He took a squint at the Bentley and walked as steadily as he could over to it. Now that he could see it properly the damage looked even worse. "I seem to have put a tiny dent in your motor." He wet a finger and rubbed it over the wing as if that would put it right.

"A tiny dent, you drunken pig? There's nearly a thousand quid's worth of damage there." Kitty gave a conspiratorial grin. "But have it on me. I'll tell the insurance company the other motor didn't stop and I couldn't get its number."

The wind wasn't so cold. The night wasn't so dark. His guardian angel had come back from holiday just in time. "You're a saint, Kitty, a bloody saint."

She grinned again. "I owe you a few favors, Jack—that blind eye you turned when I could have got into serious trouble."

Frost struggled to recall the circumstances, but couldn't. There had been so many blind eyes. "Don't remember it, Kitty, but whatever I did, it was a pleasure." He gave her a wave. "I'd better get off back home before the filth start sniffing around." He tried to walk back to his own car, but found his legs weren't interested in taking his orders; he had to grab the Bentley for support.

Kitty threw back her head and laughed. "You're too bloody drunk to drive. Hop in my car. I'll park your heap down that side street, then I'll take you back to my place and try to sober you up."

Her place was down a murky side road leading off Vicarage Terrace. From the outside it looked down at the heel and scruffy, just like Frost, but the front door was fitted with the most sophisticated security lock, a lock which looked as if it cost more than the house.

"Through here, Jack." The hall light was on and the inside was a revelation, everything new and expensive . . . very expensive. Kitty took his arm and steered him through to the lounge where she sat him down on a deeply cushioned Chesterfield settee and pushed a solid silver cigarette box toward him. She retired to the kitchen while he sat, feeling warm and happy, savoring the rich coffee smell that floated through the open door. She emerged carrying a tray holding cups, saucers, and a percolator. Two cups of hot, steaming black coffee were poured and then she settled down in the armchair opposite him, sipping from her cup and watching him drink.

"It's flaming hot," said Frost.

"Stop your bloody moaning—just drink it."

He spooned in a shovelful of sugar and stirred. He hated black coffee. "So you packed the old game in, then, Kitty?"

"I had to, Jack. I was getting past it."

He sipped and swallowed. "I'm well past it, but I'm still carrying on."

"My," she said, pulling a face, "we *are* feeling sorry for ourselves, aren't we?"

A wry grin. "I was, but not any more." He unwound his scarf and unbuttoned his mac, then drained his cup in one gulp and shuddered as if he had taken a dose of medicine. To his dismay she leant over and immediately refilled his cup. He ladled in more sugar and took a sample sip. "Whatever men found irresistible about you, Kitty, it certainly wasn't your lousy coffee. . . . It tastes like horse pee."

"You're always moaning. Just drink it down and sober up. I'm not sending you back to your wife in that state."

"My wife's dead."

Her expression changed. "Oh, Jack, I am sorry. It must be lonely for you without her."

"I was lonely with her, love. We didn't get on too well, I'm afraid." He loosened his tie and tugged at the tight, petrified knot. The heat was counteracting the sobering effects of the coffee.

She shook her head sadly. "You poor old sod. You can stay here tonight if you like."

"Eh?" said Frost, feeling everything coming back to life again.

"If you're going deaf, Jack, forget it. I don't sleep with deaf men." Rising from the armchair, she collected the coffee cups and carried them back to the kitchen. When she returned, she studied him, her head to one side, hands on well-padded hips. "You wouldn't look so bad if you got yourself a decent suit."

Frost looked down at his jacket and scrubbed away a patch of spilt coffee. "I thought this was a decent suit. I paid a bomb for it."

"When—before the First World War? Look at it: frayed cuffs, your trousers all shiny. And there's a button coming off your sleeve. I'll sew it on for you, if you like."

He fingered the loose button. "You sew too?"

Kitty's smile was full of meaning. "You'd be surprised at the little services I can perform."

He was in the mood for being surprised. Sod the kidnapper. Sod Mullett. Sod everything. He stood up and moved toward her and that was the moment Control chose to page him.

"Control to Inspector Frost. Come in, please."

The sudden strange voice made Kitty start. "What the hell is that?"

Frost fished the radio from his pocket and sighed deeply.

"It's an electronic chastity belt." He pressed the transmit button. "Frost here, over."

"Can you come back right away, Inspector? We've got a man on the phone claiming to be the kidnapper. He's demanding to speak to the investigating officer. . . . Hold on . . ." There was a brief pause, then Lambert was back, sounding excited. *"We've traced the call to the public phone box outside the main post office. He's still on the line. Jordan and Simms are investigating."*

"I'm on my way," said Frost. He stuffed the radio back in his pocket, then looked regretfully at the woman. "Sorry, love. It's not only my button that's going to be left dangling. Duty calls."

"Well, you know where I am," she said, helping him on with his mac and brushing cigarette ash from the collar.

But as the front door closed behind him, she knew he wouldn't be back.

The kidnapper call was a hoax. The caller was blind drunk and was being egged on by his equally drunk mate. They were both brought back to the station and charged with wasting police time.

A disappointed Frost drove back home and tried to get some sleep, but Kitty's black coffee kept him awake until just before the alarm went off.

CHAPTER THIRTEEN

He arrived at the station early, anxious to check progress and then get well out of the way before Mullett arrived. Liz had beaten him to it and was already at her desk, hunched over a stack of reports and a complicated-looking form which she was meticulously filling in. The office smoldered with her resentment.

Frost peeked over her shoulder. She was doing the quarterly crime clear-up rate statistical return. "I thought Mr. Cassidy was doing this?"

"No," she snapped. "I've been ordered to do it."

Frost rasped a match down the front of the filing cabinet. He offered a cigaette to Liz, who refused. "Too much to hope the boy's been returned?"

"I wouldn't know—I'm only the clerical assistant." She fanned away the smoke which was drifting over her figures.

Frost thought he'd better take a chance and give Cordwell a ring in case the kidnapper had made contact, but at that hour of the morning, all he got was the answerphone. He hung up, frowned, and then yelled, "The answerphone! Of course—the bloody answerphone!"

"Eh?" said Liz tetchily. She'd hoped that by coming in early she could get the return done without interruption.

"The answerphone!" repeated Frost. "Something's been bugging me about Grover's alibi and I've just realized what it was!"

"Oh, yes?" she said, flatly. He should be telling Cassidy, not her. She was only fit to fill in forms. "Don't forget we're going to see the woman in the cottage this morning."

Frost frowned. "What woman?"

"Primrose Cottage—where Lemmy Hoxton was supposed to have pulled his last job."

"Later," said Frost, impatiently. "One case at a time. You spoke to their boss about his phone call to the store that night, didn't you? What did he say?"

She paused, pen hovering over a column of figures, and sighed. How many more times was he going to go over the same ground? She put the pen down and checked her notebook. "He spoke to Mark Grover at around twenty past midnight, which was round about the time his wife was killed and round about the time the neighbors heard the sounds of a quarrel." She snapped the notebook shut and went back to the return where she was trying to transfer some of Frost's figures to the main sheet. "Is this a three or a five?"

Frost squinted at it and shook his head. "Could be either. Does it really matter?"

Another sigh. Frost's figures were probably spurious anyway, so what the hell did it matter? She made it a five.

"The point is," Frost continued stubbornly, "on the night the kids were killed I asked young Collier to phone the store to check with the security guard. But all he got was the answerphone. The phones are switched off at night. So how could their boss phone them?"

Liz tapped her teeth with her pen. "But why should he lie?"

"I thought we might go and ask him."

She looked down at the mass of papers on her desk, most of them with Frost's scrawled, indecipherable, and mainly fictitious figures, and decided anything was better than that. She reached for her coat. "Why not?"

Frank Maltby, the owner of Denton Shopfitters, was not at home. His wife told them he was over at Bonleys Department Store supervising the counter fittings. Which is where they found him, a pugnacious little man with a loud voice, standing in the center of acres of brand-new red and blue carpeting which had been laid by Grover and Collard on the night the children were murdered. Workmen on piece rates were hammering and sawing.

Liz showed her warrant card while Frost was still digging down in his pocket among the cigarette ends for his.

Maltby scowled. "Now what?" His face went angry and he yelled over Frost's shoulder at a workman wielding a saw. "Mind what you're doing—that's solid bloody mahogany you're ruining, not plywood." Back to Frost. "What is it now?"

Frost had to shout over the clatter of the hammering. "Just checking. Are you sure you phoned Mark Grover at twenty past midnight?"

"Of course I'm sure—I told the tart—the lady—her!" Maltby jabbed a thumb at Liz.

"Well," yelled Frost, "in spite of what you told the tart, the lady, her, we seem to have a problem."

"And what's that?"

"The store switchboard shuts down at eight and all calls go to the answerphone."

Maltby gave a smug smile. "I didn't use the store's line. I called him on his mobile phone."

"His mobile phone?" echoed Liz in dismay. "I assumed you used the normal phone."

"Then you assumed wrong, darling, didn't you?"

"You told me he was definitely at the store."

"And so he was. Where else would he be?"

"Any bloody where he liked," said Frost. "He could have been having it away in bed with the tart, the lady, her, or he could have been back at home."

"Well he wasn't, smart-arse. He was here working."

"And how can you be so bloody positive?"

"Because he bloody told me, that's why. Now, if you'll excuse me, some of us have got work to do."

"All right," said Liz defensively as they walked back to the car. "It no longer proves he was at the store, but that doesn't mean he wasn't. We've got two other people who confirm he was there."

"You're too negative," Frost said. "He started off with three people supporting his alibi, and now there's only two. Let's go and see the night security guard."

They heard the radio squawking away as they neared the car. It was Cassidy at his smuggest. *"Thought you'd like to know, Inspector, I've got the case all tied up. Snell has confessed."*

Frost stared at the handset in disbelief. "Confessed?"

"Coughed the lot—the mother and the kids. Said it all happened in a haze, he didn't know what came over him." There was a long pause. Frost, so sure Snell didn't do it, so bloody sure, couldn't think of a thing to say. *"Are you still there?"* asked Cassidy.

"Yes," said Frost hastily. "Sorry . . . Congratulations. Good work." He did his utmost to sound sincere, but knew he hadn't succeeded. The speaker rustled as someone else took the microphone. It was Mullett.

"Whatever you are doing, Frost, I want you here, now. No excuses."

Frost switched off. "The bugger's confessed," he told Liz, still unable to believe it. "Which rather tends to shoot my theory that the father did it right up the arse."

She felt sorry for him. "You spotted an inconsistency that no one else did, Inspector, not even Mr. Cassidy. You checked it out."

He flashed her a wry grin. "For a tart, a woman, a what-it, you're not at all bad, Sergeant. Ah, well, it's bollock-chewing time, folks . . . back to the ranch."

Mullett was waiting for him. He managed a quick jab with his finger at the chair just before Frost decided to sit anyway.

"Two things, Frost. The press have somehow got hold of the fact that you suspected Snell before the killings but did nothing about it. They're clamoring for a statement. Secondly, I've had Sir Richard Cordwell on the phone. May I take it you have not yet been in touch with him?"

"Not yet," said Frost.

"Not yet?" echoed Mullett in a tone of exaggerated disbelief. "You're telling me that you haven't even phoned to ask if, by some remote chance after last night's fiasco, the kidnapper had kept his side of the bargain?"

"I'm sure Sir Richard would have told us if he had," replied Frost.

"Pathetic!" snapped Mullett.

Frost nodded wryly. This time Hornrim Harry was right.

"You will not, I am sure," continued Mullett, "be surprised to learn that there has been no such contact. Cordwell is convinced it is because of your clumsy intervention after promising to stay out of it." He leant forward. "You assured me nothing could go wrong. You gave me a categorical guarantee."

Frost did a mental playback of his conversations with the superintendent and was damn sure he had given no such assurance.

Mullett removed his glasses and polished them. "I can't save you from the wolves this time, Inspector." He oozed insincerity.

When have you ever? thought Frost.

"Now that he's laid out the money, Cordwell wants his pound of flesh. He was hoping to be fêted as the savior who paid the ransom and saved the child, but now that that is no longer possible, he is content to be the benefactor whose excellent intentions were thwarted by police bungling. He has called a press conference for ten o'clock to tell everyone about the fiasco."

"There was no fiasco last night," said Frost. "We didn't show ourselves until long after the kidnapper had left with the money. The fact that the old boy Finch turned up on the scene with his flea-bag of a dog had nothing at all to do with us."

A thin, wintery smile from Mullett. "I imagine Sir Richard will tell the story slightly differently. But hear this, Frost"—and he jabbed his finger at the inspector—"you are not dragging me down into the mire of your foul-ups. I am already drafting my report to the chief constable." He waved a sheet of paper filled with his neat handwriting.

Frost nodded curtly as he got to his feet. "Don't take too much of the blame on yourself, sir, just to get me out of trouble . . . and don't overpraise me—you know how embarrassed I get."

Mullett shrugged as he pulled the cap from his Parker fountain pen. This time, he would let it go. With luck, the inspector wouldn't be with Denton Division much longer.

In the outer office the clatter of the typewriter started up abruptly as Ida Smith, Mullett's devoted private secretary, quickly returned to her typing after straining her ears to hear the music of her boss giving Frost a dressing-down. Ida was loyal to Mullett and if he didn't like the inspector, then neither did she. In any case, the man was uncouth. That filthy seaside postcard! And she certainly wasn't bending down anywhere within jabbing range of that stubby finger. If it wasn't so embarrassing she would have put in an official complaint. She gave a malevolent smirk as Frost ambled past her. To her surprise he stopped and put a hand on her shoulder. "It's good to know I've got at least one friend in this place, Ida," he said, giving her a little squeeze.

Like her boss, it took her a little time to recognize sarcasm. She returned to her typing, hammering the keys as if they were nails to be driven in Frost's coffin.

Sergeant Johnnie Johnson waylaid him as he was on his way to his office. "Jack, guess who's here to see you?"

Frost furrowed his brow as if giving this serious consideration. "Not Princess Di again—I told her never to bother me at work."

"No."

"Then I give up." He was in no mood for guessing games.

"Tommy Dunn. He wants to see you."

"Well, I don't want to see him. He's dropped me right in it, thanks to his bloody sticky fingers."

"He says it's urgent," insisted Johnnie, trotting behind him into the office.

Frost dropped into his chair, flicked through his in-tray, and weeded out the two latest memos from Mullett which he consigned to the rubbish bin. "What does he want?"

"He was charged with stealing last night. He wants you to get him off the hook."

"I want someone to get me off the bleeding hook. Tommy knows damn well I can't help him." He sighed. Dunn was a shit and a bastard, but he had done Frost one or two good turns in the past. "All right, wheel him in . . . but for Pete's sake don't let Cassidy know he's here."

Dunn was an overweight, useless-looking man. A red-faced Oliver Hardy without the little moustache. He waited for Johnnie Johnson to leave before sitting down. "Sorry about last night, Jack."

"You dropped me right in it, Tommy. Right flaming in it!"

"Wouldn't have had it happen for the world, Jack," mumbled Dunn. "Look—you've got to help me. I don't want to go to prison. You know how they love ex-cops inside."

"You won't go to prison for a first offense."

"It's not a first offense, Jack. I had a similar unhappy experience when I was security guard over at Casheasy's in Lexton, then there was—"

Frost cut him short. "Then how did you get a job with Savalot? I thought they vetted their security staff?"

"I fiddled my reference. I got some of their letterhead—"

Frost held up a hand. "Spare me the details, Tommy. So what happened this time?"

"Silly mistake. I came out without any money so I took a couple of bottles from their liquor store. It wasn't pinching —I intended buying two bottles to replace them, but they caught me before I could do it."

"And what happened when they searched your house?"

"Another misunderstanding. They found some bottles of whisky and tried to make out I'd nicked them. But I'd bought them, Jack—days ago."

"If you had bottles in the house, then why did you have to take two more without paying? I'm sorry, Tommy. You're not only a silly sod, you're a lying bastard as well. I'm pretty gullible, but even I can't swallow that."

Dunn pulled a handkerchief from his pocket and mopped his brow. "I can't go inside, Jack. I couldn't face it. You're in with Cordwell. You've got to get him to drop these charges."

Frost gave a scoffing laugh. "Me in with Cordwell? He wants my head and my private parts on a platter, and with Mullett's help he's probably going to get them."

Dunn looked round to make sure the door was shut, then leant across the desk to Frost, his voice lowered. "A deal, Jack. I've got some dirt against him that you can use as a lever."

"I'm not getting involved in your bloody blackmailing capers," said Frost. "Forget it, Tommy. I can't help."

"At least listen to what it is, Jack."

Frost chucked him a cigarette and poked one in his own mouth. "All right, but make it quick."

Dunn took a long drag at the cigarette, squirted a stream of smoke, then perched it on the edge of Frost's ashtray. "Do you remember those forged ten- and twenty-pound notes we had in the town about eighteen months ago?"

Frost nodded. Some thirty thousand pounds' worth had been passed before the bank discovered it and the shops were put on the alert. They had never caught the gang, who had moved on to somewhere else and were eventually arrested in Manchester. "Mr. Allen's case. What about it?"

"Savalot got lumbered with about twenty thousand quid's worth of the forgeries."

"Too bad," said Frost, not giving a damn.

"If you remember, the gang started passing on a Friday—Savalot's big shopping day. We whammed the takings into the bank on Saturday morning. Monday was a bank holiday and we were open on that Sunday as well—three days of peak trading. Tuesday morning, first thing, the bank phones us: The money we paid in on Saturday morning included four thousand quid's worth of forgeries. They told us how to spot them so we wouldn't take any more, but it was a bit bleeding late . . . we'd another three days' worth in the safe ready to pay in. Cordwell did his nut."

"I'm glad it had a happy ending," said Frost.

"You haven't heard the punch line yet, Jack. We didn't even get the forged notes back—they were confiscated. So we check the weekend's takings and there it was: another fifteen thousand quid's worth of phony tens and twenties."

"There's going to be some point to all this, I hope."

"Patience, Jack, patience. Anyway, once Cordwell realized we had all this duff cash and if he tried to pay it into the bank he would lose the lot, he went berserk, so he packed it all away in his safe. He's been hoping for a robbery or a fire so he can claim it off the insurance as genuine. And

over the months he's been passing small amounts of it out to
all his branches. It goes in the tills and gets handed out to
customers in change. He's got rid of nearly two thousand
quid that way. Anyway, let's jump to the ransom. . . ."

A gleam flashed in Frost's eye. He was way ahead of
Dunn now. "You're not trying to tell me Cordwell used the
forged notes to help make up the ransom money?"

"Almost fifteen thousand pounds' worth. I don't suppose
it's a crime to pay off a kidnapper in forged currency, but I
bet he wouldn't want the public to know."

Frost leant back in his chair and beamed up at the ceiling. "Tommy, if you're telling me the truth . . ."

"I am, Jack, I am."

"Then not only are you off the hook, I might be as well."
He opened the door and ushered Tommy out. "I'll be in
touch—but bake a cake with a file in it just in case." As
Dunn turned the corridor, Frost was yelling for Burton.
"Keep an eye on the shop, son. I'm off to see Cordwell."

Sir Richard Cordwell looked at Frost, his eyes glinting ma-
levolently. "You've got two minutes, then I'm going to the
press conference. Have you caught the kidnapper or got the
kid back?"

"No," said Frost.

"Then start scouring the Help Wanted ads, because you'll
be out of a bloody job after today."

"I don't think so," said Frost.

"You sodded it up. You mounted an inadequate surveillance after assuring me you would not get involved. You let
the kidnapper get away with my money, and because the
police were there, he won't release the kid, so you've got that
on your bloody conscience."

"There's a rumor going around—" began Frost.

Cordwell banged his fist on his desk. "I am not interested
in bloody rumors."

"You'll be interested in this one. The very strong whisper is that the reason the kidnapper hasn't kept his side of the bargain is because he didn't appreciate being paid out with forged bank notes."

Cordwell jerked back, wincing as if he had been hit, but quickly composed himself and picked up a paper knife which he gently tapped on his desk. He spoke quietly, looking at something behind Frost as if the matter was of no importance. "And who has been putting about these malicious rumors?"

Frost gave him a sweet smile. "A couple of nasty bastards —me for one, Tommy Dunn for the other."

"Dunn? My crooked security man? The guy who's been emptying out my liquor warehouse? Is this where you got your information from?"

"We never reveal our sources," said Frost. He stood up. "I'll see you at the press conference."

Cordwell's eyes narrowed. "The press conference . . ."

"I want to suggest a few headlines for them," said Frost. "How about: 'Supermarket Chief's Swindle Costs Child His Life'? It would take more than a penny off a tin of beans to make the public forget that. . . . Then, of course, the press will want to know about possible criminal charges, like being in possession of forged bank notes, withholding information from the police." He looked at his watch. "Better not keep them waiting."

Cordwell stabbed the paperknife into the desktop and left it quivering. "You're a bastard, Frost!"

Frost smiled. "It takes one to know one."

"I presume I can buy my way out?" Cordwell brought out his checkbook and tapped it suggestively with a gold fountain pen.

"A lot cheaper than you deserve," said Frost. "Forget the press conference and drop the charges against Tommy Dunn."

"Dunn's an ex-copper, isn't he? You bastards certainly look after your own."

"No one else looks after us," explained Frost. "Lastly, I want full details of the duff notes . . . denominations, numbers, the lot . . . and I want them now. And warn your staff to be on extra alert for the forgeries. If our luck's in, he might try to start passing them." He slid the antique phone across the desk. "Do it now, please."

Cordwell picked up the phone. A tap at the door and his secretary looked in, cringing as she received the full force of his laser-beam scowl. "Sorry to disturb you, Sir Richard, but the press conference is in two minutes."

"Get out of here, you idiot! Tell them it's canceled," yelled Cordwell.

As he breezed through the lobby, Frost was beckoned over by Johnnie Johnson. "What have you done to Mr. Mullett, Jack? He's been in a foul mood ever since you phoned him."

"It's relief coupled with joy," explained Frost. "He was heartbroken because he thought he was going to lose me and now he's over the moon because he isn't." He pulled the list of forged notes from his pocket. "Have this photostated, then taken round by hand to all banks, stores, garages, discount warehouses, public toilets, the lot. Get them to pay particular attention to anyone paying cash for large purchases, even in genuine notes. If anyone passes any of the duds, we want to know right away."

Johnson took the list and, in return, passed over a thick wad of computer printouts. "And this is for you, Jack. Details of all registered owners of Ford Escorts in Denton and the surrounding area."

Frost flicked over the pages. It went on and on and on. . . . There were hundreds of names and addresses. "What silly sod asked for this?"

"You did, Jack. You're looking for the Ford Escort you saw just before that ransom money was taken."

Frost stuck the printout under his arm. "I must have been bloody mad. Still, I won't be short of toilet paper this week—it'll make a change from Mullett's memos."

Liz, her coat buttoned, was waiting for him in the office. "Ready when you are, Inspector," she said.

"Ready for what?" asked Frost. "If it's sex, then shut the door, I'm sorry I kept you waiting."

She didn't even flicker a grin. The return she had so meticulously prepared had been snatched from her without a word of thanks by Cassidy and she had heard Mullett praising him for such a good job. "You said we were going to Primrose Cottage, where Lemmy Hoxton was supposed to have pulled his last job."

Frost hesitated. It was Cassidy's case, but Cassidy would have enough on his hands with Sidney Snell. He glanced at the computer printout and wondered if he should get people checking. But they didn't have the manpower and the list was too bloody long. "Primrose Cottage? Right, let's do it now."

Primrose Cottage, standing on its own at the end of a long winding lane, was a detached two-story building erected in the sixties, but tarted up to look as if it dated from the 1700s. The doors were oak, stained black to give the appearance of age, the tiny bow windows were chintz-curtained, and the walls were painted a fading buttercup color. A white wooden gate opened onto a path to the front porch. Frost ducked to miss the hanging flower basket and rapped at the well-polished brass knocker.

"Who is it?" called a woman's voice, raised over the

sound of a dog yapping. "Police, Miss Fleming," answered Frost. "Nothing to worry about—just checking."

The door opened slightly on a length of stout chain and the proffered warrant cards were studied. Then, relectantly, she let them in. Millie Fleming was in her early fifties, slightly plump, dark brown hair, and wearing a pink woolen cardigan over a floral dress. The dog was a small spaniel which hid under a chair the minute they walked in. She smiled. "Not a very good house dog, I'm afraid, but we hope his barking might frighten any burglars away." They were in the living room with its dark oak and chintzy furniture.

Frost patted the dog, which looked at him with big brown eyes filled with apology for its cowardice and licked his hand. "Seems friendly enough," he said. "How old is he?"

"About four months. We haven't had him long."

"You're pretty remote up here," said Frost. "You need a dog. Is it just you and your sister?"

"Yes. How can I help you, Inspector?"

"Won't take up too much of your time, Miss Fleming. Did you have a visit from a man from the Water Board—or someone who said he was from the Water Board?"

"A long time ago," she said. "About five years—when we first moved in here. He turned on the water for us."

"This would have been a bit more recent than that— about three months ago—early August?"

She shook her head. "I don't think so."

"He might have called when your sister was here," suggested Frost. "Is she in?"

"No. Julie works at the hospital—she's a nurse. She should be back soon, though." She turned to Liz. "Can you tell me what this is about?"

"We had complaints of a man preying on women like yourself," said Liz. "He claimed to be from the Water

Board. Got the women to turn on the kitchen taps while he stole jewelry and money from the bedroom."

"Oh, dear," tutted Miss Fleming. "How awful! If anyone comes here saying they are from the Water Board, I'll phone the police right away."

Frost fished in his pocket for the photograph of Lemmy Hoxton. "This might refresh your memory. Has this man ever called here?"

She took it to the window and studied it carefully, returning it with a shake of her head. "I'm pretty certain I haven't seen him before. Can I ask why this is considered so important that an inspector and a sergeant have called on me?"

"He was found dead," said Frost.

She clutched her dress. "Dead?"

"We're trying to trace his movements. We believe he intended to call here on the day he died."

"To rob us? Well, he didn't, I'm relieved to say."

A car drew up outside, then they heard the sound of a key turning in the front door. The dog emerged from under the chair and raced out of the room, barking joyously. Millie Fleming stood up. "That will be my sister. Perhaps she might remember him."

She left them and went to the passage. A brief murmur of conversation, then she returned, followed by a dark-haired, vivacious-looking woman wearing a nurse's uniform. Her hair gleamed and her face had a well-scrubbed look. She wore black tights which, as Frost was pleased to observe, showed off terrific legs.

The two women sat side by side on the settee opposite him. "This is my sister, Julie," said Millie.

The nurse smiled, showing perfect teeth. I'd love to have them nibbling round my earhole, thought Frost. "Millie says it's something about a man calling here?" she asked.

Frost quickly filled her in and showed her the photograph, but her response was the same as her sister's. "I'm pretty good at faces, but I can't recall seeing this man before."

"Is it possible he called, but you were both out?" asked Frost. "The afternoon of Friday, August sixth. Any way of checking if you were here?"

The nurse moved a stray wisp of hair from over her eyes. Frost was finding her disturbingly sexy and he wriggled uncomfortably in his chair. "Depending on what shift I was on, I would either be at the hospital or in bed asleep." She consulted a diary from her pocket. "Nights that week. I'd have been at home."

"And I'd probably be doing some gardening," said her sister. "I certainly didn't go out."

Frost exchanged shrugs with Liz. It didn't look as if Lemmy made it to Primrose Cottage that day.

They took their leave. "I didn't half fancy that little nurse," said Frost, settling himself in the car. "She can give me a blanket bath any time she likes."

Liz gave a knowing smile as she jerked the car into gear. "I don't think she would be very interested in you, Inspector."

"Oh?" said Frost, deflated.

"I think she might be more interested in me."

"Eh?" It took a few minutes for the penny to drop, but he wasn't prepared to accept the insinuation. "Oh, come off it. How can you tell?"

"Women have a way of knowing."

He pictured the nurse again in his mind, then firmly shook his head. No way! He looked out of the window as they took a bend. "Stop the car!"

They were at a turnoff where a rut-ridden lane meandered down to a small farm. This was the spot where Duggie Cooper claimed he parked the van when Lemmy went cycling off into the sunset to Primrose Cottage. Frost peered down the lane, then looked back the way they had come. "If Duggie is telling the truth, Lemmy would have to come back this way. There's no where else for him to go." He scratched his chin. "The two women say he never arrived and Duggie says he never came back, so who is lying?" He signaled for her to drive on. "I think we had better talk to Duggie again."

Duggie was adamant. "I'm telling you, Mr. Frost, he pedaled up to the cottage on the bike and he never came back while I was there. Why should I lie?"

Before Frost could come up with his reasons, there was an urgent tap at the door of the Interview Room. An excited DC Burton beckoned him over.

"Some of that funny money's turned up!"

"Already?" asked Frost. This was bloody marvelous. He'd thought they might have to wait days.

"The bank phoned. They've just had nearly seven thousand pounds paid in, over a thousand of it in forged notes."

"Who paid it in?"

"Someone called Philip Mayhew, forty-seven Haig Avenue, Denton. I've checked with Records. Nothing known about him."

"Then let's make the sod's acquaintance," said Frost, twisting his head back into the room and yelling, "Interview suspended!"

It was a semidetached house, newly pebble-dashed. Two cars, a Jaguar and a Ford Sierra, were parked in the road outside and there was a Range Rover in a driveway which led to closed garage doors.

"A lot of motors for one house," commented Frost as they cruised slowly past, surveying the situation. The curtains to one of the upstairs rooms were drawn. He wondered if the boy was up there. They drove round the block. There seemed to be no rear exit from the property, except by clambering over about six garden fences to reach the side road. In one of the gardens a large, rippling-muscled rottweiler paced up and down, looking eager to tear any intruders to shreds. Little chance anyone would risk that, but to be on the safe side Frost posted a couple of men in the side road. His mind raced over all the things that might go wrong, but there were too many of them to worry about. They stopped outside the front of the house. "All right. Let's go, go, go."

Followed by Liz, Burton, and two uniformed officers, Frost trotted up the path and hammered on the knocker. The door was no sooner opened than he slammed it back and the others raced inside.

"Police!" yelled Frost as the man, a brawny individual sporting a beard and brandishing a baseball bat, tried to push the door shut, shouting for someone inside the house to call the police.

The bearded man swung the bat at Frost, but Liz, leaping on him from the back, managed to grab his arm and twist it. "Drop it!" The bat clattered to the floor.

"Police," repeated Frost, showing the man his warrant card. "And we've got a warrant to search these premises."

"You've got the wrong house!" bawled the man.

"Are you Philip Kenneth Mayhew? Then we've got the right house. Let's go inside."

He pushed Mayhew through the first door leading off the hall, which took them into a spacious lounge with an enormous five-speaker, cinema-sound television set that made the one Duggie had bought on Lemmy's card look like a portable. Suddenly, a woman in a tightfitting black dress charged in, swinging an iron bar. Her long fingernails were painted silver. She looked as if she would happily use them to scratch Frost's eyes out. "I've called the police, you bastards!" she screamed.

"We are the police," yelled Frost.

She lowered the iron bar, but kept it swinging in her hand, warily. This scruff looked nothing like a policeman.

She was only half convinced when she studied his warrant card. "What's this all about?"

"That's what I want to know," said the man. "They claim to have a warrant."

"We have got a warrant," said Frost. He gave it to Mayhew, who skimmed through it and passed it over to the woman. "Call our solicitor," he told her.

"You paid a large sum of money into the bank today," said Frost.

"No I didn't. I haven't left the bloody house all day." Mayhew jammed a cigarette into his mouth and lit it with a table lighter in the shape of a vintage Rolls-Royce Silver Ghost.

"I'm telling you that you paid six thousand nine hundred and ninety-seven pounds into Benningtons Bank in the High Street at ten fifty-four A.M. today," insisted Frost.

"And I'm telling you I did not," spat the man.

"If you must know, *I* paid it in," shouted the woman. "Why don't you get your bloody facts straight? No wonder innocent people get sent to prison." The sound of thuds and bangs upstairs suddenly intensified and sent her head jerking up. "What are those buggers doing?" She started to charge out, only to be stopped by Liz. "Let me go, you cow!"

Frost borrowed the Silver Ghost lighter for his own cigarette. He smiled sweetly at the woman, whose eyes were spitting bullets. "I don't give a sod who actually paid it in," he said. "All I'm concerned with is that over one thousand pounds of it was counterfeit."

This stopped the woman in her tracks. She stared wide-eyed at her husband, whose jaw had sagged, showing his gold fillings. "Counterfeit?"

Frost nodded.

The man smashed his cigarette out in a round glass ashtray which was enclosed in a miniature rubber car tire. "The bastard. The lousy, rotten bastard. I'll break every bone in his body."

"What particular bastard are we talking about?" asked Frost.

"The bastard I sold the car to."

Frost frowned. "What car?"

"The Honda Accord. He paid six and a half grand in cash and drove it away this morning."

"You sold him a car?"

"Hoo-bloody-ray," said the man, giving a mock clap. "A brilliant deduction. Yes, I sold him a car. That's what I do. I sell used cars—didn't you damn well know?"

Frost didn't damn well know. Mayhew pushed a copy of the local free paper over to him. There was a block of cars for sale ringed round in the classified section. One of them was a Honda Accord priced at £6,750.

The clatter of footsteps down the stairs and Burton looked in. His face told Frost they had found nothing, neither the ransom money nor any trace of the missing boy. "You'd better do this room," Frost told Burton. "The other two can do the garden and the shed."

He ushered Mayhew and his wife into the kitchen, a beautifully fitted room with expensive units, but empty bottles and unwashed crockery sprawled all over the place.

"It might speed things up if you told us what you were looking for," said Mayhew. "We might even be able to tell you where it is."

"We're looking for the rest of the money."

"What money? That's all he gave me. I paid it all into the bank."

Frost leant against the dishwasher. "Let's get this straight. You sell secondhand cars. So why did you try and attack us with a baseball bat?"

"Some people are dissatisfied with their purchase. Some come back very stroppy. We have to defend ourselves."

"So this has happened before?"

He shrugged. "Now and again. Some niggling little thing goes wrong and they want their money back."

"Niggling little things? Like the wheels falling off or saw-dust leaking from the gear box?"

"The condition of the cars we sell is reflected in the price. You can't expect an ex-showroom Mercedes for three hundred quid."

"Tell me about the Honda Accord," said Frost.

"This bloke phone me."

"When?"

"This morning. Said he'd seen my ad for the Honda in the local rag. If it wasn't sold, he wanted to come round and have a look at it. I told him it hadn't been sold, but it was such a snip, he'd better get round quick before someone else snapped it up. He said he'd be round in half an hour."

"And was he?"

"Half an hour, forty-five minutes . . . not long, any-way."

"And how did he come—on foot?"

"No, in a grey Ford Escort. There was a girl with him. She drove."

"Did she come in with him?"

"No, she waited outside."

"Then what?"

"I showed him the motor—it was parked where the Rover is now, and gave him a test drive round the block. He had a look at the engine and gave the tires a kick. He asked how much I'd knock off for cash—as if I'd take a bleeding check! He told me he'd had a win on the horses. I said then it's your double lucky day because I'll let it go for six-five. He said 'Done.' We shook hands and he fetched a plastic carrier bag from the Ford. I brought him into the house to give him the logbook and his receipt, while the wife tipped the money out and counted it. There was a fiver short, but I wasn't going to quibble over a lousy fiver. He took the log-book and his receipt, then drove off, followed by the tart in the Ford. End of story."

The two uniformed men came in from the garden. "Nothing," they reported.

"You come back in a couple of days' time," Mayhew told them. "If I lay my hands on the bastard you'll find his body buried there."

Burton also reported he had found nothing in the lounge, but Frost didn't seem too worried. "If you gave him a receipt, you'll have his name and address?" he asked Mayhew.

They followed him back to the lounge where he tugged open a sideboard drawer overflowing with papers. He gave Frost the carbon copy. "Jack Roberts, one eighty-seven Kitchener Street, Denton."

Frost passed it to Burton. "See if we know him."

Burton moved to the back of the room and whispered into his radio while Frost stubbed out his cigarette in the motor-tire ashtray. "Describe him," he said.

Mayhew thought for a moment. "Twenty-five, twenty-six. Hair in a ponytail. Not much meat on him . . . slim build, about five feet eleven. . . . He was wearing jeans . . . frayed cuffs, dirty trainers."

"A bloody Beau Brummell," said Frost. "You weren't surprised he had six and a half grand on him?"

"In this game, nothing surprises me."

"When we pick him up, I'll want you to identify him."

"If I get to him first, he'll be the man with his dick ripped off."

Frost grinned. Things were going right for a change. With luck they could make their arrest and have the kid back within the hour. He looked up expectantly as Burton clicked off the radio. But the expression on the constable's face sent his hopes nosediving.

"House numbers in Kitchener Street only go up to ninety-two," reported Burton. "That name and address is as phony as his money."

CHAPTER FOURTEEN

Frost sat on the corner of the desk in the briefing room, an unlit cigarette dangling from his mouth. He filled everyone in on the latest position with the kidnapping. "I'm getting worried," he told them. "He's got the ransom money, he's spending it, but he hasn't returned the boy. This could mean that Bobby is dead." There were nods of agreement. Most of the team were beginning to share this view.

He lit the cigarette and took a deep drag. "We've got one bit of luck on our side. The kidnapper has no idea that some of the money is dodgy and that we've got the numbers, so he's got no qualms about spending it. He's bought himself a red Honda Accord and we've got its registration number. He's local, and he's going to be driving it around, so everyone keeps their bloody eyes open." He nodded at Arthur Hanlon, who had his hand up to ask a question. "Yes, Arthur?"

"How do we know he's local?"

"He spotted the ad for the Honda in the *Denton Free Advertiser,* which is only distributed locally. It only took half an hour for him to reach the bloke who was selling it. We know a bit more about him. He's got a girlfriend who drives a grey Ford Escort, in which she is not averse to having it away, although, sadly, that probably applies to half the population of Denton. I'll lay money that he's local and that he won't be able to resist driving his new motor around. Unless he's got a garage, the Honda could be parked out in the street, so go over every bloody street and back alley in Denton. Find the bastard. But remember, as much as we want him, more importantly we want to find the kid. If we spot him, don't pick him up: Follow and keep me informed. Off you go . . ."

He watched them file out, then winced as Mullett came bowling in.

"Another lead fizzled out, then, Inspector?"

"Yes." Frost grunted. Go and gloat somewhere else, you vindictive sod.

"Pity you don't have the success Mr. Cassidy seems to be enjoying. It might not be a bad idea if you let him take over this case."

Frost tightened his lips, but said nothing. He stood up and squeezed past Mullett. "I think that's my phone ringing," he said.

He barged past Mullett, who strained his ears, but he couldn't hear a phone.

Bill Wells grabbed him just as he was going out for a drive around. Anything to get away from Mullett. "Sidney Snell wants to talk to you, Jack."

"Not my case," Frost said.

"He says it's important."

"Where's Cassidy?"

"Out somewhere."

Frost shrugged. What the hell—it wouldn't hurt to find out what Snell had to say. He followed Wells down to the cells and waited while the door was unlocked. Snell, sitting on the bunk bed, hugging his knees, looked up plaintively as Frost came in.

"I didn't do it, Mr. Frost."

"You haven't dragged me down here just to hear that same old cracked record, I hope, Sidney. I know it by heart. 'I didn't do it, Mr. Frost . . . honest . . . on my mother's grave.'"

"Well, this time it happens to be true."

"Even if it is, so what? You're a scumbag, Sidney . . . for that alone you deserve to be banged up."

"But not for something I didn't do. I don't kill kids and I don't kill women."

"But you do sign bleeding confessions," said Frost.

"He made me, Mr. Frost. Mr. Cassidy kept on and on telling me I did it, and that I'd feel better if I got it off my chest. In the end I just signed that confession to get a bit of peace."

"I reckon you'll get twenty-five years' worth of peace, Sidney—perhaps a couple of days less for good behavior."

"I confessed, but I didn't do it," Snell insisted.

"The Guildford Four, the Birmingham Six, and now the Denton One. Face up to the facts, Sidney. One of the dead kids was stabbed, the way you stab little kiddies. Your blood and chunks of flesh are over the plywood on the back-door panel. You were seen running away afterward. And if that wasn't enough, you're a slimy little bastard and I hate the sight of you. We don't need your confession to get you sent down for life."

"I was there that night, Mr. Frost, I don't deny that. I followed her about when she took the kids out to the park, and I used to stare at her through the windows . . . but I never killed her or the kids."

"So why did you break in at one o'clock in the morning? To apologize?"

"All I intended to do was look through the window. As God is my witness, Mr. Frost, that's all I intended doing, but sometimes I can't control myself . . . The devil talks to me."

"And what did the devil say—'Kill them all, just to spite that silly sod Mr. Frost who should have had you arrested, but was too bleeding lazy'?"

"He drew my attention to that loose sheet of plywood. He said I should push my hand through and unbolt the door." He rubbed his bandaged hand. "I just meant to look at them . . . I like looking at kiddies asleep in their cots."

"I like looking at naked nymphomaniacs, but I couldn't promise I'd just look at them. You had your stabbing knife with you, and you bloody used it."

Snell buried his face in his hands. "Just enough to break the skin, Mr. Frost. I can't help myself. I don't know why, but I like it when I see the blood . . . tiny drops of red on their little arms."

"Look out, Sidney, you're dribbling," said Frost.

Snell wiped his mouth. "I get a sexual kick out of it, but I don't kill—I couldn't."

Frost sat down on the bunk beside him and lit up a cigarette. "According to your statement, the kids woke up and started screaming . . . all three of them. You had to silence them, so you used the pillow . . . and then their mother came running in and you had to kill her too."

"No!" Snell was almost shouting now. "Mr. Cassidy put those words in my mouth. I couldn't kill anyone. I'm terrified of death and dead bodies." He waved away the cigarette Frost was offering. "They made me look at my mother's dead body in the hospital. She was all shriveled up. She looked horrible."

"She looked pretty bleeding horrible when she was alive," said Frost.

"I thought they were showing me the wrong body . . . but it was her. I ran out and never went back. Do you think I'd want to see any more dead bodies after that, Mr. Frost?" He shook his head firmly. "No way . . . no way!"

"If you want to withdraw your confession," said Frost, "then tell Mr. Cassidy. This isn't my case."

Snell ignored him, eyes glazed in recollection. He was back in the house that cold, frosty night. "I tiptoed over to the kids' room. I pushed open the door and held my breath. It was so quiet—that should have warned me something was wrong. You can usually hear kids . . . they make a hell of a row when they're asleep, snorting and snuffling. But I was too excited to worry. There was this little boy. He had little pudgy arms lying on top of the eiderdown. I pulled back the sleeve of his pyjamas and pricked him, very quickly. It doesn't hurt them, Mr. Frost . . . they get frightened when they wake, but it doesn't hurt them. I broke the skin, but he didn't murmur or wake up. I let go of his arm and it just dropped down. And when I touched his face, he didn't move, and I couldn't hear him breathing. None of them were breathing. Then I realized he was dead . . . they were all dead . . . I was in a room with three dead kids. I panicked. I charged straight out through the front door and into the street."

"Was there anyone about in the street at the time?"

"An old boy with a dog. I nearly sent him flying."

"We know about him. Anyone else?"

"I didn't see anyone. I just raced for the car and got the hell out of there. You've got to help me, Mr. Frost. I'm innocent."

Frost dropped his cigarette and stamped it to death on the cell floor. "You're not innocent, Sidney. You're a perverted little bastard who interferes with kids. We might have got you for the wrong crime, but so what—the end result's the same—you get put away and everyone's happy."

"But if I'm banged up for this, Mr. Frost, it means the real killer gets away with it."

Frost sighed. "All right, Sidney, I'll have a sniff around and see what I come up with—but don't hold your breath." He yelled for Bill Wells to let him out. "Gross miscarriage of justice," he told the sergeant.

"The only miscarriage of justice would be if they ever let the sod out," retorted Wells.

The tottering heap in his in-tray looked ready to fall over at any minute. He skimmed through it to see what he could throw away. A thick wad turned out to be the crime rate detection statistical analysis that Liz had prepared with the request that he should check through them and sign them as correct. He signed them unread and hurled them into his out-tray. Then all the papers on his desk fluttered as Cassidy, his face distorted in anger, burst in and jabbed an accusing finger. "You've been talking to Snell?"

"He asked to see me."

"Whether he asked to see you or not, he is my prisoner and this is *my* case. You ask me first. Understand?"

"All right." Frost shrugged. "Keep your hair on." He was getting more and more fed up with Cassidy.

"What did he want to see you about—or did you intend keeping that to yourself?"

"He said he didn't do it."

Cassidy fluttered pages of stapled typescript in Frost's face. "He has signed a confession!"

"He wants to withdraw it."

Cassidy's face went a dirty brick-red. His fists clenched and unclenched as if he was ready to punch Frost on the chin. "It may not fit in with your crackpot theories, but Snell, the man you *refused* to arrest, has admitted everything. He did it . . . the kids and the mother. So stay away from him. This is my case and I don't want you ruining it to satisfy your own personal ego!" With one last sizzling death-ray of a glare, he spun round and stamped out of the office, nearly sending Burton flying as he did so.

Burton had to clear his throat to attract Frost's attention. "Mr. Cassidy sounded a bit upset." He tried hard to keep the pleasure out of his voice.

"You noticed it too?" said Frost in mock surprise. "I thought it was just me. What can I do for you?"

"You told us to keep an eye on Ian Grafton's place."

Frost frowned. "Then I'm sure I had a good reason for it—but who the hell is Ian Grafton?"

"The bloke who took Tracey Neal to the bank when Carol Stanfield was abducted."

"Ah, the bloke with the pigtail. What about him?"

"A lot of expensive hi-fi equipment was delivered there this morning. Nine hundred and ninety-five quid's worth."

Now he had Frost's full attention. "Right, check with the shop. Find out how he paid for it."

"I did," said Burton, sounding hurt. It was the first thing he'd done. "Cash . . . spot cash."

Frost unhitched his scarf from the hatstand. "I think he's worth another visit, son."

"What—now?" asked Burton.

Frost paused. His mind was still on Snell and the three dead kiddies. "No. There's something I want to do first. That security guard who said Grover and his mate never left the store. I want to talk to him."

"But that's Mr. Cassidy's case," Burton pointed out. "Didn't he just say—"

Frost's hand flashed up to cut him short. "I didn't quite catch what Mr. Cassidy said, son. He was shouting so much. But I'll check with him when we get back."

The security guard, Paul Milton, lived in a small three-bedroom terraced house on the far side of the golf course. If it wasn't for the swirl of damp mist clinging to the green, the bungalow where the tragedy took place could just about be seen from his upstairs window. Milton's wife, a six-month-old baby in her arms, let them in. "He's just gone up to bed," she told them. "He's on nights this week."

They followed her into the dining room where a chubby boy of two was sitting in a high chair chewing solemnly on a slice of bread and jam.

"We would like to see him," smiled Frost. "It won't take a minute."

"Paul!" she yelled, as she plunked herself down next to the high chair and started shoveling Heinz baby food down the infant's throat.

"What is it now?" replied an irritated voice from above. "I've only just this bloody minute gone up."

"Police!"

"What do they bloody want?"

"If you bloody come down you'll find out."

Paul Milton, tucking his shirt inside his trousers, staggered into the room. He was bleary-eyed and unshaven. "I should be asleep," he moaned to Frost. "I'm on duty tonight." He sat in a chair next to his wife. "What can I do for —Shit!" The baby had spat a mouthful of food all over him. The little boy in the high chair dropped his bread and jam on the floor and started to wail. "It's like a flaming madhouse in here," Milton yelled as his wife placidly retrieved the slice of bread, picked off the worst of the fluff, and returned it to the child. He stood up and buttoned his shirt collar. "We'll go into the lounge."

He led them out into the passage, but as his hand reached for the door handle to the lounge, he hesitated and did a U-turn. "Perhaps the kitchen would be better."

But nothing could have been worse than the kitchen, which was a dump, even by Frost's low standards. Unwashed plates and saucepans piled high on the draining board, bits of food on the floor alongside a long unemptied cat's litter tray. A nappy bucket, filled to overflowing, was parked alongside the washing machine. Milton shook a chair to dislodge a heap of mucky bibs and nappies and waved a hand for Frost to sit. The invitation was hastily declined, as was the offer of a cup of tea.

Frost lit up a cigarette. He wasn't sure if it was the cat's litter tray or the nappy bucket that was getting to him, but he hoped his cigarette smoke might improve the atmosphere. "Couple of questions to ask you, Mr. Milton. I know you've covered all this ground already, but I just want to be absolutely sure. It's about Mark Grover."

Milton sighed and shook his head in sad disbelief. "Those poor kids. His wife must have been right round the bend." He pulled a face at the howls from the dining room. "I often feel like wringing my own kids' necks, but I'd never actually do it."

Frost gritted his teeth against the noise. "If you feel like doing it now, Mr. Milton, don't let us stop you." He consulted his notes. "Grover told one of my officers that he and Phil Collard arrived at the store around eight to do the carpet and didn't leave until around half past one in the morning. Is that correct?"

He yawned, not bothering to cover his mouth. "Quite correct."

"Any chance either of them could have left the building without you knowing?"

"No way. It's all electronically controlled. I'd have to operate the switch."

"They were working on the top floor. Where were you?"

"Either in my cubicle by the back entrance, or doing my rounds. I have to cover every floor at half-hour intervals and click a key into time locks."

"While you were on your rounds, could they have got out?"

"Not without setting off the alarms when the door opened. And they'd have to have the master key and that was with me all the time. If they wanted to go out, they only had to ask . . . it's a store, not a flaming prison."

"And they didn't ask?"

"No." Another yawn.

Frost accepted this gloomily. He was convinced Mark Grover had found a way to leave the store without anyone knowing, but he couldn't see how he could prove it.

"Thanks for your trouble, Mr. Milton. We'll let you get some sleep."

At the door to the lounge he stopped. Why didn't Milton want to take them in there? What was he hiding? Stuff nicked from the store perhaps? He reached for the door handle. "Is this the way out?" he asked innocently.

"No, not in there," called Milton, running forward, but he was too late. Frost was already inside.

The strong aroma of expensive new wool filled the room, a smell Frost had noted earlier in Bonleys Department Store. Woolen carpeting. He switched on the light. . . . And there it was, on the floor, red, blue, and expensive, stretching from wall to wall. The pattern was very familiar. It was the design for Bonleys new restaurant, an exclusive design, specially made and imported for them.

"I spy," said Frost, "with my little eye, something that has been nicked."

"An odd remnant that was left over," spluttered Milton. "It would only have gone to waste."

Frost sat down on the settee and prodded the carpet's springiness with his foot. "Tell me about it."

"Someone must have made a mistake with the measurements because there was this great chunk of carpet left over . . . so me and the fitters had half each."

"How did it manage to find its way from the store to here?"

Milton shuffled his feet and wouldn't meet Frost's eye. "They dropped it off for me."

"So Grover and Collard did leave the store that night?"

"Well—yes. But not for long . . . hour or so, at the most."

"And you lied to us?"

"A white lie. I'm supposed to be the security guard. If Bonleys ever found out I was party to sneaking out a thousand quid's worth of top-quality carpeting, I'd have been for the high jump."

"You still might be for the flaming high jump. We're investigating a murder and you are making false statements to the police. Unless you want to get deeper into the mire than you already are, you'd better tell me everything . . . right from the start . . . and the bloody truth this time."

Milton rubbed his chin and sighed. "All right. They turned up just after eight, like I said, and they worked like the clappers—didn't even stop for anything to eat. By midnight they were well on the way to finishing and they find there's a dirty great chunk of carpeting left over . . . worth around a thousand quid, so Mark Grover reckoned. We made a deal. They laid it in my lounge for me and they kept the rest. Just before midnight I let them out. They dropped off my bit of carpet and took their own piece. They were back again around half past one and finished off at the store. Yesterday afternoon the fat one—Phil Collard—called here to lay it for me. He stressed we should all keep our mouths shut about the other night, in case we got found out."

Frost gnawed away at his thumb knuckle. "How did they seem when they came back?"

"Same as always. I didn't pay them too much attention as I was due for my next round of clocking on. I could hear them working away up there and just before two they came down and went off home. You won't tell my firm, will you?"

Before Frost could reply, Burton was hammering at the front door. "Control have radioed through. The red Honda —Jordan and Simms have found it parked in Whitmore Avenue."

As the car sped through the traffic, Frost brought Burton up to date regarding his talk with the security guard. "That's Mark Grover's alibi shot right up the fundamental orifice."

"So he could have done it," said Burton grudgingly, inching the car forward in anticipation of the traffic lights changing, "but that doesn't prove that he did do it."

Frost grunted. "You're too bloody finicky. Mr. Cassidy won't like it, but I'm having Grover and his fat mate in for more questioning." They turned a corner and Frost pointed. "There's the area car . . ."

PC Jordan, in Charlie Bravo, was waiting for them down the side street while PC Simms, a mac over his uniform, was in Whitmore Avenue keeping an eye on the Honda. "Let's take a look," said Frost.

He went with Jordan and cautiously peered round the corner. Whitmore Avenue was a broken-down terrace of three-story houses, some of them with basements. Many of the buildings had been split up into flats, others, beyond repair, were boarded up and empty. The road was jampacked with cars, mostly old bangers, but the nearly new red Honda, gleaming under the light of a nearby lamp post, screamed at them as the odd man out.

"About as inconspicuous as a topless tart in a monastery," commented Frost.

Simms wandered down to join them. "We're presuming the kidnapper is in one of the houses," he told Frost, "but we don't know which one. He's probably stuck it where there was a vacant parking space and not necessarily outside where he lives."

"He may not even live in this street," said Burton. "He could have parked it well away from his own place."

"No," said Frost. "A shiny new motor in this bloody neighborhood. He'll park it where he can keep an eye on it. A fiver says he lives in one of these houses."

They went back to the side street to await reinforcements. In three minutes another car shuddered to a stop behind Frost's Ford and Liz Maud, accompanied by two other officers in plain clothes, got out. A burst from the radio. Another car with four more officers was on its way. Frost directed them to go round the block and wait at the opposite end of Whitmore Avenue. It might be overkill, but this time he was taking no chances.

Back with Burton to take another look. There were twenty three-storied houses on each side. "Damn," muttered Frost. "We can't go knocking at bloody doors asking for the owner of the red Honda to come out. If he's got the kid holed up here, we could end up with a hostage situation."

"So how do we get him out?" asked Burton.

Frost thought for a moment, then he walked over to the ramshackle-looking waist-high brick wall that protected the basement area of a boarded-up property. The cement was crumbling and most of the bricks were loose. He worked a brick free and walked casually over to the red Honda. A quick look up and down the street, then with a hefty blow he smashed the brick down on the driver's window, shattering the glass.

Immediately the car-alarm system screamed out and the car lights flashed on and off. Frost stuck his hand through the broken door window and tried to reach the cassette player on the dash.

A shaft of light sliced across the street as an upstairs window shot up. A man leant out. "Get away from my car, you bastard!" Frost ignored him, still reaching for the cassette player.

The head disappeared and a few seconds later the street door opened and the man burst out, charging across the road, his ponytail flying. "Go, go, go!" yelled Frost into his radio, realizing even as he said it that he hadn't positioned his team properly.

The police thudded down from each end of the street. Halfway across the road, the man hesitated, spotted the stampede, and turned to run back to the house.

"Shit!" snarled Frost. He hadn't made certain someone was near to cut off his escape. If the man got back inside and slammed the door, they could be faced with the very hostage situation he had tried to avoid. He started to chase after the man, but quickly realized he was not going to make it in time. To his relief, he saw that Liz had had the foresight to run down the other side of the road, ready to block his path.

"Stop . . . Police!" she yelled.

"Out of my way, you bitch," screamed the man, his fists flailing.

It wasn't quite clear what happened next. Like a terrier after a rat, Liz darted forward, grabbed the man's arm. Her knee came up, the man yelped with pain and collapsed to the ground, clutching his groin. Before he had time to recover, Liz had him facedown and was pinning his arms behind his back. Then Burton and Frost were with her.

"Get this fat cow off of me," yelled the man.

Burton leant down and snapped the cuffs on his wrist. "You're nicked," he said, rather redundantly. Liz stood up, dusting herself down, while Burton hauled the man to his feet and went through his pockets. He found a driving license and flipped it open, then handed it to Frost.

"Craig Hudson. Is this you?"

The man, white-faced, nodded.

"And is this your car?"

"Yes—and you'll pay for the damage, you bastard." Then the pain gave him a jab, making him hiss through clenched teeth. "That bloody cow—I need a doctor."

"Play your cards right and she might kiss it better," said Frost, grabbing him by the arm. "Let's go inside and have a talk."

They marched him back into the house and up a flight of stairs covered in dark green lino. The door to the first-floor flat was wide open and they walked into a largish room, barely furnished with a TV set and a three-piece suite in a faded floral moquette. The floor was littered with empty foil takeaway food containers and the spicy reek of takeaway curry battled with marijuana for supremacy. At first they thought the room was empty, but a puff of thick smoke billowed above the back of the settee. Lying full length, a dark-haired young girl, eyes half closed and a look of utter euphoria on her face, was dragging at the fat parcel of a hand-rolled joint. She had on a grey sweater which had been rolled up to her neck, exposing gorgeous breasts and a flat stomach. "I hope we haven't interrupted your meal," murmured Frost politely, his eyes bulging.

The girl smiled blissfully and offered Frost a drag on her joint.

"Get yourself covered up," hissed Liz.

"Leave her," said Frost. There had been too few perks with the job recently. He dragged his eyes away and turned his attention to the man. "Sit!" he commanded. Burton pushed him down into the chair.

Sounds of a commotion from downstairs, then heavy footsteps and Cassidy came barging in. "Mr. Mullett thought I should be in on this," he announced.

"Great," said Frost flatly. Cassidy was Mullett's blue-eyed boy at the moment. Quickly, he filled him in, then got Jordan and Burton to thoroughly search every room in the house. And next they would have to check every house in the street. The boy could be bound and gagged in any of the derelict properties. "Where is he?" he asked the ponytailed man.

"Who?"

"Don't sod us about!" shouted Cassidy. "You know damn well who we mean. Where is the boy?"

"Boy? What boy?"

The girl on the settee had let her cigarette go out and was now humming a little song to herself. Frost was finding it increasingly difficult to concentrate on the matter at hand.

"Bobby Kirby," said Cassidy. "Where is he?"

"Never heard of him," said the man. "Can I have these handcuffs off now, please?"

"When we're ready," said Cassidy.

"Take them off," said Frost. Hudson wasn't going to try anything now.

Burton unlocked them, watched by a scowling Cassidy, furious that Frost had undermined him.

Hudson rubbed his wrists to restore the circulation. "I demand to know what this is about."

"Shut up!" snarled Cassidy. "I do the bloody demanding, not you."

Jordan signaled to Frost from the front door. He'd done a quick check through the flats in this house. No sign of the kid. He was moving on to the other houses.

Cassidy was about to interrogate Hudson further when Frost suddenly came out with the stupid question: "Where did you get the takeaway?"

Cassidy gaped and stared in disbelief. What the hell did that matter? They were looking for a missing kid, for Christ's sake!

Seeing Cassidy's annoyance, Hudson grinned. "The Taj Mahal round the corner—why?—do you want some?"

"Did you collect it, or was it delivered?"

"Delivered. What the bloody hell is this about?"

Frost took Liz to one side. "Nip round the Indian and find out what was delivered."

She looked at him the same way Cassidy did. "Why?"

"If they've got the kid here somewhere, I'm hoping they'll feed him. Miss Curry-tits on the settee doesn't look as if she could butter a slice of bread without getting it all over her nipples, so I'm hoping they might have got three meals in from the takeaway."

Begrudgingly, she acknowledged the sense of this and left to make her inquiries.

Cassidy went back to his questioning. "You paid six and a half grand for a car. Where did a scumbag like you get that sort of money?"

"I had a win on a horse."

"What horse?" barked Cassidy.

Hudson fired the answer straight back. "Dancing Foam, two-o'clock race, yesterday."

There was a morning paper on the floor by the settee. Frost opened it at the racing page and checked. "He's right. Dancing Foam won at five to one."

"You see!" smirked Hudson.

"But at five to one," pointed out Frost, "you'd have to stake over a thousand quid to win your motor money. To quote my good friend Mr. Cassidy, where did a scumbag like you get a thousand quid?"

"I saved it up."

"I knew there was a logical explanation," said Frost.

Burton came into the room triumphantly brandishing the travel bag. "Look what I found stuffed behind the wardrobe," he said.

Frost unzipped it. It was packed tight with ten- and twenty-pound notes. "Did you save this up too?"

Hudson stared at the bag, then jerked his head away. "Nothing to say," he mumbled.

"You'd better bloody say something," snarled Cassidy. "This money was used to pay the ransom for Bobby Kirby. You're in serious trouble, my friend. So where is the boy?"

"I don't know anything about the boy." He slumped back in the chair.

Frost leant over him and pointed to the near-naked girl on the settee, who was now grinning inanely at them. "Take a good look, son. You won't get any more of that if you're doing twenty years in the nick. I'd start answering a few questions if I were you."

Hudson looked over at the girl, who grinned back at him and wriggled her body provocatively. "All right. I'll tell you the truth. I found that money."

"Where?"

"Dumped by a rubbish bin, just outside the car park in the Town Center."

"You're a bloody liar," yelled Cassidy. "Where is the boy?"

"How many more times do I have to tell you? I don't know anything about the damn kid."

The girl on the settee had now decided to try and sit up. The effort made her giggle. Frost went over to her and shook her by the shoulders roughly. Her head snapped from side to side and her hair fell all over her eyes. A bonus was her breasts, which swayed delightfully from side to side like the head of a questing snake. Frost found a part of him enjoying the view, the other deeply concerned about the boy. "Where is he?"

She gaped up at him, trying to focus through wisps of stray hair, her expression one of bemused delight. "I love it when you get rough. . . ."

"I haven't started getting rough yet," snapped Frost. "Where is the kid?"

"I haven't got a kid," she giggled. "I'm on the pill."

Frost let her drop. This was useless. He beckoned Burton over. "Get SOCO and Forensic down here . . . and tell Sergeant Wells I need a lot more men down here." He turned to Cassidy. "Take Hudson and Miss Curry-belly down to the station and try and get them to tell us where the kid is. I'll follow on as soon as we've got things organized here."

Blankets from the bedroom were draped over the girl and she was hustled out with Hudson.

Frost smoked and watched and tried not to get in anyone's way as he waited for Forensic and SOCO. "Go over every inch of this place," he told them. "We want to know if Bobby Kirby has been here." Car doors slammed outside as more men arrived. He went down to meet them. "Search every building in the street. Search every flat, every basement, occupied or not—kick in doors if necessary, I'll carry the can if anyone complains." Frost waited while Burton organized them into search groups, then drove back to the station.

Hudson, in the white one-piece boiler suit they had forced him to put on while his clothes were taken away for forensic examination, sat in the Interview Room rubbing his wrists and his groin. If he ever met up with that cow of a police-woman on a dark night . . . He stared moodily at the uniformed officer leaning against the green-painted walls. "How much longer?"

The officer shrugged.

"Where's Cindy, my girlfriend?"

Again the officer shrugged.

"Can I have a fag?"

"I don't smoke," said the officer, sounding pleased he was able to deny this to the prisoner.

Hudson looked up as Cassidy, followed by Detective Sergeant Hanlon, came in. "About bloody time!"

Cassidy gave the prisoner his long, hard stare and waited for Hanlon to load up the cassette recorder. "My name is Cassidy, Acting Detective Inspector Cassidy. Also present is Detective Sergeant Hanlon. Where is the boy?"

"You don't bloody listen, do you? Watch my lips: I know nothing about no boy."

"You demanded a ransom. You paid for a Honda Accord vehicle with part of that ransom money."

"I told you, I found it!"

"You are lying."

"Prove it!"

"Where's the kid?"

"I don't know anything about any kid. . . ."

Frost waited impatiently in his office for the results of the search, a cigarette smoldering away in a disgusting-looking ashtray, piled high with grey ash. Liz had phoned through to report that the Indian takeaway had delivered a meal for two, not three. If they had the kid, surely they would feed him . . . or perhaps the kid was dead, so they didn't have to. Hudson wasn't intelligent enough to have organized the kidnap. Perhaps someone else was behind it . . . the girl? She was still in no state to be interviewed, so it was up to Cassidy to try and get something from the man.

"Any news?"

It was flaming Mullett in his smart, TV-interview uniform. He'd been sticking his head round the door every five minutes.

"Nothing yet," Frost told him.

Mullett scowled as if the lack of progress was Frost's fault. "I want a quick result on this one."

"I believe you have mentioned it, sir," muttered Frost. The phone rang. He snatched it up. Burton calling from the flat. "Forensic have crawled over every inch of the place. Not a damn thing to link Hudson with the kidnapping—apart from the ransom money, of course."

"And how is the search of the other properties going?"

"No joy so far. A couple of people have refused permission to let us in to their premises."

"Sod their permission. Go in anyway. We can always apologize afterward." He hung up. Mullett pretended not to have heard Frost's instructions so he could absolve himself from any involvement in the event of a comeback.

Frost glanced at his watch. What the hell was Cassidy playing at? He'd been questioning Hudson for well over an hour. A clatter of footsteps down the corridor and Cassidy came in, looking angry and frustrated.

"I can't get anywhere with him. He denies any knowledge of the kidnapping and repeats over and over again that he found the bag of money dumped in the car park."

"Why don't we set up an identity parade—get Finch to identify him?" Mullett suggested.

"I'd prefer to avoid that if possible," replied Frost. "Finch has already identified the wrong man. His defense would pull any subsequent identification to shreds . . . and the silly sod could well pick out another flaming look-alike."

"What have Forensic turned up?" asked Mullett.

"Slightly less than sod-all." Frost picked up his ashtray and emptied it into the waste bin. "Right. Back to Hudson. We forget the niceties and scare the shit out of the bastard."

"Wait," called Mullett. "We don't want any of your famous shortcuts and corner-cutting, Frost—things that won't stand up in a court. The important thing is to secure a conviction."

"No," said Frost. "The important thing is to find the kid . . . and that's what I intend to do."

"I'm warning you," said Mullett. "If we lose a conviction because of your underhand methods . . ."

"If my underhand methods result in us finding the kid, then we'll get a conviction anyway. Don't worry, sir, I'll be taking all the blame if things go wrong." He knew he'd get the blame anyway.

"On your own head be it," said Mullett as Frost brushed past him on his way to the Interview Room. "If this blows up in your face I shall deny all knowledge of this conversation."

Cassidy gave a sympathetic smile to Mullett as he followed Frost out, his smile saying "I'm with you all the way, sir, if things go wrong." . . . But if they went right, he was determined to grab his share of the glory.

"Now what?" asked Hudson as Frost entered the Interview Room with Cassidy.

Frost dropped into the chair opposite him and banged a folder on the table. Cassidy had the cassette ready to insert into the machine, but Frost stopped him. "I don't want this recorded." He smiled sweetly at Hudson. "Where is Bobby Kirby?"

"I'm not wasting my breath answering this same question any more. For the last time, I know nothing about no kid."

"Right," said Frost. "I haven't got time to sod about." He swung round to the uniformed man. "Would you wait outside, please, Constable?"

The constable hesitated, but did what he was told, closing the door firmly behind him.

Frost beamed at Hudson. "Isn't this cosy? Just the three of us."

Hudson's eyes flickered apprehensively between the two detectives. "What's going on?"

Frost beamed at him and pulled two photographs from the folder. He slid them across to Hudson.

"Recognize them?"

Hudson gave them a halfhearted glance. "No."

"That's funny," said Frost, as he tapped the photograph of Bobby Kirby. "This is the boy you kidnapped."

"I've already told—"

"Shut up!" Frost's voice rose to a bellow. "I'm tired, I've been up half the night, and I'm not in the mood for any more sodding around. I don't give a toss what you say, I'm telling you what happened." He banged a finger on Bobby Kirby's photograph. "You kidnapped this kid and you killed the other one. You sent the ransom demand and you went with your slut of a girlfriend to the common to collect it. You knocked the old boy out and snatched the cash. You thought you would get away with it. You thought the money would be untraceable . . . but it wasn't. We've got you to rights, so we don't give a sod about all your lies that you know nothing about it. We're not even bothering to record them any more."

"Look, I don't know what you're talking about. I found that money. If you think you can prove otherwise—"

"Shut up!" roared Frost again. "You don't know me, sonny. My name is Jack Frost. I'm not a very good cop and I'm not a very smart cop, so I have to cut corners. Sometimes I might even have to lie to secure a conviction, so I'm prepared to tell all the lies going about you, you toe-rag. I've got no compunction because I know you are guilty."

To show his lack of concern, Hudson pulled a comb from his pocket and flicked it through his hair. Frost stretched out a hand. "Can I borrow that?"

With a bemused smile, Hudson handed it over, then watched in bewilderment as Frost tugged a few hairs from the comb and slipped them into a small transparent envelope which he tucked inside the folder. "What's that for?" Hudson demanded.

"We've asked our Forensic lab to do a thorough check of the dead kid's clothes to see if there is anything on them that would help us identify the killer . . . like hairs, for example." He patted the folder.

The smirk had slid from Hudson's face. "You are going to fit me up, you bastard."

Frost looked apologetic. "Only if I have to, son. You're guilty anyway, so I wouldn't lose any sleep over it."

"You wouldn't dare."

Frost smiled sweetly. "Just watch me."

Hudson spun round to Cassidy, hoping for support. He sensed the antagonism between the two men. "You heard what he said. You're my witness!"

Cassidy stared straight ahead, saying nothing. If this thing blew up, he would drop Frost right in it.

Hudson's face was ugly. "You bastards!"

"Sticks and stones," reproved Frost. "Where's the kid?"

The man folded his arms and leant back in his chair. "All right. I'll tell you the truth. Yes, I nicked the money. I was with Cindy . . . she loves having it away out in the open. We see this green Nissan pull up and a bloke nips out with a travel bag and hides it in the bushes. I thought I'd take a look-see, so after about a quarter of an hour—"

"Why did you wait so long?"

"First, because it was peeing down with rain and I was

hoping it might ease up, two, I had no trousers on at the time, and three, Cindy was demanding seconds. By the time I got over there, this old boy was ferreting about. He pounces on the bag, so I nip in quick and try to grab it from him. He puts up a bit of a fight. I don't want no aggro so I welt him with a chunk of wood, grab the bag, nip back in the car, and we sod off back home. When I saw all that money inside, I just couldn't believe my rotten luck. That is all I am admitting to and I know nothing about no bleeding kids. . . ."

CHAPTER FIFTEEN

Frost was in his office gloomily staring at his ashtray with its mountain of fluffy grey ash studded with cigarette ends. The room was fogged with smoke, his mouth tasted horrible, and his fingers glistened with oily nicotine. He had smoked himself sick and didn't want another cigarette, but the urge to punish himself for his lack of progress was overwhelming, so he lit up yet another of Mullett's specials as he waited for Liz to return from questioning Hudson's girlfriend. He knew she would confirm Hudson's alibi and absolve him from any connection with the kidnapping and yet another lead would come to a dead end.

It hadn't been a good day so far. Mullett had finally stamped off home in high dudgeon when he realized he wouldn't be able to make his television announcement that the Kirby boy had been found safe and well, and the kidnapper had been arrested. On top of that, Snell had got himself a solicitor and had withdrawn his confession, saying it was obtained under duress, and for that Mullett and Cassidy definitely blamed Frost and had lost no time in telling him so.

Liz came in, coughing and fanning the air with her hand

against the smoke. "She's told you where the kid is?" asked Frost hopefully.

Liz shook her head and sat at her desk. "No. She bears out everything Hudson said. They were both having it away when they saw the money being dropped. They nicked the money, but that's as far as they were involved. She also swears that the night the boy was taken, she and Hudson were at a disco in Levington until gone midnight. She's given me a string of names of people who can confirm this." Liz offered him the list, but he wasn't interested. "Check it out," he said, but he knew it would confirm their statements.

Frost yawned. He felt deflated. The second day of the investigation and they were exactly nowhere. He tossed a screwed-up Mullett memo into the air and headed it into the wastepaper bin. "Do you like fish and chips?" he asked.

Liz blinked her surprise. "Yes—why?"

He pulled his scarf from its hook. "Let's go and get some."

The door to the Incident Room crashed open and Frost came in clutching a greasy brown paper bag to his chest. He pulled packages from it and tossed them around the room. "Cod and chips . . . plaice and chips . . ."

Bill Wells, who had wandered in for a chat, was appalled. "Fish and chips? You know Mullett has forbidden them in the station. They stink the place out."

"No more than his poncey after-shave." Frost held up a package. "I take it you don't want this—it's cod and chips."

Wells hesitated, then grabbed it. "As you've bought it— but open the windows afterward."

Frost perched himself on the edge of a desk and began eating cod and chips with his fingers as he addressed his team. "Fish is supposed to be brain food, so let's see if it does anything for us. Now, we're checking their alibi, but it looks as if Hudson and Miss Twin Peaks are out of the frame."

"Which puts us right back in square one," said Cassidy, who had been staring sullenly out of the window. Thanks to Frost, his case against Snell wasn't looking as strong as it did, and he was now being associated with another of Frost's abysmal failures. He hadn't demeaned himself by ordering fish and chips and now regretted it. His stomach was rumbling and the heady bouquet of chips and vinegar was making him drool.

"More or less," grunted Frost, spitting out a fish bone. "Just in case we have missed something, let's go over it again. The kid was snatched for the sole purpose of obtaining the ransom money. Dean Anderson, the first kid he snatches, dies, so he calmly goes out and grabs another one. Why didn't he pretend Dean was still alive? He would still have got the ransom money. Don't tell me he was worried about contravening the Trades Descriptions Act?"

"The kid had to be alive to make the taped message for the press," suggested Burton.

Frost nodded. "I'll buy that. Which convinces me we are dealing with a methodical sod, not a tearaway like Hudson. His plan demanded a taped message, so there had to be one, even if it meant going after a second kid." He opened his mouth and tipped in the crumbs from the chip bag, then threw away the greasy paper and wiped his hands down the front of his jacket. "Okay. Puzzle number two. Everything proceeds as planned, all his demands are met. But he doesn't turn up to collect the money—why?" He scratched his chin in thought as he sent his cigarettes on the rounds.

"Something must have happened that prevented him," suggested Liz.

"It must have been at the last flaming minute," said Frost, "because he was on the phone to Cordwell almost as soon as the money was dropped."

"A heart attack?" offered Burton.

"Don't be a fool!" snarled Cassidy.

"Hold on," said Frost. "That could be it. You get a phone call telling you there's a quarter of a million quid waiting to be picked up . . . you could either wee yourself or have a heart attack." He pointed to Burton. "Phone Denton General and find out if anyone suffering from a heart attack was admitted last night."

"Why just a heart attack?" said Cassidy sourly. "He might have got run over—or broken his leg."

"Or had his dick cut off." Frost nodded his agreement and told Burton to check with the hospital for details of everyone admitted as an emergency last night. Collier came in and handed Frost a sheaf of papers. They included carbon copies of the statements made by Hudson and his girlfriend. Frost shuffled through the rest of the papers. There was a list supplied by Denton Council of the people who used to live in the old shacks where Lemmy Hoxton's body was found. A name on it screamed out at him. He jabbed it with his finger and showed it to Liz.

Liz whistled softly. "Millicent Fleming? The woman from Primrose Cottage."

"It's a small world, isn't it!" commented Frost. "Strange she never mentioned this when we called on her. We'll pay her another visit tomorrow."

The phone rang. Hanlon answered it and relayed the message to Frost. "Jordan and Simms have contacted three of the people who were at the disco. They all confirm that Hudson and Cindy were there until after midnight. The girl threw up in the lobby so it rather sticks in their mind."

Frost shrugged philosophically. He had written them off as suspects anyway. He took a quick look through Hudson's statement before deciding to call it a day, then suddenly straightened up. He flapped his hand for silence as he read it through again, then he beamed. "Our unanswered question was, why didn't the kidnapper pick up the ransom money?" He slid off the desktop and started striding around the room. "The answer is so bloody obvious, even Mullett could have spotted it, but we've all missed it!"

"And what have we missed?" Cassidy's tone implied that whatever it was, it was a load of rubbish.

"The kidnapper *did* pick it up," said Frost. He paused dramatically. "But it was taken from him."

He was met with blank stares, everyone trying to work out what he meant.

The penny dropped for Burton first. "You mean Finch— the old boy with the dog?"

Frost nodded.

"Just because he happened to be there," scoffed Cassidy.

"It was peeing down with rain. No one with any sense would have been out in it, but Finch was chucking a ball for his dog."

"I checked with his neighbors," said Burton. "They confirm he's been taking the dog out for a run every night, come rain, hail, or shine."

"Building up a pattern," said Frost. "We know the kidnapper is methodical."

"Thousands of people are methodical," said Cassidy. "That doesn't make them kidnappers."

"Thousands of people don't chuck the dog's ball at the very spot where a quarter of a million quid is stashed."

"Coincidence!" said Cassidy dismissively.

"I don't believe in coincidences," said Frost, "not unless it suits me . . . and this time it doesn't suit me. Finch is our man!"

"You'll have to come up with something a lot more than this to convince me," said Cassidy. He was looking at the cigarette Frost had given him. It was not the inspector's usual brand. It was the expensive brand Mullett reserved for special visitors.

"Then how about this?" said Frost, and he read aloud part of Hudson's statement: " 'I saw this bloke wandering around to where the bag had been dumped, so I nipped across there smartish. He was kicking at the grass, looking for something. He picks up this bag from out of the long grass. He hadn't heard me coming, so I tried to grab it.'" He looked up at blank faces and frowned. "I'm supposed to be the dim twot here. How come I'm the only one to spot it?"

"To spot what?" demanded Cassidy.

"Hudson says he saw Finch kicking at the long grass, looking for something."

"The dog's ball," said Cassidy, as if explaining to a child.

"But when we found poor Mr. Finch, knocked out cold, he already had the dog's ball in his pocket. So if he'd already found the ball, what the hell was he still looking for?"

"The money!" exclaimed Burton.

"Yes, son," agreed Frost. "He was looking for the money."

Cassidy chewed this over, testing it for weaknesses, but he grudgingly had to agree it held water.

"It was bloody clever," continued Frost. "If the police weren't watching, Finch'd pick up the money and no one would be any the wiser. But if the Old Bill was there, he could claim he found it by accident and who the hell could prove otherwise?" He turned to Burton. "You chatted up the neighbors. What do we know about him?"

"He's a self-employed accountant, does the books for some small businesses in and around Denton. His wife used to work for Savalot on the checkout. She was with them for fifteen years, but when they moved to the big new super-store, they sacked all the old checkout girls."

"Why?" Frost asked.

"They wanted youngsters they could train to the new system from scratch. The neighbor said her job was her life. She got depressed and eventually took an overdose about eighteen months ago."

"So Finch would have a very good reason for hating Cordwell?"

Cassidy shook his head. He couldn't accept this. "You're not suggesting this whole kidnap was done for revenge? The woman died over eighteen months ago."

"Revenge has to smolder before it bursts into flame," said Frost. "It's all coming together."

"All you've got at the moment," objected Cassidy, "is a theory—and you're bending the facts to support it."

"That's the way I always work," said Frost happily. "And if Finch isn't our man, then it's hard bleeding luck, because I am going to give him the works. What else do we know about him, Burton?"

"Not much . . . He keeps to himself and he hasn't had the dog long."

Frost's eyebrows shot up. "How long?"

"Two, three weeks."

Frost chewed this over, then pounded his fist into his palm. "I said he was a calculating bastard. I bet he got the dog as part of his plan. It's all been worked out to the smallest details." He chewed his knuckle, then waggled a finger at the team. "And that's why Dean Anderson had been stripped naked. Finch is not going to leave us with a single clue. I bet there were dog's hairs on the kid's clothes . . . so off come the clothes." He was now warming to his theme, getting more and more excited. "And the indentation the pathologist noticed on Dean's forehead—I bet that was the marks of an elasticated shower cap. He was covering up the kid's hair so it wouldn't pick up traces of anything that could lead us back to him."

Liz shook her head. "I can't believe Finch is such a calculating bastard. He doesn't look it."

"Don't go by appearances," said Frost. "Mullett doesn't look like a prat."

Cassidy compressed his lips. This was not the way one should speak of senior officers to the lower ranks.

"We know it's Finch," continued Frost. "So how do we play it?"

"Slowly and carefully," urged Liz.

"We can't go slowly," Frost objected. "Time isn't on our side. Finch's killed one kid, so he's got nothing to lose by killing the other." The phone rang again. He watched as Cassidy answered it.

It was the casualty officer from Denton Hospital. Apart from a pregnant woman who had fallen down a flight of stairs, no one came into Casualty between nine and ten-thirty the previous night with anything serious enough to keep them away from a quarter-million-pound ransom. Cassidy relayed this to Frost, then stood up and flexed his leg, which was stiffening up. He wanted to go home, but was determined not to leave before Frost.

"What is this terrible smell?"

Flaming hell! groaned Frost. Where had bloody Mullett sprung from? "I noticed it the minute you came in, sir—have you trod in something?" He signaled for Burton to open up the window, then took Mullett by the arm and led him outside. "I'd like a quick word."

"And I want a word with you, Frost." The superintendent said nothing more until they reached his office. "I've had a phone call from the chief constable and he is very concerned about our lack of progress with this kidnapping. He understands the boy's mother has given an interview to one of the papers complaining the police are doing nothing."

"We're not doing nothing, sir, we just haven't come up with anything . . . until now."

"Until now?" Mullett's head came up and his eyes gleamed. "You've got a lead?" If this was true, he'd get straight back to the chief constable.

"A good one." He quickly told Mullett about Finch.

"Finch? The man who was attacked?"

"Yes, sir."

Mullett scratched his chin thoughtfully. "The boy could be at Finch's house? We could get him back to his mother tonight?" That would be a triumph. It would make the papers look absolute fools in the morning.

"It's possible, Super," said Frost. "I doubt if the boy is hidden in the house, but we should find something that would lead us to him."

"So what do you suggest?" Mullett consulted his watch. "It could take some time getting a search warrant."

Frost gave him a knowing wink. "Just leave that to me, sir."

Mullett stared at Frost. He had no wish to know about the underhand methods Frost intended to use. "Stick to the rules, Frost," he said, "and let me know how you get on." When Frost had left, he smiled a smug smile of satisfaction as he practiced what he would say to the chief constable if Frost pulled it off. "I know it was bending the rules, sir, but the child came first. . . . I realized my career would be on the line, but that wasn't a consideration. . . ." He practiced saying it silently, but with the right degree of modesty. Then his expression changed and his eyes narrowed as he rehearsed what he would say if things went wrong. "I specifically told Frost to play it by by the book . . . there was a child's life at stake and no reason for taking chances. . . ." He congratulated himself. This was the sort of situation he liked. Either way, he couldn't lose.

In the Incident Room, Frost was briefing his team. His cigarette packet was empty, but he found a fair-sized stub in his top jacket pocket and poked it into his mouth. "Finch mustn't know we suspect him. If we don't find the kid in his house, then we'll put him under constant surveillance in the hope he leads us to him."

"You don't want him to know we suspect him?" said Cassidy. "But the minute we turn up with a search warrant, of course he'll flaming well know."

"We *don't* turn up with a search warrant," said Frost. He puffed a mouthful of smoke up to the ceiling and watched it get sucked out of the open window into the cold night air.

"We use a bit of tact and subtlety, for which I am world-famous."

The dog barked incessantly at the knocking at the door and wouldn't be hushed as Finch switched on the passage light and demanded, "Who's there?"

"Police," replied Frost. "Can you spare us a moment?"

Finch opened the door and there was that scruffy man with the mac and the trailing scarf. "Mr. Frost, isn't it?"

"That's right, sir. Sorry to bother you, but we've had a bit of luck. We've caught the man who attacked you and stole the money."

Finch's face lit up. "Good work, Inspector." He led them into a living room, all neat, tidy, and polished, the room of a methodical man.

"Going out, sir?" asked Frost. Finch had his jacket on.

"Just taking Czar for a run. I do it every night. So how can I help you?"

"We need formal identification of the travel bag and we'd like you to identify the man."

"Does he admit to kidnapping that poor child?"

"He's lying his head off, sir. He says he found the money by chance and you tried to take it away from him."

"That is ridiculous. He put me in hospital. Of course I'll identify him. If you could hand me my overcoat . . ."

It was hanging neatly over the back of a chair. Frost passed it across. Seeing his master getting ready to go out, the dog began yapping its excitement and leaping up and down at the prospect of an outing.

"Take him with you, sir," suggested Frost. He wanted the dog out of the way. "Oh, and there's just one more thing, sir." He smiled his most frank and open smile. "You're probably going to think it a bloody cheek, but do you think I could do a quick search of your premises?"

Finch's eyebrows shot up. "Why?"

"Once you've identified this man, he is going to deny all knowledge of the kidnapping and try and involve you in it. He'll claim you were there for the sole purpose of collecting the ransom."

"But this is preposterous," spluttered Finch. "I found the bag simply by chance."

Frost nodded sympathetically. "Of course you did, sir. But he's going to say you've got the boy hidden away. What I'd like to do—with your permission, of course—is do a token search of the premises, so we can refute his allegations right from the start."

"Do you have a warrant?"

"It hardly justifies a warrant, sir. I'm not really taking it seriously. I can get one if you like, but it won't take more than a couple of minutes." He opened a door and clicked on the light. "Is this the lounge?" He peeked inside. "Well, he's obviously not in here." He pulled the door shut. "I'd better see the kitchen in case you've got him hidden in the bread bin."

A knock at the front door. The dog went haring up the passage, barking again. PC Jordan stood on the doorstep. "Sorry to bother you, Inspector. The station have radioed through. They've moved the time of the identity parade— they want us there now."

"Damn!" said Frost. "I want to get this finished. Can it wait five minutes?"

"Sorry, sir," said Jordan, "but they say it's got to be now. They've got everyone lined up."

Frost turned to Finch, who was trying to calm the dog. "Do you think you could go with the officer, sir? I'll finish off here and follow on in a couple of minutes."

Finch hesitated, then shrugged and hurried out to the car. "Don't forget to close the front door."

"I won't, sir. Don't worry."

He watched Finch, followed by the terrier, climb into the back seat of the area car. As soon as it turned the corner he was whispering urgently into his radio. "He's gone. Let's have you!"

Two cars that had been waiting round the corner disgorged eight men, mostly from Forensic, who swiftly entered the house.

Frost gave them a quick briefing. "Be bloody thorough, but put everything back where you found it, because Finch mustn't know. We are looking for anything that could prove the kid was here . . . hairs . . . fibers . . . blood. And look for a cassette recorder, a dot matrix printer, bottles that could have contained chloroform. If you find the kid, tied to a chair, watching the telly, I'd even settle for that."

They went about their task with practiced efficiency while Frost mooched about, opening and closing cupboard doors, trying not to get in anyone's way. Finch was an extremely methodical man. Everything was in its proper place and this made the search relatively simple.

On the wall of the living room was a framed photograph of a younger Finch and a fair-haired woman taken at a dance of some sort. Frost studied it. Both looked very happy.

"Sir!" Burton called from the hall, where he had found a door under the stairs. His torch revealed stone steps leading to a cellar which exuded a musty smell of long disuse. "There's nothing there," Frost told him, "but look anyway." He stayed at the top, watching halfheartedly as Burton slowly descended, his torch beam bouncing off heaps of stored junk. Jordan was called in to help and together they shifted as much as was necessary to ascertain there was no child, alive or dead, hidden there. Carefully, they moved everything back to where it was. Burton's foot kicked a blue fluted bottle which rolled across the stone floor. He pulled out the stopper, sniffed at it hopefully, then with a twitch of disappointment replaced the stopper. It was turpentine substitute.

"Jack!" Arthur Hanlon was calling him from a first-floor room. Frost thudded up the stairs.

One of the bedrooms had been converted into a small office and Arthur Hanlon was excitedly indicating an Amstrad word processor on a wooden desk. A dot matrix printer was alongside it. Hopes were quickly dashed by Harding, who pointed out it was a nine-pin machine and the ransom demand had been printed out by a twenty-four-pin model.

Frost mouthed a silent expletive and looked through some of the printouts at the side of the machine. Stock records and account details. The wastepaper bin contained only a torn window envelope. He peeked through the curtains to the darkened street below. Just inside the front gate a rubbish sack awaited its morning collection by the refuse van. Frost pointed it out to Hanlon. "Get someone to pick it up and take it to the station." He pulled a desk drawer open. Neat clipped stacks of bills and statements. A quick riffle through, but nothing of interest.

He was hindering Hanlon, so he went downstairs to the kitchen where two men from Forensic, on their hands and knees, were painstakingly checking for prints and fibers. "Mainly dog hairs so far," they told him.

"Probably from the dog," said Frost, ever anxious to help.

The kitchen table bore further testimony to Finch's methodical habits. One cup, one saucer, and one spoon laid out alongside a cereal bowl and a bread and butter plate, all ready for the next morning's breakfast. "I bet there's one senna pod and one sheet of toilet paper in the loo," grunted Frost, who was never impressed by neatness.

He consulted his watch. Nearly ten minutes had passed since Finch had departed. "I'd better get down to the station before he becomes suspicious. Let me know the minute you find anything, but please, put everything back exactly where you found it."

. . .

Finch was becoming impatient. He knocked back the dregs of the cup of tea Liz had brought him and gave the custard cream to his dog. "I thought it was all ready."

"Last-minute hitch," Liz told him, and was so relieved when Frost walked in.

"Sorry I'm late," said Frost. "Got another call on the way back. Have you identified him yet?"

"It still hasn't started!" snapped Finch. "I'm not very impressed at police efficiency."

"Go and see what the delay is, Sergeant," Frost said to Liz.

"Did you find anything?" said Finch.

"Eh?" said Frost vaguely, as if he didn't know what Finch was on about.

"The search."

"Oh, that?" He gave a short laugh. "I found six boys in the fridge, but none of them was the one we wanted." He was relieved when Finch grinned back. "I shut the front door as you asked."

Liz returned. "Hudson has signed a statement admitting taking the money and assaulting Mr. Finch," she said. "So there's no need for an identity parade."

"What about the kidnapping?" asked Frost.

"He strongly denies that."

"Let's see if he still denies it after I've finished with him," said Frost grimly. "Get Mr. Finch to formally identify the travel bag. It's in the Exhibits Stores."

"Won't take long, sir," said Liz, leading Finch out. As soon as they had gone, Frost was on the radio to Burton at the house.

"We've found nothing that would tie him to the kidnapping and nothing that would suggest the boy was ever in the house," reported Burton.

"The car . . . did you check his car?"

"Forensic gave it a proper going-over . . . nothing."

"Right." It was a sod, but what the hell. He'd have to think out his next move. "Get out of there. He'll be back soon."

Cassidy walked in on the tail end of the conversation, taking secret delight at Frost's downcast expression. "Doesn't look as if your theory was right, then, Inspector."

"I'm not wrong on this one," said Frost stubbornly. He bent to pat the dog, which was asleep under the table. "It's your bloody master, Fido, and I'm going to get the bastard." The dog opened one eye and licked his hand.

Finch returned. "All right for me to go now?"

"Yes, sir. Thank you very much for your help. Our lady sergeant will drive you back." Frost tried to sound as if his mind was on other, more important, matters.

Mullett waylaid him on his way to the Incident Room. "Frost!" He sounded angry. Very angry. He had been sitting in his office, the phone in the center of his desk, ready to ring the chief constable with the good news. "The Denton team have done it again, sir," he would announce. "No, no," he would add modestly after the chief had congratulated him. "I can't claim all the credit." But his speech had remained unspoken. He had seen Finch come and long faces all round but no one had bothered to tell him what had happened.

Bloody hell, thought Frost. I was supposed to keep him informed. "Just on my way to see you sir," he lied.

"You've let Finch go? Do I take it you found nothing?"

"Not a bleeding thing," said Frost.

"Nothing at all?" persisted Mullett.

"That's what 'not a bleeding thing' means," said Frost sweetly.

"All this time and effort," snapped Mullett. "All those men—a full Forensic team—all on overtime. Do you know how much this little jaunt has cost?"

"I neither know, nor care," Frost snapped back. "If

there's a cash limit on the amount we must spend to find Bobby, then let me know."

"An expensive success I can accept, Frost, but not an expensive failure." Mullett stamped back to his office.

Frost joined his dispirited team in the Incident Room. "All right, so we found nothing. But that doesn't mean we're on the wrong track. Finch is our man." He ignored the scoffing snort from Cassidy. "Take it from me. Finch has got that kid. The only question is where the hell is he? Can anyone come up with some bright idea, because I'm blowed if I can."

"Assuming Finch is the kidnapper," said Burton, "why hasn't he come up with a second ransom demand?"

"He's probably got to work out another way of collecting the money. He's been seen at the collection point once, a second time would be too much of a coincidence even for dim twots like us."

Lambert raised a hand. "Do you think he's got an accomplice looking after the kid?"

"No," said Frost. "Finch is a loner. He's in this absolutely on his own. He's got the kid gagged, blindfolded, and trussed up somewhere. So how do we find him?"

"We tail Finch," suggested Hanlon. "Twenty-four-hour surveillance. Let him lead us to the kid."

"Why should he go to the kid?" asked Frost. "It would be too dangerous."

"He's got to feed him—see if he is all right. The poor little sod is only seven."

"Finch is a callous bastard. I don't think he gives a toss about the kid," said Frost.

"If there's nothing to connect him to Bobby and he doesn't lead us to him, then what do we do?"

"We worry ourselves bleeding sick," replied Frost. Then he stopped dead. He'd remembered something. "I know where the boy might be."

"Where?" asked Cassidy, without enthusiasm. Nearly all

of Frost's bright ideas had fallen flat on their faces up to now.

"I was looking through some invoices and bills in his office. One bill was for the ground rent for the parking of a holiday caravan. A holiday caravan in the autumn . . . what better place?"

"Worth a look," said Cassidy begrudgingly. "So where is it?"

Frost spread his palms. "I don't know. I wasn't paying that much attention at the time."

Cassidy shook his head in exasperation. "So how do we find out, short of asking Finch?"

"Leave it to me." Frost glanced up at the wall clock. Liz should still be driving Finch back. He snatched up the internal phone and told Control to radio through to her in the car. She was to phone Inspector Frost urgently as soon as she reached the house. He hoped she would realize that this was something he didn't want mentioned over the radio in Finch's hearing.

The next few minutes crept by as he waited for her to ring back. It was a few minutes to midnight. The phone rang. Liz.

"Can Finch hear us?" He found himself whispering although there was no need.

"No. He's in the kitchen feeding the dog."

"If he asks, tell him it's about a rape case. This is what I want you to do. There's a room upstairs he uses as an office. In the left-hand desk drawer there's a bulldog clip of bills waiting to be paid. One is from a caravan site. I want the address of that site."

"How do I get it?"

"Tell him you want to do a Jimmy Riddle—the bathroom's upstairs next to his office. If he offers you a bucket we'll have to think again. Do your best, love. It's bloody important."

"I'll try."

"Good girl! Don't forget to pull the chain afterward—he's a suspicious sod."

She radioed back from her car in eight minutes. The invoice was for the ground rent of a caravan at the East Seaton Holiday Caravan Park.

"That's nearly forty miles away!" protested Cassidy.

"So?" replied Frost. "About an hour's drive. He could get there and back to Denton in good time to take the dog out for a walk." He walked over to the regional map. "There it is! Forty miles from Denton, remote, and no one staying there in the autumn. If I wanted to hide a kidnap victim, I couldn't think of a better place."

Cassidy studied the map. The caravan parking site was tucked away well off the beaten track. It was a possibility. "We'll need a search warrant," he said.

"No time for that," said Frost, already winding his scarf around his neck.

"Then Mr. Mullett will have to be told."

"No time for that either." Mullett would only say no.

"Seaton is in Felford Division. Shouldn't we let them handle it?" asked Burton.

It was Cassidy who answered. If the boy was there, no other division was going to steal the glory for finding him. "It's our case," he said firmly.

"There could be trouble," said Burton, shaking his head doubtfully.

"Not if we play our cards right," said Frost.

But Frost rarely played his cards right.

Burton coasted the car up the bumping approach to the caravan site and switched off the lights. A high chain-link fence enclosed a field, its grass overgrown and sagging with the weight of rainwater. Huddling under the shelter of a group of trees to the rear of the site was a line of caravans of all shapes and sizes. The wind rattled the fencing and caused the trees to groan in protest. In this weather the caravan park was a cheerless, desolate place.

There were four of them: Frost, Burton, Cassidy, and Liz. Frost had considered bringing at least another four in a second car, but Mullett's dire threats about overtime payments decided him against it. In any case, for this clandestine operation, the fewer people involved, the better. "What a dump!" He grunted, holding out his hand for the night glasses. Burton gripped his arm and pointed. A light had come on in one of the caravans. But he'd already seen it.

He fumbled at the focusing control and panned across the front of the caravan. The curtains were tightly drawn, but a thin crack of light seeped out into the night. He located the door and the number shimmered into focus: 12. It was Finch's caravan. Frost grinned. "I think our luck's changed," he told the others.

The chain-link fence was too high for them to scale and the heavy padlock on the main gates refused to yield to any of Frost's skeleton keys, so they watched impatiently as Burton, his face contorted with the effort, clamped the cutters across the chain and squeezed. The jaws bit through the chain and the padlock dropped into the mud. The gate creaked and ploughed a groove in the muddy ground as they pushed it open.

Crouching low, the long, wet grass slapping at their legs, they squelched past the silent row of dark caravans to number 12.

Frost checked to make sure the only exit from the caravan was by the main door, then he mounted its two wooden steps. From inside they could hear a voice babbling, then music. A radio playing. He banged the door with his fist. "Police! Open up!"

Almost immediately, the light went out and the radio was silenced. "Don't sod us about," Frost called. "We know you are in there." He waited. Silence. He stepped to one side so Burton could smash the glass of the door panel with the heavy-duty cutters and slip his hand inside to turn the catch. The door swung open. A stale, empty smell. They stepped gingerly into darkness and silence.

"Torch!"

Burton's torch beam sliced through the darkness and picked out a light switch. Frost tried it. It worked. The dim bulb revealed a plastic-topped table that could be folded back and two bunk beds stripped of clothing. There was a lamp and a small radio on the table, both connected to an electronic control programmed to come on at different times during the night. Frost pressed the manual button. The lamp lit up and the radio came on. A burglar deterrent.

The bottom bunk was over a storage area. They opened the doors to reveal bedding and table linen. A partitioned section was the kitchen, its oven powered by propane gas. Opposite the cooker was the sink. Frost spun the tap and a jet of rust-colored water hammered out, bouncing off the sink and splashing everywhere. He quickly turned it off and wiped water from the front of his mac. The carpeting on the floor was sodden. "I don't know why I did that," he said.

"It doesn't look as if anyone's here," observed Liz, rather redundantly.

"I was beginning to come to that conclusion myself," sighed Frost. "Let's get the hell out of here."

"What about the broken door glass?" asked Cassidy.

"It was already broken when we got here," said Frost. "Bloody kids!" It had been a long day. A fruitless day. He wanted to get home and put an end to it and hope that the morning would bring something marginally better.

He switched off the light and closed the door behind them as they descended the wooden steps. Then he stopped dead, a finger to his lips. "I heard something," he whispered.

A rustling in the grass. Someone moving about. Burton's head turned from left to right, trying to locate the source, then he nudged Frost and pointed. "There!"

A dark shape loomed, then another. A white, blinding glare as torches were shone straight into their eyes.

"Hold it! None of you move. Police!"

"Oh, shit!" groaned Frost.

Mullett was almost foaming at the mouth. "You went into another division's area and you neither sought my permission nor had the common courtesy to let them know?"

"I forgot," said Frost, edging toward the door. He was too tired and fed up to think of a decent excuse and, in any case, this sort of escapade was excusable only if it produced results. They had been dragged off to Seaton Station by the uniformed men, who ignored all their protests, but luckily their station sergeant recognized Frost. "Why didn't you let us know, Jack?" he'd asked. "We've had a spate of break-ins on those caravans, so when someone phoned to report four suspicious-looking thugs creeping about and we find the padlock cut off . . ."

"I have been dragged out of bed in the middle of the night, phoned personally by the Seaton divisional commander," continued Mullett. "He was absolutely furious—and justifiably so. Fortunately, he is a personal friend of mine, so I apologized profusely on your behalf."

"Good," grunted Frost, reaching for the door handle. "No harm done, then."

"No harm done?" Mullett's voice had soared to a screech. He pointed to a chair. "Sit!" He was getting his second wind. "You've done lasting harm, Frost. There are certain basic procedures, procedures that even the rawest recruit would automatically follow. You do not leave your own division without telling me. You do not enter another division without permission and you do not break into other people's property without a search warrant."

"I was sure the kid was there. There wasn't time to get a warrant."

"There was plenty of time. You just couldn't be bothered. In my division, you do things by the book—understand?"

"Yes, I'll bear it in mind," said Frost vaguely. His mind was elsewhere and he was only giving the superintendent a small part of his attention. He stood up.

"And what is worse, you dragged Cassidy along with you, giving him the impression you had my permission."

Frost's lips tightened. Cassidy knew what the score was and had obviously got his own version of events in first. "That was unforgivable of me, sir," he said flatly.

Mullett glared. He never knew how to take it when Frost agreed with him. The sooner he could find a way of replacing him with Cassidy, the better. "There are going to be some changes in this division," he warned grimly.

Frost visibly brightened at this. "They're not moving you on, are they, sir? It's not fair, you're doing your best—"

"No, Frost," snapped Mullett icily. "They are not moving me on."

"Oh!" Frost tried not to sound disappointed, but failed. "Well, if there's nothing else . . ."

Mullett sighed. What was the point? "No, Inspector. There is nothing else." The man was impossible, but this strengthened his resolve. Jack Frost would have to be transferred.

Frost climbed into his car, his mind churning over the events in the caravan park. Something in the caravan had flashed the briefest, subliminal message . . . something important. He yawned. Whatever it was, it would have to wait. Three o'clock in the morning and he was dead beat. Sod everything.

He dug into his pocket for a cigarette. The packet was empty. Panic surfaced as he searched deep into every pocket and scrabbled through the glove compartment. The ashtray held only ash. Sod it! He couldn't get through the night without a cigarette and the knowledge that he didn't have any made the craving almost unbearable. No shops open in Denton at this hour of the morning. Nothing else for it, then. He spun the wheel and took a detour.

She hadn't been able to sleep and was in bed reading when she heard the car draw up outside. She picked up the bedside clock. Sixteen minutes past three in the morning. Footsteps up the path, then the ringing of her doorbell. She slipped on her dressing gown and cautiously made her way down the stairs.

A quick peek through the spyhole and a deep sigh as she opened the door. A scruffy, apologetic-looking individual stood on the doorstep, shuffling his feet and grinning hopefully.

"Jack flaming Frost!"

"Hello, Shirl. Sorry I'm so late."

"Late? Only three flaming days late. You were supposed to be taking me out for dinner."

He clapped a hand to his forehead. "So I bloody was! Sorry, Shirl—this missing kid—"

"You could have phoned. I was all dressed up, sitting, waiting, stomach rumbling. . . ."

He hung his head in contrition. "I'm truly sorry, Shirl. I've been on the go nonstop ever since that kid went missing. I had no sleep at all last night."

She shook her head in mock sympathy. "You poor old git. You'd better come in, then."

He shuffled in after her into the lounge and took off his coat. She switched on the electric fire with its flickering-flame log effect. He felt warmer, happier, and perhaps a little less tired as he dropped down on the settee. "Better late than never," he murmured. "I just had to come and see you."

Her expression softened. She sat down on the settee beside him and snuggled in closer. "Perhaps you're not such a rotten old sod after all," she murmured.

He silently counted up to ten, then nuzzled her soft, warm cheek. "You wouldn't have a packet of fags on you by any chance?"

She jerked upright. "You bastard!" she said.

The bed was hard and uncomfortable and as he lay there a thousand thoughts hurtled around his brain, making sleep impossible. Wearily, he clicked on the bedside lamp and lit up one of the cigarettes from the packet Shirley had hurled at him and lay back, watching the smoke curl to the ceiling.

His mind kept replaying the abortive visit to the caravan. There was something there, something that tried to jog his memory, but his thoughts just kept going endlessly round and round, getting him nowhere. He tried to switch to something else, but again his mind insisted on replaying the search . . . the stripped bunk beds with the thin mattresses . . . about as uncomfortable as the one he was lying on . . . the cupboards full of bedding . . . the kitchen . . . the rusty water belting out and soaking the carpet . . .

At last tiredness began to envelop him and the bed suddenly became warm and comfortable and the outside cold and unfriendly. He stubbed out his cigarette and sank back, sinking down, down, down into a deep sleep, his brain fading on the picture of the caravan . . . the tap . . . the sodden carpet . . .

He sat up with a start. The carpet! The bloody carpet! That's what his mind was scratching and nagging away at, trying to nudge him into action. The right clue for the wrong bloody case!

He was in the car within minutes and back at the station in a quarter of an hour. As he pushed open the door into the lobby the siren smell of frying bacon lured him up to the canteen where he was pleased to see Bill Wells and Burton sitting together, finishing off the standard fry-up breakfast before they ended their shift. He joined them, dumping his loaded tray in front of the empty chair.

Wells looked at his watch. Half past five. "What's the matter, Jack? Did she kick you out of bed?"

"She kicked me out before I got in," said Frost, dipping his piece of bread into Wells's fried egg. He turned to Burton. "I've got a job for you, son."

"I'm just going home," said Burton.

"No you're not," said Frost. "You're on extended overtime." A clatter of trays made him spin round. Jordan and Collier from the night shift, stoking up with food before going back to the Police House. He called them over. "Job for you . . . overtime."

"Mr. Mullett's got to authorize overtime, Jack," protested Wells.

"Sod Mr. Mullett. It can't wait." He dragged his chair back so he could include Jordan and Collier at the adjoining table in the conversation. "Remember when you were dragging the canal for the kid—all that junk we found and chucked back? I want some of it out again."

"Not the dead goat?" said Jordan.

"No, that roll of carpeting."

"It'll never fit your lounge, Jack," said Wells. "And it will be stinking to high heaven by now."

"Especially if that bag of offal has leaked over it," added Jordan.

Frost ignored the wisecracks. "Go and hire a rowing boat."

"We need Mullett's authorization for that," objected Wells.

"Or that of the senior officer, which is me," replied Frost. "So let's get cracking before he comes in and says no."

• • •

It was still dark. Lights from the road bridge reflected off the oily black velvet of the canal and broke up into tiny shimmering dots as the oar blades cut through.

"I think I've got it," called Burton to Frost, who was standing on the towpath, watching. Collier stuck his pole down alongside Burton's and they heaved up a dripping bundle.

Frost's heart started to hammer. Not another bleeding body, he pleaded. If so, they can chuck the bugger back. The smell of decay seemed to confirm his worst fears. But they had dredged up the bag of butcher's offal. "Dump it!" yelled Frost. "I've had breakfast." They let it slither back into the depths where it belched evil-smelling bubbles.

"It was more to your left," said Frost.

They followed his pointing finger and tried again. Half an hour later they found it, nowhere near where Frost had said. They had to remove the putrefying goat carcass to get to it, but managed to drag up into the boat a sodden bundle of folded carpeting, about four by four meters, tied with string and stained with stinking black mud.

"Now what?" called Burton.

"Let's have a look at it."

They rowed to the bank and heaved the squelchy bundle onto the towpath. It stunk to high heaven. Holding his breath, Frost bent over and teased out a corner of the carpet material so he could see the pattern. At first he was disappointed. It was far too dark, almost black, and the sodium lights from the bridge distorted the color. He illuminated it with his torch and this time he knew he was right. He straightened up and beckoned to Burton, who was climbing from the rowing boat. "Recognize it, son?"

Filthy, sodden red and blue carpeting. What was he on about? Then Burton frowned. A frown of puzzled recognition. Yes, he did recognize it. "This is the carpet they laid at Bonleys?"

"Top of the class, my son. The special, exclusive pattern

obtainable nowhere else." Frost's penknife slashed at the string. The bundle fell open, disgorging a flood of stinking water all over his shoes. "Knickers!" The expletive would have been stronger, but his attention was snatched by a couple of large chunks of colored paving slabs used to weigh the bundle down.

"They wanted it to sink. Brand spanking new carpeting worth about twenty quid a square meter." He looked across at Jordan and Collier, who were manhandling the rowing boat up to the towpath. "Your luck's in, lads . . . another lovely job for you." He prodded the bundle with his foot. "Get this over to Forensic. If there's no one on duty get someone in . . . sod the overtime bill. I want them to go over this with a fine-tooth comb—stains, marks, dribble, jam, wee-wee, or even bloodstains. . . . Tell them it's urgent."

Jordan regarded the waterlogged bale with a marked lack of enthusiasm. "It's wringing wet, sir, and it will stink the car out. . . . Couldn't we get a van or something?"

"No," said Frost. "And when you've done that, there's another job for you. Go to the house where the kiddies were killed . . . take those bits of slab with you. Check if it's the same as their new patio and see if you can spot where in the garden this came from." He yawned. A quick check on his watch. Quarter to seven. No point in trying to get any sleep now. "I'm off to the station," he announced.

"Shall we drop you off?" asked Jordan.

Frost backed away from the smelly carpet. "No, thanks. I'll go in Burton's car."

CHAPTER SIXTEEN

Frost sat in the Incident Room smoking the cigarettes Shirley had flung at him and waiting for Forensic to get back to him with their report on the carpeting. They were taking their flaming time. He reached for the phone, but hesitated. They had given him a right mouthful the last time he rung them—"We're going as fast as we can and we'd go a damn sight faster if we didn't have to keep answering these stupid phone calls every five minutes. Don't call us—we'll call you."

Buckets rattled outside. The cleaners had arrived. Through the grimy windows, dawn was giving the sky an orange glow to start off another cold day. He extended his arms and yawned, a long, drawn-out yawn. He felt sticky and grubby. His eyelids were scratching his eyes. He was so damn tired. If he hadn't asked Shirley for those fags he would be tucked up alongside her, warm and happy, not sitting all on his own in this cheerless Incident Room. He raised his wrist and tried to focus on his watch. Just past seven. Mullett would be here in a couple of hours, all clean-shaven and gleaming, ready to start the day off with a moan about the boat being used and the overtime agreed to without his authority. And he'd moan even more if there were nothing to show for it. Frost shook his head and looked pleadingly at the phone. Come on, Forensic. Do your bloody stuff.

As he poked another one of Shirley's cigarettes into his mouth, his nose wrinkled. He couldn't get rid of the smell of that flaming goat, which was almost as bad as one of Drysdale's choicest autopsies. Even the cigarettes tasted of it.

Bill Wells brought in the local paper. "Thought you'd like to see this, Jack." A photograph of Bobby Kirby's tear-stained mother took up most of the front page, with an insert of Bobby. Above it, the headline read "Police Dragging Heels in Search for Little Bobby Claims Weeping Mother." Farther down, a subheading read "Millionaire Supermarket Chief Offers Reward for Boy's Return." A publicity photograph of a grinning Sir Richard Cordwell headed the story that he was offering a reward of £10,000 for information leading to the return of the boy. "Thanks," said Frost, consigning it to the rubbish bin, "I needed cheering up." He turned his attention back to the phone. "Ring, you sod, ring . . . I haven't got all day." As if answering his plea, the phone gave a throat-clearing. He snatched it up even before it rang properly, but it wasn't Forensic. Jordan reported that he and Collier had searched the Grovers' garden and had found a heap of broken patio slabs, a couple of which matched those used to weigh down the carpet. "You did say we were on official overtime?" asked Jordan, sounding worried. "Yes, yes," Frost assured him. He thanked them and told them to go to bed. Again he yawned and wished someone would tell him to go to bed.

He banged the phone down, then jumped as its sudden, immediate ringing caught him off-guard. This time it was Forensic.

"Bloodstains," reported Harding cheerfully. "Quite a lot of blood."

Suddenly the cigarette tasted fine. "I'm all ears."

"Blood group AO."

Frost exhaled a stream of smoke in a long sigh of relief. "The same as the dead mother! Don't let anyone call you a load of useless twots again."

"The overtime has been authorized on this?" queried Harding. "I've had to get a couple of men in."

"Of course it has," Frost replied, wondering how the hell he was going to get Mullett to agree. He picked up a pencil and practiced writing Mullett's signature on a scrap of paper. A little judicious forgery might be required. Then he hurled the pencil up in the air with a whoop of delight. He didn't give a damn if Mullett moaned about the overtime. It had paid off. Blood, the same group as Nancy Grover, had been found on the carpet retrieved from the canal. He looked again through the window at the lightening sky. It wasn't going to be such a lousy day after all, although Mark Grover wasn't going to enjoy it. He no longer felt tired, but wished there was someone with whom he could share his triumph. He grinned with delight as Burton came in with two steaming mugs of tea. "You're early, my son. I'm afraid your lady love isn't in yet."

Burton smiled and placed one of the mugs on Frost's desk.

"Did you see the way she kneed that bloke in the goolies yesterday?" asked Frost, stirring his tea with a pencil. "You'd better watch it if you take her out—that could have been you squirming on the floor."

"If my luck's in," said Burton.

Frost laughed and took a sip of the tea. "Talking of luck, we've had a break with the Grover case." He told Burton about Forensic's examination of the carpet.

"So Grover's involved?"

"Right up to his bloody neck, son. Let's start the day off by arresting him."

He phoned the hospital, but was told by the staff nurse that Mark Grover had discharged himself last night and was staying with his sister. Yes, she did have the address. . . .

He sent Burton to the Forensic Lab to bring back the carpet, then sauntered out into the car park.

A plump little woman answered the door to his knock. Mark Grover's sister was some ten years older than her brother and her face was full of concern when Frost announced himself. "I don't think he's up to answering any questions. The poor boy is absolutely shattered. He loved those children, just idolized them."

Frost nodded in sympathy. "I know, love . . . I know. . . . If it wasn't important I wouldn't bother him."

Mark Grover didn't look well. The pallor of his face emphasized the dark, bruiselike rings round his eyes. He greeted Frost without enthusiasm. "Any news?"

"Couple of promising leads," said Frost. "I know you don't feel up to it, but it would help if you could come down to the station and look at some of the things we've found and tell me if they came from your house."

Grover hesitated. "I don't know."

"Go with the man," urged his sister. "The fresh air will do you good." When he went off to fetch his coat, she whispered to Frost, "Mark could do with cheering up."

"I'll see what I can do," promised Frost, leaving her thinking what a nice man he was.

Grover kept fidgeting in the car, gazing blankly out of the window, not listening to Frost's aimless chatter. He frowned and turned to the inspector. "Are we going the right way?"

Frost had deliberately detoured to go down Cresswell Street. "Just wanted to take a look," he told Grover. He drove slowly past the house where a mass of wreaths and floral tributes from neighbors were laid out in the front garden. One wreath was in the heartrending shape of a teddy bear. Grover swallowed hard, then snatched his eyes away and shuddered. "I'm never going back in there again. I couldn't."

Frost nodded sympathetically, but he wanted Grover to be emotional and unprepared for the big surprise Frost had in store for him.

"What exactly do you want me to identify?" Grover asked.

"Won't take long," said Frost vaguely as he turned the car into the station car park, pulling up by the large storage shed at the rear. He opened the shed doors and ushered Grover in. "This way." The smell greeted them as he switched on the fluorescent lights. They flickered on and Grover stepped in to face the large section of exclusive Bonleys carpeting hanging to dry by the end wall, covered with chalked circles to outline the siting of the bloodstains located by Forensic. Grover stood stock-still, his mouth gaping open, then he turned, shouldering Frost out of the way as he charged out of the shed and into the car park.

"Don't be a twot," yelled Frost, making no move to follow. "Where can you go . . . where would you hide?"

Grover faltered, then stopped and slowly turned, shoulders slumped, his face the picture of despair. He was trembling violently. "My God," he said. "Oh, my God!"

Frost ambled over and took his arm. "Let's talk about it, son. It'll make you feel better."

Mullett, who had learned of the unauthorized overtime and had seen Frost arrive, met him in the corridor. "I want to see you," he snapped.

"Later," said Frost, moving him to one side so Grover could pass.

"Now!" shouted Mullett, quivering with rage.

"Later!" snarled Frost. "Bloody later!"

· · · ·

He sat Grover down in the small Interview Room, which smelled stalely of sweat and unwashed socks. Burton brought in mugs of tea, then started up the recorder while Frost lit up a cigarette and shook out the match. "Right, Mr. Grover. You've been cautioned. You know you don't have to say anything, but let me tell you how I see it. You had a row with your wife. You were sick and tired of her and the kids. You went off to Bonleys, but returned later with the chunk of carpet you had nicked and your wife was waiting, ready to start the row again. Something snapped. You grabbed up a knife and you killed her. The kids saw you do it and started screaming, so you had to silence them, so you killed them as well."

Frost knew this fitted few of the facts, but his intention was to stir the suspect up. It worked.

"No!" Grover was standing up and shouting at Frost. "I wouldn't harm my kids! I loved them!"

Frost took another deep drag and continued doggedly. "Her blood was all over the nice carpeting you'd brought, so you had to get rid of it. You dumped it in the canal on the way to the railway tunnel where you chucked your wife's body in front of a train to make it look like suicide. Then you went back to work to earn an honest crust and establish your alibi."

"No!"

Frost beamed up at him. "Sit down, son, you'll be more comfortable." He waited for Grover to sit. "I'm open-minded. If you've got a better story, I'm willing to listen, but if not, I'm perfectly happy with my own version."

"It didn't happen like that." Grover turned to Burton, who seemed to have a more sympathetic face. "It didn't happen like that. . . ."

"Then tell us how it did happen," said Burton.

Grover wiped hair away from his forehead. "Yes—we'd been rowing. We were always bloody rowing . . . that was our life, one long bleeding row! She said the kids were getting her down and I was never there when she wanted me. I told her I had to earn the bloody money for her to spend and I couldn't do that sitting at home all day. Then we had this rush job at Bonleys. That really got her going. She said that if I went out and left her on her own, she'd kill herself. I said, 'Good—then we'll have a bit of peace and bloody quiet.' I stormed out, slamming the door."

"Had she threatened to kill herself before?" asked Frost.

"It was her bleeding theme song. She'd get hysterical . . . the kids would cry . . . she'd shout at the kids and I'd shout at her. Happy bloody families! It used to end up with me saying, 'Kill your bloody self, then—it'll do me and the kids a big favor!' "

Frost's expression must have registered. Grover lowered his head and stared into his empty tea mug. "I know. I was a bastard. Nancy hadn't been well. She'd go to the doctor, then she wouldn't take his bleeding pills—said he was trying to poison her. I suppose I should have felt sorry for her."

"I don't suppose she got many kind words," said Frost.

A door slammed outside somewhere. Footsteps clattered up the passage. The motor of the cassette deck whirred as Frost shot smoke up to the ceiling and waited for Grover to continue.

"There was this chunk of carpet left over. Some silly sod had messed up the measurements. It was good quality stuff and would only go to waste, so we did a deal with the security guard. Half for him and we would keep the rest. Phil didn't want his share, but the kids had messed up our old lounge carpet so we were going to drop it into my place. Just after midnight we took one piece round to the security bloke's place, then went on to my house. I didn't want any nosy gits to see us, so we went in round the back way. The house was all dark so I thought Nancy was in bed. I got a knife from the kitchen to cut the string and me and Phil carried the carpet through to the lounge. I switched on the light and spread it on the floor to see how it looked. Then I realized Nancy was there. She'd been sitting in the dark. She had that smug expression on her face and she was giggling away as if she knew something funny that I didn't. I said, 'What's the joke?' She said it was a very funny joke. She said, 'We won't have to shout at the children any more because they are all dead.' " He shook his head, registering the disbelief he felt that night. "I said, 'What are you talking about, you silly cow?' And she pointed to the kids' room and giggled. I charged into their bedroom—" He couldn't go on. He buried his face in his hands and his body shook convulsively.

Frost waited. The cassette recorder counter clicked to its next number. Burton raised his eyebrows, tacitly suggesting they should break off the interview at this point. Frost shook his head. A break could give Grover a chance to compose himself, to change his story. He lit up another cigarette and waited. The shuddering subsided. Frost pushed a cigarette across to Grover, who snatched it up gratefully, dabbing at his eyes with a handkerchief.

"Thanks." He leant across to receive a light.

"You went to the kiddies' room," prompted Frost.

Grover knuckled his eyes and nodded.

Frost waited.

Grover stared at the glowing end of his cigarette, swallowing hard.

"And . . . ?" prompted Frost again.

Grover glared angrily. Then he was shouting. "You know bloody well what I saw . . . !" He sniffed back the tears.

"The children?" said Frost softly.

Grover nodded, suddenly calmer. "They were lying in their cots, still and quiet. I thought they were sleeping. I prayed that they were sleeping. But . . ." Again he couldn't go on. His body shook and he screwed up his face as if in intense pain. "It was a bloody nightmare."

"They were dead?" asked Frost.

"Of course they were. She killed them. That bitch had killed them. Aren't you listening?"

"I'm listening," said Frost.

"I could hear her in the lounge, laughing. I charged in there. She was sitting in the chair, rocking from side to side and sniggering. She said, 'I told you I would do it. You wouldn't believe me.' She said it as if it was something to be proud of. I still had the knife in my hand. I went berserk."

"You stabbed her?"

"Yes. The next thing I knew, Phil was dragging at my arm, yelling at me to stop. But it was too late. She was dead."

"Where had Phil been all this time?"

"Out in the kitchen. He saw there was going to be a row and didn't want to get involved."

"He went out there, when?"

"Immediately after we brought the carpet in. When he heard her screaming he came running back."

"And she was already dead?"

"Yes. There was no pulse . . . nothing. I said call the police. He told me not to be a bloody fool. He said they'd bang me inside for murder. She kills my kids and I end up in the nick for life. He brought me some clean clothes and made me wash and change. He said if we dumped her in front of a train it would look like she killed herself."

"And the carpet?"

"It had her blood all over it. He said we should chuck it in the canal."

"And you did what he said?"

"I was in no state to argue. He poured me a couple of brandies and we manhandled her out to the van. Then we rolled up the carpet and Phil put some bits of patio slab in it to make sure it sank. We dropped it in the canal on the way to the railway cutting."

"What happened to your bloodstained clothes?"

"Phil burnt them. He's got a coal-fired boiler."

Frost scratched his chin. "Good old Phil."

"She killed my kids," said Grover defiantly.

"I know," said Frost.

"She was pregnant. She wanted an abortion. I said no. I didn't want an unborn child killed." The irony of this made Grover bow his head and sniff back more tears.

Frost said nothing. Whatever the reason, whoever was to blame, the poor sod had lost his wife and his children. "We'll get this typed up, then you can sign it."

Suddenly Grover looked small and helpless. "Will I be let out for the funeral? The kids'—not hers. I want them buried with their favorite toys."

"I'm sure that can be arranged." Frost stood up. This was a mucky case. Nothing would bring those kids back and there was no satisfaction in cracking it.

"What happens now?" asked Grover as Burton took his arm to lead him out.

"I think you'd better get yourself a solicitor," said Frost. "You're going to need one . . . and so is good old Phil."

In the corridor outside the Interview Room, Cassidy was pacing up and down. He watched Grover being led out, then angrily marched over to meet Frost. "Do you mind telling me what the hell is going on? This is supposed to be my damn case, don't forget."

Frost filled him in about dragging the canal, finding the carpet.

"You didn't think to inform me? You just went off on your own . . . on my case!"

"It's still your damn case," said Frost. "He's confessed. She killed the kids and he killed her. His mate Phil Collard is an accessory after the fact." He handed Cassidy the cassette. "It's all on tape—get it typed up."

He never made it back to his office. Bill Wells came running up to him. "Jack. We've got a couple in the front office who reckon they know where the kidnapped boy is being held."

Frost was unimpressed. They'd had so many false leads from people absolutely positive they had seen Bobby.

"These two sound genuine," Wells assured him.

"All bloody nutters sound genuine," grunted Frost. Sod it. It was probably another time-waster, but he daren't ignore it. "All right, I'll see them."

They were eagerly waiting for him in the spare Interview Room. The man, in his late fifties, was small and sharp-featured, his head constantly moving from side to side like a terrier looking for a rat. His wife, a few years younger, was short and plump. Her light brown hair worn with a little girl's fringe and her short-skirted dress revealing tubby legs made her look like a retarded schoolgirl. Frost introduced himself and sat down. He glanced at the information sheet Wells had given him. "Mr. and Mrs. Mason, eighteen Fullers Lane. You reckon you have information about this missing boy."

"It's not the reward," said Mason. "I want you to understand it's not the reward."

"Of course it isn't," said Frost, thinking, I bet it is, you bastard.

"We should have come sooner, but one hates sneaking on one's neighbors . . . and they used to be so good to me."

"When were they ever good to us?" asked his wife.

"Well, he lent me his lawn mower."

"His old rusty one—he wouldn't let you have his precious new one. And those tight clothes his wife wears . . . you can see her nipples."

Frost cleared his throat. "If you could get to the point."

"Yes, of course," said the man. "This missing boy." He looked from side to side, as if checking on eavesdroppers, then leant over the table, lowering his voice. "They'd be the last people on earth I'd suspect of doing anything like this, but—"

"Who are 'they'?" asked Frost.

"Oh—sorry. I'm talking about Mr. and Mrs. Younger. Twenty Fullers Road."

"Mrs. Younger—she's the one with the nipples?" asked Frost, wishing it was her who was sitting opposite him.

"That's right. We live at number eighteen, they live next door," explained the woman. "They've got this shed—"

"Let me tell it, dear," said her husband, glaring her to silence. "It's a shed at the end of their garden. Nice little shed—he keeps his lawn mower and stuff in it." He hesitated and looked at his wife. "No, dear, we must be wrong. They're such a nice couple. They wouldn't hurt a fly."

"All right," snapped Frost. "They're living bloody saints and she's got terrific nipples. Now, for Pete's sake tell me why you think they've got the boy."

Mason exchanged hurt glances with his wife, but decided to overlook Frost's outburst.

"This shed. Last week he ran an extension lead from the house so he can have electric light in it. And yesterday I noticed they'd put curtains up."

"It was me that noticed it," corrected his wife. "I told you about it." She turned to Frost. "Curtains in their shed! And they're kept drawn so you can't see inside. So what I want to know is, what has he got to hide?"

An enormous dick, thought Frost wearily, slumping down in his chair.

"The light comes on at all hours of the day and night," added her husband.

"So?" asked Frost, getting fidgety. What a waste of time.

"I've seen him taking food down there," said the woman. "Hot food on a tray."

"Food?" Now Frost was interested. He sat up straight and gave them his full attention. "Go on."

"The last couple of days, just before he goes to work and just after he comes home at night, he sticks his head out of the back door, checking that no one's watching, then he scurries off down the garden as fast as he can with a tray of food and he's inside that shed with the doors shut and the curtains drawn."

"And you reckon he's taking food there for the boy?" asked Frost.

"Well, he's not feeding his bloody rusty lawn mower," said the man. "And apart from the food, he's taken bedding down there . . . a big heap of bedding, I saw him."

Gleefully, Frost rubbed his hands. This was getting more and more promising. "And what does Mr. Younger do for a living?"

"He's a paramedic . . . drives around in an ambulance treating people for strokes and helping girls who have babies on buses."

"If you swallow your false teeth, he's the man to call on," added his wife. "There was that woman round the corner— the one who had her womb scraped."

Frost winced and held up a hand in protest. It was too early in the morning for scraped wombs. "You've actually seen him taking food down to the shed?"

"Come down to our house now and you can see for yourself," said the man. "He does it half past eight on the dot."

Frost checked the time. Quarter past eight. He drummed his fingers on the table with excitement. Bedding, food, drawn curtains, and, as an ambulance driver, Younger would have access to chloroform or ether. Knock out the kid and bung him in the back. Who would suspect an ambulance?

Frost smiled at the couple. The dislike he had felt when he first met them had almost gone. "Hold on a moment— be right back."

He raced off to the Incident Room. "Got a strong lead on the kid. A couple of nosy neighbors reckon he's hidden in a shed in the garden of 20 Fullers Lane." He gave Liz, Burton, and Collier the details.

"So it looks as if you were wrong about Finch?" said Liz.

"Infallibility is not my strong point," answered Frost.

"I've been wrong before and I'll be wrong again." He moved over to the wall map. "Where the hell is Fullers Lane?"

Burton showed him.

"Right." He studied the location. "One car round the front and one round the back ought to do it. Burton—you take the back-up car. Liz, Collier—you come with me."

They were in the Masons' bedroom with its cute pictures of puppies on the wall and zip-up pussycat pyjama cases on both pillows of the bed. Two large windows overlooked the rear gardens and a comfortable chair was already in position at each. Hanging from the back of each chair was a pair of field glasses in a case. Between the chairs was a coffee table holding fruit, snacks, and a thermos flask. "The complete nosy bastard's outfit," commented Frost, picturing the Masons, side by side each night, spying on the neighbors through the curtains, chomping away at their snacks and nudging each other when something tasty clicked into focus. Frost sat in one of the chairs and picked up the field glasses. Liz sat in the other.

A creaking of stairs and the chinking of crockery as Mr. Mason came in with mugs of tea on a tray and a plate of chocolate digestive biscuits. "Thought you might like this." He peered through the curtains and pointed. "That's the shed, there!"

At the end of the next garden stood a shed about eight feet by six, in creosoted wood with a green felt roof. The drawn, thick red curtains looked incongruous. Frost swung the glasses to the door. It was fitted with a heavy padlock which looked new and far too hefty for a garden shed.

"How long has that padlock been there?"

"We saw him putting it up last week," said Mason. "Probably frightened someone will steal his lousy lawn mower that's too good to lend to people."

Frost slowly panned across the window, but nothing at all could be seen through the curtaining.

"Look out! He'll see you." Mason jerked Frost back, letting the lace curtain drop into place. "He's coming out."

By pressing his face close to the windowpane Frost was able to see the back door of the adjoining house open and a man's head emerge to look furtively around. The man stared up suspiciously at the window of the Masons' bedroom and Frost jerked back. Younger must know what a pair of nosy bastards he had as neighbors. He hesitated, then came out carrying a tray covered with a cloth. He hurried to the shed, unlocked it, and was inside in a couple of seconds. The light came on, but the curtains remained drawn.

"Good enough for me," grunted Frost. He clicked on his radio and told Burton to hold his position at the rear of the property. He jerked his head to Liz. "Come on. We're going in."

The woman who opened the door was in her mid-thirties, a hard-faced blonde in an electric-blue dress. "Yes?" Her expression changed to anger as Frost and Liz barged past her, Collier following behind. "What the bloody—"

"Police!" snapped Frost, flashing his warrant card. "We're going to search your premises."

"You are bloody not." She parked herself in front of Frost, blocking his way, but was yanked off by Liz.

"Calm down or I'm putting the cuffs on you," she threatened.

"Cuffs? In my own flaming house? Where's your search warrant?"

"We don't need a warrant if we believe there's a life in danger," Liz told her.

"Danger? What bloody danger?"

"Look after the lady," Frost told Collier. "We're going to take a look in their shed."

As he and Liz went out to the garden, the blonde yelled after them: "Arrest the bastard . . . lock him up . . . it's nothing to do with me!"

They charged up the garden and burst into the shed. A man was sitting inside eating beans on toast from a tray. A portable radio was playing. As they burst in, he leapt up, sending the tray on his lap clattering to the floor.

"Police!" yelled Frost.

"Oh, shit!" said the man.

Along one wall was a camp bed. Stacked at the rear was a pile of hospital sheets, blankets, and medical supplies. There was no one else.

"Where's the boy?" demanded Frost.

"What boy?"

Frost radioed Burton, who scrambled over the rear fence. "Bring him into the house."

The blonde was at the back door, trying to get past Collier. "Keep that bastard out of my house," she yelled. "I'm having nothing to do with him."

"Isn't this your husband?" asked Frost.

"Until I divorce the sod, yes. Until then, he cooks his own meals and has them in the shed and he sleeps in the shed. I am not having him in the house."

"Why?" Frost asked.

"The bugger's only been having it away with a tart in the back of his ambulance."

"Once—it happened once," moaned the man.

"You were only found out bloody once," she snapped back. She turned to Frost. "Do me a favor. Arrest him. Lock him up. Throw away the flaming key."

"On what charge?"

"You've seen that stuff in the shed. All the gear he's nicked from the hospital. It's no bloody use to anyone, but he nicks it."

Frost's shoulders slumped. Another false lead. "You can

have this one," he told Liz. "I'm sure the hospital will want to press charges."

Liz radioed for a van to collect the loot, then marched Younger out to the car. "I suppose it was those two nosy bastards next door who shopped me?" he said, glaring up at their bedroom window where the curtains suddenly twitched and sunlight flashed on the lenses of two pairs of field glasses. "I'll get you, you sods!" he yelled. "I'll bloody get you!"

"Another false lead, Frost?" said Mullett, striding into Frost's office and pulling a face to show his disapproval of its untidiness. He had the local paper in his hand.

"Yes, another false lead," agreed Frost, swinging his legs off the desk. Why did the bloody man always have to state the obvious?

"You probably haven't heard," continued Mullett with a sadistic smirk, "but Cassidy has obtained a confession from the husband in the child-killing case."

"Yes, I had heard," muttered Frost.

"The wife killed the children and the husband murdered the wife."

"Something like that."

He's jealous, thought Mullett, jealous of Cassidy's success in the face of his own failures. Well, let's twist the knife a little more. "And this clears Snell—the man you refused to arrest?"

Frost nodded and started patting the layer of papers on his desk to locate his cigarette packet.

"Cassidy got you off the hook with this one, Frost. You should be eternally grateful."

"I am," said Frost, lighting up. "Anything else?"

Mullett frowned. He produced the local paper and dropped it on Frost's desk. He tapped the front-page item.

"Police Dragging Heels in Search for Little Bobby." "Have you seen this?"

Frost picked up the paper. "Flasher at Pensioners Tea Party," he read aloud. He frowned in pretended puzzlement. "Is he a friend of yours, sir?"

Mullett banged his finger on the correct news item. He knew Frost was just trying to be aggravating. "That is what I mean, Frost. 'Police Dragging Heels.' Not the sort of thing I want to read about my division. So what is the position on the kidnapping?"

Frost rubbed his face wearily. "After Cordwell's magnanimous offer, we're being flooded out with more sightings and leads from the public who hadn't said a word before the reward was offered. We're following them all through, but I don't expect they will lead anywhere."

"We can't waste time or money or manpower on false leads," said Mullett. "But if it transpires we ignored one that would have led us to the boy . . ." A typical Mullett instruction, making sure he was covered whatever happened.

"And I'm going to have Finch followed," said Frost.

"Finch? You've gone over every inch of his house, his caravan, his car . . . you've found nothing."

"He's our man." Even as he said it, he had his doubts. Earlier today he'd been damn sure Younger was the kidnapper. He took a drag at the cigarette. "He'd better be our man . . . he's all we've bloody got."

"And what do you hope to achieve by following him?"

"I'm hoping he'll lead us to the kid."

"And if he doesn't?"

"Then we're in trouble."

"You will be in trouble," said Mullett grimly. "Make no mistake about it, Inspector. You will be in serious trouble." He made no attempt to suppress his smile of satisfaction as he turned and marched out of the office.

"When am I never in trouble?" sighed Frost, swinging his feet up on the desk again.

.   .   .   .

Liz Maud led Harold Younger out of the Charge Room and walked him to the main entrance. He had been charged and released on police bail and was free to return to his shed at the bottom of the garden. He had been warned that if he tried to make trouble with his neighbors his bail would be revoked.

Harold Younger was a toe-rag. He thought he was God's gift to women. He kept calling her "sweetheart" and in the car on the way to the station had slyly rested his hand on her knee. She had given him a sweet, encouraging smile, then stubbed her cigarette out on the back of his hand. He had sucked the burn and sworn at her, but didn't try anything else.

She ushered him out of the door, then returned to the Incident Room. Liz was not very happy. Cassidy, the same rank as her in spite of his temporary promotion, was tidying up on a murder investigation, while she was stuck with the petty theft of items from a hospital storeroom.

She found Frost in the Incident Room, seated at a desk, holding the phone away from his ear while a stream of angry abuse buzzed and crackled into empty air. When the noise stopped, he put the phone back to his ear. "I appreciate your concern, Mr. Stanfield. The inquiries into the abduction of your daughter are proceeding. I have every hope we will be able to make an early arrest." More angry buzzing, so he put the phone down on the desk and lit up a cigarette, then when it went quiet, picked the phone up again. "Got to go now, sir . . . urgent call." He hung up and swung round to Liz. "That was Mr. Stanfield. He read in the paper how we're dragging our heels over the kidnapping and intends telling the paper how we're dragging our heels over his daughter's abduction." He stood up and stretched. "So I suppose we had better do something about it. Let's find out how—" He clicked his fingers. "What was his name, the one with the pigtail?"

"Ian Grafton?" suggested Liz.

"Yes, how an out-of-work layabout can afford an expensive hi-fi."

"We were going to call on those two women at Primrose Cottage again," Liz reminded him.

"Primrose Cottage?" Frost frowned, trying to recall what it was about.

"Lemmy Hoxton. They lived in the area where he was found."

"Oh, flip, yes." He'd completely forgotten about that case. Too much happening at once. He couldn't keep up with it.

Jordan came in with PC Collier trailing behind. "You wanted to see us, Inspector?"

"Did I?" asked Frost. "What the hell for?" Then he remembered. "Finch . . . I've promoted him to my number one suspect in the kidnapping case again." Noting their surprise, he added, "All right—so he's my *only* bleeding suspect. I want him tailed. I'm hoping he'll lead us to where the kid is, but for Pete's sake don't let him know you're following him. If he suspects anything he'll probably sit tight, stay indoors, and let the kid die of starvation. You can call on other cars to help if necessary."

He sat down again at the desk, then realized Liz was still standing there. "Primrose Cottage?" she said.

"No." He shook his head. "Lemmy's been dead for months, another couple of hours won't make any difference. We'll go and see Ian Grafton."

He was feeling too fragile to let Liz drive, so he took the wheel himself. She glanced at him out of the corner of her eye. The poor old sod looked dead tired and much older than when she had first seen him when he turned up out of the blue at Patriot Street. "Do you mind if I ask you a question?" she said.

"As long as it's not rude," said Frost.

She grinned. "It's about Mr. Cassidy's daughter."

"Oh, yes?" said Frost, guardedly.

"He seems to blame you for the failure of the investigation."

"Yes," agreed Frost. "He thought I should have tried harder."

"Can you tell me what happened?"

"He idolized his daughter," said Frost, "but he was always very busy those days. He was never able to spend much time with her. That night he'd arranged to take her out for a treat or something—I think his wife was away. Anyway, he had to call it off at the last minute as something boiled over on a case he was working on. The next thing we know is a call from Tommy Dunn that the girl had been knocked down and killed by a hit-and-run driver outside the Coconut Grove."

"The Coconut Grove? What was she doing there?"

Frost shrugged. "God knows! She might have tried to get inside the club—you know what kids are like—but Baskin would never allow that: He knows how keen we are to take his license away. I went straight down there. Plenty of people who heard the car hitting her, not a soul who saw it." He sighed. "So—another of my failures—we never caught the driver and Mr. Cassidy has never forgiven me."

"Mr. Cassidy suggests you didn't follow up the case with your customary vigor," persisted Liz.

"I bet he didn't put it that politely," said Frost. "Let's drop the subject." He turned the car into Fairfield Road. He couldn't park outside Ian Grafton's house. The battered old van was missing. In its place was a gleaming black Porsche.

"When they come into money, they buy fast cars," said Frost with a smirk of satisfaction. He had no doubt now who had abducted Carol Stanfield.

Ian answered their ring. He was disconcerted to see them and had to shout over the sound of heavy-metal music rolling down the stairs. "You can't come up—I've got someone with me."

"Only take a couple of minutes," breezed Frost, barging past him.

As he opened the door the blast of noise from the massive Tannoy speakers almost hit him in the face. The speakers and the state-of-the art hi-fi unit almost filled the room. But there was still room for the bed. And sitting on the bed, her expression changing from delight to utter dismay when she saw it was Frost and not Ian, was Carol Stanfield. Spread on the bed around her were heaps and heaps of bank notes.

She said something, but he couldn't hear. The noise from the hi-fi was deafening and when he struggled to turn it off he only succeeded in turning up the volume. Liz pushed past him and cut the power off from the mains. In the sudden, stunning silence they were slow to hear the sound of running feet taking the stairs two at a time. Ian and Carol were dashing for the front door.

By the time Frost and Liz reached the street, the Porsche was roaring round the corner.

Liz started to run for the Ford, but Frost stopped her. "We'll never catch them in that, love. They've got no money and nowhere to go. They'll be back."

They went back inside the flat to gather up the bank notes. He radioed the station to ask all units to keep an eye out for the Porsche and report its position. "Apprehend the occupants if possible, but I want no Brands Hatch speed chase."

He dropped Liz off at the station with the money, then went on his own to Primrose Cottage.

CHAPTER SEVENTEEN

It was the younger sister, the bubbly nurse, who opened the door. Julie Fleming blinked her surprise at seeing Frost back again so soon.

"Trivial matter," he said, following her into the chintzy lounge where her sister, Millicent, was watching television. She pressed the remote control to switch it off, then turned to greet their visitor. She did not seem at all happy when she realized who it was. "Sorry to bother you both," said Frost, lowering himself down into an armchair and loosening his scarf. He started patting his pockets, smiling apologetically. "Now where did I put it? Ah!" He located it in his mac pocket and produced the typed list of names, which he unfolded and studied. "You used to live at Woodside Lane?" The nurse kept her face impassive, but from the corner of his eye he saw the older woman visibly start: She snatched up some knitting, then pushed it away.

"That's right," said Julie. "A long time ago." She sounded almost too casual.

"I'm a bit puzzled as to why you didn't tell me you used to live there."

Julie frowned. "Why on earth should we?"

Still watching the older woman, whose hands appeared to

be shaking vigorously, Frost said, "Because that's where we found the body, right near where you used to live . . . the man you said never called here."

"Good Lord!" exclaimed Julie, wide-eyed and incredulous. "He was found there?"

"You know damn well he was," snapped Frost. "In a coal bunker, right opposite your old garden."

"How on earth were we to know that?" replied Julie. "You never told us where the man was found."

He tried to hide his dismay as his mind raced over their previous conversations. She was right. He hadn't told them. Damn, damn, and bloody double damn! His one ace trumped.

Julie sat on the settee next to her sister and took her hand. "Millie isn't very well, Inspector. We've told you we know nothing about this man, so unless there is any other way we can help . . . ?" She stared at him, her expression frank and open, but somehow, he knew she was lying. All right, he thought, if it's lies you want. . . .

"I hate to suggest you're not telling me the truth, Miss Fleming, but we have a witness . . ."—he looked again at the sheet of paper as if confirming details—"a witness who saw the dead man, Lemmy Hoxton, come into this house on the day in question. And he never saw him come out again."

The nurse flushed angrily. "I resent the implication. If this man called here, why on earth would we try to pretend he hadn't?"

"Why, indeed?" Frost gave his enigmatic smile which implied he knew everything. But he knew damn all. He was floundering. He stared at Julie, a long, hard stare. She returned it, her gaze unwavering. Game, set, and match to her. His bluff had failed.

But he hadn't been watching her sister.

"Tell him, Julie! For God's sake, tell him and get it over with."

Millicent Fleming was standing, shaking, her face white.

"Tell me what?" asked Frost.

Julie moved protectively in front of Millie. "You can see she's not well. Would you please leave now?"

"What does she want to tell me?" repeated Frost.

Julie signaled her sister to keep silent, then glared defiantly at the inspector. "It's nothing. She doesn't know what she is saying."

Frost stood up and sighed wearily. "It might be better if we all went down to the station."

"All right," said the nurse, patting her sister's hand and gently pushing her back onto the settee. She sat down beside her. "Yes, that man came here. Yes, he robbed us, and then he left."

"He robbed you?" exclaimed Frost. "And you did nothing about it?"

She stared at the floor. "We didn't want anyone to know what he had taken."

"Which was . . . ?"

She hesitated, drew a breath, and put an arm round her sister, who had started to sob quietly. "Photographs."

"What sort of photographs?"

"Explicit photographs. Photographs of . . ." She looked at her sister. "Photographs of us doing things . . ."—she lowered her eyes and her voice was a whisper—"using things."

Frost's jaw dropped. He wasn't sure he had heard correctly. Then he remembered what Liz had said about them. "What sort of things?"

She flushed brick-red. "Do we have to go into details?"

"You use these things on each other?"

"Yes." She was now staring straight through him to the far wall.

"But you are sisters!"

"No. We live together. . . . We have a circle of friends . . . we go to the church. . . . We thought it best to give the impression that we were sisters, but that isn't the case."

"So Lemmy discovered your secret?"

"Yes. He took the photographs and jewelry and money. He threatened to blackmail us if we told the police."

"And where were the photos and jewelry and stuff kept?"

"In the bedroom."

"The connubial bedroom?"

An angry frown. "Of course."

Frost pushed himself out of his chair. "Show me."

"I protest. Surely this isn't necessary . . . ?"

But Frost was already halfway up the stairs. Still protesting, Julie followed him, leaving Millie, face tearstained, on the settee. He opened a door to a daintily furnished room with a double bed. He felt disappointed. He had expected mirrors on the ceiling, black sheets, whips, and leather knickers. Instead, it was comfortable and chintzy, like the lounge. He tugged at the top drawer of a mahogany dressing table. "He took the jewelry from here?"

She was standing by the door. "Yes."

He looked in another drawer. Tucked away under a pile of neatly folded underwear was a grey plush-covered box with a gold clasp. He opened it. Inside were gold neck chains, a locket, two jeweled brooches, a cameo watch, and a heavy gold and ruby bangle. "How come he missed these?"

She looked away and said nothing.

"I'm waiting for an answer," said Frost. "You said he took your jewelry, but your jewelry is still here." He smiled at her. "Perhaps you went out after and bought some more, in which case just show me the receipts and I'll slink away with my tail between my legs."

She was engrossed in the pattern on the carpet.

He pulled open other drawers. In the bottom one he found a wad of colored Polaroids bound with elastic bands. He flicked through them. "You take a good picture," said Frost. At the back of the drawer, the sex aids. The object he brought out and held aloft was obscenely realistic. "Alas, poor Yorrick," he declaimed, "I knew him well."

She winced. "Must you be so unpleasant, Inspector?"

"If I'm pleasant, people lie to me," he said. "He didn't take your jewelry, he didn't take your family snapshots, and I'm damn sure he didn't take your money. Lemmy would never leave without them . . . not unless he was dead." He picked up the pink and red-tipped appliance, waggled it, then slapped his palm with it. "This wasn't the murder weapon, I hope?"

She looked away. "You're quite disgusting, Inspector."

"Lemmy's body was pretty disgusting when we fished it out of that coal bunker . . . you know the one I mean . . . next to your old house."

"We've got to tell him, Julie."

They hadn't heard her come in. Millie looked drawn and was holding tightly onto the door frame as if she was about to collapse.

"Yes," said Frost. "You've got to tell me." He waited while the nurse took the other woman's arm and gently led her over to sit on the bed, then sat beside her, tightly gripping and patting her hand. Frost nodded for Millie to begin, but it was the nurse who spoke.

"I was home when he called. He must have thought it was only Millie in the house, but I had a migraine and was lying down in the back bedroom where it was cooler. It was so hot that day. All I had on was a nightdress. Millie let him in. He did all the things you said . . . got her to turn on the kitchen taps while he came upstairs to the bathroom, ostensibly to flush the toilet. I heard him in our bedroom, opening drawers, so I got up and went to see what he was up to. He was at the dressing table, his back to me."

"This dressing table?" pointed Frost.

"Yes. He'd opened the bottom drawer and found the photographs and the other things. When I shouted at him, he spun round, a dirty grin on his face. He wouldn't hand over the photographs. He said if I wanted them back, I would have to pay. He said . . ." Her voice dropped and Frost had to lean forward to catch what she was saying. "He said, 'Why not try the real thing?' Then he grabbed me and tore off my nightdress. I struggled and tried to get away, but he was too strong. He pushed me over to the bed. He was going to rape me. Thank God, Millie heard the noise and came running in." She turned and smiled at the other woman, who took up the story.

"I heard Julie screaming so I grabbed the rolling pin and ran up. His trousers were gaping open and he was forcing Julie back onto the bed. I hit him . . . hit him . . . again and again. He turned and stared at me, then he collapsed on the floor. I prayed he was unconscious, but Julie said he was dead."

"You didn't call an ambulance, or a doctor?" asked Frost.

Julie looked up. "There was no point. I'm a nurse. I know when someone is dead."

"And you didn't consider calling the police?"

"No."

"You were being attacked . . . he was trying to rape you . . . you were screaming in fear of your life. I can't see any jury convicting you, especially when they learnt what a bastard Lemmy was."

Julie shook her head hopelessly. "Too much personal detail would have come out."

"But it's all going to come out now, isn't it?" said Frost. "All the lip-smacking details." He put a cigarette in his mouth, but didn't light it. "You hid the body?"

"We wanted to put him somewhere where he wouldn't be found for a long time. Millie thought of the coal bunker near the old house."

"A good place," said Frost. "If we hadn't been looking for a missing boy, we might never have found him." He lit the cigarette. "You did something else to him. His fingers?"

The nurse shuddered. "Yes."

He dribbled out a stream of smoke. "Why did you do it?"

"We'd just painted the bathroom. He must have touched the paint. It was all over his fingers. We tried to get it off, but we couldn't."

"Why was it important you got it off?"

"It was our own special color. The shop mixed it for us to match the bathroom curtains." She saw Frost still looked mystified. "The shop keeps all the details of these special mixes in case you want a repeat order. If the body was found, we thought you could have traced the paint back to us."

Frost gave a wry smile. "You wasted your time, love. I wouldn't have been that bleeding clever."

"We scrubbed and scrubbed, but it wouldn't come off," said Millie. "Then Julie said we would have to . . ." She left it unsaid. "We waited until it was dark, then took him to our old place. Every day from then was a nightmare. We kept expecting to read in the papers of someone who hadn't returned home. Nothing. So we thought he had no relatives . . . no one who would miss him. We were lulled into a sense of false security. We even began to fantasize that it never really happened. And then you came. . . ."

"Yes." Frost nodded in sad agreement. "And then I came." He pinched out the cigarette and dropped it in his pocket. "Grab your coats, ladies. Let's go to the station." He kneed shut the drawer with the photographs. Bloody hell, he thought. The press are going to have a field day with this one.

In the car the older woman was sobbing bitterly, tenderly comforted by her companion. Frost said nothing. There were occasions when it gave him great satisfaction to bring a case to a conclusion, but plenty, like now, when he wished he hadn't been so bloody efficient or lucky.

"What will happen?" Julie asked.

"We'll take statements," he said. "You'll be charged and you'll more than likely be granted bail."

"And then?"

"A half-decent lawyer and you'll probably get a suspended sentence."

"The trial," sobbed Millie. "It will all come out."

"It doesn't matter," said Julie. "It doesn't matter."

Poor sods, thought Frost. The photographs as exhibits and all the details of their relationship . . . he could see the tabloid headlines now. . . . Of course it bloody mattered.

They were on the main Denton road. The line of traffic seemed to be moving very slowly and they were just crawling along. The car in front of Frost showed its brake lights and stopped. There was a holdup ahead. He wound down the window and stuck his head out, but all he could see over the long line of vehicles ahead was flashing blue lights. He wound the window down, resigned to a long wait. "Don't know how long this will take, ladies," he said. "Looks like an accident."

It took nearly three quarters of an hour for the traffic to start moving again. The older woman had stopped sobbing and sat, head bowed and red-eyed, staring blankly through the car window, while the nurse, deep in her own thoughts, absently patted her hand. Vehicles slowed down again as they reached the cordoned-off scene of the accident. A large chemical-carrying tanker had slewed across the road and was lying on its side. There didn't appear to be any leakage of fuel, but firemen were standing by. An ambulance was parked on the hard shoulder to the rear. In front of it, another group of firemen with a mobile crane were trying to raise the tanker so they could get to the crushed car underneath. It was a Porsche. A black Porsche. Hovering alongside the firemen, a team of paramedics waited, ready to dash in.

Frost braked abruptly and got out, ignoring the angry blast of car horns behind him.

A traffic policeman hurried over. "Please get back in your car," he ordered. "There's nothing to see here."

Frost flashed his warrant card. "What happened?"

The traffic policeman shrugged. "We don't know yet, Inspector. It looks as if the Porsche was going too fast and crashed over the central barrier smack in the path of the tanker coming the other way."

"Couple of teenagers—a chap and a girl—in the Porsche?"

"Yes." The traffic policeman was looking over Frost's shoulder, where the firemen had managed to raise the tanker and were now using cutting gear on the Porsche.

"Alive or dead?"

A screaming of metal as the roof of the Porsche was torn off. Two of the paramedics pushed forward and looked inside, then moved back, shaking their heads and signaling for the firemen to carry on.

"I think they are dead, sir," said the policeman.

Frost sat them in separate interview rooms and asked a WPC to bring them mugs of tea, which they looked at with obvious distaste and pushed away after the first sip. "I'll be back soon," he said and went off to find Liz to tell her about the Porsche. He hoped she would be in his office, but it was Cassidy who was waiting for him, pacing up and down to work off his anger. Frost wasn't in the mood for Cassidy, but he masked his feelings and gave an inquiring smile.

"The Lemmy Hoxton case is mine," hissed Cassidy. "You told me you wouldn't interfere and yet you've been off to see those women, without a damn word to me. You're deliberately keeping me out of it. . . ."

Frost thudded down into his chair and rested his chin on his palm. Cassidy was right. One hundred percent right.

Cassidy was chuntering away with his moan, nonstop, just like Mullett. So Frost applied his anti-Mullett technique, switching off his ears until Cassidy ran out of breath.

A pause, so he got in quick. "I'm sorry, son. I forgot."

"Forgot?" echoed Cassidy incredulously. "How the hell could you forget?"

"Because I'm stupid," said Frost. "I shouldn't have done it. The two women are in the interview rooms and they're ready to make statements confessing to the killing." He told Cassidy the details. "So it's all yours."

Not in the least mollified, Cassidy stomped to the door, turning for one final snarl. "You haven't heard the last of this," he said.

"I'm sure I haven't," murmured Frost wearily.

PC Collier yawned. He liked working for Frost and he welcomed the overtime money, but the inspector always kept everyone up late, then expected them to be bright-eyed and bushy-tailed, with hardly any sleep, the next day. The succession of late nights was taking its toll and the warm interior of the car was whispering how great it would be to close his eyes, just for a few minutes, and drift off. Collier jerked his head up and wound down the window. They were parked at the end of Finch's turning, tucked away well out of sight, but from where they were they could just see the blue Austin Metro.

At his side, Ken Jordan was slumped in the driving seat, eyes closed, breathing heavily in a deep sleep. It wasn't fair. There should be two of them watching. They'd nearly missed Finch earlier when he had slipped out of the house, but didn't take the car. Collier had followed him on foot to the supermarket, where Finch bought some food and returned home. If he sneaked out again . . . Collier stiffened and nudged Jordan sharply. "He's coming out!" Immediately, Jordan was awake and alert. He snatched up the radio to report to Control, then slipped out of the car. It was his turn to follow on foot if Finch didn't use the Metro.

The front door slammed as Finch and an excited yapping dog walked to the car. Finch was carrying a carrier bag which he slung onto the back seat. It looked like the food he had bought earlier at the Savalot Supermarket. When it was clear Finch was taking the car, Jordan slid back into the driving seat and picked up the radio. "Subject in car driving south into Market Street. We are following. . . ."

Frost located Liz in the main Interview Room. She had Tracey Neal with her, the travel bag with the money between them on the table. Tracey didn't look so cocky as when they had last seen her.

"Tracey's told us about the abduction," said Liz.

"It was Carol's idea," insisted Tracey. "I just went along with her. I haven't had any of the money."

Frost sat next to Liz. "Stealing from her own parents. Why?"

"They're not both Carol's parents," said Tracey. "Her father divorced her real mother and married again. He spends all his money on her—furs, expensive clothes, jewelry. Carol said she'd only married him for his money."

"So Carol was jealous?"

"The new wife would get his money when he died. Carol didn't think that was fair."

"So you staged the fake abduction?"

"Yes."

"Why did you dump the jewelry and furs and stuff?"

"We didn't know what to do with it. Ian thought we'd bound to be found out if we tried to sell them."

"So why take them in the first place?"

"It was Carol's idea. To spite her new mother, I suppose."

Frost intertwined his fingers behind his head and studied the ceiling. "All right, love, you can go," he said at last.

Liz looked at him as if he had gone out of his mind. "Go?"

"I don't think Carol's father will be pressing charges," he said. "If he does, we'll think again."

Liz showed the girl out, then came back, clearly piqued and ready for a row. She wanted to tie this one up herself. Cassidy seemed to be getting all the successful cases and she was getting nothing. But when Frost told her about the accident she was stunned. They were little more than children.

"We'll have to break the news to her father," said Frost. "Double bad bloody news. It was his daughter who stole his money and now she's dead." He sighed. "I wish Cassidy had grabbed this flaming case as well."

Burton chased after them in the corridor and called them into the Incident Room. "Finch is on the move. He's got a carrier bag of food with him. He could be on his way to the kid."

"Let's hope he's not on his way to the park to feed the bloody ducks," said Frost, glad of the chance to put off calling on the Stanfields.

In the Incident Room he snatched up someone's mug of tea and settled down in a chair in front of the speaker.

"Jordan to Simms. Subject heading north to Bath Road. Can you take over?"

"Simms, receiving. Affirmative. We are at first turnoff in Bath Road." A pause, then, *"We see him. Taking over now."*

"Right. We'll move ahead of him and wait at the Lexton turnoff."

Jordan pressed down the accelerator and the car shot forward, flashing past Finch's Metro. They resisted the temptation to turn their heads as they passed, not wanting there to be any hint they were interested in him. No side roads for the next ten miles or so and the first possible diversion was just past the Fina service station near the Lexton turnoff. When they reached the service station, Jordan drove up onto the forecourt and waited.

"Am following," reported Simms. *"Not much traffic about and road fairly straight, so I'm having to keep well back."*

"Be careful," urged Frost. "He mustn't know he's being followed."

"He's putting on some speed," reported Simms. *"He's roaring ahead."*

Frost frowned anxiously. "He hasn't spotted you?"

"I don't think so."

A quick glance at the road map. "He can't go anywhere but straight ahead. Drop well back and let Jordan take over when Finch reaches the service station."

"Roger," said Simms.

"Roger," said Jordan.

The radio went quiet. Frost scrabbled at the cellophane on a fresh pack of cigarettes, cursing when the damn stuff refused to tear. At last he ripped it off in several pieces, stuffed a cigarette in his mouth, and passed the pack around. Another check with the wall map. No way yet of knowing where Finch was heading, but it was clearly well outside Denton. The speaker was making little crackling sounds. "Come on, come on," Frost muttered, "Finch ought to be with you by now." He clicked on the mike. "I haven't bloody offended you, have I, Jordan? Talk to me."

"No sign of Finch yet," reported Jordan. *"I . . ."* A pause, then, *"Oh shit!"*

"What is it?" roared Frost.

"I can see Simms . . . but Finch hasn't reached us."

"He must have flaming well reached you. Simms was behind him. He can't have bloody vanished!"

"He was ahead of me," said Simms.

"Well, he hasn't passed us," said Jordan.

Frost killed his cigarette in the ashtray. "The bastard's got to be somewhere. Jordan—stay put. Simms—double back and see if you can spot him." Another cigarette. He dragged smoke deep into his lungs and waited. A burst of static.

"Simms to Control. I see him!"

"Where?" pleaded Frost. "Share it with us!"

"He's parked up on the grass verge where the road bends."

"Is he in the car?" Frost was concerned that Finch might have parked the car and gone on foot to where the boy was.

"Yes . . . him and the dog. Just sitting, doing nothing. What do I do?"

"Drive on," said Frost. "When you're out of his sight, do what he's done—get up on the verge and wait." He changed channels. "Jordan. Stay put. He's in between the two of you. Unless the sod's got a helicopter in his boot, he must go one way or the other."

He stood up and stamped around the room. The tension was getting to him.

"Finch has just passed me," called Simms. *"He's done a U-turn. He's heading back to town."*

Frost's shoulders slumped. He knew where Finch was heading. "Follow him."

"What's he up to?" asked Burton.

"I hope I'm wrong, son, but I reckon he spotted us."

A few minutes later Simms reported: *"He's gone back to his house. I'm parked at the end of the road. Finch is getting out . . . and the dog. He's picking up the carrier bag of food . . . now he's gone inside."*

"Bum-holes!" said Frost mildly. This confirmed what he suspected. "Tuck yourself somewhere at the end of the road and keep watch. A hundred to one he won't be coming out again today, but we can't take any chances."

"What happened?" Liz asked.

"Finch was testing us," said Frost. "He wanted to find

out if he was being tailed and we screamed out to him that he was. Damn! I've blown it."

"I don't see what else you could have done," said Burton.

"I should have had more bloody cars. Sod Mullett and his economy drive. Finch notices a car behind him. He gets off the road and waits. The same car does a U-turn and comes back again. You'd have to be as dim as flaming Mullett not to know you were being followed." He knuckled his eyes. "Come on, Liz. More job satisfaction. Let's break the news to Stanfield about his daughter."

Stanfield opened the door to them. "Why—it's PC Plod," he sneered. "I bet you haven't come here to tell me you've got my money back?"

"We have got it back, as it happens—" began Frost.

Stanfield wouldn't let him finish. "What?" he shouted. "That's bloody marvelous!" He jerked his head round and yelled back into the house. "It's the police. Marvelous news! They've got the money back!" Almost dancing with delight, he ushered them in. "Come in, come in . . ."

In the lounge, his wife, all smiles, came to meet them. "This is wonderful," she said. "First the jewelry, now the money. . . ."

"It's a bit early in the day," said Stanfield, opening up the cocktail cabinet, "but this definitely calls for a drink."

But his wife, looking over his shoulder, had seen the expression on Frost's face. An expression saying that something was terribly wrong. She went white. "What is it?" she whispered. "For God's sake, what is it?"

They saw themselves out, quietly closing the front door on the bitter sound of sobbing. "I properly sodded that up," said Frost. He felt shattered. Another of his complete and utter shambles. He radioed Control in the hope that Finch had thrown caution to the wind and driven off to feed the kidnapped boy. But Finch was staying put in his house. Frost drummed the steering wheel with his fingers, then came to a decision. "No use pussyfooting around. Finch knows we're on to him, so let's bring the bastard in."

Frost pulled out a chair and shook off some loose papers, which fluttered to the floor. He waved a hand for the man to sit. "Good of you to come, Mr. Finch."

Finch sniffed, and sat down. "The way your officer spoke, it seemed as if I had little choice."

Frost frowned and tutted. "I'm sure he didn't mean to give that impression."

"Well, that's the impression he conveyed."

"Then I apologize on his behalf. Just a couple of things I want to get clear. Back to the other night, when you found the money. Did you see anyone else in the vicinity?"

"Yes—the thug who attacked me and sent me to hospital."

"Anyone else?"

Finch folded his arms. "If there had been anyone else, Inspector, don't you think I would have mentioned it?"

Frost switched on his disarming smile. "Forgive me for asking apparently stupid questions. Our difficulty is that the kidnapper went to a lot of trouble to ensure the money was dropped where he wanted it, but then—unless we consider two strong possibilities—completely failed to collect it."

Finch smoothed his moustache. "And those two strong possibilities are . . . ?"

"We were watching the money. Only two people turned up in the appointed spot—you and the man who assaulted you. Hudson has got a cast-iron alibi for the kidnapping, so we've cleared him. Now we'd like to clear you."

"I see." Finch gave a curt nod. He didn't seem at all worried.

Frost leant back in his chair. "Your wife worked for Savalot Supermarkets?"

Finch frowned. "What has that got to do with it?"

"The supermarket provided the ransom money. We're just wondering if there could be any link."

"My late wife worked for them for more than fifteen years."

"Why did she leave?"

"The new supermarket opened and her smaller shop was closed down."

"Did she want to leave?"

"No."

"Why didn't she move to the new supermarket?"

"The new store was fully computerized. They needed computer-trained staff and considered my wife was too old to learn new methods."

"And this upset her?"

"Yes."

"She ended up by taking her own life?"

"Yes." Finch stared straight ahead.

"How long after she lost her job?"

"Eighteen months. She became very depressed at being thrown on the scrap heap after fifteen years of loyal service. The job was her life."

"She took an overdose?"

"Yes." His face was tight, trying to suppress emotion.

"Did you blame Sir Richard Cordwell for her death?"

"Yes."

"Enough to want revenge?"

"Yes."

"Was that why you chose Savalot to provide the ransom?"

"No." Finch stared up at the ceiling, then took his glasses off and polished them carefully. "I loved my wife, Inspector, and I hated Cordwell as being the root cause for her death. It was an intense hatred and not one that could be satisfied by getting them to pay two hundred and fifty thousand pounds. It was a hatred that made me feel like setting fire to all their stores . . . or running Cordwell down in my car. . . . A hatred that, to my eternal shame, I did nothing about. The pain is still there, but time has numbed it. I did not kidnap the child."

"We know the kidnapper used chloroform. You do the accounts for a couple of chemists. You could have helped yourself to the odd bottle."

"I could have, but I didn't."

"Do you possess a cassette recorder, Mr. Finch?"

"My wife had one a long time ago. I don't think I still have it."

Frost offered a cigarette, which Finch waved away. "There's another point that puzzles me. Hudson says that when he charged across to grab the money, he saw you kicking the grass as if you were looking for something."

"That's right—the dog's ball."

"But that was already back in your pocket, sir."

Finch creased a puzzled frown. Then his brow unfurrowed and he smiled as if the explanation was so simple. "Of course—I'd forgotten. My foot touched something hard in the grass. I was looking to see what it was, and that's when I discovered the travel bag."

"I see, sir," said Frost, trying not to show his disappointment. Either Finch was innocent, or he was bloody clever, and he was sure Finch wasn't innocent. He shook two photographs from the folder and slid them across the desk. "Seen either of these boys before, sir?"

Finch adjusted his glasses and studied them. "No."

Frost tapped one of the photos. "This little boy choked to death on his own vomit. I'm sure the kidnapper did not intend his death. When it comes to a charge, we probably would not be talking murder."

Finch nodded vaguely as if this was of no interest to him. "If we got the other boy back safe and sound, I think we might be able to say a few kind words on the kidnapper's behalf to the judge."

"You should be telling this to the kidnapper," said Finch, "not to me. Are you accusing me?"

"We have to keep an open mind, sir," said Frost. "Explore all possibilities."

Finch stood up. "You've searched my house, you've searched my car, and you've found nothing. If you have anything at all to tie me to this crime, then please charge me. If not, I take it I am free to go?"

"Of course you're free to go," said Frost. "I'll get someone to drive you back."

"Don't bother," snapped Finch. "I'm quite capable of finding my own way home." He strode out of the office.

Frost hurried back to the Incident Room. "Well, sir?" asked Burton.

"Guilty as hell," said Frost. "I want the bugger tailed everywhere he goes."

"All in hand," said Burton. He had assigned Jordan and Collier to watch the house.

"Finch is a glib bastard," said Frost, with almost a hint of admiration. "Always comes up with a clever answer for everything."

"Perhaps it's because it's the right answer?" suggested Cassidy, who was feeling pleased with himself now that he had taken the confessions from the two women which tied up the Lemmy Hoxton case. "Perhaps he's innocent."

"He's guilty!" said Frost firmly. But even he was beginning to have doubts.

Collier nudged Jordan. They were parked at the end of the road, watching Finch's house. Jordan yawned and opened his eyes. "What is it?"

"How much longer are we supposed to be stuck here?"

Jordan shrugged. "Until we're relieved, I suppose." He

was glad to have a nice easy job for a change where he could catch up on lost sleep.

"For all we know they've arrested him. It's been more than three hours since they took him in. No one would think of telling us."

"I'll check," said Jordan, reaching for the radio.

"What do you mean what's happening with Finch?" demanded Control. *"Isn't he back?"*

"If he was back, I wouldn't be asking," said Jordan.

Frost had returned to his office where he slumped down in a chair and closed his eyes for a couple of seconds. He had plunged instantly into a deep sleep, a sleep boiling with jagged dreams involving Finch and the body of Bobby Kirby, hand flopping limply, the severed finger dripping blood. The phone woke him. He jerked up with a start, trying to work out where he was, groping for an alarm clock that wasn't there. Of course . . . he was in the office. He hooked the cord round his finger and bumped the phone off its rest and across the desk. "Frost."

Lambert in Control. He had Jordan on the radio and he wanted to know what was happening with Finch.

Frost yawned and shook his head to try and wake himself up. What was Jordan on about? He and Collier were supposed to be watching the house and Finch should have been back long ago. "I'm coming," he yawned into the phone, and made his way to the Incident Room.

"What do you mean he never came back to the house?" he asked Jordan over the radio. "He left here hours ago."

"I don't know about him leaving you, Inspector," replied Jordan. *"All I know is, he certainly hasn't come back here."*

Frost creased his brow, trying to remember what had happened when he let Finch go. He couldn't remember allocating anyone to drive him back. Then he went cold. Finch had turned down the offer of a lift and he had let his number one suspect—his only bloody suspect—wander out of the station on his own. "You're sure he hasn't returned to the house?"

"Positive," said Jordan. *"We've been watching."* Collier, at his side, reacted to the "we."

"Then be even more bleeding positive," said Frost. "Go and bang on his door. That should set the dog barking. See if someone who isn't there tells the flaming thing to keep quiet."

"I know he isn't there," said Jordan.

"Just do it!" barked Frost. He waited impatiently, listening to little bursts of static from the speaker until Jordan returned.

"He's definitely not in the house," reported Jordan with an air of "I told you so."

"You needn't sound so bloody pleased about it," said Frost. "What happened?"

"I knocked. The dog inside went mad . . . yapping and whining. I can still hear it barking from here. No one told it to be quiet, no one came to the door."

"Is his car still there?"

"Yes."

Frost sighed. What else could go bloody wrong? "Stay put. I'll get back to you." He clicked off the radio, conscious of everyone watching him, waiting to be told what to do. Control was instructed to order all patrols and mobiles to actively search for Finch. Bill Wells was to send every available man out to scour the town . . . pubs . . . cinemas . . . everywhere. He told one of the WPCs to phone all the firms Finch did accounts for, in the hope he was with one of them. Then he contacted Felford Division for someone to keep an eye on the caravan, should Finch decide to return there.

He briefed his team in the Incident Room, stressing how important it was to find him. "He's a calculating sod. If he's gone missing, there's a reason. If he's done a bunk, we'll never know where the kid is, so we've got to find him. Someone check buses and the railway station." He paused, trying to think of anything he might have missed. "And if anyone thinks of anywhere else he might be—public lavatories . . . knocking shops . . . sex-change clinics . . . Toys "Я" Us . . . don't tell me, just go and look."

They bustled out, passing the divisional commander on his way in. Mullett always managed to appear when things were going wrong. "What's the position with Finch?"

Frost told him.

"You just let him walk out of here?" said Mullett, his voice shrill with incredulity. "You said you were having him followed. You said he would lead us to the boy."

"I know I said that!" snapped Frost. "But I sodded it up."

"Something you seem to be doing a lot of lately," said Mullett. "Strange that Cassidy seems to be having all the success while you have all the failures." He marched to the door. There he turned to fire one last bullet. "If you mess this one up, Frost . . ." The slamming of the door punctuated the threat.

"Thank you for your encouraging words," Frost muttered to the closed door.

He waited impatiently by the radio. Nothing. He got Control to radio out to everyone in case their radios had failed. Everything in order. Then the negative reports began flooding in. No sign of Finch anywhere.

Another half hour passed. No news. He radioed through to Jordan. "Please," he pleaded, "say Finch has come home, he's safe indoors, but you forgot to tell me."

"*Sorry, Inspector,*" said Jordan.

Burton and Liz returned, tired and unhappy. "Sorry, Inspector," said Liz. "I don't know where else we can look."

Frost stood up. "You and Burton, come with me."

"Where are we going?" she asked.

"To Finch's house. Let's go over the place again."

"But we didn't find anything before."

"Then let's hope we bloody well find something this time."

CHAPTER EIGHTEEN

The dog began barking again the minute they walked up the path. They could hear it scratching furiously at the kitchen door, trying to get out. Frost rang the bell and hammered on the door, just in case. He waited a couple of seconds, then gave the nod to Burton, who moved forward with the heavy hammer. Two blows were enough. The door shuddered and screws squealed as they were wrenched from the woodwork. Burton kicked the door open and they entered the house, where the dog was barking itself into a state of hysteria and Frost had to raise his voice to make himself heard.

"This is make-or-break," Frost told his team. "Strip the place bare, peel the bleeding wallpaper off if you have to, but find me something that leads us to the kid."

He left them to it and wandered out to the Austin in the drive. Burton, with the help of an enormous bunch of keys borrowed from Traffic, had got the door open and was sitting in the front seat, going through the contents of the glove compartment. Car handbook, road map, old parking tickets . . . Frost took the handbook, which was of Denton and the surrounding area. His pulse quickened when he saw a section carefully ringed, but it was simply showing the location of the caravan that Felford Division were already keeping an eye on. Burton rummaged through the dash compartments. They yielded nothing. Frost returned to the house and the barking dog. He told Collier to try and get the animal to keep quiet.

Collier wasn't too happy about this. The terrier was yapping nonstop and scratching frenziedly at the door, sounding ready to tear the intruders' throats out. Gingerly, Collier opened the kitchen door inch by inch. The barking stopped. Collier froze. A danger signal. He had been told that when the barking stopped, the animal attacked. The dog waddled toward him, growling menacingly, then leapt up and licked his hand. He gave it a pat, and fed it some tinned food from the larder which the dog gulped down; then it went off to sleep oblivious to the house full of strangers. "Bloody good house dog," commented Frost.

In the lounge Jordan was on his knees by the magazine rack, taking each magazine out, shaking it, then leafing through the pages. Frost wanted to tell him not to bother— Finch wasn't going to hide the boy's location in a magazine —but he didn't want to discourage enthusiasm, no matter how misplaced.

Everyone was bustling with their own search areas. No need now to put everything back exactly as it was. Upstairs, in Finch's office, Burton was now studying the items on the cork-based pinboard, taking each off and checking the backs. Nothing very exciting. A few business cards . . . a hand-written list of his premium bonds, a picture postcard from Spain . . . the telephone number of a plumber. In the bedroom Liz was going through the pockets of all the clothes in the wardrobe.

Frost was in the lounge. On a coffee table was an answerphone, its little green light flashing to signal that a message had been left. He played it through . . . it was a call from a firm asking if Finch could do their accounts a week earlier than planned. Frost switched it off. The phone had several numbers stored in its memory so he tried them all, only to get other people's answerphones. They were connected with Finch's accounting business. The man didn't seem to have much of a private life.

Bill Wells called him on the radio. *"We've just had a complaint from the woman who lives next door. She says there's a gang of scruffs in Finch's house acting suspiciously."*

"Okay," said Frost. "I'll see to her." Everyone else was busy, so he ambled over to the next house himself and charmed his way into a cup of tea.

"Knock the dog off the chair," said the little grey-haired woman, pouring hot water into a cup and adding a tea bag. As soon as Frost sat down, the animal, a fat, snuffling bulldog, was up on his lap dribbling all over his trousers.

"You're honored," said the woman. "Alfie doesn't take to everyone." She added milk and passed the cup, with its floating tea bag, to Frost. "Why are the police here?" she asked. "Mr. Finch isn't in any sort of trouble, is he?" She said it as if she hoped he was.

"Good Lord no!" said Frost. "Mr. Finch kindly gave us permission to search his house in case we overlooked something." He didn't elaborate further.

"I saw him go out earlier," said the woman, "but I didn't see him come back . . . and I usually notice."

I bet you do, you nosy cow, thought Frost. "Any idea where he might be?"

She shook her head. "Hardly know anything about him. I used to chat with his wife, but that stopped when she died."

"Yes, I suppose it would," said Frost.

"Killed herself," she said confidentially. "He never got over it."

Frost nodded sympathetically, then his nose began to twitch. A most foul aroma. He hated to suspect the woman, but the dog was looking very innocent.

"Oh, dear," said the woman, catching a whiff. "Alfie's

not being naughty, is he? He suffers from the odd touch of flatulence."

"He's not selfish. He shares it around," said Frost. He lifted the dog off his lap and stood up. "I'd better make a move." The woman followed him to the front door where he bent and gave the dog a pat to show he bore it no grudge. "How does Alfie get on with Mr. Finch's Jack Russell?"

"That's not Mr. Finch's dog," she said. "He's looking after it for someone while they're on holiday."

He gave her a wave and returned to Finch's house. A glum-faced team awaited him. "Nothing," reported Burton. "Not a damn thing."

Frost sat on one of the bottom stairs and fumbled in his pocket for a cigarette to give him time to think. This was his last hope. There just had to be something here.

"I hate to say it," said Hudson, "but could it be you've made a mistake about Finch?"

Frost shook his head. "It's him," he said stubbornly. He was at his lowest ebb. The investigation had come to a dead end, it was peeing with rain, and a seven-year-old was out there somewhere and he hadn't the slightest hope of doing anything about it.

"It's all a mess here," said Liz. "Shall we tidy up?"

"No," Frost said. "Leave it. Let's all go to the pub and get pissed."

From the kitchen a salvo of barks.

Something must have disturbed the dog. Frost stopped dead. The barking triggered the memory of what the next-door neighbor had said, something that hadn't seemed important at the time. "It's not his dog!" he exclaimed. "It's not Finch's bloody dog!"

They looked at him as if he was insane. "Have I missed something?" asked Liz.

"No, but I nearly did," said Frost, beckoning to Burton. "Up on that pinboard in his office there's a holiday postcard from Spain. Go and get it."

With a puzzled shrug to the others, Burton galloped up the stairs and brought down the card, which he handed to Frost. A highly colored beach scene with towering hotel blocks in the background. Frost turned it over and read the message. " 'Dear Henry: Very hot here. We pity you shivering in Denton. Yes, please pay the phone bill for us and I'll settle up when we get back next week. Ethel and Wilf.' "

Frost looked up at them expectantly, only to be greeted by a wall of blank stares. "Flaming hell!" he moaned. "I'm supposed to be the dim one." He jabbed his finger on the card. " 'Please pay the phone bill for us . . .' Doesn't that suggest anything?"

They looked at each other, eyebrows raised in bewilderment. "It means they want him to pay their phone bill," said Jordan, as if answering a stupid, self-evident question.

"So how would Finch know about their phone bill?"

It was Liz who saw what he was getting at. "Finch is keeping an eye on their place while they're on holiday. He's checking their post for them."

"Which means he's got the key . . . to an empty house. A perfect place to hide a kid."

"Possible, I suppose," said Liz grudgingly.

"It's all we've got, so it had better be bloody probable. So let's find out where Wilf and Ethel live. Did anyone spot an address book?"

They all shook their heads.

"His computer!" said Frost. "People keep names and addresses in their computers."

"I tried to access it," said Burton, "but it's password-protected."

"What does that mean?" Frost frowned.

"It means you've got to key in the password to gain access to the information. We could probably crack it, but it would take time."

"Time is what we haven't bloody got!" He paced up and down, pounding his palm with his fist. "They must live in or near to Denton otherwise Finch couldn't keep popping in to check all was well."

"If we knew their surname it would help," said Burton.

"So would their bloody address," snarled Frost, "but we haven't got it." Then his head came up slowly and he smiled. "I've got it. I know how we can find them. The Electoral Register."

"How would that help?" Liz asked.

"The Electoral Register lists everyone living in the Denton area eligible to vote and I'm damn sure that anyone called Ethel and Wilf have got to be of voting age. All we've got to do is look through it until we find an Ethel and a Wilf living at the same address."

"But there's thousands of names on the register!" moaned Burton.

"Then the sooner we start checking, the better. Let's go."

A blue haze of cigarette smoke was rolling around the Incident Room. The silence was broken only by the drumming of rain from outside and the rustle of turned pages from within. Everyone available had been dragged in to help, even patrols dropping in for their meal break, who had to take sections of the register up to the canteen with them.

"I've got a Wilfred and Elizabeth Markham," called Jordan.

"Check it out," said Frost, blowing cigarette ash from his sheet. "People sometimes use a different name from that on their birth certificate." But he wasn't optimistic. No one changed their name to Ethel by choice.

"What is going on?"

Frost raised his eyes from the page and groaned. Mullett again, scavenging around, trying to find something to complain about. Still, he was an extra pair of hands. . . . He quickly explained and pushed a section of the register across to the divisional commander.

"Delighted to help," boomed Mullett. "We are, after all, a team." He settled himself down at an empty desk, which made Frost's heart sink, as his stomach was rumbling and he was hoping to send out for another feast of fish and chips. "You'd be more comfortable in your own office, sir," he suggested hopefully.

"I'm quite happy here," smiled Mullett. "What were those names we were looking for . . . George and Mildred?"

"Wilf and Ethel."

"Of course, of course." Mullett coughed pointedly. "I'm sure we'd all work a lot better if people didn't smoke."

They had three false leads. Two Wilfred and Ethel's that seemed promising, but were at home watching television when the car called to check. At the third, the house was empty, but the next-door neighbor said they were at the pub and would be back in half an hour.

Frost rubbed a weary hand over his face. The names were beginning to blur and wriggle in front of his eyes. At one stage he suddenly realized he had turned a page but hadn't consciously read any of the names on it. There must be an easier way.

"What names did you say again?" asked Mullett.

Bloody hell. The man had a memory like a bleeding sieve and how could he have been checking away for half an hour without knowing the names he was looking for? "Wilf and Ethel," said Frost patiently.

"I've got a Wilfred and Ethel here," said Mullett, tapping the page with his finger. Frost dashed across and snatched it from him. "Wilfred Percival Watkins and Ethel Maureen Watkins, 2 Wrights Lane, Denton." He checked the map. Wrights Lane was a fairly exclusive area with a few detached Victorian houses in extensive grounds on the outskirts of Denton, not too far from the woods and the river.

After three disappointments, no one got too excited.

They plodded on with their own lists while Frost sent an area car to check this one out.

Within five minutes came an excited radio message: *"Charlie Baker to Mr. Frost. Checked the Wrights Lane address. Lights are showing, but as you instructed we did not approach. Neighbors say the owners are a retired pharmacist and his wife, holidaying in Spain. They also confirm they have a Jack Russell terrier which is being looked after by a friend."*

"Bingo!" yelled Frost, throwing his list up in the air, where the papers fluttered and autumn-leafed to the ground. He grinned broadly at Mullett. "Thank you, Super. I always said you weren't entirely useless."

By the time Mullett had worked out that this wasn't the wholehearted compliment he had assumed, Frost and his team were racing across the rain-swept car park, leaving empty desks and sheaves and sheaves of printed lists.

The car slithered and bumped up the unpaved road that led them to Wrights Lane. Rain bounced and drained off the road into an overflowing ditch which ran along its length. The road dipped sharply as the car went beneath a small iron railway bridge and churned its way through a deep puddle. A slight bend and there was the house, just to their left behind a fringe of trees. Its lights were on.

They turned into the drive, skidding to a splashing halt by the front door, the second car with the rest of the team having to brake sharply to avoid running into the back of them. Out of the car, heads down against the driving rain, and Frost was hammering at the front door after sending Burton and Jordan round to the back. No answer, but through the frosted glass of the door he could see someone moving about inside the hall.

He was about to knock again when Finch called, "Who is it?"

"Police—open up."

"Just a minute."

A brief pause, then the door was opened by Finch, his jacket off, a sponge mop in his hand. He raised his eyebrows in pretended surprise. "Inspector Frost! Twice in one day—what an unexpected pleasure!"

"We want to search these premises," said Frost.

"Do you have a warrant?"

"No, but it won't take long to get one."

"Is it about the missing boy?"

"Yes."

"Then I waive my right to demand a warrant. Please search where you like." He moved back so they could pass. "Do wipe your feet . . . and don't make a mess. This isn't my house."

He's too cocky, thought Frost, hoping and praying this wasn't going to turn out to be yet another wasted exercise. He's too bloody cocky.

They thudded past him. Liz went straight through to the back door to let in Burton and Jordan, who were shivering in the rain. They stepped thankfully into the dry and onto gleaming checkerboard linoleum tiles, dripping pools of water which Finch hastily sponged up with the mop. "Please," he admonished. "I've gone to a great deal of trouble to tidy this place up. It belongs to friends of mine who return from Spain tomorrow." He checked the washing machine, which was churning away. "I've got so much to do before then."

Liz allocated areas of search, while Frost sat with Finch in the lounge, a large, high-ceilinged room, its gleaming furniture reeking of polish.

"How did you find me here?" asked Finch, slipping on his jacket. Then he smiled. "Of course—the address on the dog's name tag. How clever of you!"

Bloody hell, thought Frost. Don't tell me it was on the flaming dog's name tag all the time! He smiled back modestly as if pleased at his cleverness. "That's right."

"Why do you think the boy is here, Inspector?"

"Because you are here, Mr. Finch." He took a cigarette from the packet and lit up.

Finch grabbed at a heavy glass ashtray and pushed it over to him. "This smacks of harassment. I have already told you I know nothing about the boy. You have nothing to suggest otherwise, yet I am constantly having to put up with this cavalier treatment."

"Where is he?" asked Frost.

"I wish I knew," said Finch. "The poor little mite, away from his parents . . ."

An urgent call from upstairs. "Sir—here!"

Burton had found something. Frost shot a glance across to Finch, who remained impassive. He was carefully blowing flakes of cigarette ash from the polished top of the table.

"In here, sir." Burton was waiting on the landing outside a grey-painted door. "Put your cigarette out, please." Frost, puzzled, did as the DC requested. He exhaled smoke, which Burton fanned away before opening the door a fraction, pushing Frost in, then quickly closing it behind them both.

They were in a small bedroom at the back of the house. An oak wardrobe, a small matching dressing table, and a single bed which was pushed tight against the wall. The bed had been stripped down to the ticking on the mattress and pillows. A smell of wet wool came from the carpet, which had been shampooed recently and was still slightly damp.

"Take a sniff, sir," said Burton.

Frost sniffed. "Polish? Carpet shampoo?"

Burton looked disappointed. "Nothing else?"

Frost tried again, then frowned. A sickly, sweet smell. Very faint, but it was there. "Chloroform?"

Burton nodded in agreement. "That's what I think."

"The kid's been in this room," said Frost. "On that bed!" He lowered his nose to the mattress and sniffed, but could detect nothing. He went to the door, opened it briefly, then called for Liz to bring Finch up.

Finch came in and stood in the middle of the bedroom. "Smell anything?" Frost asked him.

With a cocky smile, Finch took a deep breath, his nose twitching delicately as if he was savoring the bouquet of a rare wine. "Furniture polish . . . carpet shampoo . . . ?" he suggested. His nose wrinkled in distaste. "And stale tobacco smoke, which I imagine is coming from you. May I open the window?"

"No," snapped Frost. He gave a tentative sniff, but by now the dying linger of the anesthetic had expired. "We could smell chloroform!"

Finch gave a knowing smirk and shook his head. "Dry-cleaning fluid. There was a stain on the carpet—the dog—I cleaned it off and shampooed it." He bent over and peered. "It's completely gone now."

Frost pointed to the stripped bed. "Where's the bedding?"

"In the washing machine. The dog—he was sick over the pillow."

Liz was told to dash down to the kitchen and rescue the bedding from the washing machine in the hope Forensic could do their stuff on it.

"Inspector!" Jordan called from below. It sounded important. Frost scuttled down the stairs, two at a time, hoping and praying that it was something that would wipe the supercilious smile from Finch's face. Under the stairs an open door led to steps to the cellar. Jordan was calling from there.

A large cellar, its floor of flagstones, the bare brick walls whitewashed. An unshaded seventy-five-watt bulb swung in a holder, flickering grotesque shadows on the walls, along which ran metal shelving stacked high with cardboard boxes, bottles, drums, stock left over from when Finch's friend sold his chemist shop.

"I found this," said Jordan, handing the inspector a large bottle in blue fluted glass with a label that read "Trichloromethane ($CHCL_3$—Chloroform)."

Frost held the bottle up to the light. It was about a third full. Removing the stopper, he lifted it to his nose. Not white spirit this time. Definitely chloroform. He nodded grimly, then looked down at the floor, stamping his foot on the flagstones, pointing out a couple that appeared loose. Where better to bury a body? "Have them up, son. All of them . . . especially the ones that don't look as if they have been moved."

Back up the cellar steps, squeezing tight against the wall to get out of the way of the Forensic team who were crawling everywhere. Harding didn't look very optimistic even when Frost told him about the chloroform. "You'd expect to find it among a chemist's stock. It doesn't really prove anything."

"How's the search going?" Frost asked.

"He seems to have made sure there's nothing for us to find. This place has been scrubbed, sponged, polished, and vacuumed. The vacuum cleaner is a wet-and-dry model, so it's had water through it which has removed nearly all traces of dust and fiber."

"What about the bedding from the washing machine?"

"We'll have a go at it at the lab, but I reckon it's been too well washed to yield anything."

"The kid was here," said Frost firmly. "I'm pretty certain he was here up to a couple of hours ago."

"Would he have had the run of the place?" asked Harding.

"Hardly," replied Frost. "I reckon the poor little sod was trussed like a chicken on that bed."

Harding shrugged. "Then he wouldn't have left much trace in the rest of the house, would he?"

"Inspector!" Liz, this time calling him from the landing. Another bloody clue that would probably lead nowhere. Harding followed Frost up the stairs. Liz took them into a small boxroom which had been converted to an office. It was very similar to the one in Finch's house. A small desk had been jammed up against one wall. On the desk was an IBM 286 PC connected to a printer. Liz pointed. "A twenty-four-pin dot matrix printer, the same type as the one used for the ransom demand."

Frost grinned with delight. "Then we've got him." He turned to Harding. "Can we prove the ransom note was written on this machine?"

Harding swiftly disillusioned him. "All we can say is that the note was printed on a machine of the same type. There is no way we can prove this was the actual machine used."

Yet again Frost was deflated. "There must be some way."

"I don't think so." Harding sat himself down at the desk and peered at the printer. Its was a Star 24–10, some five years old. "There's no typeface, only little pins."

"The ribbon," suggested Frost. "Wouldn't it leave an imprint on the ribbon?"

Harding sniffed his doubts. "The ribbons are a continuous loop. They go round and round with subsequent letters printed on top of earlier ones. It would be almost impossible to separate them out."

"Try anyway," said Frost.

Harding lifted the printer cover. "If it's a fairly new ribbon I suppose there might be a chance." He took out the cassette and examined it, then shook his head and passed it over to Frost. "Out of luck again, Inspector. It's too damn new. It hasn't been used. The old one has been replaced. As I said, your Mr. Finch is determined not to give us anything to go on."

Frost thudded down the stairs with the cassette and held it aloft. "We're looking for a used printer ribbon, just like this one. Check waste bins, rubbish bags, dustbin sacks. We've got to find it." But he knew Finch was too damn clever to replace the ribbon without making sure there was no way they could get at the old one.

In the living room Finch was sitting, watching the proceedings with a cynical smile, a smile which said, all too clearly, "There's no way you dumb policemen are going to find anything that would incriminate me."

"We found chloroform downstairs," Frost told him.

"That's hardly surprising. My friend used to run a chemist shop. Old stock, I imagine."

"Chloroform was used on the first boy."

"So you said." Finch looked at Frost in mock reproach. "You are surely not suggesting my friend had anything to do with it? I think you will find he was in Spain at the time."

"You seem to be finding this all very amusing, Mr. Finch. A boy of seven kidnapped, mutilated, frightened . . . a boy who might even be dead."

"I don't find it remotely amusing, Inspector. What I do find amusing—although I suppose 'pathetic' is the right word—is that you should be wasting your time here . . . all these men . . . all these resources." He stared at Frost. "Can you tell me one thing—one single thing—you've found that proves I had anything to do with it . . . just one . . . ?" His superior smile made Frost fight hard to control the urge to smash his face in. "You can't, because there isn't anything."

"We'll find it," said Frost, trying to believe it himself. He jerked his head at Liz and told her to take Finch to the station. "We'll question him again there," he told her.

Clanging noises echoed from the cellar and drew him down the stairs to investigate. Jordan and Collier, both sweating profusely, were levering up flagstones. It was a tiring job. The flagstones were big and heavy, needing all their efforts to lift and move without crushing their fingers. Two stacks of removed flagstones stood in one corner. A large rectangle of earth was exposed. Dry earth, untouched since the floor was laid. Jordan wiped sweat from his brow. "Nothing yet, Inspector."

Frost went over to the stacks of stones. The flags were nearly three inches thick. He thought for a second. "Pack it in—forget it. If it's taking two of you to lift one of them, he could never have done it on his own." The smug look on Finch's face had convinced him they could tear the place apart and not find anything. They would have to look elsewhere. But where . . . where?

When he went back into the lounge to check progress, one of the Forensic team going over the upholstery with a hand-held vacuum cleaner kept moving him on from wherever he tried to settle. He took the hint he was in the way and yelled that he was going back to the station.

He was standing in the shelter of the porch, turning up his mac collar ready for the plunge through the rain to his car, when he noticed the garage door was slightly ajar. It had already been searched, but on impulse Frost splashed across and went inside. A chocolate-brown Renault took up most of the space. He squeezed through and checked the boot in the remote hope that the original searcher had been as slapdash as he usually was and that he would find Bobby curled up, fast asleep, happy to be rescued. All the boot yielded was a spare tire, some tools, a metal petrol can, and a towing rope. He flashed his torch to the ceiling and the beam caught a shelf high up on the wall. On the shelf were a couple of bulging blue plastic bags which didn't look as if anyone had had them down to check. Frost reached up and managed to grab the corner of one bag. He tugged, then a bit harder. The entire shelf tipped up and the bags slithered off and thudded to the ground, bouncing off his head on the way. Hitting the cement floor, the bags burst open, spewing out packs of cotton wool and tins of slimming foods, which rolled and clattered everywhere. More junk from the chemist's shop.

Frost rubbed his head ruefully, then kicked one of the tins to relieve his feelings. It rolled underneath the car. He dropped on his hands and knees to retrieve it and it was then he noticed there was mud in the tread of the tires. Fresh mud, still wet. Finch had been out in the car, very recently, and then must have dried off the bodywork to disguise the fact. Frost stood up. The kid. Finch had used the car to move the kid. That was why he was so smug and unconcerned when they were searching the house.

He yelled for Harding, who was annoyed at having to run through the rain and glared at Frost with his hair streaming and his jacket soaking. Frost indicated the mud and asked if there was any way of determining where it came from. "Some little six-inch square of Denton which has this unique type of mud, found nowhere else in the universe?"

Harding squatted and studied it, then he stood up. "I can tell you exactly where this came from, Inspector." He pointed. "From the lane just outside the front gate. Wherever he went, he picked that up on the way back but I don't suppose that is much help."

"About as good as the sort of help Forensic have been giving me all bloody day," snarled Frost, plunging out through the heavy curtain of rain back to the house. He went to the bedroom. The smell of chloroform had completely gone. He wondered how long it would have lingered. He was guessing that Finch had chloroformed and removed Bobby not too long before the police turned up. Chloroformed him, driven and dumped him somewhere, and then driven back. Burton came in to join him. Frost told the DC of his theory.

"You're saying that wherever he took the kid, it isn't very far away from here?" said Burton.

"That's exactly what I'm saying," said Frost. "Otherwise we wouldn't still have been able to smell chloroform." He went to the window and looked out. The wind was blowing the rain almost vertical. A few dotted lights of houses could be seen, but beyond them, just visible, lay the dark, sprawling mass of Denton Woods. The woods! That had to be it. That's where the boy was. "He's dumped the kid in the woods, somewhere," said Frost.

Burton joined him at the window. The woods stretched on and on. "If you're right, he could be anywhere."

"I know," said Frost.

"We'll have to wait until morning. We'll never find him in the dark in this weather."

"By the morning the poor little sod could be dead," said Frost. He tugged his radio from his pocket and called Mullett.

Mullett wanted an almost cast-iron guarantee from Frost that they would find the boy before he agreed to authorize a full-scale search party.

Frost gave it to him.

"Two hours," added Mullett, quickly checking the balance of the overtime account. *"If they haven't found anything in two hours, call it off."*

"Of course, sir," said Frost.

In the Interview Room Finch had been reunited with the dog, which was stretched out on the floor at his feet. "Where did you go in the Renault?" demanded Frost.

"Out to the lane and back. I wanted to check if it was functioning all right. If so, I would drive back home in it, if not, I would call a cab."

"And?"

"It spluttered a bit—water in the carburetor, I think—so I decided I would take a cab when the time came. I didn't anticipate you would kindly provide me with transport."

"Why did you dry the car off to conceal the fact you had been out in it?"

Finch waggled a reproving finger. "You attribute the basest motives to me, Inspector. It is my friend's car. When I borrow things, I return them in the state in which I receive them. The car was clean when I drove out. I made certain it would be clean when my friend returns from Spain tomorrow." He smiled. "Satisfied?"

Frost concealed his irritation. The bastard had a glib answer to everything, all delivered with that snide, unconcealed smile which showed his satisfaction in putting one over on the police. "You took that kid to the woods, didn't you?"

Finch raised his eyebrows in mocking query. "Did I? That's news to me."

"We've got teams with dogs searching the woods now," said Frost. "It won't be so bloody funny when we find him."

"I hope you do find him," said Finch, "but if you think I put him there, you are wasting your time."

Frost saw no point in pushing it further. "Interview suspended." He marched out to his office. Forensic must have turned something up by now, something that would wipe the smile off the face of this smug bastard.

He pulled the phone toward him, then hesitated. If they had anything they would have been through to him. He stared moodily at the rain cascading down the window, blurring the view of the car park.

The phone rang. He grabbed it. It wasn't Forensic, it was Arthur Hanlon.

"Radio message from Johnnie Johnson," reported Hanlon. Johnson was leading the search team in Denton Woods. "He says it's absolutely hopeless. The dogs are useless in this weather, the team can hardly see a hand in front of their faces, and they're slithering and sliding all over the place. Unless we can pinpoint a precise search area, they want to pack it in."

Frost looked out again at the atrocious weather. He could sympathize. Soaking wet, stumbling through sodden undergrowth in the dark, brambles snagging and slashing, visibility down to a few feet. They'd have to stumble over the poor little sod to locate him. Hardly any chance of finding him in those conditions, but no chance at all if they packed it in. "Tell them to give it another couple of hours," he told Hanlon, completely forgetting Mullett's limit of two. "Tell them I am sure the kid is there."

"But don't tell them I'm equally sure the poor little bugger is dead," he muttered after he had hung up.

He steeled himself to phone Forensic. Let's get the bad news over. Harding answered the phone. He was most apologetic.

"That house has been cleaned so thoroughly, we've found nothing that would help, but there were a few fibers that could have come from the child's clothing."

Frost gripped the phone tightly. His luck had changed at last. "Then we've got him."

"I'm afraid not, Inspector. The fibers mean nothing on their own. Find the child and from his clothing we can prove he's been in the house . . . but we need the child."

"If I had the child I wouldn't bleeding need you!" growled Frost.

"We can't find what isn't there, Inspector."

He banged the phone down, but Harding was right. Finch was being too clever for all of them. He had stripped Dean of his clothing to avoid leaving any clues and had probably done the same with Bobby.

"How is it going, Frost?"

Bloody hell! Bang on cue when things were going wrong, there was Mullett ready to twist the knife in the wound.

"Not too brilliant," he replied. "Without proof it looks as if the bastard is going to get away with it."

"Have you heard from Forensic yet?"

"Yes. They haven't come up with a flaming thing."

Mullett stared at Frost, his lips tightening. This, of course, was all Frost's fault. "So tonight's expensive exercise has achieved precisely nothing? In fact you've achieved nothing right from the moment you took on this case."

Frost smiled sweetly. "Thank you, Super. You have the God-sent gift of stopping me from feeling big-headed." He barged past him out of the office. He'd had all he could stomach of Mullett for one night.

Back to the Interview Room for another crack at Finch,

but he found Liz there on her own, patting the dog. "Toilet break for Mr. Finch," she explained.

"Let's hope the seat falls down on his dick," Frost grunted. He sat down and immediately the dog leapt up on his lap. He patted it and it licked his hand. "Friendly little sod, isn't he?" His eyes narrowed. He wondered if the dog had been friendly with the boy. If it had got on the boy's lap . . . nuzzled against him, licked him . . . could some hairs from the boy have got onto the dog? He scooped the animal up and dashed off to the Incident Room where he phoned Harding, catching him as he was just ready to go home.

"Worth a try, Inspector," agreed Harding. "Extra over-time, of course."

"Of course," said Frost. An area car was called in to rush the dog off to the laboratory.

Finch, escorted by Burton, was led back into the Inter-view Room. He looked around. "Where's Czar?"

"He's helping us with our inquiries," Frost told him.

Finch stood up. "I want him here—now!"

"Sit down," snapped Frost. He shook a cigarette from the packet and offered one to Finch, who waved it away in annoyance.

Frost lit up and grinned. "Friendly little dog, isn't it? Did he jump up to the kid . . . was he the only friend the poor little sod had?"

"I've already told you—"

"—that you don't know anything about the kid. Well, you've been bloody clever with your sweeping and scrubbing and vacuuming, but I bet you didn't give Rin-Tin-Tin a bath. Our Forensic Lab are checking the dog over now. Want to bet they find the odd hair or two from the kid . . . the poor little kid whose finger you chopped off? Come on —I'll give you ten to one we find something."

The briefest flicker of concern blinked on Finch's face, but was swiftly suppressed. He stared at Frost, expressionless. "You won't find anything, because I know nothing about the kidnapping. I have already made a statement to that effect. I have no intention of saying the same thing over and over again. Unless you intend to charge me, I want to go."

"Give my colleague another statement explaining your movements tonight," said Frost. "We'll get it typed up and you can sign it . . . but it might be best to wait until we get the results from the dog first in case you want to change it to a confession."

If this was meant to ruffle Finch, it failed. I'd hate to play poker with you, thought Frost, making his way back to the Incident Room.

Burton sat by the old Underwood manual typewriter on the end desk in the Incident Room pecking out the statement for Finch to sign. Frost had told him to take his time so they could hold on to Finch until the results from Forensic came through. Burton didn't need telling. He was a very slow typist at the best of times and this snail's progress was his top speed. . . . Frost came in and looked hopefully at Hanlon, who had just put down the phone.

"They're still looking, Jack. It's the wrong sort of weather for a search."

"It's the wrong sort of weather to be on holiday, but that's where I ought to be flaming well be, not here." Frost hurled himself down into a chair and realized one of their party was missing. "Anyone seen Mr. Cassidy?"

"No, thank God," muttered Burton.

The external phone rang. Hanlon answered it, listened, then put his hand over the mouthpiece. "For you Jack— Forensic."

Frost took the phone, pausing before he raised it to his ear. He didn't think he could take much more bad news

without something to cheer him up, like Mullett falling over
and breaking his neck. "Frost."

"We've taken samples from the dog's fur," reported the
lab technician flatly. "We've found three hairs that could
have come from a young boy"—Frost's elation flared, but
was instantly doused—"but they do not come from Bobby
Kirby. . . . Sorry, Inspector."

Frost held the phone and stared blankly as waves of despair washed over him. Then his head snapped up. They'd
only tried to match it with Bobby. "The other boy—Dean
—the dead boy . . . see if they come from him!" he roared
into the mouthpiece. "No—don't ring back . . . I'll
hold."

The phone at the other end went down with a bang and
he could hear mutterings, echoing footsteps, and then silence. He thought they had forgotten him and started
whistling into the mouthpiece. Someone picked up the
phone, said, "Be with you in a minute," and immediately
dropped it down again.

He hunched up a shoulder to hold the phone to his ear
while he fished out his cigarette packet. Before he could
light up, however, Harding was back. This time he wasn't
apologetic. He was downright jubilant. "You were right, Inspector. Those hairs come from the first boy, the dead one,
Dean Anderson."

It was so long since he had heard good news, Frost didn't
know how to take it. "Are you sure? Lie to me if you're
not . . . but please say you're sure."

"Positive. Absolutely positive."

A hot surge of relief flooded his body. "You're not so
bloody useless as I thought." He spun round in his chair
and yelled in triumph: "We've got the bastard! We've got
him!"

Frost bumped into Mullett, nearly spinning him round,
as he sprinted down the corridor to the Interview Room.
"You look absolutely ravishing tonight, Super," he cooed to

a puzzled and gaping superintendent. "We've got the bastard!" he explained. "I'm going to charge him now."

Finch was sitting, looking bored, as he waited to sign his statement, when Frost burst in. Right, thought Frost. Now we wipe the smile off your face, you supercilious sneering sod.

He crashed down in the chair opposite Finch and leaned forward. "It's the end of the line, you sod. Man's Best Friend has let you down. There are hairs from the dead boy all over it."

Finch flinched as if he had been hit. He struggled to keep his face impassive, but he was clearly shaken. "I don't think I want to say anything," he said carefully.

"Is the boy still alive?"

Finch didn't answer.

"Don't sod about," said Frost. "It's all over. We've got you. Where is the boy?"

Finch sank his head and squeezed his chin in thought. Then he straightened. "I want the tape recorder switched off."

"Why?" asked Frost.

"Turn it off and I'll tell you."

Frost nodded to Liz, who stopped the recording and removed the cassette tape.

"I would now like the young lady to leave," said Finch. "What I have to say is for your ears only."

Frost nodded. They waited until Liz went out, scowling. "Well?" Frost said.

"You believe me to be the kidnapper."

"I bloody *know* you are!"

"But your first concern is for the boy."

"So?"

"Only the kidnapper would know where the boy was, and in telling you, he would be sealing his guilt."

"Go on," urged Frost.

"If I were the kidnapper, I would want a deal. An assurance, in writing, that if I reveal the boy's whereabouts, all charges would be dropped and any evidence you might have against me would be destroyed."

"We don't make deals," said Frost.

Finch shrugged. "Well, in that case the boy will most certainly die." He looked up to the ceiling; overhead the rain could be heard bucketing down on the roof. "Such shocking weather. If that poor boy is out in it, he'll be dead by the morning."

"You're telling me Bobby's still alive?"

A thin, mirthless smile from Finch. "Only the kidnapper would know that, Inspector." He moved his chair closer to the table. "You've got nothing on the kidnapper. If he keeps his mouth shut, the boy will die and the kidnapper will walk free. Do a deal and the kidnapper will still walk free, but the boy will live. As they said in *The Godfather,* surely an offer you can't refuse?"

"But you wouldn't walk free," said Frost. "We have evidence."

The supercilious sneer returned and Frost began to worry again. What did the swine have up his sleeve? "Are you talking about the hairs from the boy you say you've found on the dog? I hardly think that would stand up in court."

"It's good, solid forensic evidence." But even as he said it, he saw the flaw, the gaping hole in the evidence that he now knew Finch had spotted first.

"It is only evidence that the hairs taken from the dog came from the dead boy. But how did they get there, Inspector? You were at the scene of the crime when the boy's body was found . . . you could have picked up the hairs and when the dog jumped up on your lap, they could have been transferred. I wouldn't be at all surprised if many of the constables who have been in contact with this dog were also at the crime scene . . . the hairs could even have been picked up from the car that took the dog to your laboratory.

Hardly good, solid evidence against me, Inspector, especially as it is all you have."

"You bastard!" said Frost.

"Do we have a deal?" asked Finch.

"I'll see," said Frost.

He went out to find Mullett.

CHAPTER NINETEEN

He barged out of the Interview Room, crashing into Cassidy, who was hovering outside. "I want a word," he said.

"Later," said Frost.

"It's about my daughter," hissed Cassidy, "and it's got to be now!"

"Your daughter's dead," Frost snapped. "Bobby Kirby might still be alive." He pushed Cassidy out of the way and almost ran down the corridor to the Incident Room. Cassidy, his eyes spitting venom, followed him.

Hanlon was hanging up the phone. He didn't look very happy. "The other search party, Jack. They want to pack it in. In this weather it's hopeless."

"The kid's still alive," said Frost. "They've got to carry on. I'll talk to them."

Before he could do anything about it, Mullett charged in, his tongue hanging out for the good news about Finch. Frost told him.

Mullett groped for a chair and dropped into it. "He admitted he had taken the boy?"

"Off the record, no witnesses, with the tape switched off. He'd deny it in open court."

"And he said the boy was alive?"

"Yes, but the kid probably wouldn't last the night."

"Do you believe him?"

"Yes."

Mullett knuckled his forehead, trying to think. "You haven't enough evidence to charge him?"

"Nothing that would stand up in court. The choice is that we do a deal, let Finch go and the boy lives, or no deal, we still have to let him go, but the boy dies."

Mullett turned to Cassidy. "What would you do?"

Cassidy was only too eager to tell him. "I wouldn't have got myself in this position in the first place."

"Quite," said Mullett. He turned angrily on Frost. "This is all down to you. I absolve myself from all responsibility for this mess."

"I'll take all the bloody blame if it makes you happy," snarled Frost, "but what are we going to do about the kid?"

"I've no authority to do deals," Mullett replied. "That's a matter for the chief constable."

"Then ask the flaming chief constable!" Frost picked up the phone and banged it down in front of the superintendent.

Mullett looked at the phone as if it was a live bomb, then, steeling himself, stretched out his hand. Then he flinched, anticipating what the chief constable would say. He snatched his hand back. "No, Frost. You got us into this mess. You get us out of it." He strode to the door, then spun round, pointing a finger at the inspector. "I want a result on this, Frost. I want a watertight case against Finch and the boy returned safe and sound. The boy's safety is paramount. I don't care how you do it . . . but stick to the rules."

"Thanks for sod-all," muttered Frost. He stood and stretched wearily. He'd have to have another word with Finch, try a bit of subtlety . . . like threatening to tear his dick off.

His path was again blocked by Cassidy.

"Whatever it is, it can wait," said Frost.

"It can't wait," insisted Cassidy, "and it won't take more than a second of your valuable time." He unfolded a small sheet of paper and waved it at Frost. "Something you might recognize."

Frost bent forward to read it. A car registration number. His stomach tightened. He knew what it was.

"This," said Cassidy, waving it in front of Frost's face, "is the registration number of the car that killed my daughter. The BMW, the car you said didn't exist. The car whose driver Tommy Dunn was seen talking to."

"How did you get it?"

"Never mind how I got it. You were given this registration number at the time. You conveniently lost it." He pushed his face right up to Frost. "How much did the drunken sod of a driver pay you and Tommy to keep him out of it, you bastard?"

Frost said nothing.

"I'm going to trace the driver and I'm having the case reopened," said Cassidy, his face a mask of disgust. "See if your damn medal can get you out of this!"

"Hold it, Cassidy!" Heads jerked round. Arthur Hanlon, who had been sitting quietly by the radio, was coming over. Normally placid, his face was as flushed and angry as Cassidy's. "You don't know the facts."

"Facts?" echoed Cassidy. "Frost lied his bloody head off and a drunken pig of a motorist was let free. Those are the facts!"

"If he lied," said Hanlon, pushing between Cassidy and Frost, "then he did it for you, you bastard."

"For me? What are you bloody talking about?"

"How well did you know your daughter?"

"How well? I was her father, for Christ's sake!"

Frost tugged at Hanlon's sleeve. "Leave it, Arthur." But he was shaken off.

"You were her father," said Hanlon, "but how often did you see her? You were career-mad. The job came first, seven days a week, twenty-four hours a day—sod your family, you hardly ever went home. You didn't know what your kid was getting up to."

"Getting up to? She was fourteen bloody years old . . . what the hell could she get up to?" shouted Cassidy. "What are you daring to say about my daughter?"

"Your daughter was on drugs! Your lovely, pure fourteen-year-old daughter was on hard drugs."

Cassidy's knuckles whitened as he clenched his fists tight. "You're lying!"

"And to support her habit," continued Hanlon doggedly, "your fourteen-year-old daughter turned to prostitution."

"You take that back, you bastard!" Cassidy had lunged forward and grabbed the front of Hanlon's jacket.

For a small man, Hanlon showed unusual strength. He pulled Cassidy's hand away. "What do you think she was doing at the Coconut Grove that night? She was stoned to the eyeballs and plying for trade to pay for her next fix. Tommy Dunn saw her and hustled her out. He put her into his car and was about to drive off when she opened the door and flung herself out, right into the path of an oncoming car. The driver had had a few drinks, but there was no way he could have avoided her."

Cassidy stared straight ahead as if he wasn't listening, but the muscle on the side of his face was twitching uncontrollably.

"She was killed instantly. Nothing could bring her back, but Jack Frost wanted to spare your feelings. He didn't want the facts to come out in court, so he let the driver go. Then he got the doctor at the hospital to do a very cursory post-mortem, ignoring the drug abuse, the sexual activity, the disease. Jack Frost wanted you to have that pure fourteen-year-old daughter you had always boasted about, so he lied and he covered up."

Cassidy was a man who had been stunned. He stared blankly and shook his head as if it would shake away everything he had just heard. He turned to Frost. "He's lying, isn't he?" Then back to Hanlon. "You're lying! The old pals act. Everyone covering up for everyone else—just like Mullett and his mates lied when Chief Inspector Formby wrapped his car round that lamp post." He walked to the door. "Sod you all!" he yelled, almost in tears. A flutter of paper as he tore up the registration number and hurled it to the floor. "Sod you all!"

The door swung shut behind him.

"I wish you hadn't done that, Arthur," said Frost. "But thanks, anyway." He poked a cigarette into his mouth and tried to think. What was he going to do before Cassidy sounded off? Oh, yes. Have another word with Finch.

Liz looked tired and washed out so he sent her home. "Burton will drive you," he said. Burton seemed pleased at this. Frost kicked the door of the Interview Room shut. Just him and Finch.

"No deal," he said tersely.

Finch shrugged. "A pity, but I gave you your chance."

Frost scraped a chair across the brown linoleum and sat down. "I might be able to get the court to go lenient with you. The first boy's death wasn't intended and you cooperated in letting us recover Bobby. You could be out in five years."

"According to my doctor, I haven't got five years," said Finch. "Any prison term, no matter how short, would be a life sentence, so you've got no carrots to offer me."

"Tell us where he is," said Frost.

"Only the kidnapper would know that," replied Finch.

Frost stood up. He called for a uniformed constable to take Finch back to the cell. "I'll make you a promise," he told Finch before the constable arrived. "Whether we find that boy alive, or dead, or never, I'm going to nail you. I hope your doctor is right, because you are going to die in prison, you bastard."

Fine bleeding words, he told himself, but how the hell am I going to do it?

Frost helped himself to a mug of tea from Bill Wells's thermos flask, then paid for it by having to listen to the sergeant's moans about the way Mullett kept blocking his chances of promotion and putting him down for duty on Christmas day. He was only half listening. Bobby Kirby was out there somewhere in the cold, torrential rain, and teams of men were looking for him. He was toying with the idea of driving over to Denton Woods to help, if just to be doing something constructive, but he knew he'd just be getting in the way. He looked up as Burton returned from driving Liz back to her digs.

"Get any, son?" he asked.

Burton grinned. "Never had the nerve to ask her."

"Did you hear about the bus conductress who married a bus driver?" asked Frost. "On their wedding night she stripped off and said, 'Room for one on top.' When he'd finished he said, 'But you didn't tell me there was room for five standing inside.'" He cackled at his own joke, then stopped abruptly. It didn't seem right to be laughing while that poor little sod . . . Wryly, he recalled the empty threat he had made to Finch. Well, there was no way he was going to find the kid, drinking tea and telling dirty jokes. He swilled down the dregs and banged down the mug. "Come on, son," he said to Burton. "Let's go for a drive."

He sometimes thought better in the car, so he lay back in his seat, smoking, eyes half-closed, letting Burton drive through the rain. The little buzzer in his brain started to sound off again. The house. There was something that puzzled him when they went into the house in Wrights Lane. But what the hell was it?

"What happened when we banged on the door to get in there, son?" he asked Burton.

Burton couldn't help. "You sent me and Jordan round the back."

Frost leant back and gazed up at the roof of the car for inspiration, but none came. "Drive me to her digs," he told Burton. "I want to talk to Liz."

"She'll be in bed," said Burton.

"Then she can get out of it again," said Frost. "I've got to talk to her."

He banged on the door and kept his thumb jammed in the bell-push. At last a light came on from an upstairs window, then the sound of footsteps descending the stairs. Bolts slid back and there was Liz, an unfastened dressing gown over her nightdress, a police truncheon swinging menacingly in her hand.

"Bloody hell!" gawped Frost. This was a transformed Liz. Her hair, usually screwed back tightly, was now free-flowing down her back. It was gorgeous hair and she had a lot of it.

She had scrubbed off her makeup and her skin looked fresh and dewy. Her flimsy nightdress didn't conceal very much. "What do you want?" she hissed to the dark shape standing in the doorway.

I'd love to tell you, thought Frost. "It's me, Liz. Sorry it's so late." He told her what was worrying him.

Liz shook her head. "We knocked at the door, Finch let us in, and then we searched the house."

"All right, love," he said. "You go back to bed. I'm going to take another look around that house."

"Wait—" Liz said. "I'm coming with you."

He waited in the car with Burton, who wanted all the tantalizing details.

"She had a dressing gown on," said Frost, embroidering the facts to suit his audience. "Nothing on underneath . . . she must sleep in the nude . . . and it kept flapping open."

"Flaming heck!" breathed Burton.

"And her Bristols," he added. "I've never seen such nipples."

"Tell me, tell me!" pleaded Burton.

"Have you ever seen ripe Royal Sovereign strawberries, warm from the sun with the dew still on them?" said Frost.

"No, but I can imagine it," said Burton, wriggling in his seat.

"Well . . ." His expression changed abruptly. "Look out, she's coming."

Liz sat in the back seat. Burton kept eyeing her with renewed interest. She certainly looked different with her hair hanging loose. As they paused at the traffic lights he turned and gave her a smile. "You look smashing with your hair like that."

"Keep your eyes on the road, Constable," she said icily.

The house was unguarded. With the search party out in force they didn't have enough men for that luxury. They went inside, where Frost mooched from room to room, not knowing what the hell he was doing there or what he was looking for. Fingerprint powder was everywhere, but the only prints found were those of Finch and a few of the householder and his wife which had survived Finch's vigorous polishing and cleaning operation. In the bathroom and the kitchen, the sink traps had been removed and the contents taken away by Forensic for examination. The couple returning from Spain were going to have a shock when they arrived home tomorrow.

Frost opened and closed closet doors aimlessly and dug through the pockets of clothing swinging from hangers. From the back bedroom he stared through the rain-shimmering windows to the garden. An enormous rain puddle made the lawn a lake. In the distance, a few smears of lights flickered as the poor sods in the search teams floundered about in the woods. He wondered if the little boy was under cover. A mental picture of the seven-year-old, bound, gagged, probably with masking tape over his eyes, made him shudder. And they were nowhere near to finding where he was.

Downstairs, in the kitchen, Liz was rummaging through drawers that had already been thoroughly searched. "I wish I knew what we were looking for," she murmured.

"You and me both, love," Frost muttered, pulling open a drawer next to the sink. It held cutlery and a bread board. He took out the board and a long, razor-sharp carving knife and wondered if this was what Finch had used to cut off the finger for the ransom demand. The board, well grooved with knife cuts, had been scrubbed white. He dropped them back, nudging shut the drawer.

Burton came in, dusting himself off. He had been up in the loft, crawling behind water tanks. "We did a thorough job on the search first time," he said. "I don't see how we missed anything."

Frost stared into space. "It was right at the start. Right at the start. We banged at the door." He looked at Liz. "Then what?"

She frowned as she tried to remember. "We knocked . . . he opened the door . . . we all charged in."

Frost chewed his knuckle. There was something else. But what? "We knocked. Finch was already in the hall. He said, 'Who is it?' I said, 'Police,' and then . . ." He snapped his fingers in triumph. "I've got it! He said, 'Just a minute.' He made us wait before he opened the door . . . only a few seconds, but he made us wait. . . . Why?" He hurried out into the hall, Liz and Burton following. A pile of letters stood on the hall table awaiting the return of the couple from their holiday. Some of them, the ones that looked like bills, Finch had opened. Frost checked through the envelopes carefully, then pulled the table away from the wall in case anything had slipped behind it. Nothing.

A door under the stairs led to the cellar, but there had been no time for him to nip down there. The only other things in the hall were the clothes hanging from the coatrack.

"Did we go through the pockets?"

"Yes," said Liz.

"The women's clothes as well as the men's?"

"We went through them all," said Liz. "Nothing there that shouldn't be there."

"Unless his dick was hanging out and he tucked it away before coming to the door, I reckon he hid something." Frost looked again at the clothes on the rack. "Let's go through these. Take everything out of the pockets and check the linings."

The pile of odds and ends from the pockets mounted. Old receipts, bus tickets, scribbled shopping lists . . .

"What's this?" Frost had found something in the inside pocket of a woman's grey and white woolen coat. A black plastic credit card holder.

"Her credit cards," said Burton. "I checked them earlier."

Frost was about to add it to the heap when an impulse made him look inside. He smiled grimly at Burton. "You didn't check it thoroughly enough, my son." He showed him the credit cards inside. They were all in the name of H. A. Finch.

Burton stared, shamefaced. "I don't know how I missed that. . . ."

"It doesn't matter, son," said Frost. "If you had found it earlier we wouldn't have attached any importance to it." He went through it. "So why was Finch so anxious to hide this?" Tucked in the end pocket were two Visa receipts. The first was for Finch's shopping the previous day at the supermarket. But the other bore that day's date: "Hatters Garage, River Road, Denton . . . Petrol £12.74."

He phoned the garage. "Can you tell me what time this receipt was issued?"

"Some time this evening," said the garage man. "Latish."

"Can't you be more precise? It's important."

"If you can give me the registration number, I might be able to pinpoint it precisely. We've got a security video camera running all the time . . . too many people driving off without paying."

Burton was sent off to get the number of the Renault. Frost relayed it.

"Just a minute." The sound of the phone being put down . . . noises while the man dealt with a customer, then the clicking of controls as the video was wound back. . . . "Hello . . . Is it a Renault?"

"Yes."

"Ten twenty-three this evening."

"Thanks," said Frost. "Don't erase that tape. We're on our way now to pick it up."

It took just over twenty minutes to reach the garage, where they sat in the manager's office as the garage man loaded up the tape. "We get all sorts of things recorded on these," he said chattily. "Caught a bloke doing a number two behind the Derv pump last week. Want to see it?"

"No, thanks," said Frost. "It might be me."

"There you go!" The man found the approximate place and pressed the play button. Black-and-white images of single shots jerked across the screen like old silent films. The man pressed the pause button and there, quivering on the screen, was Finch using the pump. Frost rose from his chair and almost pressed his nose on the screen as he studied the car. If he was hoping to see the missing boy grinning out of a window, he was disappointed. The running time was shown on the corner of each frame. Finch arrived at 10:23 and left at 10:27. They commandeered the tape.

"So what does it all mean?" asked Liz when they were back in the car.

"He hid that receipt," said Frost, "which means he didn't want us to know he'd bought petrol here. Why not? Because he had Bobby Kirby in the boot. Finch was taking him to where he was going to hide him."

"And where was that?" asked Liz.

"Definitely not in the woods," replied Frost. "There's plenty of filling stations he would have passed going there. Hatters Garage is in the opposite direction."

"He could have gone on to the woods afterward," Burton pointed out.

"So why go to great lengths to hide the petrol receipt? No, son. All those poor sods falling over each other searching the woods and running up our overtime bill have been wasting their time. The kid isn't there."

"Then where is he?" asked Liz.

Frost sighed. "All we can do is guess. The road past the filling station leads straight down to the river."

Liz paled. "You believe he's dumped the boy in the river?"

"Alive or dead, I reckon that's where he is." He told Burton to drive down there while he fished his radio out of the glove compartment. "Frost to Control . . . over."

"We've been trying to get hold of you, Inspector," said Lambert. *"Message from Mr. Mullett. He wants to see you in his office right away."*

"Message for Mr. Mullett," said Frost. "Tell him to get stuffed. This is urgent. Contact the search team in the woods. Tell them to stop immediately and get over to the top of River Road bloody quickly. I'll meet them there. And try and rustle up a couple of frogmen. We could be fishing for a body."

"Right," said Lambert. *"Mr. Cassidy wants a word."*

A rustle as Cassidy took over the microphone. *"What's happening?"*

Frost gave him the details. "I'm getting a team over to search the river area in case he's still alive."

"I'm on my way," said Cassidy. If there was a chance of a successful outcome to this case with the boy still alive, he wanted to be part of the winning team.

"Great," said Frost, trying to sound enthusiastic. "The more the merrier."

The river, some twenty feet across at this point, was little more than an open sewer, receiving the effluent from the various factories on the far side who found it cheaper to pay fines than conform to the stringent requirements of the Rivers Authority. Its surface was usually a sluggish mass of discolored foam and oil-rainbowed scum, but the heavy rain of the past few days had made it overflow the sluice gates and now the flow was galloping past.

The road ran alongside the river for about a quarter of a mile and it was in this section that Frost intended to concentrate his search. He stood, watching the boiling river, drenched to the skin, while Burton and Liz, heads down, almost blinded by the torrential rain, looked for places where a small body might be concealed. Frost shouted Bobby's name in the forlorn hope the boy might be able to answer him, but all he could hear was the machine-gun bullets of rain making snapping noises, almost like the crackling-twig sound of a forest fire, as they pockmarked the river.

Headlights reflected off the water and he turned to see cars approaching. The search parties from the woods. From the first car, Arthur Hanlon, his hair plastered and dripping, squelched over to Frost. He eyed the current tearing past carrying broken branches and floating debris. "Don't like the look of that, Jack."

Frost nodded gloomily. "All it needs is bleeding Lillian Gish on an ice floe."

"You reckon Bobby's somewhere near here?" Hanlon had to shout over the noise of rushing water.

"Yet another one of my inspired guesses," said Frost. "If he's dead"—he hurled a stone into the water—"he'll be on the bottom, sharing a sack with some bricks."

He went with Hanlon over to the members of the search party. Most still sat inside their cars, not wanting to get any wetter or colder until they had to. All of them looked tired and dispirited, but they climbed out of the cars to huddle round him. "Isn't this better than being stuck inside a stuffy office?" Frost asked, which produced a few laughs. "All right. I've sodded you about up to now, but this has got to be our best lead yet. I know you're tired and fed up and hate my guts, but the poor little sod we're looking for is seven years old, shit scared, and he could die if we don't find him quickly. Search everywhere, even the most unlikely places. If you're not sure, search again. Good luck."

Hanlon split them into groups and directed them to various search areas while Frost made his way back to the bank. More voices and car-door slammings. The mobile lighting unit and the frogmen. Hanlon sent a couple of men over to help them unload their gear and get the lights set up.

Frost walked up and down the bank. The rain beat down heavily on his bare head and soaked through his shower-proof, water-blackened mac. The rigged lights shone down on the river, making it look like black velvet, and bounced off the oilskins most of the men were wearing. A false alarm was raised as debris floating past looked just like a body, but when it hit the lighted area it turned out to be clumps of vegetation and earth from where the bank had collapsed into the river.

Jordan, in the small rowing boat with Collier at the oars, was prodding the muddy bottom with a pole. The monotonous, grating creak of the rowlocks as Collier fought to keep the boat steady against the drag of the current was setting Frost's teeth on edge.

"Something here, Inspector!" Jordan calling from the boat, leaning over the side, dragging something from the dark water.

Frost's heart stumbled and skipped a couple of beats as an ominous-looking black plastic dustbin sack was hauled up and brought over to him. Don't let it be the boy, he pleaded silently. Please, don't let it be the boy. His knife slashed it open and it spewed stinking river water all over his feet. A long, low sigh of relief. Rotting household rubbish, dumped a long time ago.

Frost wiped the rain from his face and eyes and tried to concentrate to see if he got any feeling that the boy was somewhere near . . . that he was alive.

"Any luck?" called a familiar voice.

Bleeding Cassidy. He hoped he wasn't going to go on again about his daughter. "We haven't found a dead body yet . . . that's about as lucky as we've got."

"I had another word with Finch," said Cassidy.

Did you? thought Frost. He's supposed to be *my* bloody prisoner, but be my guest. . . .

"Mr. Mullett thought I might be more successful than you."

"Mr. Mullett isn't questioning my infallibility, I hope?" muttered Frost.

"Finch is keeping mum. I told him you were searching the river. He didn't seem at all worried."

"He's hardly going to say 'Oh, my God, not the river!', is he? If he looks blank and acts dumb, we can't pin anything on him."

"But if we find the boy . . ."

"There'll still be no proof Finch put him here. The fact he filled up at a garage in the vicinity is hardly bloody conclusive." He pulled off his scarf, which was soaking wet and making him uncomfortable. "I'll be happy if we find the kid alive, even if it means letting Finch go."

The area was adazzle with all of the floodlights working;

the generator throbbed away out of sight somewhere. Oars creaked, rain drummed, and one of the floodlights sizzled and flashed intermittently as rain found a faulty connection. Searchers on the bank in oilskins bent low as they flattened and prodded the long wet grass.

"Put some bloody beef into it," roared Cassidy, walking over to one of the groups who had been out in the rain and cold all night. Backs stiffened, but no one said anything. They were too tired.

"Looking for the boy, Jack?"

Frost groaned. Sandy Lane from *The Denton Echo* with one of his photographers, ready for one of his "Police Fail Again" stories.

"Hello, Sandy." He grunted. "Been listening in to the police wavebands?"

The reporter grinned. "No, Jack. We just happened to be driving past and we spotted all the lights."

"Oh," sniffed Frost. "I thought there was an innocent explanation. Yes, we're looking for the boy."

"Any reason why you chose this particular spot?"

"No. We just happened to see the lights and we thought we'd have a look. Now leave me alone, Sandy, there's a good boy. We're busy."

The photographer took a couple of pictures of the searchers, then retired out of the rain to the car with Sandy to wait for the body to be fished up, or the boy to be found alive. The reporter began working out alternative headlines to cover either eventuality.

The search had moved farther down, leaving in its wake a trail of flattened grass and odd heaps of rubbish dredged from the river. Frost threw away the sodden cigarette that dangled from his mouth and tried to light up a fresh one from the damp pack in his pocket. He managed a couple of drags of bitter-tasting smoke before it sizzled and died. The feeling that the kid was here, almost within reach, was strong, but only as strong as the feeling they probably wouldn't find him. He felt like hurling himself in the car, tearing back to the station, and doing a deal with Finch. Tell us where he is and we will drop all charges, give you a pension for life and all the Cup Final tickets you want. He pulled back a sodden cuff to consult his watch. One o'clock in the morning. He could hear Cassidy shouting, redirecting one of the teams back to an area they had already searched. He thought of Finch in his nice, dry cell, snug and warm, and probably working out how much he could sue the police for harassment and wrongful arrest.

"Frost!"

A shudder quivered through him. Just what he needed to make his misery complete. Mullett, immaculately turned out in his tailored raincoat, which, in some mysterious way, seemed to repel the rain. Frost forced a smile. "Hello, Super."

Mullett gaped at the floodlights, the frogmen, the teams of off-duty men and tried to mentally work out the cost. He transferred his glare to the drenched, drowned-rat figure of Frost. "Who authorized this?"

"I tried to get you," said Frost. "I rang your house—no one answered."

"I haven't been more than six feet away from the phone all night," snapped Mullett.

"I must have got a wrong number, then," said Frost. "It rang and rang . . . and I knew you would have authorized it."

"So Finch told you where the boy was?"

"Not exactly, sir." He told Mullett about the petrol receipt.

Mullett stared at him in openmouthed incredulity. "And on the basis of that flimsy piece of so-called evidence you have committed us to an overtime bill far in excess of our resources, even after I had specifically told you—" His lips tightened. "You deliberately didn't phone me, Frost, because you knew I would say no."

You clever bastard, thought Frost. That's exactly why I didn't phone you.

"Inspector! Over here."

A welcome diversion. Arthur Hanlon, Jordan by his side, was bending over something fished out of the river. "Excuse me, Super." Frost brushed past Mullett and hurried down.

Another dustbin sack. Hanlon had cut the white plastic tie. He tipped out the contents. A pair of fisherman's waders, plus a muddy stone to ensure the bag sank. Frost lifted them up and examined the heavy rubber soles. No sign of any wear—they could have been brand-new.

Cassidy, determined not to be left out, came running over. "What have we got?" he demanded. Frost showed him. Cassidy shrugged. "So what does it mean?"

"Why would anyone want to chuck away a pair of brand-new waders?" asked Hanlon.

"A fisherman could have dropped them in by accident," suggested Cassidy.

"With a flaming brick inside to make sure it sank?" snorted Frost. "Besides, fishermen don't come here. Any fish that survived through the chemicals being shunted in the river would be purple and shine in the dark." He shook his head. "I'll lay odds Finch dumped these."

"Why?"

"Because he didn't want us to know he'd been paddling in the bleeding river." He was getting excited now. "He's found a place to hide the boy, but he had to get in the river to reach it."

"Another possibility is that he waded in the river to dump the body in the deepest part," said Cassidy.

"My brain can only deal with one possibility at a time," said Frost. He looked over to the far bank. "Could anyone wade across to that bank?" he asked Jordan.

Jordan shook his head. "Far too deep."

"Then we concentrate on this side." Frost looked down

at the cold swirl, steeled himself, then stepped into the river. It came well above his knees. He didn't believe in asking people to do things he wouldn't do himself. "We need to search the bank from the river," he told Hanlon. "Get all the volunteers you can. Tell them they'll have to get their feet wet . . . their dicks too, if it gets any deeper." The water was icy and the current threatened to knock him off his feet, but, unsteadily, he pressed on, pushing aside the overhang of vegetation from the bank which was now bobbing in the raised water level. Behind came a splash as Jordan joined him. Cassidy remained on the bank, keeping pace with them.

At one point Frost got his foot stuck deep in the mud and in pulling it free lost his shoe. There was no time to retrieve it, so he cursed softly and limped on.

He nearly missed it. It was at the point where the river curved and the current was at its strongest and nearly kicked his feet from under him. He clutched at a clump of reeds to stop himself falling. And there it was, no longer hidden. An opening in the bank. Water was lapping almost halfway up a brown glazed pipe, some eighteen inches in diameter. "Jordan!"

Jordan splashed over to him. "It's part of an old drainage system to run off rainwater from some of these fields at the back of us. They're blocked off now." He pulled back the overhang of long, dank grass so Frost could look inside.

"Torch!" called Frost. Cassidy, from the bank, handed one down.

The beam ricocheted off something drably white. Passing the torch back to Cassidy, Frost squeezed his arm through and touched it. Cloth of some kind. Woolen cloth. He managed to get a grip on it and tugged. At first it didn't want to move, then it slid forward. The weight was right. His heart pounded. He now had it out and raised it out of the water. It was a child, cocooned in a sodden blanket which was bound round with cord. Brown plastic tape sealed the mouth and eyes. The flesh was cold. As cold as the riverwater. "I've got him!" Frost yelled.

"Give him to me!" Cassidy, bending over, held out his arms for the bundle. Frost passed it up.

Helped by Burton, Frost managed to clamber up on the bank. He was still on his hands and knees, shivering with cold, as Cassidy cut the cord and stripped off the sodden blanket. Under it the child was naked. Cassidy shrugged off his greatcoat and swaddled the boy. Then, he carefully peeled off the plastic tape. The eyes were tightly closed. Rain pelted the pale face. He could detect no sign of breathing.

He's dead, thought Frost, hugging himself for warmth. The poor little sod is dead.

Liz pushed through the huddle and bent her ear to the child's mouth. Her eyes narrowed as she listened. "He's breathing," she announced. "Just barely, but he's still breathing."

"Ambulance!" yelled Mullett. "Get an ambulance!"

Frost took charge. "No!" He grabbed Cassidy. "It will be quicker to get him straight to the hospital. Take him in an area car. Radio ahead and let them know you are coming."

Cassidy nodded and, clutching the child tight to his chest, pushed through to the area car. Electronic flash guns crackled as Sandy's man took photographs.

Mullett was beaming. He couldn't wait to get back to phone the chief constable. "A most satisfactory ending," he told Frost.

"Thanks, Super." The wind on his wet clothes was chilling him to the bone. "Pass me the blanket. I'll get it over to Forensic."

Mullett bent and picked it up. He frowned. "Hello—what's this?" He was looking at something caught up in the folds. "Seems to be a receipt of some kind."

"Show me," said Frost excitedly. Mullett gave it to him. Frost studied it carefully. Soaking wet, but still readable, it was a till receipt for the purchase of petrol. Hatters Garage.

That day's date and paid for by credit card. Finch's credit card.

He looked up at Mullett and smiled. "You clever old sod," he said. "We've got him. Thanks to you, we've got him."

A doubtful smile flickered on and off Mullett's lips. He wasn't quite sure what it was he had done.

"The evidence we wanted," explained Frost, slipping the receipt between the pages of his notebook to protect it from the rain. "Now we can tie Finch to the kid." He beckoned Liz over. "Ever charge a man with murder and kidnapping?"

She shook her head.

"Then here's your chance. Get that bastard Finch banged up."

"Aren't you going to do it?" asked Mullett.

"I'm soaking wet," answered Frost. "I'm going home to change." At the car he yelled his thanks to the search team. "Booze-up in the Incident Room in an hour. I'll bring some bottles, but don't let that stop any of you from bringing your own!"

Clutching tightly to his chest bottles which clinked and threatened to slip from his grasp, he backed through the swing doors and into the lobby. From the raucous sounds seeping from the Incident Room the celebration party was already in progress. Bill Wells on the front desk beckoned him over.

"Finch wants to see you."

"What about?"

"He didn't say," said Wells. "No one takes me into their confidence."

Frost left the bottles on the front desk, reminded Wells he had counted them, then went down to the cells.

Finch was lying on his bunk. He got up when Frost entered. "You bastard!" he hissed.

"Sticks and stones . . ." said Frost, waggling a finger.

"You framed me. You fitted me up!"

"Fitted you up?" said Frost, his face a picture of injured bewilderment.

"That petrol receipt."

"What about it?"

"You planted it! You found it with my credit card and you planted it."

"My divisional commander found it—not me."

Finch pushed his face close to Frost's. "I don't care who found it—*you* planted it to be found."

Frost shook his head. "I know you like to think yourself as infallible, Mr. Finch, but you slipped up this time. The receipt must have fallen from your pocket as you were stuffing the poor little git up that drainage pipe."

"There's a flaw in your reasoning, Inspector, an insurmountable flaw. I drove to the river, I hid the child, and I filled up with petrol on the way back. So how on earth could that receipt have got there?"

Frost shrugged and gave an enigmatic smile. "One of life's little mysteries." He paused. "Do you want to make an official complaint?"

Finch barked a scornful laugh. "What use would it be? You'd lie your head off."

"How well you know me," murmured Frost.

CHAPTER TWENTY

He woke with a raging headache, feeling stiff, cold, and uncomfortable. The alarm was shrieking, chewing through his brain like a rip saw. He fumbled to switch it off, but his hand floundered about in empty space. One eye creaked open to a confusion of images. He wasn't in his bedroom. The window was in the wrong place. And he wasn't in his bed, he was curled up on a hard, rigid-backed chair. Slowly, slowly, realization filtered through to his alcohol-deadened brain. The party last night. He was in the Incident Room and the ringing was the phone. He squinted at his watch, moving his arm to bring it into focus. Eight-thirty A.M. Reaching for the phone sent his headache throbbing anew. "Frost." He winced as he spoke into the mouthpiece.

"Wakey, wakey, campers," chirped a disgustingly cheerful Bill Wells.

"What do you want?" growled Frost, his eyes crawling round the Incident Room. Ashtrays overflowed with half-smoked broken-backed cheroots, empty glasses and bottles everywhere, on desks, rolling about the floor. Jordan and Arthur Hanlon were asleep on separate desks, snoring loudly. The atmosphere was thick with stale tobacco smoke and whiskey and—God, his stomach churned at the thought of it—jellied eels. At five in the morning someone had been sent to an all-night stall which sold seafood and had come back with containers of cockles, whelks, winkles and . . . jellied eels.

A small color television set in the corner was on, its sound off. It was the early morning news and, in eerie silence, Cassidy, carrying the child, was seen dashing into the hospital . . . being hugged by the mother . . . making modest speeches to the press.

Frost snatched his attention back to the telephone. "Sorry, Bill . . . what was that?"

"I said the good news is that the hospital reports the kid is pulling through. The bad news is that Mullett is in."

"You haven't woken me up just to tell me that?"

"No, Jack. The solicitor for those two women who killed Lemmy Hoxton is here. He wants to see you."

"It's Cassidy's case, not mine."

"But it's you he wants to see."

Frost sighed. "Right. I'll be along."

He staggered into the washroom, kicking aside an empty jellied-eel tub on the way, and splashed cold water on his face. His rumpled hair was smoothed back, a cigarette stuck in his mouth and lit. His first cough of the morning, then he ambled out into the corridor.

The door to Mullett's office was swinging open. He could hear the divisional commander oozing false modesty as he spoke on the phone to the chief constable, so he paused, ears cocked, hoping to pick up some tidbits to pass on to Bill Wells.

". . . I know the overtime level had been exceeded, sir, but my only concern was for the missing boy, so I took the risk in the belief that a human life was worth it, no matter what the outcome might be for me. . . . You're too kind, sir, I was just doing my duty. . . . Thank you, sir. . . . Thank you very much." A click as the phone was replaced.

Frost tiptoed a few steps back the way he had come, then, rather noisily, resumed his walk.

Mullett called him in as he was passing. "Frost!"

He shuffled in and dropped into a chair.

"Take a seat," said Mullett, too late as usual. He gave an ingratiating smile. "You'll be pleased to learn that I've managed to get you off the hook regarding the excessive unauthorized overtime."

"Thank you very much, Super," mumbled Frost. "I don't deserve you."

He said this with such sincerity that Mullett saw no double meaning and beamed happily. "Cassidy did well." He tapped *The Denton Echo* on his desk. A huge picture of Cassidy, the boy in his arms, was under the enormous headline Policeman Hero Saves Child from River."

"Didn't he just?" said Frost.

"Unfortunately, Lexford Division want him back again."

"Tough," grunted Frost.

"So I might have some good news for DS Maud regarding a temporary promotion."

"She deserves it," said Frost.

George Perry, the solicitor for the two women, was white-haired and stooped. He looked benign, but he was shrewd. Very shrewd.

Frost led him to his office. As he opened the door he nearly tripped over a heap of clothes. Liz and Burton were asleep on the floor near the radiator, locked in each other's arms. Neither was wearing very much. Frost backed out, closing the door firmly. "We'll try next door," he said.

They went into the office Cassidy was using. Frost sat at the empty desk and offered Perry a chair. "So what can I do for you?

The solicitor unzipped his solid leather briefcase and pulled out two typed statements. "I am acting for Miss Millicent Fleming and Miss Julia Adams. You took statements from them yesterday?"

"Not me," said Frost. "My colleague, Inspector Cassidy."

"The statements were taken without a solicitor being present."

"They were asked if they wanted one, they both declined."

Perry smiled. "I am sure everything was explained to them. The thing is, my clients would like to withdraw their statements."

"Can't be done," said Frost.

Another smile. "Come now, Inspector. All things are possible. They admit the crime but the prurient details . . . the sexual relationship . . . those photographs . . . They are going to cause such a stir."

"I'm afraid so." Frost nodded.

"These women have families . . . friends . . . they are respected members of the church. They would much prefer that these details were not part of the case against them."

"So what are you suggesting?"

"Hoxton came to rob them. He tried to rape Julie. Millicent struck him to stop him and he died. That is not in dispute. But surely there is no need for the sexual aspect to come out. They are both most concerned—almost suicidal about this."

"Their statements will have to be read out in court."

"I'm suggesting we tear up the original statements and destroy the tapings of those interviews. They will give you fresh statements that will omit the sexual aspect."

"I don't see why we can't do that," Frost said. "I'll have a word with my colleague, it's his case—"

As if on cue, Cassidy came in, scowling his annoyance to find his office being used by Frost. "Can I ask what's going on?"

Frost explained.

"No way," said Cassidy emphatically. "No flaming way."

"It wouldn't harm our case," said Frost.

"It would be bending the rules," said Cassidy, "and I don't bend rules for anyone." He stood pointedly by his desk, waiting for Frost to give up his chair.

Frost pushed himself up. "Sorry, Mr. Perry."

Perry gave a sad smile. "I tried," he said. "They'll be terribly disappointed, but I tried."

In the corridor outside, Frost watched Perry, shoulders sagging, walking toward the custody area. He chased after him. "Mr. Perry!"

The solicitor paused and turned.

"I shouldn't be surprised if the original tapes and statements get lost," whispered Frost. "I'm well known for losing things. Give me a call later today. We might need your clients to give us fresh statements."

Perry twisted his head up and down, making sure no one could hear. He lowered his voice. "Your colleague is dead against it. I wouldn't want to get you into trouble, Inspector."

"I don't need outside help to get me into trouble," Frost told him. "I can do that very well on my own."

He sailed past Perry and out into the lobby.

"Have you seen Wonder Woman this morning?" called Wells. "Mullett wants her."

"She might be taking things easy this morning," said Frost. "She had one winkle too many last night."

He turned up the collar of his mac and stepped out into the pouring rain. There was a dead firework on the pavement. He kicked it away.

About the Author

R. D. WINGFIELD was born in London within screaming distance of the scenes of the Jack the Ripper murders.

Until 1970 he worked in the sales office of an international oil company, writing crime plays for radio in his spare time. The success of his radio work meant the day job had to go, and he became a full-time writer. His plays have been broadcast all over the world and translated into many languages.

R. D. Wingfield is married with one son, and lives in Essex. He is the author of four mysteries: *A Touch of Frost, Night Frost, Frost at Christmas,* and *Hard Frost,* all available from Bantam Books.